KU-533-007

THE MIDNIGHT COUNTRY

by the same author

KELLY
FESTIVAL OF FOOLS
THE HUNGRY LAND
RITES OF INHERITANCE
THE HOUSE OF MIRRORS

THE MIDNIGHT COUNTRY

Michael Mullen

HarperCollins*Publishers*

HarperCollins*Publishers*
77-85 Fulham Palace Road
Hammersmith, London W6 8JB

Published by HarperCollins*Publishers* 1995

1 3 5 7 9 8 6 4 2

Copyright © Michael Mullen 1995

The Author asserts the right to
be identified as the author of this work

A catalogue record for this book
is available from the British Library

ISBN 0 00 224523 X

Set in Sabon

Typeset at The Spartan Press Ltd
Lymington, Hants

Printed in Great Britain by
HarperCollinsManufacturing Glasgow

All rights reserved. No part of this publication may be
reproduced, stored in a retrieval system, or transmitted,
in any form or by any means, electronic, mechanical,
photocopying, recording or otherwise, without the
prior permission of the publishers.

For
Alisa Shachter
Tel Aviv

Chapter One

Alma and Sophie Schmerling stood on the balcony of their hotel suite, wrapped in sable coats. Below them lay the enchanted city of Vienna. It was the final day of the century and that night they expected to attend the grand ball at the Hofburg Palace, the most important event in the Viennese social calendar.

Now they were at the centre of empire.

'Your place lies in Europe,' their mother, Margit Schmerling, had insisted in New York when they were growing up. It had been a firm and continuous theme. 'You belong in Vienna. Your blood is noble. Of that have no doubt.'

She had old scores to settle in Vienna.

The sky above the city was charged with snow. The sisters hoped that, on this New Year's Eve, it would begin to fall on the imperial capital.

Their eyes rested on the spire of St Stephen's Cathedral, rising protectively above the city roofs. It stood in the Inner Stadt and was the central point of the city, with its high-pitched roof and coloured tiles. To the north lay the Schönbrunn, where the Emperor, Franz Joseph, lived his spartan life. His remote presence held this shambling empire together.

Alma and Sophie turned their backs on the city and entered the elegant suite where they were staying. Draped on the armchairs lay their ballgowns, light as down and purchased from the best couturier in the city.

Their mother was sitting by a blazing fire, reading a

newspaper and indifferent to their nervous feelings. She searched through the social columns for interesting court gossip. Margit Schmerling, now in her fifties, was dark-eyed, with rich black hair and soft skin. When she had arrived in New York almost twenty years before, she had been penniless, with three daughters. Joseph Steiner, overcome by her beauty and European roots, had married her. She had been attracted to his great wealth.

'Is it possible that Papa could fail to obtain invitations?' Sophie asked. 'Perhaps we might spend New Year's night alone in the hotel. I could not endure it. He must arrange for the invitations to arrive.'

'Do you not realize that the great court ball is restricted to the aristocracy and the diplomatic corps? You have set him an almost impossible task,' Margit told her daughters.

'Then what will we do with our ballgowns. It will be all so embarrassing,' Alma sighed.

'Be patient. Your stepfather is a most persuasive man. I have never known him to make a promise that he could not fulfil.'

'But it is getting late. For three days he has attempted to obtain the invitations. If he fails I shall never forgive him.' Alma could not rest. She took up the papers, tried to read them, then cast them aside.

The youngest of Margit's daughters, she had inherited her mother's beauty and part of her strong character. Her black hair was worn in ringlets in the style of the late Empress Elizabeth and, since their arrival, many in the city had noted the likeness.

Sophie, the middle daughter, was thick-set and possessed an opulent beauty. She lacked the refinement of her sister.

Marie was not present. The eldest sister, she had disappeared during the afternoon. She had no wish to attend the ball, so there had been a furious row between mother and daughter. They had hurled abuse at each other:

'You have broken my heart and dishonoured your name.

I tried to educate you and you rebelled. You speak of socialism. You preach in halls. Your mind is filled with communistic nonsense. I know what it is like to be poor. Do not tell me about the dispossessed. I have been one of them.' Margit had fired the opening salvo.

'I am tired of your regal notions. I have no wish to attend the ball and fawn before the idiot ascendancy of Europe. Your title will never be established. We all know that.'

'I am entitled to the title Countess. It will be contested in the courts. I belong in the imperial city. They all know that, although they may not admit it. I know my worth and I will not have a rebellious girl tell me my business.'

It had been a quarrel which had been seething ever since they had arrived in Europe. Now it had erupted into open hostility.

'I am leaving,' Marie had called.

'Good. Go and live with one of your anarchists.'

For her sisters, it had been a nasty incident, but it was soon forgotten. The thought of the imperial ball was on all their minds as they waited anxiously for the invitations.

The civil servant was a quiet man, with glasses and a tidy moustache. His face had the tight, worried expression of a minor civil servant. He approached the table where Joseph Steiner sat drinking his coffee.

'Herr Steiner, I believe,' he said, bowing his head.

'That is correct.'

'I am instructed to bring you to Commandant Liebmann,' he announced curtly. He seemed uncomfortable in the café. His fingers on the edge of his hat were nervous.

Joseph Steiner followed the civil servant. Joseph was a thin, small man, with sad eyes and sharp features. His appearance was neat, almost insignificant.

In a quiet street a cab was waiting for them which they entered and set off for the Arsenal, the headquarters of the imperial army. As they moved through the streets, a regiment of Hungarian Lifeguards with white cloaks falling from their shoulders rode past in precise order. Joseph Steiner observed them with a cynical eye. They were soldiers from the past. They would stand little chance against the Prussian army.

As the cab passed through the Arsenal gates, Joseph reflected that he was not impressed by the immense amount of ammunition stored in a single place. An anarchist could blow the heart of Vienna apart with well-placed explosives.

They arrived at the back entrance to the office of Commandant Liebmann. Descending from the cab, Steiner followed the civil servant up a series of shallow steps to a central hall. He stood in a quiet corner and looked about him. Flags of various regiments fell limply from poles. They all bore the insignia of the imperial eagle with outstretched wings.

He watched the officers, dressed in their regimental colours, pass through the hall and up the great stairs to various offices. Steiner studied their appearance. They seemed like characters from a light opera. He carried information in his pocket which could wipe them out in a single engagement.

He waited patiently. Dressed in dark clothes he drew little attention to himself.

Finally, the civil servant appeared. He was agitated. 'I should have brought you directly to Commandant Liebmann. My apologies,' he stammered.

People always underestimated the power of Joseph Steiner. It was one of his best assets.

He followed the civil servant along a corridor which led deep into the building. It was a sober place and had a dry, silent air. They turned a corner and two guards who stood before a plain door drew aside. The civil servant opened the door and they entered.

It led into a magnificent room, ornate and gilded. On the

walls hung military paintings in vivid, celebratory colours. Commandant Liebmann was sitting behind a desk.

The civil servant disappeared.

'Take a seat, Herr Steiner. Welcome to Vienna. Have you come for the winter season?'

'I may settle here eventually. I would like to divide my time between my interests in America and Europe,' Steiner told him.

'You would be welcome in Vienna,' Liebmann laughed, then quickly became serious. 'You have brought the papers, I presume.'

'Yes. I believe they might be of great interest to you.'

Commandant Liebmann looked at Joseph Steiner, wondering if he possessed any feelings. 'And what is the price for this information?'

'An invitation to the court ball.'

'The court ball is reserved only for the diplomatic corps and the military. Franz Joseph himself will be present. It is impossible,' Liebmann began.

'At the outset everything is impossible. Then it becomes possible. So I have found in all the capitals of Europe,' Joseph Steiner told him directly.

Commandant Liebmann reflected for a moment. 'You could, of course, be made a representative of the American government. I could have words with the American consulate. Show me what can you offer me in return for such invitations.'

Joseph Steiner took two sheets of paper from his pocket. He slipped one across the great table.

Commandant Liebmann examined it closely. Only a nerve in his jaw twitched. It was noted by Joseph.

'And the second page?'

'It gives the formula and the universities in Germany where the gas is being prepared.'

'Consider the invitations already issued. I will have them delivered to your hotel,' Liebmann said.

'Good. Here is my address and here are the names of my wife and daughters.'

'I thought you had three daughters.'

'I am afraid one shows no interest in these matters.'

'Not interested in meeting Franz Joseph?'

'Sadly not.'

'May I have the second page?' he asked.

Joseph Steiner passed it to him. Liebmann examined it closely. 'I think we have made a fair exchange,' he said, his eyes scanning the document.

The meeting was at an end. The civil servant was summoned. Joseph Steiner was led along the gloomy corridor to the cab. He passed quietly out of the Arsenal. He had other business to attend to.

Prince Dmitri Shestov had received his invitation to the Court ball a week previously, as he was attached to the Russian embassy. A diplomat, he spoke German and French fluently. He moved easily in court circles, where he was known for his wit and horsemanship.

However, Vienna cast restraints about him, with only the arrival of winter to bring some vigour to his life. He rose early on the cold mornings, dressed in the heavy sheepskin clothes of the Russian peasant and rode furiously through the woods. There, with his servant Nikka, he spent days hunting. At night they sat in some lodge drinking vodka and playing cards.

Now, on the eve of the new century, he was preparing to visit his favourite brothel on the Rotentürmstrasse, close to St Stephen's Cathedral. It was almost dark and the lights gave the city a mute intimacy.

Dressed in his regimental uniform he set out by coach, passing through the Ringstrasse, the heart of the city.

He crossed a cobbled courtyard and entered the brothel. It was lit by gaslight and already several officers had gathered in the large waiting room. Madame Scholl directed that champagne be brought to the prince.

Moving languidly about the large room were high-class prostitutes. Sometimes they joined the company, at other times they sat on the chaise longue, waiting for one of the officers to choose them for his pleasure.

At half-past eight Prince Dmitri called to his favourite prostitute and they moved up the wide stairs to one of the apartments. He sat on an armchair and watched her undress. She possessed a full body and, as her chemise fell to the floor, he studied her: the heavy breasts, the full thighs, the luxurious hair reminding him of peasant women on his father's estate.

He made love to her with a certain amount of tenderness. Later she told him of the conversations she had heard amongst the officers. He listened attentively. In the brothel he could discover more than in any other house in Vienna.

Before he left the room he paid her for her information. He descended the stairs, put on his cloak, and returned to the waiting coach. Then he set out for the ball.

In the Jewish section of the city, the high-gabled houses were built along narrow streets. Above the doors were painted Jewish names. The place possessed a familiar smell which Joseph Steiner had almost forgotten. Memories began to flood through his mind, fragmented and bright and following no sequence: a great minora with its seven candles burning in a small room; his father reciting prayers in Yiddish; his mother baking in the kitchen. He clinging to her long dress; a dog barking in the small yard. He remembered attending a wedding, where the fiddler was playing as a crowd danced about a married couple. He had a long pointed chin which curved upwards like a sickle; his face was sad even when he played joyful music. Then there was a funeral. They were carrying his father's coffin to the cemetery. Later his mother was dying, in a gloomy room with heavy furniture. And then his uncle was taking him away from the ghetto. They seemed to travel forever; through a countryside which never ended, across a sea which had no limit.

He arrived at Esner Strasse and stood and looked about him. The houses were not as tall as he had remembered. Some he recognised. His heart began to beat with excitement. He had not expected to be so moved by his return to the ghetto.

As he entered the street where he had lived so many years previously images became more certain. He tried to recall the names. 'Ruban the tailor and Mikah the jeweller lived in this house,' he told himself as he stopped in front of a narrow house with a high gable. 'I remember them both.' He stopped before the house where he had lived and for a moment he hesitated. Then he raised the iron knocker and knocked on the door. It fell with a dull sound.

A woman appeared. She had a hostile face.

'I was born here. May I enter?' he asked.

'You are not from Vienna,' she remarked.

'No. I am from America.'

She studied him for a moment in his expensive overcoat, his patent-leather gloves, his felt hat.

'The house is untidy. I have many children. My husband is a drunkard,' she said starkly.

'I just wish to walk through the rooms. That is all. I will pay you for your trouble.'

'Very well. Excuse the state of the place. My husband is a hatter but he refuses to work,' she continued.

The house was impregnated with the stench of urine and sweat. Steiner passed down a corridor and looked into the kitchen. He remembered it vaguely. He then walked quickly through the rooms, but he could not recognise them. When he reached the attic he noticed a photograph on the wall. It was faded and the glass in the frame was broken.

‘Who are these people? he asked.

‘I do not know. The photograph was here when we moved in.’

He examined it closely and his heart missed a beat. He remembered it from his childhood. It was a portrait of his mother and father. It had survived the years.

He tempered his excitement. ‘I would like to purchase it,’ he told her in a controlled voice.

‘You can have it if you pay for it,’ she said, knowing that it was of value to the man.

Steiner took some money from his wallet and handed it to her. Then he took the precious photograph from the wall and looked at it. His throat was dry with emotion.

Thanking the woman, he returned to the street. She watched him from the door, a dirty child in the crook of her arm.

He walked further into the ghetto until he came to the small synagogue. Following a rare practice he entered and spent some time in prayer. As he was about to leave, an old man entered. Steiner studied his appearance. He was obviously the rabbi. He carried a great beard which flowed down his chest and his hair stood out from his head like a ragged halo. His back was bent.

Joseph Steiner walked to where he sat and tapped him on the shoulder.

‘You interrupt me in the house of prayer,’ the rabbi said crossly.

‘I have to talk to you.’

‘Then wait until I have attended to my duty.’ He bowed his head and continued to pray. There was a palpable stillness in the synagogue. Steiner had almost forgotten that such places of tranquillity existed.

When the rabbi was ready, they left the synagogue and sat on a rustic bench.

‘What can I do for you?’ the rabbi asked.

'Do you recognise these people?' Steiner showed him the photograph.

He held it up to his weak eyes and scanned it for a moment. 'Isack and Sarah Bikel. I remember them well. They arrived here from Russia. They were quiet people, kept very much to themselves. Isack was a shoemaker, I think. Both died of cholera. Many died of cholera at the time. They had a son and he was taken to America. That is all that I can tell you. It is such a long time ago.'

'And where are they buried?' Steiner asked.

'Let me see now. There were so many funerals at the time that I can barely remember. We had to remain indoors. We were afraid. But there is one who can tell you. He survived the pestilence and he buried the dead. He remembers as if it were yesterday. But his mind is strange. Come with me.'

The rabbi led him down an alleyway, a dark and filthy place. He banged upon a door and a woman answered.

'Tell David that there is a gentleman here who wishes to see him. He will pay him well for his services.'

'He is not well. His mind is ravelled.'

'Bring him here. We wish to ask him a question.'

The madman appeared. His eyes were out of focus. 'I am a poor man. I cannot pay taxes,' he began.

'We bring you money,' the rabbi said.

David's mind sharpened, and the rabbi explained the nature of their visit.

'I remember. I remember now. Many died during the plague. The officials directed me to bury them in one large grave. They are at the west wall of the cemetery.'

'You must show us the exact location,' the rabbi said.

They discovered the cemetery at the end of an alleyway. It was surrounded by a wall and had been abandoned many years previously. The iron gate had rusted and they walked through a wilderness of weeds and rank grass. The earth was ridged beneath them.

'We walk on the nameless dead. We walk on the nameless dead,' the madman intoned. 'Ah, here we are. The west wall. They are buried here. It is the largest grave in the cemetery.'

Joseph Steiner stood in reverence beside the wide mound as the rabbi chanted the prayers for the dead. When he had finished Steiner remained beside the grave. Later, he returned to the synagogue and made the rabbi a large offering.

Then he left the ghetto. He had solved part of the riddle. He had picked up traces of his past.

The young women grew more anxious. Perhaps Joseph Steiner had not succeeded in obtaining invitations to the court ball. But at five o'clock there was knock at the door and they rushed to open it. Outside stood a young lieutenant. He clicked his heels and saluted, and handed Alma the precious invitations.

They rushed to their mother. 'They bear the imperial seal,' they said excitedly, filled with relief. Now they could begin to prepare for the court ball.

The old century was moving towards its end. Soft flakes of snow began to fall on Vienna.

Chapter Two

Joseph Steiner returned to the hotel at eight o'clock, clutching the photograph which he had placed in a thick envelope. A tentative contact had been made with his roots in Europe. He knew now that the ashes of his parents lay in a small, forgotten cemetery in Vienna and that he belonged to its earth.

He was in a pleasant mood when he entered the rooms. His stepdaughters rushed to him and threw their arms about him. 'It is wonderful, Papa. Perhaps we may meet the Emperor,' Alma announced, her eyes bright with expectation.

'Very few meet the emperor. He is an old man and finds public occasions tiring.'

'How did you succeed in obtaining the invitations? We were getting quite nervous,' Sophie told him. She noted that he seemed happy. The downcast turn of his lips and the tight lines of his forehead had relaxed. She wondered if he had made some lucrative deal in the city or visited a brothel. Perhaps he had purchased some masterpiece for his collection.

'We had better prepare for the great occasion,' he told them, 'In two hours the most luxurious carriage in Vienna will arrive in the courtyard. We cannot afford to be late.'

As he spoke the hairdressers arrived, the women went to their rooms and the preparations for the ball began.

Steiner closed the door to his bedroom and opened the envelope. He looked at the photograph of his parents once more.

He dressed slowly, recalling his good fortune in the ghetto.

When he was finished he returned to the great drawing room. His daughters and his wife had put on their ball-gowns and jewellery and now the maids were fussing about them making the final preparations.

He did not interrupt them, but took a glass of champagne and went out onto the balcony. It was now dark above the city. Snow was gently falling on the roofs and on the square, muting sound. The streets, lit with gaslights, seemed magical. Somewhere a small orchestra was playing a waltz. He looked at his watch. Three more hours and the old century would end.

Marie Schmerling had left the hotel early in the day. She was dressed in a long cloak which she drew about her against the cold. She was a tall woman of twenty-five, with red hair and the imposing figure of her mother.

She had given the cab driver an address in Vienna and he brought her to the old part of the city, drawing up eventually outside the Grossen Keller. She descended a flight of stairs and entered a long arched basement which had once been the crypt of a church. It was now filled with tobacco smoke. About the tables men and women sat drinking cheap Hungarian wine. Candles gave off a small, intimate light.

'Ah, Fräulein Schmerling, you have kept your promise,' a young man called. 'Come and join the company.' Pieter was an artist whose work she admired. Earlier that week she had visited his studio and had sat with others on broken furniture discussing the future of art and the future of Europe.

She passed down through the narrow space between the tables. 'I have kept my promise,' she said, 'I have come to join you for the ending of the old century'

Pieter invited her to join the group. They provided her

with a seat and she sat down. She studied the company. They were artists and writers who lived in cheap attics or small apartments.

'And what has brought Fräulein Schmerling to Vienna? Surely we have nothing here to offer a rich American?' one of the women asked in a sarcastic voice. One of those women who lived at the edges of the bohemian world, she liked to smoke a cheroot and drink rough brandy.

'I have Viennese blood in my veins, thicker perhaps than yours,' Marie responded tartly. 'I am interested in the city and in Europe. Great changes are taking place here at present.'

'If they are, I have not noticed them,' the woman retorted.

'Then you are blind, and you have neglected your socialist reading,' Marie replied.

There was silence for a moment. Then Pieter, the young artist, intervened. He poured her a glass of red wine. 'To the old century,' he said. 'It is ninety-nine years old and will soon die.'

They toasted the death of the year.

'And may the tyrants die with it,' a man opposite Marie said. He possessed a deep voice and it was the first time that Marie had noticed him. He had a stubborn brown beard and bright eyes and smoked a pipe contentedly.

'The tyrants will never die, Fieldmann. You must live under the Hohenzollerns, the Hapsburgs and the Romanovs. They are as solidly placed as the Urals. Nothing can shake them,' somebody else replied.

'You are wrong, my friends. You are wrong. Things are changing. The lady is correct. There is nothing certain any more. Tonight Franz Joseph may attend the court ball and everyone in Vienna will dance to the music of the waltz in the confident belief that everything will remain so, but I can assure you things are changing,' he said in a serious tone.

'You are vague about everything. Give us an example,' Pieter asked.

'Yes. Give us a single example of change,' another asked.

Fieldmann reflected for a moment. 'You would not understand if I told you,' he replied and drew contentment from his pipe.

'You underestimate us. Do you think we are lunatics from the asylum,' the bohemian asked in a mocking tone, and put on the face of a crazed person.

'Perhaps it is the lunatics that have given us a vision of what we are. Have you read Nietzsche and have you looked at Klimt's latest paintings. They will tell you what is happening.' He returned to his pipe.

The conversation would have continued but the waitress brought them more wine. They searched through their pockets for money.

'Let a liberated lady pay for your drinks,' Marie told them. She put her hand in her pocket, took out a pouch of money and handed the waitress several coins. 'When the bottles are empty bring us some more,' she directed.

They were impressed by the gesture. They were penurious but shared their few pennies.

An old man dressed in a rough army coat entered the café. He made his way from table to table, begging. Under his arm he carried a battered violin case. He approached the group, his cap held out to them.

'Ah, Stephan. You must play for us,' Pieter said.

'You would not listen to my music. It is peasant music I play. Even at the markets they scorn me,' he told them.

'No, Stephan. You play for us. We like your music. It has feeling. It smells of the earth. This waltz to which they all dance is trivial.'

The old man placed his case on the edge of the table and opened it. He produced a cheap violin, thumbed the strings to test their concordance and tightened them until he was pleased with their sound.

Then, closing his eyes, he began to play. He had little talent but his music was plaintive and moving.

'Shall I play more?' he asked hesitantly after he had finished his first tune.

'Yes. We like it very much,' one of the students told him.

Stephan played some more tunes. Then he placed the fiddle in the case and closed it.

Marie Schmerling handed him a coin. He looked at it in wonder. 'This will buy many meals,' he said.

'Good. Have a happy New Year,' she told him.

He walked out of the Grossen Keller with slow, dragging steps and made his way across the road to another cheap café. The snow was falling heavily.

In the Grossen Keller the talk continued. It was vigorous and fragmented. Marie began to enter into the spirit of the place. The wine seemed to lighten her mind. She would welcome in the New Year in a vaulted cellar beneath Vienna. Fieldmann, whom she discovered was an artist, continued to smoke his pipe quietly and drink alone. For some reason Marie could not take her eyes off this wide-shouldered man with the hands of a peasant.

As they set out for the court ball, Joseph Steiner felt content. He had hired the finest carriage in Vienna and he intended to arrive in style. Both his wife and daughters looked resplendent in their gowns.

They passed down the Ring Strasse towards the Opera House, then their pace slowed. Other carriages were before them. Everywhere there were bright lights catching the flakes of snow and turning them into ephemeral leaves of gold. People dressed in heavy clothes had gathered to watch them pass.

The women were afraid to move in case they creased their dresses which had been so carefully arranged by the servants. Their hearts were pounding as they neared the

Hofburg Palace; they felt they were about to enter into an enclosed society.

Finally, the carriage swung into the crescent in front of the palace. A liveried servant rushed forward, opened the door and drew down the steps. He took the ladies' hands and helped them out. They looked in awe at the great steps and the brightly lit doors, with the promise of immense space within.

As they ascended the steps, ahead of them walked members of the diplomatic corps and officers in their regimental uniforms. And then they were on the very edge of brightness. Joseph Steiner took the invitations from his coat and handed them to the doormen. They studied them for a moment then bowed and indicated that they could proceed and they moved into the great hall of the imperial palace. They could hear the music of an orchestra playing. The sound was light-hearted and delightful. Their father had fulfilled his promise.

Alma and Sophie tried not to be too curious as they moved forward along the hall. Everywhere soldiers in regimental dress stood about casually talking with elegant women. The conversation seemed light and frivolous, but never loud. Flags and penaces bore Vienna's ruling sign, an outstretched eagle with predatory beak and proud eye. Gilded wall mirrors reflected the easy movement of people about the polished floors.

'All the royal families of the vast empire have representatives here tonight,' Margit Schmerling remarked triumphantly.

To the young women, as the old century neared its end, life was enchanting.

At eleven o'clock they moved quietly into the great ballroom, the sound of rustling dresses filling the air. They were dazzled by the splendour of the lights, the high ceiling bearing heroic frescoes. At the far end of the great ballroom a full orchestra was playing music by Strauss.

However, they found themselves confined to a quiet corner surrounded by the least important members of the assembly. Alma and Sophie felt embarrassed; no-one had come to invite them to dance. They feared that they might spend the whole night alone, standing by a great window.

'I feel terrible, Mother,' Sophie said, 'I wish I had remained at home. Marie was correct. We do not belong in such a place.'

'You must appear as if you are unconcerned, my dear,' Margit Schmerling replied, her face grim with a forced smile. 'Never display your feelings openly and remember I belong here. I know the social ways of the city.'

'Perhaps we might have to stand here all night and never meet a soul. I so wished to meet one of the royal household,' Alma complained.

It was now half-past eleven. The emperor had not arrived from his rooms in the palace. They listened to the conversations of others. Perhaps he would not attend. Ever since his wife, Elizabeth, had been assassinated, he lived a solitary life at the Schönbrunn.

At twenty-five to twelve there was a fanfare of trumpets. The dancers left the floor and lined up along the walls. At last the Emperor was about to make his entrance. Alma and Sophie had to strain their necks to catch a glimpse of Franz Joseph. He entered through a large, gilded door which was drawn back by liveried doormen, dressed in a red uniform and wearing some of his many decorations. His moustache and sideburns were grey and his eyes looked sad beneath the bushy eyebrows. His back was slightly bent from sitting over his desk at the Schönbrunn Palace.

He moved along the lines of dignitaries waving his hand to those he recognised. Sometimes he paused for a few words. Then he passed on to another group. It took him twenty minutes to reach the end of the ballroom.

Alma and Sophie knew they would only see him at a distance.

He stopped and spoke to some officers, asking them the names of their regiments and where they were stationed. He was about to move forward when his eyes caught those of Alma. His expression changed. He looked intently at her. Then, to Margit's surprise, he moved towards them. The crowd parted and permitted him to pass through. Silence fell about them. For a moment Margit thought that the Emperor was going to pass them by and join some other group. Instead, he stopped before her daughter Alma. He bowed slightly from his hips and turned to his equerry.

The equerry looked quizzically at them. 'Mister Joseph Steiner, his wife Margit, and daughters, Alma and Sophie,' Joseph Steiner told the equerry.

He was about to introduce them formally when the Emperor said. 'I now know their names.' He looked at Alma with a sad smile. 'You remind me of my wife when I met her for the first time in Bavaria,' he said.

'I have read the wonderful story of her life, your Majesty,' Alma told him.

'She was always a young woman. I do not think she ever left Bavaria. She carried it about in her heart. But you must come and visit me at my apartments at the Schönbrunn. I will have my secretary arrange it. Running a large empire can be a tedious thing,'

'It would be a great honour, your majesty,' Alma said almost unconscious of the words she uttered.

Women were beginning to whisper behind their fans. They had heard the conversation and were interested in this young woman who had just made her appearance in Vienna. Others, at a greater distance, wondered why the Emperor had broken his usual custom and talked with commoners.

And then it was twelve o'clock. A fanfare of trumpets

announced the advent of the New Year. All over the city the bells began to ring out. The new century had arrived.

The Emperor turned to Joseph Steiner and his family and wished them a Happy New Year. Then he passed up the ballroom to his gilded chair which was set on a daïs. The orchestra struck up the 'Emperor Waltz' and the crowd began to move onto the great dance floor.

Alma Steiner suddenly became the centre of attention. It was clear to all that she had made a great impression on the Emperor. As they studied her appearance it was obvious why he had been attracted to her. She strongly resembled his beloved Empress Elizabeth.

The young men flocked about her and Sophie. Again and again she was swept onto the great floor to the strains of Strauss. The great lights of the chandelier were reflected in the mirrors as she moved to the light measure of the music.

Alma was about to take a rest when another young man approached her.

'May I have the pleasure of this waltz?' he asked.

She accepted.

He took her in his arms and swept her on to the floor. He was a man of magnificent stature and his movements were elegant and light.

'I am Prince Dmitri,' he announced.

'From Russia?'

'From St Petersburg to be more correct.'

'Are you a friend of Tsar Nicholas?'

'Yes. He appointed me to my position here.'

'I have a secret ambition to visit the great city on the Neva,' Alma said. 'Perhaps some day I will.'

'Perhaps you will.'

The conversation was light and delightful. The Prince bowed and returned her to her seat, where others quickly claimed her attention. He had noted how attentive Franz

Joseph had been to the young woman. She could be an important contact with the Schönbrunn.

Joseph Steiner watched quietly. He had come to the very heart of a great empire and now his stepdaughters were dancing with the best society. Many of them could trace their lineage back a thousand years. His heart pounded with excitement. He was dazed at the turn events had taken.

He turned to his wife Margit. She was sitting in an armchair watching the swirling movement on the dance floor. A smile played on her face. She surveyed the scene with pleasure.

'Shall we dance?' her husband asked her as the orchestra began to play a waltz.

She hesitated. 'Perhaps I have forgotten how to waltz,' she told him.

'No Viennese ever forgets how to waltz. It is in their blood. This is the moment you have waited for. Let us not hesitate. We are at the very heart of the empire. I promised that I would bring you back to Vienna.'

He took her arm and led her on to the dance floor. He drew her into the pattern of the dance with his stiff elegance. Soon she had forgotten her doubts. She was part of the great sweep of things. It was a long time since the Emperor Franz Joseph had been in the same ballroom as her. Life could not be more pleasant than it was at that moment.

Chapter Three

It was late when they left the palace, passing with the other guests down the shallow steps to their carriage. Snow continued to fall in great luminous flakes on Vienna. The streets were bright with lights and laughter. They passed slowly along the Ring Strasse, savouring each moment.

Margit Schmerling was too overcome to speak. She hummed a Viennese tune as she gazed out at the city that now seemed so attractive. She knew every building, every shop along the great street which swung about the old city.

'It is a beautiful night,' she said. 'Why should it end? I have dreamed of this occasion for so many years. Let us drive as far as the Schönbrunn.'

As they drove along the banks of the Danube, the river lights created luminous paths on the hurrying waters. The horses' hoofs drummed softly on the snow.

Joseph Steiner opened a basket he had ordered earlier and took out a bottle of champagne and some glasses and offered them to his wife and daughters. They toasted life as they drove towards the Schönbrunn.

When they arrived at the great wrought-iron gates, only a few lights glowed in the windows. The palace had a strange, deserted air about it. Alma could imagine that, in one of the rooms, the lonely Emperor Franz Joseph was at work on his correspondence.

As they returned to their hotel, Margit recovered her composure. 'You must rent a house for us, Joseph. We cannot receive people at an hotel. After tonight they will be flocking to us.'

'So you intend to settle in Vienna, my dear?' Joseph decided to tease his wife.

'This is my home,' she said indignantly. 'This is where I belong. I believe I shall thrive here. Now that we have the ear of the Emperor, all doors will be open to us. And the girls must have proper quarters. Vienna is impressed with style and wealth.'

'It is never easy to conquer such a city as Vienna,' Steiner warned her.

'You are a pessimist. Tonight, Joseph, I will not listen to such talk. The new century has started well for us.'

There was silence again as they reflected upon the events of the night.

'Do you think the Emperor will invite me to his palace?' Alma asked.

'Of course he will. Do not fret.' Margit was sure of success.

'Perhaps he will forget.'

'He is an Emperor. Of course he will not forget.'

Nevertheless Alma was anxious. Margit decided to change the subject. 'And who is the gentleman who asked you to waltz; that dashing man with the blond hair?'

'Prince Dmitri from Saint Petersburg.'

'I do not like Russians,' Margit replied. 'They are barbarous. Are you going to see him again?'

'I do not know.' Alma looked stubbornly at her mother.

'Take care. He seems to me a dangerous man. Too handsome.'

At the hotel, the servants had fires blazing for them in their rooms, but they sat together for some time, savouring every detail of what had happened that night.

When Steiner took his leave and went to his rooms, he took the photograph from the bureau once more and studied it carefully. He was particularly impressed by the beauty of his mother's face, its restrained sweetness. He realised that, with this photograph, he had picked up the first tentative clues. Now he must search for his roots.

He lit a large cigar and poured himself a brandy. It was a luxury which he rarely indulged in. The fine taste of the brandy and the aroma of the cigar filled his mind with pleasure.

Looking out the window at the falling snow, he laid out his plans for the coming decade.

As he sat smoking there was a knock on the door. He thought that it might be his wife, come to his bed on this the first day of the century.

Sophie entered. 'I have come to say goodnight,' she said.

'Then sit and talk with me. You looked very beautiful tonight. Do you like Vienna?'

'Not as much as Berlin.'

'Berlin!'

'Yes. It has more vigour. Vienna seems so dull.'

'Alma seems to thrive here.'

'And Mother. She will become insufferable. People in Vienna will not tolerate all her nonsense.'

'It will take us some time to settle down in this city. In a year's time, when the snows are falling again on New Year's night, we will consider all that has happened.'

Sophie studied the expression on her stepfather's face. It was lonely. Despite his vast wealth he seemed in search of happiness. She knew her mother no longer slept with him and she often wondered what had attracted him to her.

'I bought you a present,' he said, smiling at her.

'A present?'

'You will find it in my bureau.'

She opened the drawer and looked at the print. The lines were sharp and well etched. It represented a German village scene.

'It is an original Dürer,' he said. 'I knew that you would be pleased with it. You can add it to your collection.'

She set it on the desk and then threw her arms about Steiner. 'Thank you. I wish you could be happy.'

'I am happy. I discovered this by chance in an attic.' He took the photograph and showed it to her. 'That is worth more to me than the finest masterpiece I possess,' he told her.

'What a simple picture. The woman is beautiful in a quiet way.'

'They are my parents just as I remember them, so many years ago. That is my New Year's gift to myself.'

He described the events of the day. 'I felt at home in that ghetto as much as your mother felt at home at the grand ball. Now, I feel firmly set here as much as she. So the New Year has been good to us all.'

'You look tired, Papa. It is time to go to bed,' Sophie said.

'The excitement of the night makes one sleepy. But I will sit and read for some time. I require little rest.'

She bent down and kissed his cheek.

'Has Marie returned?' he asked.

'No. You know there was a dreadful quarrel today.'

'There are always dreadful quarrels with Marie. She detests rank and she hates wealth. She is so firmly convinced that she can change the world. I have argued with her but she will not see reason. Vienna should suit her temperament.'

But when Sophie had left and he continued to look at the snowflakes falling past the window, he reflected that of all Margit Schmerling's daughters, he liked Marie the best.

Margit and Alma remained before the great fire in the drawing room. Margit had opened a bottle of champagne and as they drank they reminisced about the night.

'It could not have been more perfect. It was the ideal introduction to society. No later than tomorrow we shall look for a house in the best quarter of the city. Money is no object with Joseph Steiner. Soon, I expect to be flooded with invitations to the best houses in Vienna.'

Alma, though, was dubious about the invitations. Her mother had been carried away with events. Now, as she grew drunk on champagne, her imagination began to create illusions.

'The Emperor will certainly want to know about my rights to the Schmerling estates. When Count Schmerling died without issue, the title should have passed to your father, not to a nephew. They left me penniless with three children. My case must be brought to the ears of the Emperor.'

Illusions or not, Alma reflected, there was no mistaking the bitterness in Margit's voice. 'It is time for bed, Mother,' she soothed, 'You have had enough to drink. Tomorrow you must be clear-minded. We will take a trip around Vienna and look at houses.'

But Margit insisted on more champagne. This had been her night and she had no wish to go to bed.

Alma knew her mother had had too much champagne, when Marie returned, and Margit looked at her daughter with stupid eyes.

'You are not a Schmerling,' she called. 'You were got out of a common soldier. You are a bastard and you have the heedless ways of a bastard.'

Marie stood before her. Her eyes blazed with anger. 'You stupid drunken woman. You call yourself a countess? Look at you. You look like a fish woman.' She had not seen Margit so drunk before.

But her mother had placed a doubt in Marie's mind which would settle there. Perhaps she was illegitimate. Then who was her father? Perhaps he was a common soldier, as Margit had said.

Stung by her mother's words, she called out, 'If I am a bastard then you are a whore.'

But Margit did not listen to her. Excitement coursed through her veins. 'Tonight I met the Emperor. Countess Schmerling met the Emperor. We spoke together. What do you think of that, you bitch,' she asked, a smug smile on her lips.

'He is rotten with syphillis. No wonder his children were mad. His son committed suicide. His wife turned strange. Is this the company you aspire to?'

At this, Alma turned on her sister. 'You are evil saying such things about the monarch. We met this evening and he invited me to visit him at the palace. How dare you spoil such a pleasant night. I hate you. No matter how kind people are, you turn bitter towards them. We are tired of your ravings.'

'She is a bitch,' her mother said from the chair, her words slurred. 'I will throw her out on the street. That is where she belongs. She has common blood in her veins.'

They had reached the end of their insults. Marie turned and left the room.

In her bedroom, Marie looked at the night skyline of the city. It was vague and soft under the moon.

The snow had stopped for the moment.

She felt isolated. She bent forward and wept. She had not wept for a long time and she knew she would not weep again. She rocked her body to and fro until she controlled her sobbing.

She hated Margit Schmerling. She hated the social structure of Vienna. She hated the pretence of the city. Most of all, she hated her vulnerability. Who was she?

It was much later when Margit Schmerling turned in. Alma helped her to her bed.

'It was my night and I enjoyed it,' she called drunkenly as Alma closed the door.

* * *

That night, Prince Dmitri returned to the embassy. He opened his desk, took out his diary and wrote down the events of the evening. He was particularly interested in the health of the Emperor. Despite the long hours he spent administering the empire he seemed fit. Only his broad back seemed to have bent a little with the burden of office over the years. He also noted the young woman who had attracted the eye of Franz Joseph.

Having written up his account he left the embassy and returned to the villa he had rented. As he was driven through the snowy streets of Vienna he thought of St Petersburg, set out along the river Neva. It was an exciting place compared with Vienna with its rigid court rules. He wished that he were celebrating the New Year at the Winter Palace.

However, he was conscious of his important position in Vienna. At any time there could be trouble in the Balkans, then he would have to move swiftly. His orders were definite. His affiliations lay with the Serbs. Now, the massing of Croat troops along the Bosnian border was troubling.

Finally he arrived at his home where his servant, Nikka, was waiting for him. Dmitri could smell vodka on his breath.

'You have been celebrating the New Year, Nikka.'

'My heart has been full of sadness. I drank too much and I sang sad songs. When will we return to Russia, master? When will I be with my friends again?'

'Soon, Nikka. Soon.'

Nikka threw his great arms around his master and wished him a happy New Year.

Count Dmitri tapped him warmly on the shoulder. 'Happy New Year. We will return to Russia, I promise you, and we will hunt in the forests. Goodnight.'

'Goodnight, master.'

It was very late. Dmitri made his way to bed.

Chapter Four

Joseph Steiner was correct. Invitations did not flood in, as his wife had anticipated. Instead, they felt isolated in the great city. Margit Schmerling made several attempts to invite some of the lesser nobility to their new town house but her invitations were not answered.

'It was a mistake,' she told Sophie. 'We should never have returned to the city. They still resent me. I should never have married that Jew, Joseph Steiner. Vienna hates Jews. Vienna has always hated them.'

'You cannot lay the blame at his feet,' Sophie replied in his defence. 'He is a decent man. Perhaps your aspirations are too high?'

At this, Margit flew into a rage. 'Aspirations too high! Aspirations too high! My aspirations are equal to my status in this city. You side with him against your mother; Marie spends her time with poor artists and preaches revolution. Only Alma stands by me.'

'You know that is not true,' Sophie replied.

'It is,' Margit called back. 'Oh, when will I have peace,' she protested. 'I am not feeling well. I must rest.'

The arguments always followed the same predictable course and ended with Margit retiring to her room.

It was late spring when the invitation arrived. Flowers were blooming in the city parks and the trees were in bloom in the Viennese woods.

'It carries the imperial crest,' Margit Schmerling cried excitedly when she was handed the letter. She tore it open.

'You have been invited to meet the Emperor. He has not forgotten you. I knew it! I knew it! An Emperor never breaks his word. Now, how shall I dress you for the occasion.'

Alma grew angry. 'How dare you open my correspondence! I shall dress simply. I will go and meet the Emperor without undue fuss.'

Despite her mother's protestations she dressed discreetly for the occasion.

At eleven o'clock that April morning a coach drew up at the front gates of the Schmerling household. It carried the imperial crest on the door.

'Let it remain on the street for some minutes,' Margit said imperiously. 'I wish my neighbours to see it.'

'I must not keep the Emperor waiting,' Alma complained.

Finally she entered the carriage. Her mother stood at the gate and waved to her daughter proudly.

The carriage swung through the gates of the Schönbrunn Palace and across the cobbled courtyard. It passed through an archway and stopped on the gravel before an impressive sweep of steps. Immediately a servant in livery escorted her through the palace and into the presence of Emperor Franz Joseph.

His eyes brightened when he saw her. 'How delightful of you to come. I will have some tea served and you can tell me about your stay in Vienna. The Emperor hears little gossip from the city. Too busy dealing with correspondence pouring in from all over the Empire,' he smiled, indicating the massive bundles on the table.

'And do you deal with each letter, your Majesty?' she asked.

'Yes.'

'Then you carry too heavy a burden.'

'Who can I trust?' he asked, chuckling.

The tea was brought to his office and they sat and talked of city matters, the light operas she had seen and the concerts she had attended. It was pleasant talk and the time passed rapidly.

'Now we shall walk in the gardens for a little while. I love them at this time of year.'

Despite his years Franz Joseph walked briskly to the Gloriette, which stretched across the landscape above the gardens.

As they strolled back to the palace he turned to her and said, 'I hope that you will be happy in this city. You remind me of the gaiety of my youth. You must come and visit me again.'

It had been a trivial and pleasant encounter, but when she said goodbye to the Emperor and returned home in the coach, her was mind filled with excitement. This extraordinary man liked her and wanted to see her again.

'Well,' inquired her mother. 'Did he ask after me? Did you mention to him my purpose in returning to Vienna?'

'No, Mother. We spoke of pleasant things. He told me of his youth and of his first meeting with Elizabeth. Then he asked me about the gossip of the city.'

'Gossip? Why is the Emperor interested in gossip?'

'Everyone in Vienna is interested in gossip, Mother.'

However, the visit of Alma to the Emperor did have its effect. Soon, invitations arrived at the house from the lesser nobility. Margit Schmerling began to form a coterie about her.

Sophie drifted away from the petty court intrigue, more interested in her stepfather's activities.

Joseph Steiner had rented an office close to the quays. The Danube flowed past it and from the window he could study the movement of ships.

He was a secretive man. For weeks on end he did not

return to the house. Sometimes he disappeared from the city and nobody knew where he was.

'He is a wandering Jew,' Margit often said. 'So do not ask me where he is. You know the Jews. They are a furtive race. They keep to the dark alleys.'

One day Sophie arrived at his office, on the top floor of an eighteenth-century building. When she walked in, she was surprised to see two of the newly invented telephones and three secretaries working in an adjoining room.

Her stepfather was pleased to see her. 'What brings you here?' he asked.

'Boredom,' she said. 'I am tired of the circle my mother has gathered about her. They indulge in petty gossip. They have venomous tongues and all the daughters are spoiled. I cannot endure them. I wish to work with you.'

He considered her for a moment. She had a determined look on her handsome face.

'Are you certain?' he asked, looking closely at her.

'I am. I never feel comfortable in mother's society. I feel like screaming. My heart and my mind tell me that I should be doing something real, something useful.'

'And do you think that you will find satisfaction in these offices and in this old building? This is not the very best part of the city.'

'This is where money is made. This is the trading centre of the city. It is bursting with life.'

He considered Sophie for a moment. His stepdaughter did not belong in drawing rooms. Her conversations were never trivial and she had an alert mind. Perhaps he could trust her with his financial secrets. There was no other he could turn to.

'This is not easy work. Your back will ache and your feet will grow tired. As you notice I do not carpet the stairs and they are made from cold stone.'

'You are trying to dissuade me.'

'No. I am telling you the truth.'

'Well, I accept your truth. I am willing to do whatever you wish.'

'Very well,' he said. 'One of the secretaries will teach you how to type. When you have become competent I will make you my secretary.'

'Very well. I will begin this moment.' She disappeared into the adjoining room which had a glass partition.

Joseph Steiner watched her as she talked with the secretary. She seemed intent on success. Five minutes later she was sitting before a typewriter, learning the position of the central letters.

All morning she practised with grim determination.

'Let me take you for some coffee,' he told her at midday. 'You deserve a rest.'

'I will learn how to type,' she said as they walked down the stairs. 'If I am to be useful to you, I must.'

The café lay close to the quays. She had not been in such a place before. It was heavy with the scent of cigars and brandy. Men sat in conspiratorial huddles talking quietly.

'The wheat business of Vienna is carried on here. Every loaf of bread and each pastry that is consumed in the city begins here. Let me introduce you to one of my friends. He is from the Hungarian plains. He is a wheat broker.'

The broker was an old man. He smoked a large cigar and sipped from a small cup of coffee. He removed his hat and bowed to her.

'You say you can carry my wheat at a lower price than many of the others. Why is that, Steiner?'

'Simple figures. I make less on each ton of wheat. But I import a great tonnage. I can be trusted to deliver.'

'And could I trade you wheat for guns?'

'Yes.'

'And where can you get guns?'

'I have contacts.'

'I do not need guns, Steiner, but I do need machinery. We are building a great smelting furnace in my town. I need a complete smelting works. You get me a complete smelting works, crated and marked, and an engineer to install it, and I will fill all your barges with wheat.'

'Good. I will have a smelting factory ready for you within a year.'

'Six months, Steiner.'

'Very well. Six months.'

Sophie listened intently to the dealing. As yet, it was too complicated for her to follow, but she knew she would learn.

Before the old man left he turned to Steiner and said, 'I am satisfied.'

They shook hands and he departed.

'What was all that about?' she asked.

'A vast sum of money. I have purchased some barges. They will carry wheat from the Hungarian plains. All great fortunes arise out of such deals. And one piece of advice. Never try to make a quick profit in such business. It never succeeds. With the stock exchange, it is a different matter.'

'But why did you say you could produce a smelting works within six months?'

'Because I can. I have some friends in Berlin. A visit to the city and the deal will be realised. I am a go-between.'

'There is much to learn.'

'I know. But you only learn through dealing.'

'Can you trust the gentleman?'

'Of course I can. In his youth he was a bandit. I always trust bandits. I never trust politicians.' And with that he began to laugh.

Sophie loved the rough atmosphere of the place and the strong, committed scents. Barge captains, dealers, money lenders and prostitutes mixed freely in the café. It satisfied that strong, dark part of Sophie's nature.

Within two months she could type efficiently. One day

Steiner entered the office and dictated a letter to her. He took it and studied it.

'Very good,' he said. 'You have a natural aptitude for this business. Your mother will not like this, but you can move into my office. I have work for you to do. Let me tell you what I have in mind.'

He sat down and explained to her that he had acquired a large art collection over the years.

'The paintings are secured in vaults all over Europe. I wish you to catalogue them. Then I intend to bring them here to Vienna and offer them to the national gallery. They will be known as the Steiner Collection. But first, we must secure premises where they will be safe. All this I leave in your hands. But before you embark upon this task I wish you to go to visit Berlin and sign the contract for the smelting plant. It is crated and ready to be shipped.'

'It is a considerable undertaking.'

'You were bored. I can assure you that this work will be anything but boring. Will you accept the challenge?'

'Yes,' she said firmly.

'Good. I rely upon your discretion. You must be discreet in this business. There are times when I disappear. I will not let you know where I am going. You will have to trust me.'

Sophie found Berlin exhilarating. She requested that she be brought through the industrial section of the city. The magnitude of the mills and the factories surpassed her imagination. Everywhere there was activity and confidence and everything was modern. The factories were contemporary and neat and the machinery gleamed with polish and oil. The pungent odour of the smoke and the factories lingered in her mind. It possessed a sense of power and urgency.

When she returned to Vienna a week later, her stepfather was waiting for her.

'Well?' he asked when she entered.

'I signed the contracts and supervised the transport of the crates. They have arrived at warehouse C.'

'Good. And what did you think of Berlin?'

'It is filled with energy. It moves forward. I loved every moment of my visit there.'

She explained to him how she had visited all the industrial areas.

'We are becoming partners,' he smiled.

This was the beginning of Sophie Schmerling's association with Joseph Steiner.

Marie was coming to terms with Vienna. Already she had contacted several socialist clubs and had visited the slums of the city. It was a world at variance with that of her mother's romantic dream. But Marie no longer bothered to argue with her. She entered the house by the kitchen and she kept to her own two rooms. She began to study socialist literature in depth.

Yet one image often presented itself to her mind. It rankled in her memory.

She recalled the night her mother had called her a bastard.

It had been in drink but Marie knew from her mother's voice that it had been true, and she hated the manner in which Margit had humiliated her.

'Where do I belong?' she often asked herself in frustration. She did not belong with the family. Now, she knew she belonged to the great seething, homeless masses all over Europe.

She would have revenge on the aristocrats. They were pampered and useless.

Marie had one ally. Of all the men she had ever met, the artist Jacov Fieldmann had impressed her most by his character. He possessed a free spirit and a strong mind. His work possessed energy which many of the other artists lacked.

When Marie inquired after him in the Grossen Keller, his friend Pieter was dismissive. 'Fieldmann. He is restless. At this moment he is probably wandering the Caucasus studying the art of the peasants and stealing the affection of their wives and daughters. Someday he will return to the Grossen Keller again. He will take up where he left off.'

Marie devoted all her time to the socialist committees in Vienna.

The memory of the first New Year in Vienna passed. The Schmerling family, in their different ways, settled into life in the imperial city.

Chapter Five

That spring of 1903, there was a certain amount of excitement in Vienna. The charming, but wayward Prince Karl had returned after four years in self-imposed exile in Italy.

'Why did he leave the city?' Margit Schmerling asked one of her friends. Her interest was aroused. Here at last was a man with status – a true prince, and a distant relative of the Emperor.

'It is a confused story. Of course it is merely gossip,' her friend replied.

'Nevertheless, I wish to hear it.' Her curiosity had to be gratified.

'Prince Karl is a gambler among other things. One night in a casino on an island to the south of the city he shot a man, who had accused Karl of cheating at cards.'

'Murder?!'

'Yes. Nothing was ever proven of course. It is rumoured that the body was weighed down with chains and dumped in the river. His friend, Prince Dmitri, took charge of the whole affair. It seems they made a pact that they would remain silent on the matter. An inquiry was held, but of course nothing could be proven and Prince Karl quickly left the city. Rumour has it he was banished by no less than the Emperor himself.'

'And now he returns.' Margit was shocked, but intrigued.

'The affair has been forgotten about.'

'But I know this Prince Dmitri, he is attached to the Russian Embassy,' Margit realised.

'They say he cuts a dashing figure about the city.'

'And that he is one of the richest men in Russia,' Margit added, a gleam in her eye. 'But when will we have an opportunity of seeing this Prince Karl?'

'I would say that he will soon make his appearance at some of the social functions. However, it is also rumoured that the man is broke.'

'He is royalty. That is what counts. I would be delighted to ask him to dine with us.'

When Alma heard her mother's story later, her curiosity was aroused. She often found her mother's gossip petty and rather foolish, but she now felt intrigued by this shadowy figure who had just appeared in the city. Perhaps he would be interesting to meet.

Two days previously Prince Dmitri had gone to the railway station to meet his friend, Prince Karl. He was surprised at how fresh he looked when he descended from the train. He was impeccably dressed in the latest fashions and he walked with a gold-topped cane. Clearly, poverty had not forced him to change his tastes.

They immediately set off to the Russian embassy. Karl was excited by his return to the city. 'I missed Vienna with its intrigue and its gossip. Italy is a rotten place. I recall only long days in the sun and tiresome conversations.'

'And the women?'

'All titled and all poor. I did find a young widow and consoled her for four years. I helped her get rid of some of her fortune. But what is the news of Vienna?'

'Nothing new. The Emperor sits in the Schönbrunn and the empire becomes more difficult to run. Franz Joseph is not very bright. His empire needs to be tidied up.'

'Is that not to Russia's advantage?' Prince Karl remarked. At times his mind could be sharply perceptive.

It was true. Prince Dmitri was anxious about Russia, and a weak Austrian empire was an advantage. Trouble was stirring in the Balkans, the running sore on the side of the empire.

But soon Prince Karl tired of political thought. Spring was in the Vienna air and he was bent on pleasure. 'I am afraid that I am financially constrained at the moment,' he said, not daring to look at Prince Dmitri. 'I had to flee Italy before another royal scandal broke about my neck. Left a considerable sum of money behind. It will, of course, be returned to you when I get on my feet.'

'Very well. I will advance you a thousand florins.'

When they reached Dmitri's villa, Nikka opened the coach door and let them out. He looked sullenly at Prince Karl, remembering the incident in the casino. He had been called upon to carry the body to the boat and wrap it in chains. He did not mind such dirty business but Prince Karl had neither thanked him nor given him money for his efforts.

Despite having fled from Italy in a hurry Prince Karl had several heavy suitcases. Nikka carried them to his room.

'That will do,' the prince said, and dismissed him.

'I do not like your friend,' Nikka said sullenly to Count Dmitri, outside in the hallway. 'He has a cold heart. He is like a fish.' He spoke in guttural Russian.

'He is useful to me, Nikka,' Dmitri said. 'He provides me with information when he is in Vienna.'

'He is dangerous.'

'Have you made contact with Vasilj?'

'Yes. I brought him here this morning. We arrived by the back entrance.'

'Were you observed?'

'I pretended that we were two drunk peasants.'

'Very good. I will speak to him.'

Dmitri found Vasilj in the library. He was a serious young man with intense features and a heavy moustache.

'What is the news from the Balkans?' he asked.

Vasilj stood before a large map. He gave Dmitri a detailed account of the whole area, so complex it was almost impossible to understand.

'It is unstable and will tear itself apart. It is impossible to hold it together. The Turkish power is weakening. There will be a rebellion, I am sure of it. It may not happen immediately but it is evident. Austria has her eyes on the Balkans and could at any moment move her armies to the frontiers and take the peninsula.'

Prince Dmitri knew that he was looking at a powder keg. A single spark and the place could blow asunder. Then everyone would be drawn into the war.

'In the event of a war I will move immediately into the Balkans and fight with you. Tonight you can leave the palace and return to your own country. I will see you again in three months' time.'

When Vasilj left the library, Prince Dmitri sat down at his desk. Many things disturbed him. The Russian army was ill-prepared for war and Nicholas II was a weak man. Like Franz Joseph, he had little knowledge of what was happening in his empire, no great grasp of military matters and he was incapable of making a decision. He, too, could bring his house down upon him like a pack of cards.

'But Europe is firm and civilised,' a friend had argued with him a few days previously.

'It *appears* firm and civilised,' he had insisted. 'But look at Germany. With its idealist spirit, it is becoming a great force, with an elite military corps. It thinks on logical lines. We must be prepared and we are not.'

By that evening Prince Karl was ready to make his grand entrance into Vienna.

He had spent the day in bed and was now totally refreshed. He was a creature of the evening and of the night.

He was dressed immaculately when he emerged from his room. Prince Dmitri was impressed by the clarity of his skin. It was that of a young boy and his debauches had not left any trace on his face.

He opened a bottle of champagne and they toasted Prince Karl's arrival in Vienna. 'To some rich young widow who is unaware of my seductive charm,' Karl said.

They set out for the light opera, arriving just before the rise of the curtain. The members of the orchestra were dolefully tuning up, the strings of instruments complaining as they were drawn into concordance. Prince Karl checked that none of the royal family would be present so that they could sit in the royal box. Their entrance was greeted by a flutter of whispering beneath them. Opera glasses were trained on the box.

It was the first glance Alma had had of Prince Karl. Her heart stopped a beat. He was as handsome as poor Prince Rudolph, who had killed himself at Mayerling. This at last was the missing Hapsburg.

Margit Schmerling had also trained her glasses on the box. 'He is with Prince Dmitri. What a handsome pair they make. He is a close friend of the Tsar, I believe,' she whispered excitedly.

The overture began and the curtains were drawn aside to reveal the courtyard of an inn in a Bavarian village. But Alma was not interested in the pretty music. Again and again she turned her opera glasses towards Prince Karl. In his noble features and elegant dress lay the wonderful arrogance of royalty.

At the interval mother and daughter engaged in quiet chatter.

'Well, what do you think?' Margit asked.

'He is very handsome.'

'And dangerous, my dear. Remember the rumours.'

'Perhaps he has changed.' Alma continued to stare at the royal box, her face flushed.

'Perhaps.'

Finally Alma dragged her gaze from Prince Karl and turned to the stage. She feigned an interest in the third act and when it was finished and the final curtain came down they began to pour out of the theatre.

They lingered in the great entrance hall with the rest of the audience, anxious to meet some of the petty nobles or their wives. It was known that Alma was a confidante of the old Emperor and many of those who thought that she might be beneficial to them made it their business to meet her.

They were about to leave when the two princes swept down the main staircase. It was a move planned by Prince Karl. Both men were tall and Prince Dmitri was dressed in his regimental uniform; a red coat and blue trousers piped in gold. The crowd burst into spontaneous applause.

Prince Karl stopped for a moment and fell into conversation with several young women who were charmed by his presence. Meanwhile Prince Dmitri clinically surveyed the Viennese beauties. They had little to distinguish them from each other. Then his eye caught Alma Schmerling and he recalled that he had danced with her once at a New Year's Eve Court Ball. More importantly he remembered that she paid frequent visits to the Schönbrunn Palace for private conversations with the Emperor. It was a privilege accorded to very few.

As the two princes swept through the crowd again Prince Dmitri turned to Alma Schmerling. 'We danced together at the Court Ball,' he remarked

'That is correct,' she said.

'Allow me to introduce Prince Karl. He has just returned from Italy.'

The Prince bowed from the waist. Alma was aware of his fine skin, his carefully groomed figure and the scent of his perfume.

Prince Karl looked at her carefully. He was struck by her beauty.

'Alma is a close friend of the Emperor,' Prince Dmitri said pointedly.

'I hope that he is well,' the prince said. 'I have not had the opportunity to meet him since my return.'

'Yes, he is very well,' she replied.

Margit Schmerling was aware that there was buzz of conversation in the great hall. The crowd was impressed by the amount of time the two princes granted Alma. Clearly it was a social coup.

'I hope that we shall meet again,' Karl said as he bowed and left the theatre.

Alma looked after the departing princes, a bright light in her eyes.

When they were in the coach Prince Karl asked petulantly, 'How can she meet the Emperor when he has banished me from his presence? I am surprised he did not send some soldiers to turn me back at the border.'

'Did you not see that she resembles his late wife? Through her he can live his romantic past.'

'Is she his mistress?'

'No. The old emperor is beyond that.'

'And what of her wealth?'

'Her stepfather is a Jew. They say that his wealth is limitless.'

'She is not Jewish though, surely?' Prince Karl was horrified.

'No. Middle-class Viennese. A tentative connection with some title or other. The mother believes that she is a duchess. She could be your way back into the royal family,' Prince Dmitri said. 'It is a consideration.'

'I am not that desperate.'

'Perhaps someday you will be.'

The coach continued to the outskirts of Vienna to a secluded building surrounded by trees. It had been one of Prince Karl's favourite gambling haunts four years previously. When they entered, he recognised many of the gentlemen present. Well-acquainted with his reputation, they welcomed him back to the city and very soon they were engaged in a game of cards.

Prince Dmitri noted that Karl had not changed his gambling habits. At the beginning he was cautious. Then after a run of bad luck he grew nervous and began to bet on weak cards. Shamelessly he asked Prince Dmitri to lend him some money and at the end of the evening, he was fortunate to recoup his losses.

Towards morning Karl decided to visit a brothel, a low-class place where young women were forced into prostitution through poverty. Prince Dmitri waited for him while he chose a woman and took her to a bedroom. Later there were screams of pain and the young woman rushed naked into the foyer. Her face was swollen from the beating she had received.

The Madame rushed to her rescue and called out, 'I will not have my girls beaten.'

'I am a Hapsburg,' Karl roared at her. 'I have the power to close down this flea pit. Do you hear me.'

'Is this true?' she asked Prince Dmitri.

'It is.'

'Then take your friend with you and do not return. He is a brute.'

By the time they returned to Dmitri's villa, Prince Karl had regained his composure. 'It will not happen again,' he said. 'I must be careful.'

Although daylight was breaking over the city, before Prince Dmitri went to bed he recorded the day's events in his diary. The final entry read: 'I believe that Prince Karl is of such a strange, nervous disposition that he is quite mad, like his cousin Rudolph. He displays the same symptoms.'

By early summer Sophie Schmerling had grown used to

Vienna, being increasingly involved with the business of Joseph Steiner.

'It is such a tangle,' she said to him one day. 'I will never understand it.'

'It only appears to be a tangle,' he told her, 'because you are looking for some centre which holds it all together. Well, there is no centre. I have never concentrated my shares or my money in one place. This the people of my race have learned from bitter experience. And there are always the hidden sources; diamonds and gold, preferably gold, hidden in vaults.'

'And what of your art collection?'

'Paintings are valuable but they give me pleasure, too. I do not trade in art. It gives me great joy. That is why I wish to bring my paintings to Vienna. I have plans for them.'

'It will take me two more years to finish the catalogue, Papa.'

'Take your time. When it is finished I will have it printed privately. I have plans for my collection. Joseph Steiner will be remembered in Vienna. However, in the meantime I have other plans. Today we are going on a small journey. I have ordered a coach.'

'Where are we going?'

'To survey a property which is about to come on the market. A friend told me about it, and at present I do not wish anyone to know of my interest in it.'

'Where is it situated?'

'A short distance from the city. It is a baroque mansion, surrounded by mature trees.'

'You never cease to surprise me.'

'Surprise is the very seasoning of life. Let us go.'

They travelled south, until they reached the entrance to a walled estate. In the early summer sunlight, the trees cast dappled shadows on the avenue, which opened to reveal a splendid baroque villa painted with a blue wash.

In front of it was a small lake crowded with flowers and small reeded islands.

Waiting at the front door was a middle-aged gentleman who unlocked the doors and they moved into the parqueted hall. A staircase with flowing balustrades led to the first storey. The house smelt fresh and clean.

They passed through all the magnificent rooms and looked at the stucco work, the gilded mouldings, the ceiling frescoes. They opened the balcony doors and looked down on the lake and the trees beyond it.

'What do you think?' he asked.

'It has a gem-like quality. It is perfect in every way,' Sophie said excitedly.

Joseph and Sophie spent three hours in the house, taking pleasure in everything they saw. Sophie could not remember having seen any prettier building in her travels. 'You must buy it. Who owns it?' she asked.

'A Baron Von Hertling from Berlin. A military man, I believe. It belonged to his aunt.'

'Is it for sale?'

'Of course it is for sale. I have set my eye on it and I intend to buy it. Perhaps he will not sell it to a Jew, so I have arranged for an important banker to buy it for me. He will buy it in his name and the whole affair will be dignified. Later, I will purchase it from him.'

'And will the banker sell it to you?'

'Of course he will. He is using my money. He is broke. I have offered him a high commission for the transaction.'

'You are a clever man, Joseph Steiner,' Sophie said.

'I have to be. Your mother must never know, but in three or four years' time, when you and your sisters are settled, I intend to move in here. Things are not going well between us. Vienna has changed her. The poison of the city is entering her heart.'

Sophie shivered, but did not ask exactly what he meant by those words.

* * *

When Baron Von Hertling, Chief of Germany's élite military police, heard of the offer on his property, he was delighted. The bid exceeded those of all the others who were interested in it.

'I spent many happy days there in my youth. But that is past now,' he told his solicitor. When the deal was formally signed, he breathed a sigh of relief. He looked at the large cheque. He had not handled such a large sum for a long time. He would invest it in property in Berlin. He had confidence in that city and its future.

He returned to Germany as soon as his business was finished in Vienna.

Prince Karl never received his money from Italy. He sold some shares in the Austrian Railways which he did not realise he possessed until his solicitor drew his attention to their existence.

'Carefully managed, this guarantees my independence for two years,' he told Prince Dmitri, 'And with some luck at the gaming tables I will increase my wealth. I believe that luck has smiled on me.'

'Luck never smiles on him,' Dmitri told Nikka later. 'I will wager that in one year he will be broke.'

Prince Dmitri was correct. Prince Karl threw lavish parties, invited the most expensive prostitutes to his quarters and spent his nights gambling. Within a year he had frittered away his wealth.

'I was unlucky,' he said when he came to borrow more money from Prince Dmitri. 'I can remember games which turned on the twist of a card. I could have doubled my wealth.'

Despite his misgivings, Prince Dmitri advanced him a large sum of money.

'You will regret it, Master,' Nikki told him.

'No. Some day he will have to pay me back. I can assure you I have plans for Prince Karl.'

As summer turned to autumn, however, Prince Dmitri's attention was abruptly drawn towards the east. The Japanese had surprised the Russians in a night raid at Port Arthur, one of their most useful ports in Korea, and destroyed a great part of the Russian fleet there. Now the eastern flank of the empire was exposed.

He followed the course of events intently, appalled at the casualties. 'Two hundred thousand dead. This is slaughter! The generals should be court-martialled. If we cannot defeat Japan then our enemies will gather about us,' he told Nikka.

But the defeat at Port Arthur was greeted with joy in Vienna. Dmitri felt the humiliation of it in the ballrooms and in the brothels. 'The Tsar is a fool,' one of Karl's gambling friends said. 'He knows little of war and he knows little of peace. He is not a true leader.'

Despite the importance of his duties in Vienna, Dmitri asked for permission to return to his regiment in Russia urgently, but it was refused – it was deemed that he had more important business in the Austrian capital. He could only look helplessly on as the tragedy unfolded.

The carnage continued through spring of the next year, and he read all the dispatches avidly. 'We are no longer dealing with little Japs,' a correspondent had written in one of the papers. 'We are dealing with skilful opponents.'

'If the Tsar fails then we all fail,' Dmitri told Nikka. But Nikka did not understand. He possessed a peasant mind and could not grasp abstract ideas.

'We must hunt,' he told his master. 'We must shoot boar. If we do not, you will go mad. Let us leave this city and hunt the boars.'

They left Vienna and set off for a hunting lodge in the high hills.

In August of that year, Jacov Fieldmann returned from his wanderings, carrying on his back all the paintings he had done in his travels and several sketchbooks. He entered the Grossen Keller one evening and ordered a bottle of wine.

'You are back, Fieldmann,' the artists said. They noticed that his face was weatherbeaten and his hair had grown. His beard was thick and grey streaks ran through it.

'Obviously.'

'And where have you been?'

'Nowhere and everywhere. Let me tell you about it.' He took off his backpack and sat with them. He entertained them with stories well into the night. They were drunk when they reeled out of the tavern.

Marie could not take her eyes off Fieldmann. She was fascinated by his character.

As she walked home through the streets she wondered if she were in love with him.

During the last few years she had had little time for love. She had joined the Communist Party. She had studied the ideas of a revolutionary called Vladimir Lenin, in a publication entitled *What is to be Done*. His ideas had inspired her and she had begun a correspondence with him in Switzerland.

But now her mind was obsessed not with thoughts of Vladimir Lenin, but with Jakov Fieldmann.

Chapter Six

As Baron Otto Von Hertling passed through the Tiergarten towards the Brandenburg Gate, he felt that Berlin in late autumn was as beautiful as Paris and more vital than Vienna. He listened to the echo of the cannons, and it seemed that an advancing army was moving through this great park in the heart of Berlin.

Two hours previously, he had met the Kaiser at the Charlottenburg Palace, in his ornate office, hung with tapestries and made intimate by dark panelling. There he was instructed to form a new secret service, specialising in military espionage.

'A new Germany is coming into being. We must be prepared. You belong to a family who trace their bloodline back to the Teutonic Knights. I know you will give sterling service to this new Germany. You will be directly accountable to me.'

The Baron had been trained at a military academy and the Prussian discipline had given him a taut appearance. His mind was sharp and his body toned by rigorous exercise. He was ready to belong to the inner circle of Kaiser Wilhelm.

Only six months previously he had feared he would never escape the Palazzo Cafferelli, the German embassy in Rome, a city he detested. Then a telegram had been sent, instructing him to report back to Berlin.

When he had told his superior, Franz, Baron Von Kühn of his instructions, the older man had smiled wryly, 'You move into the centre of power,' he had said, turning a wine glass between his fingers. 'There is much intrigue in Berlin.

The Bismarck family is still a power despite Kaiser Wilhelm.'

'Have you no ambition to return to Berlin?'

'No. My wish is to remain here. I'm not caught up by all this new nationalism. I prefer Rome to all other cities; beneath the Christian layer lies a deeper pagan stratum that is wide and dark. To me this is civilisation,' Von Kühn gestured at the wide piazza visible through the open window. It was summer in Rome and the dome of Saint Peter's stood sharp and green against a blue sky. 'I find the landscape of Berlin flat and featureless compared to Rome.'

'Few Germans have taken so fully to the experience of Italy. They always long for home,' Von Hertling said.

'They may have their sausages and their beer. I prefer wines and good foods.' Von Kühn had been a classical scholar. During the summers he had made journeys through Greece and sailed on the Ionian Sea, learning the language as he passed through the landscape. He could recite long passages of Greek and Latin by heart and to demonstrate a political point he could search through his memory for a suitable quotation. He had the wide sympathies of a Renaissance man. Berlin with its dark intrigue, its inward-looking view of itself, did not attract him.

'You will marry a German princess, Von Hertling, consolidate your family estates, sire a large German family and feel quite satisfied with your lot,' he said pouring himself another glass of wine.

'There is much to be achieved before I settle for such bland contentment. I think you underestimate my ambitions,' Von Hertling replied.

'Perhaps I do. But you are too caught up with this German thing. It is romantic for young men to sacrifice their lives for a fatherland which is of Bismarck's creating.'

Baron Von Hertling felt anger growing within him. His friend trivialised the new German State. 'You speak dangerously. Such words will be reported back to the capital.'

'The day we have no right to speak freely concerning our feelings is the day in which darkness falls. I do not fear the Kaiser as others do. I am not one of the toadies who have to flatter him.'

'You have become Roman,' Von Hertling said dryly.

'Perhaps I have.'

They drank their wine in silence and looked at the city Von Hertling hated. He had never mastered the language and felt a stranger here. He could not relax and he did not understand the complex intrigue of the Vatican.

Baron Von Kühn was valued in the city for his taste and his learning. He knew the subtlety of the Italian mind and with apparent ease could unravel difficult diplomatic problems. He was not only a friend to the Pope but the Viennese ambassador to Rome often consulted him on delicate issues.

'Then, of course, you are a Catholic. You would understand the intrigues of this city,' Von Hertling said, breaking the silence. There was a caustic edge to his remark.

Von Kühn turned to him. 'A Catholic by intellect. A pagan at heart. Rome is a rotten city but I know small monasteries and humble convents here which house great and simple minds.'

They indulged in some theological arguments for an hour until the sun set early behind the city and they watched the light depart.

When Von Hertling left the room, his steps echoed on the marble floor and filled the rooms with an ominous sound. 'A limited and dangerous mind,' Von Kühn remarked as he listened to the sound of Von Hertling's steps grow fainter. 'And the more important he becomes, the more dangerous.' He returned to his armchair and taking up a copy of Count D'Azelglio's memoirs, he began to read.

At midnight Von Hertling left his apartments and passed across the Tiber. The night air was sharp and clarified his mind for the affairs he had to settle in the city.

He reached a dark courtyard in the inner city, crossed it and mounted several steps before he reached the top storey. He knocked on the door four times. Then he waited. After some time several bolts were slipped back and the door was opened by a stocky man. It was obvious that he was from southern Italy. His features were dark, almost African.

Von Hertling was ushered into a room which was surprisingly comfortable. A thick carpet covered the floor. Heavy mirrors hung on the wall which caught the lantern lights outside and doubled their intensity. Some books and papers were thrown carelessly on a table – timetables for all the trains of Europe; departures of ships from various ports; lists of goods which could be purchased and sold; and detailed maps of cities.

'Did you bring the gold?' the Italian asked directly. 'No gold, no deals.'

'I always bring gold,' Von Hertling snapped.

'That is why I like doing business with you.'

Von Hertling studied the large, corrupt head, the intent eyes, the heavy lips.

'This is what you asked for,' the Italian said, handing him a folder. Von Hertling opened it. It contained several blueprints of a new torpedo developed by an arms firm in Rome. He studied it carefully. It had a longer range than those developed in Germany. He never asked how the Italian obtained such secret information, but it never failed to impress his superiors in Berlin. It was accurate and to scale. He studied it for several minutes.

'My services do not come cheaply,' the Italian began, studying the intent expression on Von Hertling's face. He knew that he was satisfied with the plans.

'We are both professionals. I pay you better than all the others,' and with that he took a small belt of money from his wrist. He slipped it across the table to the Italian, who undid it and counted the gold coins.

'As agreed,' he said and pushed the three small columns of coins aside as if dismissive of their worth.

Von Hertling looked at him. 'I leave for Berlin in two days' time. I have arranged for someone to contact you here. We continue to deal on the same terms. Betray me and you are a dead man,' he said coldly.

The Italian looked at him with dark hate in his eyes. He managed to smile. 'We understand each other.'

'Good. It is time for me to leave.'

They did not shake hands. The Italian knew that the German regarded him as a social outcast that he had to depend upon to do his dirty work. The Italian unbolted the door again and let Von Hertling out. Then he returned to his desk. He took the money and counted it. Tomorrow he would lodge it in a bank vault and move south towards the sun. He detested Rome during the summer. It was a corrupt place. He preferred Sardinia, where he possessed a large estate and a crumbling villa which had belonged to an old Sardinian family. There he would exercise his horses, count his wheat bushels and the barrels of oil from his olive trees and drink the southern wines.

Von Hertling walked home. He had reason to believe that Von Kühn had given the Italian government sensitive information concerning German intentions in Africa. He had been dubious concerning Von Kühn's allegiances since he arrived in Rome. Perhaps the man should be removed from his office.

Von Hertling did not return directly to Berlin. He had some final business to settle in Vienna.

As he walked along the Ring Strasse, he was impressed by the heavy architecture of the great thoroughfare. In a sense it reminded him of Berlin. When he was a small boy, his aunt had brought him through the city on the trams which still moved along the glistening rails.

It stirred some delightful memories in his mind. His mother had been ill and he had been sent to the city for a year. It had been a long time ago and he still remembered Vienna through the eyes of a child.

He decided that he would visit his aunt's villa, in the south of the city. It would be a final leavetaking. He took a cab across the Danube and out through the leafy suburbs, until he reached the ornamental gates which led to her estate.

He felt hesitant for a moment, then he ordered the driver on. As they drove up the winding road, he looked at the arching trees and the delicate shrubs. He recalled the laughter of young women who smothered him in affection.

When they reached the crescent in front of the house, a young woman was standing on the balustrade.

He looked at her. She possessed strong, even beautiful features.

'Good day,' he said, bowing from the waist. 'I believe that I am now a trespasser here. My name is Baron Von Hertling.'

'Then you are the former owner,' she said.

'It was really the property of my aunt. But I did spend one happy year here. I wonder if it has changed.'

'You are free to visit if you wish,' she said. She looked intently at the Baron. He had controlled features and direct, Germanic manners. A duelling scar ran down his cheek.

He mounted the steps and gazed down at the vista. For a moment he did not speak.

'I was happy here,' he said simply.

'And are you not happy now?' she asked.

'Yes. But then I had no obligations.'

As she looked at this stranger, for some reason Sophie felt attracted to him, although she did not know why this was so – he was not, after all, handsome. Perhaps it was his manner or his neat gestures.

They walked through the house, the Baron conscious of the woman who walked beside him. Perhaps it was some old magic which stirred him. As he entered the rooms he explained to her what life had been like during his days in Vienna.

'You are a romantic,' she said when they had finished visiting the house.

She invited him to have a glass of wine on the veranda which overlooked the park. It was a young sparkling wine.

When they were finished he turned to her, smiling and said, 'It has been a most pleasant visit. Perhaps we shall meet again.'

'Perhaps.'

'Who purchased the house?'

'It now belongs to Joseph Steiner.'

'The Jewish banker?' Von Hertling seemed taken aback.

'You have heard of him? You will know then that he is a man with many business interests in Europe. He is my stepfather.'

Despite his obvious discomfort, Von Hertling cleared his throat and managed, 'I hope that it will be a happy place for both of you as it was for me.' He bowed and tripped lightly down the steps. She noted how supple his body was.

He passed down the avenue, unable to banish the woman from his mind. Perhaps it was the delightful occasion, the happy memories he had of the house, of young women laughing. He could not tell. But, despite her stepfather, she had left an impression on his mind.

Now as he walked through the Tiergarten in autumn he recalled his visit to the villa.

He remembered her presence on the platform; the light summer dress she had been wearing, the tone of her voice.

Now more than ever he had to banish her from his mind. With his visit to Kaiser Wilhelm there was much to consider. The secret charge of this city and the empire had been handed over to his care and he must gather young and trusted men about him. He must not waste his time with this woman and her sly father.

As evening fell, he passed out of the Tiergarten and through the Brandenburg gate. Before him stretched the broad avenue, Unter den Linden, as splendid as the Champs-Elysées.

A surprise shower of fireworks exploded in multi-coloured stars above the city.

Chapter Seven

'Are you certain?' Von Hertling asked the young man.

'I have spent a year in Rome at the embassy. I have followed him. I have heard him in conversation with Italian diplomats and I can assure you that he is working against Germany. He has disclosed the most sensitive information to the Italians.'

He was never a German at heart. I suspected that he was unpatriotic, Von Hertling thought to himself. Then he looked at the tall young man standing before him. Von Hertling had picked him because he was beautiful and homosexual. He was also certain that he had become Von Kühn's lover. But the young man was now about to be discharged from the army for immoral behaviour, and was ready to betray him.

'You will now be put to the test. I wish you to murder him. Let your method be subtle. I want no scandals attached to this office. If you are caught then we will discount any knowledge of you. You understand.'

'Yes. Give me a few days to make my plans. I have a week's leave.'

When the young man left the office, Von Hertling considered what had been discussed. His conscience did not trouble him. He was ridding the state of an enemy and wished to dispose of Von Kühn in a tidy, efficient manner.

Three days later the young man returned. There was a certain vicious excitement in his eyes. 'I wish to have this letter copied by an expert forger,' he said.

Von Hertling looked at the letter. It was in Latin. He asked the young man to translate it for him.

'Is it in perfect Latin?' he asked.

'Yes. I had a professor at the university write it for me.'

'Good. I will have it transcribed in Von Kühn's hand by one of our men.'

Two days letter the young man set out for the embassy in Rome, the letter hidden in a safe place in his luggage.

'It is snowing in Germany,' Von Kühn said from the marble bath.

The young man stood naked before the fire blazing brightly in the marble fireplace. 'So the weather reports tell us,' he replied.

'I detest the northern cold and the long winter nights. That is why we are introspective and our thoughts lack edge,' Von Kühn continued as he emerged from the bath. His body was fat and loose from an indulgent life.

He dried himself and moved towards the bed, where he lay naked and gazed at his lover. 'You should have been a Greek,' he said. 'You have a perfect body. Your mind however is evil and perhaps that is why I am attracted to you.' He watched the young man's movements. 'Shall we have some wine?' Von Kühn asked.

'Very well. I am in the mood for light wine,' the young man replied and went into one of the rooms. He appeared with two glasses of wine and handed one to Von Kühn.

'Lie beside me,' the older man said. 'I missed you when you were in Berlin.'

The young man sat on the side of the bed. Von Kühn put out his fan and stroked his back. 'What shimmering skin you possess. It is without a blemish. Let us toast your beauty.'

The young man watched as Von Kühn sipped his wine, unaware that it carried a sleeping draught. Soon he began to yawn. 'I feel overpowered by this wine,' he said. He began to grow drowsy. Soon he was in a deep sleep.

The young man placed the note on the marble table top beside the bed. Then, arranging the naked body on the bed, he quickly slit Von Kühn's wrists with a sharp razor.

He did not immediately rush from the room in panic, but watched the blood spurt from the veins and soak into the bedlinen. The stains widened and became thick with a patina of fresh blood.

He looked in fascination at the dying man. Then he dressed and left the room. Later he sent a coded message to Von Hertling.

'He died like an ancient Roman, without the service of the clergy,' Von Hertling mused.

At New Year 1905, Baron Von Hertling boarded the train south to his ancestral home in Thuringia. He had received word that his father was ill and he knew this might be the last time he would see him.

From the window of his carriage he watched the people moving along the platform. Most seemed rich and prosperous, part of the miracle of Berlin. The economic boom of the *Gründerzeit* had drawn them to the Imperial capital.

Opposite him sat a fat Bavarian, dressed in stolid tweed. His hands were plump and soft. Immediately, he began talking. His trip to Berlin had been most successful. He had clinched some deal or other at the agricultural ministry which would be of great benefit to him. He drew a large cigar from a leather case and began to smoke it, concentrating on every puff in order to derive most pleasure from it. A gentleman with a bowler hat, silver glasses and a patient face sat beside him and listened without comment.

Von Hertling looked through the window. It was a grey day. The sky was charged with snow. As the train moved slowly forwards, his eyes followed the development of Berlin. The centre was firm with imposing and monumental buildings. In the heavily industrialised areas beneath the brick chimney stacks the acrid smoke made life almost unbearable. But he cared little for those who worked in choking conditions. They fuelled the great industrial miracle.

Imperceptibly the country appeared. It was flat and featureless, broken only by forests. The great plain stretched as far as the Urals. He looked forward to a few days hunting in the forests of his father's estate.

The train continued on its journey. The Bavarian, having spoken without stopping for half an hour, at last placed his hands over his stomach in contentment, and began to snore. Baron Von Hertling could imagine him at some beer Keller in Münich, singing Bavarian songs, banging his beer mug on a wooden table in happy contentment.

Grateful for peace, Von Hertling opened the paper he had purchased in Berlin and studied it carefully, not only for its political content but for the social gossip it carried.

The Bavarian snorted awake like a sow which had been in a deep sleep. 'How far are we from Münich?' he asked from behind rheumy eyes.

'Many miles,' the gentleman beside him said.

'I was dreaming,' he began. 'I dreamt that I was walking in the Alps and that I fell into a precipice. It was dreadful. I fear such a death. I suppose that is why I often dream about it. Do you dream?' he addressed his companion.

'Sometimes.'

'You don't fall into deep precipices?'

'No. Nothing so violent. I dream that I am lost in long corridors and there is no way out. They all have the same features and are all the same length and each one is lit by a naked gaslamp.'

'And do you dream?' he asked Baron Von Hertling, who was still trying to read his paper.

'Yes. I dream that I shoot fat Bavarians. They run through the forest in regional costumes and I shoot them. In my last dream I shot five.'

There was a cold silence in the carriage.

'I must eat. I am famished,' the Bavarian said heavily. He took his leather suitcase from the rack and departed from the carriage. He farted heavily at the door.

'So much for *gemütlichkeit*. I do not believe he will return. He is a Barbarian,' Baron Von Hertling commented as he set his paper aside. He looked at the gentleman sitting opposite him. He could have been a banker or a university professor with his heavy coat, his hat and his starched collar and severe tie. 'Are you travelling far south?' he asked.

'As far as Rome; I intend to film the city.'

Baron Von Hertling was suddenly interested. He had seen short films projected onto screens in Berlin and was already building up a collection of documentaries from all over Europe. 'You will find Rome interesting. It is a delightful city if you admire Renaissance buildings.'

'The light is excellent in the south during the winter and it has not been filmed before. During the spring my films will be shown all over Germany. People who have never been to Rome can enjoy its wonders.'

'Tell me more of this new invention. I am most interested.' Even at that moment the germ of an idea was growing in his mind.

The gentleman opened the long wooden box that was beside him on the seat and he drew out an oblong object. He explained that it contained flexible film reel. Then he demonstrated how it was installed in a new invention called a cine camera

'I trundle the wheel at a certain speed, in fact at waltz speed. When it is developed and run at the same speed you have moving pictures.'

'Could you film at sea?'

'It depends upon the light. If it is good then the pictures will be clear. This is a very new and wonderful invention.'

Baron Von Hertling held the camera in his hand. It was well-tooled. He opened the side and looked at the brass wheels and sprockets within. He took the camera and set the wheels in motion. They whirred contentedly.

'Is it possible to film from the air?' Von Hertling asked.

The gentleman reflected for a moment. 'If one could mount cameras on a balloon basket it could be done on a clear day, I suppose. But I would have to have four cameras mounted in the basket, because I would not have time to change the reels. It has not been attempted before. Imagine flying over Rome in a balloon. You could look down into the city as no one has ever done before.'

He was excited at the prospect. Then he said, 'It is only a dream. I could not afford such a trip.'

'That is not a problem. I can make all the facilities available to you.'

The gentleman looked at him in surprise. 'Why should you be interested to such a degree that you would place a lot of money at my disposal?'

Baron Von Hertling considered the filmmaker. How much could he tell him about his position and his work? He hesitated. 'I am employed by the government. Berlin is expanding at such a rate that an aerial view of the city could help us in developing the lands to the west. It would further help in planning future roads through the city.'

It was a plausible answer. The gentleman was excited at the prospect. Then he remembered, 'But I fear heights. Are balloons safe?'

'Safer than our journey on this train. Should you wish to, I can assure you the very best balloonist in Berlin would fly you across the city.'

The man's desire to film the city from the air overcame his fear of flying and he agreed to Von Hertling's proposition.

They talked of many things during the rest of the journey. He discovered that the gentleman was a Jew and that he had fled from Russia, and that he believed in the opportunities of the new Berlin.

'My children can grow up in this city. We do not fear pogroms and there is an energy here which is like fresh air. There is always a new challenge. My children attend a good school. They are very bright. You must come and visit us sometime at my apartments above my studio.'

'Perhaps I shall,' Baron Von Hertling said in a non-committal way. While they were talking in such a pleasant fashion his mind was racing. He must examine the opportunities afforded by this new invention. Men must be trained who could film enemy shipping, factories, the movement of troops, cities and buildings. He must study the rudiments of filmmaking and develop it further if necessary.

Before he left the train, Von Hertling asked the gentleman to call on him when he had returned from Rome. 'And bring your film on Rome with you. I would like to see it.'

As the train drew out of the station he noted the Bavarian gentleman in the restaurant car, bent over a large plate of food. He had his fork and knife raised like drumsticks and he was about to attack it with relish.

The station of Ohrdruf was covered in a thick blanket of snow. His sister and brother, Marcus and Inge, were waiting for him and rushed to meet him, throwing their arms about him. He felt great joy in their presence. They asked him many things as they passed down the platform to the cab. It was a small, intimate station, neatly kept and the station master had known him since he first set off for the military academy in Berlin. He, too, was there to greet him.

When they reached the sleigh, Otto, the old retainer, with his heavy moustache and woollen cloak, looked at his namesake and greeted him with a rough embrace.

'You look thin and meagre. We will fatten you well here and send you back to Berlin glowing with health. Happy New Year.'

The snow had stopped. It lay evenly and deeply on everything. Otto whipped the cover from the seats of the sleigh, which were deeply sprung and comfortable. He sat between his sister and brother and set off to the Schloss.

They passed through the small town of Veld and up into the pass. On either side pines ranged up towards the steep summits, white sentinels, pointed and crisp. The air was sharp and the harsh bells filled the empty space with sound. As the horses trotted evenly up the pass, Von Hertling looked back on the village. It looked neat and pretty in the distance, bound about a church. Beneath the nave many of the Von Hertling family lay buried.

The Schloss came into sight, built on a stony outcrop. It was a towering jumble of castellated walls, that had been built and rebuilt over the years. The Romans had set their standards here as had the Normans and all the German princes of the Von Hertling line since. From the high tower the Von Hertling flag with its arms and legend hung limply from a flag pole. It was on this tower, looking at the mysterious hill slopes, the forest of dark conifers with their old mysteries, that he had been stirred to join the military academy in Berlin.

'How is father?' he asked as they approached the steep road which lead to the great castle gate. He had not written home for some time. And his brother's last letter to him had seemed hesitant.

Marcus and Inge remained silent for a moment, looking at each other, not daring to answer.

Finally, Marcus stammered, 'Father is not well. He had several bad turns during Christmas.'

As they entered the great castle and stopped in the old medieval courtyard, the baron's mind was filled with apprehension. He had suddenly forgotten the winter beauty of the landscape, the youthful memories of playing war games on the castle battlements, of the dreamy hours he had sat watching the mists pass up the valley like ghosts from some great Wagnerian opera. He left the sleigh and rushed across the courtyard, up a flight of steps and into the great hall with its brown beams and old ancestral shields. His father was sitting before the great blazing fire in his wooden armchair covered by animal skins, waiting to greet him. He rushed to his side and knelt down. He looked at the old man. His side and face were paralysed. The character had left his features, as the tears rolled down his cheeks.

'Had I known, I would have come immediately from Berlin,' he said.

His father drew words hesitantly from himself. 'No. Duty calls. I told you, duty calls. You have to attend to the business of Germany.'

The old man relapsed into silence and looked into the heart of the blazing fire. He had been an aide-de-camp to Bismarck and a close friend. Bismarck had stayed at the Schloss during the turbulent years of the 1870s and in the very room in which his father now sat, plans had been made to unify Germany.

He looked up from the fire and down at his son. 'Bismarck is gone and there is no wise or strong chancellor to guide the destiny of the new nation. Kaiser Wilhelm is an arrogant fool. He will surely lead you into war. There is no need for war. Consolidate the borders. Time is on our side.' He delivered his testament slowly, stumbling with his words, dribbling from the left corner of his mouth.

Suddenly he was tired. He looked toward the blazing fire again. Then he fell asleep. His son stood beside him, conscious of the great size of the ancestral hall, the shrunken stature of his father. Now, he had no wish to speak to his mother or the rest of his family. Instead, he mounted the steps of the old tower, his steps sounding hollow on the old worn steps. Finally he reached the flat, angled attic then let himself onto the roof. He gazed down at the wide countryside about him, his heart charged with sorrow.

Here, alone, and above the countryside which had shaped his character, he could weep.

It seemed that Von Hertling's father had held on to life until his son returned from Berlin. When he heard of his beloved Otto's promotion he retired to his room. Now, in the large bed, his head on comfortable pillows, he waited for death. He looked directly at a great hunting picture which he loved. It was filled with awkward passion, as men attacked a large-tusked boar in a tangled thicket.

He was fed on soft bread soaked in milk and lay in the bed for a week, motionless, attended by his family and a nurse. As news of his illness spread across the hilly countryside, old titled friends wrapped in heavy cloaks made their way to his chamber to say goodbye. They had been with him during the years of turmoil and they had helped to shape the new Germany. Many were there when he died.

His body lay in state in the great oak-beamed hall. A fire blazed in the fireplace and candles stood about the bier. Beside him rested the insignia of war: his polished helmet with its eagle escutcheons in gold, the ornamental sword, his uniform and military medals.

Three days after his death ten officers carried the coffin across the yard and placed it on the sleigh. Then the cortège passed out of the courtyard, through the great gate and down the tortuous road. They passed through the valley of pines until they reached Veld. Here, with military and religious ceremony, the remains of his father were placed amongst his ancestors in the nave of the church. When they emerged from the chapel the snows were falling softly about them, covering up the sleigh marks.

Chapter Eight

Marie Schmerling's life was filled with social activity. She had broken off all relations with her family and was free every night to go from her little flat to the Grossen Keller to listen to Fieldmann. He was not a handsome man, with his heavy neck supporting a square head, a thick beard covering his face and the massive hands of an iron worker. Nonetheless, she fell beneath his primitive power. His mind was anarchic and he was direct and forceful in his speech.

'You believe that this empire will hold together forever. Let me tell you that the base is rotten. The top will topple in time. I will be there when it falls and give it its final push,' he told her when they discussed social issues. Like Marie, he was firm in his beliefs.

Sometimes when he came to the city he stayed at the studio of one of his fellow artists. His conversation was extravagant and he would hold court in his friend's small room.

'Vienna is a decadent city. These great imperial buildings impress the world. And listen to the music; Strauss and more Strauss. It is like sweet, insipid wine. Look at the statues. They are as lifeless as corpses. Now, I shall cast a statue greater than all these. The stonemasons in Prague taught me the colour, the strength, the value of stone. It will celebrate man, not Hungarians or Croatians or German men, but every man.'

'Will he have Chinese features?' one of them asked.

'No but he will have Chinese balls and a German arse,' Fieldmann called out roughly.

On one occasion Marie noted that he was looking intently at her.

'You strip me with your eyes. You are arrogant,' she said directly.

'Of course I do. I am an artist. I strip every woman with my eyes. It is my business. Now lift up your chin.'

Before she could refuse he pushed up her chin and looked at it. 'I could use that chin.'

Then he felt her shoulders and her buttocks. The feel of his hands on her body gave her pleasure. Despite the coarse hair on the back of his hands, his fingers were sensitive. They played on the surface of objects, searching out their texture and their mass.

'Have you ever modelled in the nude?'

'I have never been seen nude!'

'Some day I may need you. I will let you know,' he said directly. Then he turned from her and began to speak with another.

At the end of that summer, the heat was stifling in the city.

In the wine villages the grapes ripened on the hills. All day the workers moved along the slopes tending them, watching them grow full.

Jakov Fieldmann lived in one of these small villages set in the folds of the hills to the south of Vienna. Here the wine and the food were cheap and Jakov lived among the peasants whose rough simplicity he admired.

One Friday evening Marie Schmerling set out with the others from the Grossen Keller, through the woods that surrounded the city, carrying their easels and paints with them. Most of them took lodgings in one of the cheap village inns and that evening they visited Jakov Fieldmann at his studio. It was a large, neglected building which he had purchased from one of the vineyard owners. He had restored the loft and partitioned the ground floor. In summer it was a comfortable place. At the end of Jakov's garden, surrounded by trees, lay a pond fed by a fresh stream from the Vienna woods. There the small group gathered.

'It is rumoured that you are working on a group that will put Monsieur Rodin to shame,' one of them, Pieter, said.

'I never speak of work when it is in progress.'

'Let us see this great work,' Pieter insisted.

Jakov grew angry. His eyes flashed with fire. 'I do not discuss work in progress,' he told them and they did not question him further.

'It is now time to eat and drink,' he said abruptly changing the subject.

They followed him out of the garden and up a narrow hilly road until they came to the inn. The garden was filled with revellers sitting about heavily weathered tables. Gypsy music played in the background.

'You are most welcome,' the woman of the inn told him as he approached. Katrin was a burly woman who had taken on the inn when her husband died.

Jakov put his arms about her and kissed her. 'She is sweet-fleshed,' he told them, taking a seat on one of the rough benches. 'I have given her comfort in her hour of need. I wanted her to model for me but she refused.'

Large pitchers of wine were carried to the table and set before them. They began to drink and talk.

'Come and sit by me,' he called to Marie.

Surprised, Marie left her seat and sat beside him. Her whole body felt tight and her mind seemed dry.

'Now tonight is not a night for political talk. Tonight you enjoy yourself. We were born to enjoy ourselves, not serve some old paternal Emperor who is impotent.'

Then, looking intently at Marie, he said gruffly, 'Drink your wine. Your face is tense. Your heart is not joyous.' He then began to talk of his travels through the Transylvanian Alps. His account was rapid and picturesque. He had called at villages which had little contact with the outside world; where nobody had heard of Emperor Joseph.

He described his life there with intimate detail. 'Once, I stayed in the castle of a wild countess. Here, dogs slept on the bed with her. They snarled when we made love. One bit my backside when I humped her! They thought I was assaulting her.

'Then I met a stonemason who was carving old medieval statues as great as anything in Chartres. He belonged to a long line of masons, stretching back into the medieval world. I talked with herdsmen as they tended their sheep in the mountains and ate their rough cheese. In the hills and the mountains I learned more about primitive man than I ever learned from Jean-Jacques Rousseau.'

Marie listened while he talked. More wine was brought to the table and the men and women grew drunk.

'Let us abandon talk. More important things have to be attended to.' Jakov looked at the great canteen of soup. One of the women ladled it into ample plates and they began to eat.

It was late in the night when the musicians arrived. They played the folk songs of Southern Austria and Jakov Fieldmann began to sing with them. He had a heavy, rough voice full of humour and pathos.

Before they parted, more wine was carried to the table. By now almost all of the customers had left and the group had become nostalgic and maudlin. They tried to sing in harmony but their voices were ragged and did not knit. 'It is time to go when the Viennese are out of harmony,' Katrin told them. They paid the bill and left.

As they stumbled home Fieldmann told Marie, 'You can lodge with me.'

She was startled at the suggestion.

'I will not assault you. I am tired and tomorrow I have work to do,' Jakov insisted.

They entered his garden by a narrow alley. She could hear the sound of the stream splashing into the pond. The scent of vines and wild flowers was in the air and the sky was pulsing with stars.

'It is very beautiful here,' she remarked.

'Indeed. During the summer I often sit here and listen to the sounds about me. It eases the turmoil in my head. Sometimes I have ideas which will never find their way into bronze or stone. It is difficult to wipe them from your mind.'

He lit a lantern and they entered the great barn. He took her hand and led her up to the loft.

There were two beds in the wide, low attic. He indicated that she should sleep in the larger, more comfortable one. While she was hesitating, he removed his clothes and laid them on a chair. She looked at his burly body, full of muscular strength, the great thighs, his private parts hanging from a triangle of bushy hair.

He was unconscious of his nakedness. He fell into bed and was soon asleep. She undressed, stood naked in the loft, unfamiliar with such surroundings. Then she slipped between the rough sheets of the bed and fell asleep.

The morning light poured in great shafts through the attic windows. Marie woke up and drew in the clean scent of the place.

Fieldmann came up the wooden steps and stood naked above her. She looked at his body again. It vibrated with life and for a moment she thought that he was going to pull across the coverlet and join her in the bed.

'Do you swim?' he asked.

'Yes.'

'Then, if you wish, you can have a swim in the pool. It will sharpen your body. Then we can have breakfast in the studio.'

'Naked?'

'It is the only way to swim.'

She drew aside the coverlets and stood naked before him. A frisson of pleasure ran through her body.

He looked at her carefully. 'Turn round,' he ordered. As she obeyed, she felt his fingers on her body, probing her shoulders, running easily down her buttocks and inside the walls of her thighs.

'You are the model I have been looking for. I need you to finish my work. But come, let us swim.' With that he rushed down the stairs.

Marie followed him quickly. When her bare feet touched the cool dew on the grass she felt that she was running on velvet. Jakov rushed across the lawn and with a quick dive disappeared into the pool. She followed him. The sharp water stung her body. When she surfaced he was beside her, laughing. 'It is wonderful,' she said.

Suddenly he had his arms about her and was drawing her beneath the water. He played and tumbled with her as if she were a child. When she emerged from the water she felt invigorated.

They ran back to the great barn and he threw a blanket around her and dried her quickly, rubbing the towel briskly on her body in order to make it warm. Then, going to a cupboard, he took out a long, silk kimono and handed it to her. 'It was something I received once from a Japanese gentleman in Vienna for painting his mistress.'

He dried himself as he spoke, then he put on a large woollen dressing gown and set about making breakfast. He boiled black coffee on a stove and fried ham and sausages in a pan. He placed the food on two plates beside large wedges of bread and set them on the table. Marie discovered that she was hungry. As the morning sun strengthened and poured into the garden and through the windows, she ate the coarse breakfast with relish.

'I could live here forever,' she remarked when the breakfast was finished.

Jakov had lit his pipe and was smoking contentedly, looking at the light which had flooded the garden. 'You do not have to return to your home. There is a bed in the loft for you. However, in winter it is a different matter.'

Marie considered the invitation as she looked at the garden and the woods beyond.

'Let me show you my studio,' he said suddenly. 'The others will not arrive until noon.'

He took a key from the wall and he opened a door leading off the kitchen. She followed him inside. He went to the window and drew aside the curtains and Marie looked about her. Figures in varying stages of completion lay around the bright studio – the shapes of women and men in all their tribulation and pain.

'Others deify man and woman,' Jakov began, 'I look at them as they are; I study the men who work in the brickyards of Vienna or in the mines of Silesia and the women who work in the fields. There is no great demand for these statues but I do them nevertheless. That is why I sometimes starve.'

Marie's attention was drawn to the centre of the studio, where a huge model stood hidden by white sheets. She was anxious to see what lay beneath it.

Jakov followed her gaze. 'I will satisfy your curiosity,' he told her and drew off the sheets.

Marie gasped and proceeded to examine the complex study with admiration. At its base stood the world of plants intertwined, and emerging from that an intricately carved world of animals. On the final tier stood a naked man. The work formed a close unity, each line and space in harmony with the rest. It was a vast and complex design which reached almost to the ceiling.

'When will it be finished?' she asked.

'Soon. I have been searching for a female who is equal to the man. I believe that you are that woman.'

'How do you know?'

'I know.' He removed her kimono, sat on a chair and studied the contours of her body, the way breasts and belly and buttocks ran in harmony into each other.

'Let your hair fall loose,' he ordered, his voice gruff.

Mesmerized, she followed his command.

'Yes. Everything about you is right. Will you mount the platform and stand beside the man?'

She climbed onto the platform on the higher tier of the statue. She placed her arms about the figure of the man. Jakov Fieldmann walked about his creation.

'Now let us begin,' he told her when she descended. He lit a brazier so that she would be warm, then, taking a lump of clay he began to soften it in his hands, never taking his eyes from the lines of her body. He built up a rough image of her on a circular table. Then, with his fingers he began to mould it into shape. He moved rapidly and intensely. Sometimes he came over to her and touched her body, leaving brown clay marks upon the white skin. She watched him work. Creative energy poured through his fingers. They ran across the clay easing it into delicate lines. Taking a knife, he began to smooth the clay figure. 'That is all I can do for the moment. I am dry,' he said.

Marie examined what he had made. It was perfectly executed. She looked at him and saw that he was tired. Quietly she removed his rough dressing gown and let it slip to the floor. She placed her arms about his body and held him close to her. 'You are a beautiful man,' she said.

He put his arms about her and began to caress her buttocks. She could feel the strength grow in his loins. He kissed her mouth and her breasts and licked the salt from the nipples until they stood hard in the aureole. Then, taking her by the hand, he led her through the door and up the loft stairs, easing her on to the bed. She smelt of passion.

Jakov mounted her easily, thrusting slowly into her body until she began to make small cries. She viced him into her body with her long legs as she responded to his rhythm, urging him to thrust harder into her. Then she arched up to him, cried out and relaxed. He exploded within her.

The midday sun was pouring through the window when they awoke.

Afterwards, in exile in Siberia, she would recall that autumn amongst the gentle hills of Vienna. That Sunday evening when the others piled into the carriage, she remained. She stood at the small ornamental gate, which led to the garden and watched the carriage as it moved slowly across the cobbled stones, down the hill.

She returned to the studio. Fieldmann, bare-armed, was working on a piece of sculpture. With a wooden mallet and a chisel he worked towards a fine image, his face covered in limestone dust. She sat and watched him for an hour then she took a book from his shelf and sat in the garden. She read for some time, listening to the stream falling into the pool in a full gurgle. Everywhere lay the scent of early autumn. Already some of the leaves were turning and there was copper amongst the green. The fruit on the trees was heavy and plump. Some had fallen on the matted grass.

After a while, Marie left the garden and walked in a dreamlike trance through the village. It was a place of deep tranquillity.

When she returned Fieldmann was sitting in an armchair. 'You like the village?' he asked her.

'Yes. Here, Vienna seems far away.'

'So it may appear, but the secret service have their eyes here as they have them elsewhere. Soon the local policeman will have filed your name to be sent to the city. And I am sure that some of the inns have their spies.'

Marie felt a shiver of apprehension run through her. She was so happy in this lovely place, and she wanted nothing of Vienna and its intrigues.

But, as the days passed into weeks, her happiness continued to grow. Jakov Fieldmann taught her to cook. Soon she knew how to buy meat and vegetables at the market and cook them in peasant fashion and she learned to enjoy the local, cheap wines. Each evening when the weather permitted they ate in the garden. The weekends were broken by visits from the city. A pattern formed to their lives.

During this time, she learned much concerning Jakov Fieldmann. He was an avid reader. He read all the political pamphlets from France and Germany, which he purchased in Vienna. When Marie retired to bed at night he sat beside the billy stove beneath a lamp, poring over the great classics. Copies of Tolstoy, Dostoevsky and Zola stood cheek-by-jowl on his library shelves with the works of Karl Marx and others.

He had abandoned his sculpture for weeks, saying, 'I will return to it when the time is right. It is not something I can rush. But I believe that it will always remain a plaster model. It will cost too much to cast it.'

'But surely you can find a patron?'

'Perhaps in Paris but not in Vienna. They do not welcome me here, where the statues praise the warlords and the kings.'

He was the greatest talker she had ever heard in her life. However, she suspected that there were certain things he never revealed to her.

'I wish you to stay at the inn for the next few days,' he told her abruptly one evening in October.

'But why?' she asked.

'It is nothing you should concern yourself with. I have to meet some people. Ask no further questions. I wish to keep you out of certain areas in my life. They are too dangerous.'

'I share your bed; why can I not share your life?' she told him angrily.

'I have my reasons.'

She knew better than to question him further. She packed some clothes and took up residence at the inn.

The next morning when she sat down to breakfast, she noticed two strangers at the next table. They were serious men, trying to look as inconspicuous as possible.

Marie began to sense danger. She tried to catch snippets of their conversation and on several occasions she thought she heard Fieldmann's name being mentioned. She did not know what move to make. It was clear to her that they had arrived in the village to visit the studio, although she did not know why. She knew that she must return to Jakov Fieldmann immediately.

She left quickly by the back door.

At Jakov's studio, the men busy working failed to observe her enter. On the floor stood a printing press, large posters rolling off it. The men were hanging them to dry on a line they had strung across the studio. In one of them, she immediately recognised a caricature of the Emperor.

Fieldmann became aware of another presence in the room and turned around. When he saw her, anger flashed in his eyes. 'I told you not to visit the studio. Now you know what is going on here. You are implicated.'

'I noticed two visitors to the inn. They were obviously agents. Your name was mentioned.'

'Then they must have followed us here,' one of the men said. 'We must dismantle the press and destroy the posters.'

'No. We will do the whole print run. Then I will hide them in the loft,' Fieldmann argued.

Marie helped the men to gather the wet posters and hide them in the loft while Fieldmann continued to turn the press. When he was finished, he dismantled it and hid it behind a false wall. The men slipped away.

'What is going on?' she asked.

'You have seen the posters all over Vienna. Against the Emperor and all he stands for. Well, they originate here. If the press was discovered, I would find myself in jail. You are now an accomplice. The world of revolution is a darker one than you might suspect.'

The agents never came to the studio.

The others returned to Vienna with the posters hidden in a cart.

Fieldmann became moody and they did not make love for several days. Then as abruptly as it had arrived his mood passed and a new creative energy possessed him.

Autumn passed into winter. It grew cold. Snow began to fall on the valley. The grapes had been harvested and now the wine villages took on an isolated, homely appearance. The great barn grew cold, the thin timber walls no protection against the sharp winds which wheeled up the valley from the north.

Jakov Fieldmann set out each morning and cut timber in the woods, trudging through the snow like some peasant, his breath chilled by the cold. His fingers became too numb to work. He covered his hands with mittens and stood before his stone figures with chisel and mallet, but no sooner had he commenced than he lost his accurate touch.

Even the bed in the loft gave no protection against the intense winter. At night Marie felt the chill seeping into her bones. Finally, she caught pneumonia. Her lungs torn by pain, she was too weak to leave the loft.

Fieldmann made broth and carried it to her. 'This is no place for a delicately reared woman,' he told her. 'For goodness' sake return to your home. It is comfortable there.'

'No. I have made my decision,' she insisted. 'I have chosen this way of life.'

'You will die here. I must get you to a hospital.'

'Perhaps I will grow better. I will remain here a little longer.'

'We could be snowbound. I have known these village to be isolated for weeks.'

Then the heavy winter snows came and when Jakov looked out of the window one morning the garden was covered with snow drawn into dangerous drifts by the swirling winds.

He looked at Marie lying in the bed. Her condition was deteriorating.

'I will carry you to Vienna if necessary,' he told her firmly. But by now she was too weak to take heed of his words.

He borrowed a neighbour's horse and wrapping her in warm blankets he placed her on the saddle and climbed up behind her.

The village road leading to the city was empty. Smoke rose from the houses and the inns. He urged the horse forward through the deep snow. It was a slow, dangerous journey. Several times he had to dismount and drag the horse through large drifts. Then, when the horse could travel no further, he took Marie and placing her on his back, continued by foot.

It was his stubborn peasant resolution which helped him to survive. After three hours he reached the outskirts of Vienna where he hailed a cab to carry them to a hospital. There he waited while a doctor examined Marie. He detested large buildings with endless corridors. They reminded him of prisons. He looked at the floor, his hands knotted in anxiety. Moisture steamed from his clothes.

'Well,' he asked when the doctor appeared. 'Will she live?'

'I cannot say. Her lungs are congested but she is a strong woman. We will know in the next few days.'

'Can I see her?'

'She is in a coma. She will not know that you are here.' Nonetheless, Jakov entered the great ward, which had a stale sick smell that seemed to exude from the walls. He looked at the old and the poor who occupied the beds and he felt humiliated that he could not have afforded a more private place.

He sat by her bed and held her hand. She seemed to sense that he was there. He looked at Marie's fine face with its well-bred lines and was reminded of a Romanian princess he had once seen at a religious service in Bratislava. He felt hopeless. By himself he could endure hardship and privation. But he had no wish to draw this woman into his troubled and tempestuous life.

Jakov waited until darkness fell, then he left the hospital and made his way to an old quarter of the city where a friend lived. He reached a gloomy courtyard and mounted the flights of steps until he reached his studio.

'I am with company,' the artist called.

'I don't care if you are with Elizabeth Schratt,' Jakov called back, 'Let me in. I am in no condition to return to the village.'

The artist opened the door. A naked model, draped only in a quilt, was sitting by the fire. It was obvious that they had been making love.

'I am sorry I interrupted your moment of pleasure. Marie is ill in hospital. I will sleep in the corner. Give me a bottle of brandy.' He took the bottle from his friend and began to drink it by the neck. He paid little attention to them both, and they looked at him as he stripped off his wet clothes and stood naked by the fire.

Soon he felt some warmth in his body.

He went to the window and pulled down the brocade curtains. He wrapped them about him and lay on the floor. Soon he was asleep.

Day after day he returned to the hospital. Then one day, weeks later, Marie emerged from the coma. She opened her eyes and looked at him. 'Where am I?' she asked weakly.

'At St Lazare. I brought you here. But I will explain all

that to you later. You must rest now.' Jakov looked at her tenderly.

Marie remained in hospital until her strength had partially returned. When she could walk Jakov brought her to a house he had rented in a wine village nearer the city. It was small and warm and there she regained her health. It was only when spring finally returned and the first leaves were seen on the trees that she felt some courage enter her mind. But the pneumonia had taken its toll on her health.

Chapter Nine

'The girls have been a great disappointment to me,' Margit Steiner complained to Joseph. 'I have done my best for them. They have been educated at great expense, I bring them back to Vienna and what do I get for my troubles? My eldest daughter lives with an artist – one of these days she will turn up with a bastard on my doorstep. I cannot talk to Sophie. She has become too independent. Gadding about Vienna in an automobile when she is not visiting some city in Europe. She should have been a man, and you have set her against me! Alma is my best hope. But even she will not do me a single favour.'

Joseph regarded his wife wearily. They were having tea together in her conservatory, one of these rare occasions when they sat together and talked. Joseph Steiner detested them. He had to sit and listen to her trivial complaints and when she did not complain she tittle-tattled endlessly about the royal family. Also, she was growing thick about the neck and arms. He body, which had once been opulent, was running to fat.

They had been settled five years in the city Margit so loved, but her social status had not improved. Her claim to a title had been refused. She had primed Alma to bring up the matter with the Emperor but Alma would not hear of it.

'Just one small word in his ear and my final ambition will be realised,' Margit had pleaded.

'My friendship with the Emperor does not justify such requests. It would be a breach of trust.'

'Well, then approach it in some indirect way. Do it discreetly.'

But Alma would not listen to her request, saying firmly, 'That is the end of the matter, Mother.'

Now Margit was growing anxious. She had formed her own coterie, but it was only frequented by minor royalty or those who claimed a distant blood link with Franz Joseph. She felt that she was not advancing into the best circles.

She turned now to her husband who was sipping tea. 'I blame you for our present condition. You could have pursued the girl's interests with greater determination.'

'I do not interfere in domestic matters. It has never been my habit. I admire the manner in which the girls lead their lives. They have each gone their own way.'

'And what of Marie? She is so wayward.'

'Even the Hapsburgs have been wayward. They have had a very exotic past, you know. One of them even joined a circus, if my memory serves me correctly. And there is a trace of madness in all European bloodlines.' There was a note of sarcasm in his voice.

She did not answer him, but the conversation abruptly changed direction.

'I need more money to run this house. The allowance you give me is not sufficient.'

'Then I will increase it by ten per cent,' he said.

'You live by per cents,' she snapped back at him. 'I am constrained by the amount you give me.'

'I think I have been more than generous. You can indulge all your tastes, I believe.'

'You are a tight-fisted Jew. Perhaps it is because I married a Jew that I am not acceptable in the highest circles of the city,' she spat at him.

A nerve in his neck twitched angrily. The poison of the city was working in her mind. Vienna had always hated the Jews. It remained hidden like a virus in the earth; something waiting for its moment. Now Margit had picked up the plague.

It was at that moment their relationship died. He looked at the heavy-bodied woman sitting opposite him and he wondered how he had ever loved her.

'What about my money?' she continued. 'What about my money? I need money.'

'Our conversation is at an end,' he told her curtly. He rose from the table, asked the servant for his coat and hat and left the house.

In Joseph Steiner's mansion outside the city, he could be free from the anti-Semitism that had poisoned the city, and his wife. His collection of paintings being catalogued by Sophie gave him great pleasure. He had also had a telephone line installed, at great expense, to contact all the stock exchanges in the world. But most importantly, he had also set up a Hebrew library in the house, inviting an old scholar from the Jewish quarter to maintain it for him. He collected books on Jewish history and discovered that here were many questions to answer, political, religious, social.

The old scholar, Steinmann, would set about his task at a quiet pace as if he had all the time in the world, working slowly, arranging books carefully in subject order.

Sometimes he spoke in Yiddish to Joseph, who discovered he had a quick ear for languages and it quickly returned to him.

'I can still recall the Yiddish voices of Vienna after all the years,' he mused.

'The language is what binds us,' the scholar said wisely.

'Perhaps it binds us too much.'

'That is a good thing.'

And sometimes when it was growing dark he left the villa in his automobile and visited the old Jewish quarter. He walked through the streets that he half remembered from his childhood and stood close to the grave where his parents had been buried.

Now, these small actions seemed more important to him than ever.

Alma's friendship with Franz Joseph ensured that most doors were open to her now. At least once a month she visited the old man at the Schönbrunn. It was a simple companionship: in summertime he would walk with her in the wide gardens and listen to the gossip she brought from the city. In winter, they sat in his suite of rooms. Gradually, she began to take an interest in the Empire which his great presence held together.

When news came through that five hundred people had been slaughtered by a Cossack regiment on the great square in front of the Winter Palace, Alma had been with him.

'Such a grave mistake,' he told her. 'I know Nicholas quite well. He is a simple man, too simple to rule a Russian Empire. He lacks decisiveness and correct advice.'

'What would you have done?' she asked.

'I would have listened to the people, taken some positive action. My Empire is less stable than his, after all. The Balkans is a most uncertain territory. I am concerned about its future.'

'Some day I must travel to the Balkans. I have heard so much about the mysterious east.'

'A very good idea. If you wish to know about the empire, travel through it. Follow the Danube.'

'I shall most certainly consider it.'

However, in the flurry of social activity which marked the beginning of the year in Vienna, Alma almost forgot her desire to travel the empire, until she met Prince Eugene for the first time.

At a small summer party given by the Emperor on the lawn in front of the Hofburg Palace, she recognised the tall, gracious man, talking to an elderly countess. Son of a Transylvanian count, the Emperor had appointed him to travel through the Balkans and report to him on the situation there.

'What an interesting mission,' she said to him when they were introduced. His life in the open spaces had given him a tanned complexion.

'Interesting, but dangerous. When I am in the mountains I long for the court life of Vienna. I am no sooner in Vienna than I wish to return to the mountains again. I have camped in mountain villages and slept in ruined castles on my way through the country. On one occasion I was taken prisoner, but it served me well. I learned how to speak a new patois. But someday perhaps you will travel to the Balkans. You will see for yourself where the west ends and the east begins.'

'The Emperor has suggested that I should travel down the Danube. He believes that the people of Vienna have no idea how complex the empire is.'

'It is true. Only the Emperor holds it together. His influence is great. If he died then there would be total confusion. There are too many questions to be solved. I see now where the danger lies.'

'Have you advised the Emperor?' Alma looked concerned.

'I advise him. But he does not listen. Nobody listens in Vienna.'

'I do.'

'Then I could not have a more beautiful confidante.' She knew that he was flirting with her and she was greatly pleased.

Alma would have like to pursue the discussion with Prince Eugene, but on a social occasion they had only a little time to talk. Somebody interrupted their conversation and he passed on to another group.

She was about to leave when a handsome, blond man approached her. He bowed from the hips and asked her if she was enjoying the gardens.

Alma had seen Prince Dmitri many times at Palace functions, and of course, he had once danced with her. 'They are always beautiful at this time of year, particularly the roses,' she smiled.

'I have developed a unique species at my palace by the Black Sea. I must present it to the Emperor.'

'Do you often visit the Crimea?' she asked.

'Not as much as I would like. At this time of year it is filled with the scent of exotic flowers.'

It was a pleasant conversation. They walked along the path towards the Gloriette.

'You have an admirer in Vienna,' he told her.

'Who, might I ask?' Alma was taken aback.

'Prince Karl.'

'But I have met Prince Karl on only two occasions, I believe.'

'Well, you have made a firm impression on him.'

She felt excited at the thought. Prince Karl was dangerous, she knew, but attractive. However, she controlled her emotions and quickly changed the conversation.

But as she made her way home in the coach she reflected on what Prince Dmitri had said.

As Prince Dmitri returned to the embassy he, too, reflected on what he had told Alma Schmerling.

His words had had an effect upon her. That he could judge from her reaction. Alma was a woman of some character and might bring some order to Karl's life. Her father, Joseph Steiner, was also immensely wealthy. Lastly, it would rehabilitate him with the Emperor, which would be useful for Dmitri. Marriage was far too troublesome for him; it would leave him less time for visiting prostitutes on the Rotentürmstrasse.

'But she is a commoner,' Prince Karl replied angrily when Prince Dmitri mentioned the idea of marriage to him.

'The old Emperor will grant her a title if necessary. It is not unknown. Besides, it might bring you back into court circles.'

'It is beneath me.'

'At this moment, my dear Karl, nothing is beneath you. The bankers will be soon knocking on your door. Your credit has been overextended. You may have to flee to Italy again. Think about it.' Prince Dmitri was determined to succeed. Very few could approach Franz Joseph; he had grown crusty and distant. Perhaps he might listen to Prince Dmitri's advice on the Balkans through Alma. A word from her could change the whole course of events.

Alma caught sight of her admirer at a ball in the Belvedere Palace.

'We have met fleetingly before,' she confided to a friend from behind her fan as she gazed at Prince Karl. He had the fine-cut features of the Hapsburgs and his contemptuous expression added to his mysterious charm.

'I believe you have attracted his notice,' her friend whispered.

'How can you be certain?'

'He has looked in this direction on several occasions.'

'I think he is the very image of Prince Rudolph who took his life at Meyerling,' Alma sighed.

'Beware of him. He has a dangerous reputation,' her friend warned.

'Is there any gentleman in Vienna who has not a dangerous reputation?'

'He is coming towards us. Pretend you do not see him.'

Prince Karl advanced towards Alma and invited her to dance. He had an elegant manner which came from his aristocratic breeding. Alma's heart was beating wildly as they moved about the floor. People took notice of this most handsome pair.

The orchestra were playing the 'Emperor' Waltz. 'I

believe you are familiar with the Emperor,' he said as they danced around the floor.
'We are friends.'
'You are lucky. He keeps very much to himself. Even I cannot have an audience with him.'
'He likes to get away from the heavy burdens of office. We walk in the gardens when it is fine and we talk about all matters.'
'Then you are privy to state secrets,' Karl laughed.
'Not exactly, but I do know what is happening in the furthest corners of the Empire,' Alma smiled.
'And how is his health?'
'Excellent for a man of his age.'
'I often worry about him. He carries a great weight upon his shoulders.'
They talked of many things as they waltzed about the floor. When she returned to her seat several women were talking behind their fans.
He asked her to dance several times during the evening.

Next morning Margit Schmerling received several telephone calls from her friends. The city was rife with rumours, they told her, that Prince Karl was in love with Alma.
As if to underline his affection he sent Alma a large bouquet of flowers the same day.
Margit Schmerling read the small note that came with them carefully. It was quite obvious that he was interested in her daughter.
'Nothing will come of it, Mother. There is no need for such excitement. He is probably sending flowers to several women in the city,' Alma told her, trying to conceal her excitement.
'Haven't you read between the lines? I can assure you he is interested.'
Each day for the next week a bouquet of flowers was

delivered to her at the same hour. The notes attached to them were warm and affectionate.

When, a week later, he invited her to ride with him in his coach through the Viennese woods, Margit Schmerling could not contain her excitement. She ordered the house to be dusted from top to bottom. Fresh flowers were cut and placed in vases. The finest linen was spread on the tables.

However, the Prince did not invite himself in. Instead his coach driver came to the door and invited Alma to join him. From behind a gauze-covered window, Margit Schmerling watched her daughter move down the path. The prince descended from the coach and helped her inside. Then they departed.

When Alma returned that evening her mother wished to know every detail of the day's events. Alma explained how they had stopped at a rustic café and had lunch and how the orchestra played especially for them.

'How romantic,' Margit sighed. 'He is sixteenth in line to the throne, you know. A most important gentleman. Has he invited you to join him again?'

'Yes, we intend to meet again.'

'I am so pleased,' her mother said.

'It will come to nothing, Mother. I barely know him.'

But during the long summer of that year, Alma fell in love with Prince Karl. Perhaps it was the strong lines of his Hapsburg features that made her blind to his reputation. Although she had heard certain whispers concerning his gambling and attraction for gypsy women, she chose to discount them.

It was Alma's relationship with Prince Karl that brought the tensions between Sophie and her mother to a head. Sophie possessed a strong stubborn nature and was less attracted by the social life than her sister. Instead, she spent her time in the offices of Joseph Steiner typing letters and studying the prices on the stock exchange. She drove her new automobile about the city with complete disdain for her mother's feelings.

That evening Prince Karl had just escorted Alma home, when Sophie drew up noisily in the driveway, swerving to avoid his carriage. Margit was furious at the spectacle. 'Have you no regard for your mother?' she demanded. 'What other woman would dare drive an automobile by herself? You should have a chauffeur. It is too mannish. Look at your sister. She frequents the finest palaces in Vienna and is invited to the best houses. You seem to have no interest in this wonderful city.'

'It is not a wonderful city,' Sophie replied. 'I detest it. I detest the arrogance of the Hapsburgs. I detest the trivial conversations, the tittle-tattle relating to titled people. You are a fool, Mother, full of nonsense. I have no wish to end my days as wife to some court official languishing in a drawing room. And you are forcing Prince Karl on Alma, when you know he is debauched. I believe you would welcome such a marriage.'

'I have regal blood in my veins,' her mother told her.

'You mean you have bastard blood in your veins,' Sophie retorted.

Her mother had palpitations. Her hands began to tremble and she had to sit on the chaise longue to regain her breath.

'I want you out of this house this very day,' she gasped. 'Out of this house. Do you hear?'

'I hear. I will have packed and disappeared within the hour.'

'And do not return. I have had enough of your arrogance.'

Sophie disappeared to her room, leaving her mother in a state of shock.

That evening Sophie left her mother's house. She had phoned Joseph Steiner and he was expecting her.

'Thank God I am finished with her,' she cried. 'I could not bear it any longer. My mother is mad. She is confusing reality with fiction.'

'She has done that for many years,' Joseph Steiner said wryly. 'You are welcome to this house. It may perhaps be a little remote but it satisfies my need for privacy.'

'I love it here. I love the refined elegance of the place. I love the paintings and I love the silence of the woods. And I will not have to listen to any more court gossip.'

This marked the beginning of a deep friendship between Sophie and Joseph. Gradually, they came to understand each other's ways.

'I have one passion,' Joseph told her some weeks later as they stood in the Italian room. 'I have specialised in the Sienese school. They were the first masterpieces I ever purchased. I possess many of them but it is the early ones I treasure most of all. They are simple and primitive and belong to the dawn of the Renaissance. There are some remaining in Italy. Others are spread across Europe. Some I believe are in Russia. It is my ambition to collect them under one roof.'

'And are they more important than money?' she asked.

'I have told you before that money is of no importance in itself. It is what you can purchase with money that is important. It is the protection you can buy for yourself. But come, let us sit and talk in the garden. What is this gossip I hear concerning Alma and Prince Karl?'

'I am sure you are well-informed of everything which happens in Vienna, Papa. You know he is a gambler. He spends his nights at the casinos. It is said that he has sold many of his properties to finance his debts. Alma is enamoured of him and mother encourages the relationship. I detest him and I detest all the others. They are worthless.'

'Then you do not like Vienna.'

'No. I would prefer to live in Berlin.'

'Berlin! What a strange choice.'

'All the power resides in Berlin. I have seen it in my travels through Europe.'

'Perhaps you are correct.'

'I know that I am correct.' Sophie was smiling as she said this, but Joseph saw the resolve in her eyes.

'Yes. You are.'

One day some weeks later, he said to her, 'I would like you to go to Leipzig. Spend some time there and while you are in the city visit the Schloss of Otto Klaus. He possesses two early Sienese paintings. Try and persuade him to sell them. Money is no object.'

Sophie was surprised at how generous Joseph Steiner could be when some painting was concerned. He would spend a vast amount of money on it, yet he would carefully check his bill in a café.

'I shall be pleased to go. If I travel by automobile, I will see more of the countryside.'

'An excellent idea,' he replied. 'The automobile is a wonderful invention. In ten years' time there will be few coaches left in Vienna.'

'That is why you have shares in the Ford Company?'

'Exactly.'

He advised her to stay at the best hotel and spend a month studying the city. 'It is a fascinating place. It has been an intellectual centre since the Middle Ages. Its printers produce some of the finest books in the world. Also, Bach and Wagner are associated with the city, so there is much to interest your mind. It is a vigorous place and you will get away from the stuffy atmosphere of Vienna.'

His familiarity with Europe often surprised her. He had a sharp memory for historical details.

'I look forward to the change and I will be far away from my mother. I am beginning to detest that woman,' she replied.

'Forgive her. She has limited vision.'

'You should be the Christian,' she laughed.

He said goodbye to her and watched her drive down the avenue in the magnificent automobile. As a daughter, she was everything he had always wanted.

Joseph was not to see his stepdaughter for three months. The visit was to change the course of Sophie's life. The city fascinated her, particularly the old section. Each morning she walked through its cobbled streets and watched the people beginning their day's work. She brought her copy of *Faust* to the Auerbach's Keller where Goethe had set one scene, and read passages from the work in a corner. She enjoyed the healthy, honest food and the direct talk.

However, she was also conscious of her business in Leipzig and so she wrote to Otto Klaus and he invited her to his Schloss. When she arrived, it was obvious to her why Joseph Steiner had sent her to the place. It was situated behind old walls, the grounds were falling into decay. The paint was peeling from the walls and grass was growing on the short avenue.

Otto Klaus was a man in his sixties, with a long, grey mane of hair and an intense and serious face. He sat on an armchair in a sunny room, protected by rugs. It was obvious that he was a frail man.

'You are welcome, Fräulein Schmerling. Excuse me for not greeting you at the door but I am afraid that I am indisposed. Be seated.'

He ordered the servant to bring them a sweet Rhenish wine. 'To your good health,' he toasted.

It was obvious to Sophie that the wine was expensive. It was sweet and aromatic and very palatable. It was also obvious to her that the ailing gentleman had now fallen on poor days.

They spoke of many things, particularly the history of the city.

'You know Bach gave dignity to religion. His music has ordered harmony. I could live in a heaven where only

Bach's music is played, on a good organ of course. As for the rest, they are bitter wine.'

Sophie was fascinated by his conversation and his view on European matters. But the hours passed and she felt that he was growing tired.

'It is time to leave. Perhaps you wish to rest,' she said with consideration.

'I know that you are interested in the Italian paintings. Let me show them to you, before you go.'

His servant wheeled him into a long gallery. It was obvious from the brighter patches on the faded walls that he had already sold several paintings. Standing together at the end of the gallery in a place where direct light did not fall upon them stood the two Sienese paintings. They were formal pictures, in delicate colours, with a gold-leaf background. Sophie knew that they genuinely belonged to the Sienese school. She looked at them in awe.

'What is your opinion?' he asked.

'Need you ask? They have a heavenly quality; almost Byzantine in their inspiration.'

'Yes there is a Byzantine influence there but it is becoming Italian. It is early Renaissance work and has a magical, spiritual quality.'

They discussed the paintings for a long time, until finally, Klaus said, 'As you see I have parted with all the others. These I held on to until the very last. Now unfortunately they must go.'

'I know where they belong,' Sophie told him. She explained that her stepfather had many paintings from the Sienese school and that they were well cared for.

'And the price?'

She made him an offer.

'They are worth more,' he said. 'My mother was Italian. She brought them with her from her family castle in Italy. There are my last link with that country.'

She felt the money was not that important to him. He

simply did not wish to sell them. 'Perhaps you do not wish to part with them?' she asked. 'I will remain in the city for some weeks and I will come and visit you. Perhaps my stepfather will raise the offer while I am here.'

'Come and visit me. I enjoy your company. Not many call to visit me now. I am unable to entertain them and the world to which I belonged is quickly passing.'

Sophie welcomed the chance to return and visit Otto Klaus. Each week she drove to the Schloss she brought him half a dozen bottles of his favourite wine. In the meantime, her interest in German culture deepened. Fascinated by Leipzig, she began to take courses in German history and culture, absorbing the spirit of the old states and the new nation. She read avidly. At the Thomaskirch she heard the Saint Matthew Passion by Bach. It had been performed in this church for the first time in 1729 and the great majestic power of the piece had a profound influence on her. Vienna had never produced such music.

But for Sophie Leipzig was more than a charming city. It was an industrial centre too, and her interest in automobiles prompted her to visit one of the industrial fairs which were held in the town at intervals.

When she arrived at the showrooms she created a stir. Many people were surprised to see a woman driving a powerful automobile.

She walked slowly from one beautiful automobile to another. She had studied the engine of her car and knew something of its power and complexity.

When she arrived at the first automobile produced by Benz she stopped and studied it carefully. It was a delightful piece of engineering, simple and clean-lined.

'As important as the Gutenberg Bible,' a voice said beside her.

She looked up and saw a man dressed in a military uniform with a blade mark on his cheek. It was Baron Von Hertling.

'Is it as beautiful as the Venus de Milo?' she asked, laughing at him.

'Yes,' he said firmly.

'You believe in these new machines, Baron?'

'I have complete faith in them. They will supersede the coach and they will change the strategy of war.'

She was intrigued with his conversation. Others would try and flatter her, but this man seemed to treat her as an equal. He spoke with such enthusiasm and knowledge. He opened the bonnet of one and explained the finer points of the engine. She was fascinated by his knowledge.

'Are you on your way to Vienna?' she asked later.

'I have just come from Berlin and am on my way to Rome. How lucky that I should stop here on the way,' he smiled.

Sophie tried not to look embarrassed. 'I have come from Vienna,' she said. 'I am attending to some business in Germany'

'Vienna is a charming city, I think.'

'Charming but vapid. I prefer Berlin. '

'Not many women would have such a preference. Why have you chosen Berlin?' Von Hertling was surprised.

'I like the energy of the city. It is filled with life.'

They continued their conversation for some time and later he invited her to have some coffee with him in the old quarter of the city. He was surprised when she told him that she would drive him there in her automobile.

The old city worked a strange charm on both of them. She told him of her studies at the university, of visits to the theatre and her interest in German music. He told her a little of himself. He talked of Germany and its future. She was fascinated by his vision.

Later she drove him to the station and he set out for Rome. As she waved to him from the platform, she could not account for her interest in Baron Von Hertling. Perhaps it was because he was different to the men she met in

Vienna. Like the car engines he seemed to possess some strong power within him.

She hoped they would meet again.

Three months later Sophie visited Otto Klaus for the last time. He was ailing and he could barely drink the white wine she brought him.

'I must leave,' she said. 'I have to return to Vienna.'

'Then take the pictures with you. I am dying. Money is no longer of any account. My relatives will suddenly appear from all over Europe and steal my possessions. They are scavengers.'

'I could not accept them without payment,' she told him and offered him the original price.

The servant took them from the wall to the conservatory, where they were held under the light. The colours seemed to glow.

'I had no idea they possessed such an ethereal quality,' Otto Klaus remarked when the sun fell upon them.

Two days later the paintings were carefully sealed into a large narrow crate and put on the train for Vienna.

In her stepfather's house she watched as they were placed on the walls beside the others. They added immensely to the wealth and understanding of the collection.

Joseph Steiner had made discreet inquiries about Prince Karl which confirmed the gossip. The Prince was a creature of the night, spending his time and money in the casinos on the islands to the east of the city.

He tried to approach Margit on the subject, writing her a businesslike note, but she would not listen to him. She became furious at his intrusion into her life.

'You have made your choice. Let Alma make hers. How dare you interfere with my daughter's happiness. She is deeply in love with the Prince and he is deeply in love with her. He has paid several visits to the house. He is a gentleman to his fingertips.'

'Have you asked him about his finances?'

'One does not discuss such subjects with a Hapsburg! That is a Jewish mentality. His title alone is his fortune.'

He dropped the subject, aware that Margit was blind to Prince Karl's faults, only wishing to be at peace in his secluded home.

Chapter Ten

Joseph Steiner boarded the train for Berlin, accompanied by Sophie. He had built up contacts with German bankers and industrialists and he wished to introduce Sophie to some of his colleagues. Money and business were moving rapidly into her favourite city and it could become the industrial centre of Europe. On the way, though, they would stop in Prague, his favourite city.

'You travel very lightly,' Sophie laughed when they settled into the carriage.

'It is an old habit. I am always prepared to depart only with a few essentials.'

'You have your notebooks?'

'In my left and my right pocket. They take up little room. It is unnecessary to carry cases of documents from place to place.' He rarely wrote anything down, but instead committed facts and figures to his precise memory. He kept some notes in two small, leather-covered notebooks which he had purchased in a cheap store.

He settled into the plush seat covered in velvet, enjoying the comfort of the deep pile against his body. He watched the people on the platform as the train pulled out, fascinated by the blend of races in Vienna.

Next, he checked his fingernails. It was an old habit with him. During his early life when he had first arrived in New York he had worked in a steam locomotive depot, oiling the great engines. The oil had matted his hair, lodged between his fingers, almost blocked his pores. Evening after evening he spent hours washing the day's filth from his body. Ever since he had checked his nails and fingers for spots of dirt when he was at rest.

The train headed north and he watched the city pass by. He belonged in cities. One could satisfy all desires in a city and hide in its narrow streets and sewers if danger arose. He was always conscious of the dangers of being a Jew. Jews were migrants, moving from place to place, dealers in jewels and gold and fine art.

In New York he had forgotten the threat to Jews. But Vienna was an anti-Semitic city. Sometimes he could see the hate in people's eyes and even his wife had picked up the poison.

He looked at Sophie. She was an attractive woman. Her face was strong and she had an independent mind.

'Are you looking forward to Berlin?' he asked.

She turned from the window and looked at him. 'Yes. Vienna has become tiresome. One runs into the same faces week after week and the gossip is always of the court. It suits Alma, but not me.'

'I can assure you that life is not as formal in Berlin,' Steiner reassured her. 'They are a hard breed, very determined and like all young countries and empires, confident of themselves.'

'It will be a challenge. I like Germans and I have studied their culture. It is solid and well based in the past,' she told him.

'And what of Prague, our first stop?' Joseph asked, amused.

'I do not know, but I imagine it lacks Berlin's energy and life,' Sophie laughed.

They were now passing through fertile countryside. The great wheat fields seemed to stretch to infinity. Here and there a village surrounding a church with a bulbous dome indicated habitation of the wide, flat expanse.

'You will like Prague,' Joseph said. 'It is like something from a fairy tale. It has a light quality which always lifts my heart.' He had an intense affection for Prague, situated almost at the centre of Europe. It was a city which always charmed his eye; and the Jews had almost found a lasting home in its old ghetto.

They reached Prague at evening time. 'I will show you some of the sights,' Joseph said. 'Of all places on earth this is the most magical. It possesses a mystical quality and I believe I could live quietly in the Jewish ghetto.'

'You could not,' Sophie retorted. 'You may believe that you could but you must be always close to the financial centres and the stock exchange.'

'Only a part of me,' he answered with an impish grin.

They set out for Prague Castle, set on a hill above the city. From here they could view the Vltava river flowing in a protective arm about the ancient part of the city. Charles Bridge, with its old arches and angled pillars, spanned the river below a weir. Great statues stood in silhouette on the parapets, like guardian spirits. The skyline of red-tiled roofs, standing above narrow streets, was dominated by spires and domes rising into the light-blue haze like gauze around the city.

They then made for a restaurant Joseph knew close to the castle, sitting at a window where they could look down on the city lights suffused by the night mist.

Sophie looked at the small man opposite her, with his tight body, intense eyes and sad expression. 'You are an extraordinary man, Joseph Steiner. You have moved quietly through our lives and never lifted a hand to harm us. You took on a great burden when you married Mother, a vain woman with three wilful daughters. We have never returned your affection to any great degree and yet you have never refused us a single request in all our lives.'

'I loved your mother very much.'

'Do you still love her?'

'Love dies. I will say no more. She should not have returned to Vienna. Any other city but not Vienna.'

'But you did not receive all the love you deserved,' Sophie insisted. 'You educated us at the best schools. You insisted that we learn European languages. You introduced us to the best society. Was it worth it? Should you not have married a rich Jewess and settled in a beautiful city like Prague?'

'Providence has set out a course for us. We must follow. We must follow a pattern,' her stepfather said fatefully. He did not wish to give her a direct answer.

'I do not believe in such a philosophy. We make our own patterns and weave our own destinies. The Germans form their own destinies. They have will and purpose,' Sophie said firmly.

'I have educated you too well. You have learned to argue against me,' he smiled.

'You are a good man, perhaps even behind the withdrawn exterior, a tender man. I do not think that life has dealt you a fair hand.'

'That is not so. I am wealthy. I am now in the most beautiful city in Europe and I am talking to a beautiful woman.'

They might have continued their conversation but a violinist came to their table. Joseph Steiner talked to him in his own language and hummed a few notes of an old tune. The violinist began to play a sad Slavonic song. Joseph listened intently.

When it was finished he gave the musician some money, explaining, 'It is a folk song. I heard it once at a railway station in Poland. It was played by an old soldier who had been wounded in some war or other. It reminds me of past times.'

'Why do you not speak of them? They are bound to be full of interest.'

'Certain memories I keep to myself,' he said vaguely. 'I thought I had laid them to rest in New York. I come to Europe and they return to me. Many of them are only half remembered.'

'Perhaps you should never have returned to Europe,' Sophie suggested, alarmed by her stepfather's sadness.

'I belong in this soil. As I grow older I realise this fact with greater clarity. We all wish to return to our origins.'

'Is it not dangerous?'

'All my life I have lived with danger. It has taught me caution. I can quietly disappear into a crowd.'

When they left the restaurant some time later, Sophie realized that her father had revealed more to her that evening than she could ever remember.

When they reached the bottom of the Castle hill they got out of the carriage and walked across the old honey-coloured sandstone bridge, with its great brooding, religious statues, where one could lean over the parapet and look down at the water. The blue mist was thickening over the city and between buildings. They lost their great mass and seemed to float like dream islands along the river, and the lights now had an aura of muted gold.

Sophie and Joseph now entered the old town with its narrow cobbled streets, arched doorways and ornamental windows. The streets were never straight and each corner revealed a new and limited perspective. They finally arrived at the old town square and felt the intensity of time as their eyes went from building to building, all intimately knit together. 'It is too beautiful,' Sophie said, her eyes bright.

'Nothing can be too beautiful.'

'Tomorrow I will return early and walk through this quarter and pass over the Charles Bridge. There is so much to see and think about.'

It was late when the cab took them to the hotel in the hilly area of Hradcany. Here, from her window, Sophie looked down on the city shimmering with lights. She remained looking out the window until the clock in the Cathedral struck twelve. Down in the lanes beneath her, lovers were making their way home arm in arm. They passed out into the light of the street lamps into the shadows and then out again. Now and then a drunkard stumbled up the lanes and stopped to urinate in some quiet corner. A party returning from a tavern sang a tune in doubtful harmony. Above it all was a smell from the city which she could not define.

She lay in bed, reflecting on the wonderful day and on her stepfather in the adjoining room. For a moment she entertained the idea of going to his room and talking with him some more. It was one o'clock before she finally nodded off.

The next morning the sun poured in the window of the hotel. Sophie drifted in and out of sleep, watching the mysterious slabs of light filled with slowly whirling motes. She rose and went to the window. The sun rising out of the east cast fresh light on the domes and towers and the tiled roofs of the city. She dressed quickly and went to the dining room where Joseph Steiner was waiting for her, dressed neatly like a businessman.

'The city is yours to conquer today. If necessary I will hire a guide for you,' he told her.

'No. I will discover it for myself. I prefer it that way. A street map and some information will be sufficient,' she smiled.

'Better so. You can form your own impressions.' He handed her a wallet of money. 'But you will need this,' he told her. 'Perhaps some piece of jewellery will catch your eye. There are excellent jewellers in Prague. I have made out a list. Hand them my card and they will give you every service.'

Sophie took the small, ornate wallet and placed it in her bag. 'How can I thank you?' she asked.

'I find your company a delight,' he said with delicate refinement. 'But you must eat a hearty breakfast. If you wish to walk through the city you will have to eat everything which is placed before you.'

They ate at a leisurely pace then Joseph ordered a cab and they drove through the district of Mala Strana to the old quarter of the city, where they stopped at the romantic square. People had gathered at the old Town Hall to watch the Horloge ring the hour. As the chimes sounded they watched a procession of the Apostles appear at the small windows above the face of the clock. Then they saw a skeleton, symbol of death, ring a fatal bell.

They stood at the heart of Prague. Here they parted.

Joseph Steiner had a definite plan in mind. He made his way north to Josef Stadt. As he walked into the quarter he felt the burden of Jewish history grow heavy upon his shoulders. As he looked about him at the shop fronts he recognised the Jewish names. In this ghetto, more than any other in Europe, their culture was still intact.

He took his notebook from his pocket and checked an address near Parizska Street. He asked for directions and found himself in front of a small arched door. He lifted the stiff knocker and banged it. It sounded empty and barren.

After some time an old woman appeared at the door. Her eyes were wet and she blinked as if unfamiliar with the light. 'Who are you? What do you want?' she asked suspiciously.

'Steiner. Joseph Steiner,' he told her, handing her a card. 'I would like to see Master Samuel.'

She closed the door on him and Joseph looked at the houses around him with their stuccoed walls, mouldering plaster, and the quiet, silent movement of Jews as if apologising for their presence.

The old woman returned. 'He will meet you. Follow me,' she said starkly.

He followed her through a corridor, a dusty, airless, place. They passed up wooden stairs to a landing, where she knocked on a small door.

'Joseph Steiner,' she called gruffly. She then opened the door and he entered.

Master Samuel sat at a great black, oak desk. Piled on top of it stood old books forming awkward piles. On the floor stood other piles of books, brown and heavily bound, with faded lettering on their spines. The room was lined with shelves crammed with more books.

'Take a seat if you can find it,' he said. Joseph made his way through the pillars of books and sat down opposite the old man.

'I intend to set this room in order. But I am always sidetracked. There are new books to purchase and I can never catch up with my reading. I received your letter, though. In fact it is here somewhere.'

He took up an old shoe box from the floor and began to rummage through it. 'Ah, here it is. It was a most difficult request but I finally tracked it down. These old Venetian Bibles are rare. Most of them have been lost or destroyed.'

He took a book from a drawer in his desk and opened it. It was in pristine condition. He handled it reverently.

Joseph Steiner then took it in his hands and looked at it carefully. He had only seen one once before, in a library in New York.

'Master craftsmen and scholars worked on these pages,' Master Samuel commented. Joseph turned each one with reverence, looking at the sacred texts intently.

They did not discuss the price. Instead they talked of the beauty of the book, its historical importance. 'I have American buyers for such books. That is important to me. I keep a careful record of them. If they go to America or England they are safe. I am never certain of Europe. When they wish to destroy us they burn our books. If they are placed in distant libraries they can survive.'

Finally, Steiner paid for the precious book and requested that it be delivered it to his hotel.

'Now I must visit the Jewish cemetery,' he said.

'I shall go with you. I often visit it. It is filled with old ghosts.'

The old man rose from his desk and left aside his prayer shawl. Then, taking his stick, he accompanied Joseph Steiner through the old quarter. They stopped several times and he explained the historical importance of the buildings, particularly the Staronnoval synagogue, part of which had been erected in medieval times.

'We have been here a long time, a long time indeed. This area is our monument. To destroy it would be to destroy the memory of what we are and what we were.'

'In every city I find such memories,' Joseph Steiner told him thoughtfully.

Samuel peered at him intently and nodded his head. They moved on to the narrow lanes and densely populated houses of the area around the Altneuschule, near the cemetery.

The Jewish burial ground was a private, secluded place. They pushed aside a rusty gate and found themselves standing amongst grey and red slabs, crammed into the ground as close together as teeth, with only narrow paths of dark, inert earth between them. Some of the stones were a great age, with Hebrew inscriptions and symbols expressing the origin of the deceased, their names and professions.

'It is a vast library in stone,' Samuel mused.

They searched amongst the crowded tombstones, bending down to decipher old names, excited by their common interest. As they left the sacred place some two hours later, Joseph said, 'I believe I could be at peace here.'

They walked the short distance to the old town square, and stood at the centre, contemplating the intimate beauty of the place.

'This city is a human size, and has a protective air about it. It has been good to Jew, and Gentile and agnostic. I hope it will always continue to be so.'

With this they shook hands and the old Jew returned to his quarter. Joseph watched him walk across the square with a slow, awkward gait.

Joseph then made his way to the commercial section of the city. As he walked through the comfortable streets he had time to reflect on some information he had received by telegraph from New York. When he finally reached the office of the broker, Joseph directed him to purchase stocks in a railroad in Iowa. Then he quietly left the building.

He returned to the hotel where the parcel was waiting for him. He opened it and took out the precious book. Setting it on a table in his room he began to study it. The richness of its contents filled his mind with pleasure.

That night he had dinner with Sophie. The conversation centred on her visit to the city. Finally, as the meal was coming to an end, she asked him how he had spent his day.

'Very simply,' he told her. 'I purchased an old Hebrew book and I visited a Jewish cemetery.'

'And what did you discover?'

'That my history has not left me. Sometimes I feel that my race is cursed. Perhaps we will never return to our homeland.' His eyes looked sadder than ever.

How could the great suffering they had endured be justified, Sophie wondered as she placed her hand over her stepfather's.

Chapter Eleven

The fishing skiff lay anchored in a small port south of Bremerhaven. Captain Wolff studied his charts carefully to calculate the distance and the time. They would have to travel for a day and a night to be in position. Then he went to his cabin to check his revolver. He hoped that he would not have to use it.

That evening he made contact with a young officer whose name he did not know, at a local inn.

He studied the young man who had arrived dressed as a seaman, carefully. 'You look too perfect,' he said. 'I will arrange for you to have some proper clothes. You can explain to me exactly what you require when we get on board.'

Carrying a battered suitcase the officer followed him to the skiff. As he approached he was surprised at its small size and poor condition. It was only when he went below deck that he realised how well-equipped it was.

The officer opened his case and took out his camera. 'You have seen moving pictures,' he began as he laid out the equipment on the table.

'Yes. I have seen a film show in the local hall,' Wolff replied.

'This is the equipment which makes moving pictures. I will need a position on the deck from which to take the pictures.'

'That can be arranged. Let us hope that the weather holds. The visibility is good this time of year. I have received orders to facilitate you in every way.'

It was obvious to the young officer that Captain Wolff

had been on several missions in the North Sea. He looked capable and intelligent.

'Now, let us have a drink,' the Captain said. 'Let us toast the German Navy.' He opened a bottle of rum and poured two glasses. He drank his own quickly and filled it again.

When he had finished he put the cork back on the bottle and pushed it down with his palm. 'I'm sure that you have to prepare your camera,' he said. 'We will set out in twenty minutes. All the fishermen have been hand-picked by me. They know the purpose of the mission. If there is trouble they know how to handle it.'

With that he left the cabin and went on deck. Soon the engine began to vibrate and the fishing skiff moved out to sea. It travelled directly north towards Heligoland then set a course west.

The officer went on board and looked at the vast and empty sea. The waves were awkward and grey and broke over the bow in spray as the small craft made its way stubbornly west. The wind was cold and salty. It penetrated his oilskins. His fingers grew numb and he rubbed them to try and keep them warm. He had no great interest in the endless sea and soon he went down to the cabin and took out a photographic manual and began to read it. At nine o'clock he tried to sleep. The movement of the small craft turned his stomach. He tried to control himself. Then a wave of nausea swept through his body. He rushed on deck and vomited into the sea.

'You get used to it,' Captain Wolff said calmly.

The officer returned to his bunk, but the waves of nausea continued. Several times he rushed on deck but he could no longer vomit. His stomach was empty.

It was very late in the night when he finally slept. Almost immediately he was shaken awake.

'It is time for breakfast,' one of the fishermen was saying to him.

The nausea had disappeared and he found that he was able to drink cups of warm tea and rough brown bread.

Captain Wolff appeared. 'We will be in position in an hour. Come up on deck when you are ready.'

The officer took his camera and checked it carefully. Holding the delicate box he went on deck. The sea was choppy and he moved awkwardly to the bow of the small craft. He sat on a wooden bench and pointed the camera directly west. Then he placed it on a stand. It moved to the uneven rhythm of the waves. When he was satisfied that everything was correct a tarpaulin with an aperture was placed over him. Only the lens showed through. He waited.

Out of the morning mist the greatest fleet of ships in the world steamed into view, like great mastodons. The skiff moved as close to their wake as it could. Hidden underneath a canvas tent the young officer's camera whirred, and his excitement mounted. He concentrated on the upper decks as he had been directed. Four times he loaded the camera, his nervous hands fumbling with the delicate mechanics. It took the great fleet two hours to pass by. It sailed into the distance and passed over the horizon and it was only when the massive procession had disappeared that he began to feel the cold.

Two days later the officer left for Berlin, four cases of film packed in his luggage.

Von Hertling had converted the large cellar beneath his offices into a cinema. He had invited several naval officers and engineers to the film and they watched closely as the movement of the British fleet was projected on to the screen. The film was shown several times. Then the lights were put on. They sat and discussed what they had seen. It was obvious that the British still held the edge over the new German navy. Von Hertling calculated that the British guns had a longer range and that the great ships travelled at twenty-one knots per hour, twice as fast as theirs. But they believed that they could improve on the British effort.

When the officers had returned to their various offices all over Berlin, Von Hertling knew that they were impressed by his methods. He had collected important information for them which they could study at length. Now, he would simply have to obtain plans of the ships. His network of spies was growing slowly and now spread in a wide web across Europe. And all the information was co-ordinated by Berlin.

By now Von Hertling had almost complete control of the secret service. His power was beginning to grow. Many ministers at the Reichstag knew of his importance. There were rumours that he had files on their private lives which he could use against them. It gave him a sense of power and importance.

He was about to leave the building when a carriage drew up at the main door. Two men got out and looked about them, then a third figure emerged and walked quickly into the building. The door was thrown open and a gentleman in a long military trenchcoat stood before him. It took him a moment to recognise the Kaiser, Emperor of Germany.

'Your Majesty,' he began, not knowing what else to say.

The Kaiser dismissed his bodyguards and told them to take up positions at each end of the long corridor. 'Be seated, Von Hertling,' he directed. He snapped open a cigarette case and offered the baron a cigarette.

Von Hertling took it and placed it in his lips, still looking at the Emperor.

'Light it, Baron. Then we can talk.'

The Baron lit his cigarette and sat at his desk. The Emperor sat in front of him.

'You wonder why I come unannounced. I should have had my secretary inform you but I do not wish to have my movements known. I believe that you are doing important work here, particularly in the photographic field.'

'We have set up a special unit which travels abroad and brings home military information.'

'Then you have knowledge of everything which is going on in Europe and you can show me this on a screen?'

'We have not built up a full picture. There is much more that I would wish to obtain but this department has only recently been established and there is opposition to it in some quarters. They dislike the secrecy attached to it.'

'One must have secrecy. Tell me about your plans. I am a good listener,' the Emperor directed.

For the next hour Baron Von Hertling explained to the Kaiser the inner workings of his information-gathering network. The Kaiser had a clear, sharp mind and only interjected on a few occasions when he wanted further information.

Finally, he said, 'Now, let us see this basement of which I have heard so much. I must know all that is happening in my empire.'

The Kaiser followed Von Hertling down the cement steps into the bare corridor which ran the whole length of the building. It was a dreary place with a series of painted doors built into the walls. Bare bulbs burned above them and shed a harsh light on the corridor, highlighting the gritty walls.

'Not a very pleasant place, Baron,' the Emperor commented wryly. 'Some of our prisons are better furnished than your basement.'

They entered the cinema and the Emperor sat down. Von Hertling showed him the recent films which had been shot in the British naval yards, explaining the significance of each piece.

'Good. I am impressed,' the Kaiser announced. 'Now, let me see your store of film.'

They entered a dark room and the Kaiser examined the labelled cans of film arranged neatly in racks along the wall. 'I see that you possess many films on the Kaiser. Could you tell me why? Am I not above suspicion?'

'Yes, your Majesty, but those about you may not be,' the baron said in a serious voice.

'You are hiding something,' the Kaiser said, turning to him. 'I demand to see the films.'

'Very well, your Majesty.'

As the films were projected on to the screen, the Emperor studied them intently. 'But they are of no importance. They are photographs of crowds. What do they mean?'

'Do you wish to know?'

'Of course I wish to know. I am your Emperor.' The Kaiser had begun to get uncomfortable.

'I have employed one young man to study every face which appears in these crowds. We are on the lookout for assassins. Twice we have been able to prevent attempts on your life.' He pointed to several insignificant figures in the crowds. They turned up in other film reels. They were always close to each other and at strong vantage points.

'The moment was never correct for them to move against you, and now we have captured them. At present they are in prison. We have extracted all the information we possibly could from them and we discovered that they were anarchists. They have no connection with any European governments.'

The Kaiser said nothing for some time then said, 'You have served both your Emperor and Germany well. I believe that I may have further work for you and I would like you to strengthen your spy rings. There are certain people whose files I may wish to see and you will bring them directly to the palace if they are requested. One can only act strongly from certain knowledge. I believe that we understand each other.'

'Yes, your Majesty.'

'Good.' With that his appearance changed and he became distant and stiff. The intimacy between them disappeared.

The Emperor turned on his heel, marched down the corridor and up the steps out of the basement.

It took Baron Von Hertling some time to recover his composure. He retraced his steps to the projection room and sat for some time considering what had happened. His organisation had received the approval of the Kaiser himself.

That night Von Hertling left his office late and decided to walk towards Alexanderplatz in the eastern area of the city. This was a place which always gave him a sense of the majesty of the empire, as did the Ring Strasse in Vienna. The lights cast a magical glow on the streets, which were noisy with the automobile, which had recently appeared in Berlin.

Baron Von Hertling felt content as he passed through the main avenue of the city towards the great imperial buildings. Normally a bodyguard would have accompanied him, but such excitement filled his mind that he wished to be alone.

It happened quite suddenly when a young man approached him from the far side of the great road. He sensed that something was wrong when he noticed how agitated the young man was. He decided to move quickly and drew his revolver. The young man noted his action and half-way across the road fired at him. The bullet passed through his left shoulder, but despite his pain Von Hertling took aim and fired. The young man dropped in the middle of the avenue and a horse-drawn carriage ran over him before he had chance to escape. When Von Hertling reached him he was dead.

The bullet hole was clean and there was no danger of infection. Immediately, Von Hertling phoned several of his agents. He had to discover who the dead man was and to what organisation he belonged.

He returned to his office. Despite the deep pain he spent two hours with his men. Then unable to endure it any longer he collapsed.

While the baron recuperated quietly in his rooms, the body of the young man was identified. The papers in his pockets indicated that he had lived in Berlin with some friends for six months. They belonged to a renegade anarchist group from Vienna.

Each member of the group living in Berlin was tracked down and interrogated. Then when they had nothing more to disclose, they were murdered, buried in the woods to the north of the city.

The names of the other members of the group operating in Vienna were given to Von Hertling, who vowed to deal with them at an opportune moment. Amongst them was a Jakov Fieldmann.

Chapter Twelve

Sophie gazed out of the train window as they approached Berlin. Here, she thought, the new energy of Europe resided.

Joseph remarked that the great city had spread to the east since his first visit there many years ago, when he had purchased some worthless land. Now it was beginning to realise a large profit for him.

He took out his notebook to consult some addresses. Having memorised them, he returned the notebook to his pocket.

'Can I not buy you a proper briefcase,' Sophie laughed.

'It is too cumbersome and too obvious. When you have to leave a place quickly it is better to have everything neatly tucked away. Carry a change of clothes, a notebook and some valuables. The smaller and more significant they are the better. I always have something valuable on me which a border guard will not recognise. Once, I travelled with a notebook from Poland which contained insignificant pious reproductions which you can buy anywhere. However, concealed among them was a small cartoon by Raphael. I sold it in Paris.'

By now the train had entered the station, a vast place with an arching glass roof. When they hailed a cab George Steiner directed the driver to take them through the city. 'It looks more magnificent than ever,' he remarked to Sophie.

They followed the great avenue through the city, passing through the Tiergarten, with its woods and avenues. Then they drove along the wide boulevard, Unter den Linden, towards the old part of the city with its great museums and governmental offices. Sophie observed that the buildings were as impressive and just as imposing as those in Vienna. She felt elated with the power of this great city.

When they returned to their hotel, close to the Tiergarten on Französische Strasse, Joseph said, 'I'm afraid that I must leave you for some hours. I have arranged a meeting with a business acquaintance. In the meantime, you must visit the shops. There is nothing which you cannot purchase in Berlin.'

Sophie went to the window and watched him depart, remarking that as always there was a cab waiting for him. He entered and it drove away.

Joseph's visit took him to the eastern section of the city, a grimy place with great smoke stacks belching smoke into the air. The streets were crooked and narrow and the workers looked tired and drawn. He walked through several similar streets until he came to a steelworks, an awkward brick building that had been built to no particular order. Inside it was dark and only the wells of hot steel in the cauldrons glowed.

Ernst Fischer was waiting for him at the door. He was a young engineer who had been trained in Paris and Berlin. His father had died six months previously and he had inherited the place. He was a tall, ascetic-looking man, with sharp features. He wore steel-rimmed glasses with thick lenses. Joseph Steiner wondered how far this young man could see.

'This is the factory you described in your letter,' Joseph Steiner began, casting a critical eye over the drab, irregular buildings.

'Yes,' Fischer replied, 'It has little to recommend it in appearance. But it is situated in one of the best areas in the city. It will increase in value.'

'And so will every other piece of land in Berlin,' Joseph Steiner announced sharply, wondering why he had come on such a foolish visit. 'And I do not see any future in continuing to produce agricultural instruments. There is no great market for such things.'

The young man looked at Joseph Steiner. His features grew tight and severe and he had to restrain his anger. The Jewish gentleman had not even listened to his proposals and he wondered if he should end the conversation and leave him.

'I never suggested that there was. I have other plans. I did not bring you this far to show you a run-down factory with a tired labour force. If you could come with me to the office I believe that I can show you something that will be of interest.'

Joseph walked with the tall, gangling young man across an open space where scrap-iron rusted in great mounds. Few words passed between them. Joseph Steiner looked in disgust at the chaos and misuse of space. The dilapidated factory was standing on four acres of valuable property!

In a corner of the yard stood a new building, a formal place, newly built, with large windows and without any suggestion of ornament. When they entered it was warm inside and light filled the place. Two young men sat at drawing boards in a large office. They were clean-shaven and tidy like the office itself. The place was uncluttered with heavy furniture. Only the blueprints standing on easels around them seemed to add colour to the place.

Ernst Fischer did not ask Joseph Steiner to sit down. Instead he brought him to a large easel, where he flicked over the first page and began to explain.

'With proper finance this is how the area would look. All the old buildings would be levelled and these would take their place. There is no waste of space. There are delivery areas and storage space. Everything is logically positioned and there will be no waste of time.'

He flicked over the pages. 'And this is what I intend to produce,' he said showing Joseph a final drawing.

Joseph studied it for a moment. Sophie had one of the new motor cars that were the plague of Vienna, but then he looked again more closely. This was a different sort of machine, several times larger. 'Will it work?' he asked.

'I have done all the mathematical calculations, down to the last pound. In fact I believe that in a year's time this vehicle will carry more weight. Every week there is some new improvement in the field of mechanics. There is no going back. The horse has no future.'

'And what of the army? Will they go to war in these machines?'

'Yes. But they will be even greater and stronger. The combustion engine is improving rapidly. I have other drawings but they are in no way detailed. They belong to the realm of the imagination.'

'Let me see them,' Joseph Steiner directed. It was the first time in this meeting that a note of enthusiasm entered his voice.

The young man grew excited. His fingers began to move as if he were playing a keyboard. He drew out several drawings and placed them in front of Joseph. When Joseph Steiner looked at them his instinct told him that he was looking at the future.

He sat down with Fischer and began to discuss how much it would cost to finance the modern factory.

'There are young architects in Berlin bristling with new ideas,' Fischer told him. 'They laugh at the Reichstag and the Royal Palace. They believe that they are a waste of good material. I can draw on some of the brightest young minds, eager to produce something new. I know them.'

'I will remain in Berlin for a fortnight. I have some business to attend to. I will meet you in ten days' time in this room, when I would like to see a model of the factory and a model of this machine you wish to build. Then I will make my decision.'

* * *

When Joseph returned to his car, he gave the driver an address in Kreuzberg. Then he sat back in his seat and reflected on the young man he has just met. Ernst Fischer had an inner intensity which he admired. Money invested in Berlin would yield a high reward.

Steiner fell into a light sleep and when the cab halted he found himself in front of number 10 Mehringdamm. He alighted and paid the driver. He studied the stucco facade of his friend, Levi Belkind's, townhouse. Masses of flowers hung over the balconies adding lightness and charm to the place. He knocked on the door and waited, until a servant answered. He had been expected and was ushered into the great hallway. While he waited for his friend Joseph studied the rare paintings on the wall.

'Ah, Steiner,' a voice said behind him. 'Do you approve of my paintings?'

'Very much so. You have a good eye.'

'My dealer has a good eye. But come with me into my study and let us talk.'

Levi Belkind exuded life. He was a portly man but carried his weight with dignity. He was wearing a silk smoking jacket and smoked a strong cigar. In fact the whole house seemed to smell of cigar smoke.

They entered a large study, lined with great bookcases filled with massive volumes. Joseph Steiner looked at them for a moment with some curiosity. His friend was no reader.

'I buy them by the yard. I believe they are of some value. Never have time to read them, but they are reassuring,' Levi Belkind said, reading his thoughts.

He directed Joseph to sit in a deep leather armchair and poured him a brandy. 'It is far too much. I prefer a light white wine,' Joseph protested.

'You are in Berlin not in Vienna,' Belkind laughed and sat down in front of the fire.

Joseph looked at Belkind's heavy face, the chin set in a soft jowl. The man was totally dedicated to the pleasures of life. He had homes in three great European cities. In each city he had a mistress.

'How have you been keeping since we met in Vienna?' Levi asked.

'Keeping an eye on business,' Joseph told him.

'Always an eye on business. Levi Belkind here keeps an eye on business. He also has an eye for a young woman. You should take a young woman, a Russian princess. They are passionate creatures, soft-skinned and luxurious.' He would have continued to develop his point but he noted that Joseph Steiner was uncomfortable.

'Tell me what you have been doing since you arrived in Berlin.'

'Today I visited a young man in the Zehlendorf district. He has inherited a run-down factory from his father. It is a rambling, useless place but he has plans for a new factory. I studied them in his office. They appear sound enough to me.'

'In the Zehlendorf district you say? Let me think now. How many acres does he possess?'

'Four, perhaps five.'

'And what does he intend to produce?'

'A type of motor vehicle. He believes that they will carry troops into war.'

'War. War. They speak of nothing but war,' Levi Belkind said with disgust. 'These Prussian Junkers will eventually make a war necessity, and Kaiser Wilhelm will be only too delighted to oblige. If there is no war there will be a revolution. But these are only my feelings. Invest with the young man. In fact I will raise half the capital and I will keep an eye on our investment.'

This was the precise reason why Joseph Steiner had come to visit. If Levi Belkind invested with him, then his business would thrive.

'Now that we have this piece of business out of the way tell me about the scandals at court. One is always interested in such matters.'

Joseph had little gossip for him, so Levi Belkind told him all the scandal of the Berlin court. Joseph was shocked at some of the revelations.

'It is life. The Empress Dona believes in domestic bliss. Little does she know that the palace reeks of immorality. It is always so.' Then Levi Belkind became serious: 'Immorality I tolerate but I do not like the anti-Jewish feeling that lies beneath the tolerant face of this city.'

Joseph Steiner was surprised. For years the Jews of eastern Europe had taken refuge in the great city, bringing their crafts and skills with them. They had been bankers to Bismarck and the Kaiser.

'What is the reason?'

'There is the old reason and the new reason and no reason at all. The Jew has always been a scapegoat. Has there ever been a time when we have not been hated? Most of the professional people in Vienna are Jews and in Berlin most of the Jews are in banking. As bankers we are seen to control the purse strings of the nation. If there should be hunger or unemployment then the rabble rousers will point to the Jews. I have already noticed it in small ways. Some of the newspapers in the city are making noises. The gutter press print cartoons which do not flatter us. So be careful. Be a person of the shadows. Watch the way the political winds are blowing.'

Disturbed, Joseph turned again to financial matters.

Levi Belkind was a shrewd observer of the European scene. His business sense was sharp and accurate. 'Money invested here cannot fail. At present there is stability, but the Kaiser, despite his brilliance, is a wayward fool. This is becoming a military state. The army is gathering power. And when the army grows powerful then it will look for a war. Mark my words.'

'I have often been invited to watch the military manoeuvres,' Joseph Steiner told him.

'Observe them carefully. Every year they become more impressive and more deadly. They are well organised and give the army a purpose. Krupps can turn out the finest cannons in the world.'

Belkind gave him a long list of facts and figures. Joseph observed the ponderous man, fleshy in every part of his body, looking into the fire. Periodically he stopped and drank some brandy and puffed on his cigar. His life possessed a sensual quality which Joseph admired.

Finally Levi took a watch from his pocket and examined it. 'Will you dine with us? I have some friends coming to dinner, artists and writers. They stimulate the mind.'

'I am afraid that my daughter is waiting for me. I promised to bring her to the theatre tonight.'

'You should have told me that she was with you. She could have come to supper. I am sure she would have enjoyed the company. We could speak further about the deal. I am interested in it. Soon land will be impossible to buy in Berlin.'

'Well, Sophie is waiting and I must call a cab, but thank you.'

'Not at all. My chauffeur will drive you to your hotel. I have invested in one of these new automobiles. They are exciting inventions.'

'My stepdaughter owns one and she knows all about the internal combustion engine. It is quite amazing,' Joseph laughed.

'And can she drive this automobile?'

'Yes.'

'Then she must be quite an amazing woman.'

'She is. I intend to place her in charge of my affairs in this city.'

'We must be introduced then. Most of the women I meet

are playthings. I would like to meet a woman of such independence.'

'I believe that you will soon be doing business with her.'

Belkind took up the telephone which stood on an onyx-topped table and called his chauffeur. Some minutes later Joseph Steiner left the Kreuzberg district of Berlin in a new automobile. Like Levi Belkind's house it smelt of cigars.

Chapter Thirteen

The mist lay lightly on the valleys and on the hills, where birch and larch trees grew in small coppices. At five o'clock military bugles echoed through the woods and men began to stir and wipe the sleep out of their eyes. For three days many of them had been on the march from their barracks following the commands of captains and generals. They were neither certain of their position nor their purpose.

Field kitchens had been set up in village squares and in farmyards and on this morning the men formed querulous lines and waited for their breakfast, which was ladled onto large tin plates. Having received two ladles of food each and taken heavy slices of brown bread they sat down and began to eat. They complained of the early-morning call, the cold conditions of their billet, the urgency with which they had been marched forward. They always complained in the morning time, when their heads were heavy with drink and they lacked sleep.

'I'm certain the Kaiser is still in bed in Berlin,' one of them complained, scraping the remains of his breakfast from the plate.

'Probably donning one of his fancy uniforms and deciding what medals he will pin on his chest. And it is the same with the Prussian generals. We are only pawns in their war games,' another soldier added.

'There will be changes. I've been to Berlin. The workers and others feel discontent. The middle men make the money and eat the gravy. The working man sweats his guts out in these great factories. I've been through them. The great furnaces are like the fires of hell.' The soldier who spoke had a sharp, unhappy face.

'You watch your tongue,' a young recruit told him. 'You could be court-martialled for talk like that.'

'Not unless there is an informer amongst us,' he replied bluntly.

As the mist thinned the men began to stir. They harnessed the horses to great guns and cannons and at half-past six began to move onto the road which led to the valleys where the manoeuvres were to take place. They formed a long line which stretched for twelve miles. Their leaders had received their orders, had consulted their maps and knew the battle formation.

In Berlin the generals had risen at dawn. Already they were making their way from their various barracks and offices to the railway station. They gathered informally into smart groups and talked of the day ahead. At ten minutes to nine it was announced that the Kaiser was on his way to the station and they quickly drew into formation. At three minutes to nine exactly he entered the station, surrounded by his generals. They moved quickly along the platform and climbed into the imperial carriage. The others took their positions in the remaining carriages, amongst the invited observers, Joseph Steiner.

At nine o'clock the train steamed south. Joseph sat with some reporters from German national newspapers and noted that they were filled with the military arrogance which seemed to possess the German mind.

As they approached their destination they could see the great armies moving into position. They had set up camps and hospitals behind the lines and smoke seemed to rise from a thousand campfires. He looked at the intent faces of the young men, all bent on some small purpose or other.

When they reached the small station it was festooned with colours and the whole town had turned out to greet the Kaiser. A military band started up and from the carriage Joseph could see the Kaiser descend from the imperial coach. He wore a silver helmet with a golden spike and his coat was covered with ornamental braid and medals. Outside the station his horse was waiting for him. He mounted quickly and was followed by others including the Prince Regent of Bavaria and a blond man Joseph recognised from Vienna, Prince Dmitri. They set off at a fast trot through the village. Joseph, with others, followed in carriages.

The vantage point was on a hill overlooking a slight valley where the corn had recently been cut. The meadows were empty of cattle and as far as the eye could see squadrons of men were set out in neat formations across the hills.

When both the Kaiser and his generals were in position the guns began to boom out. Immediately, the vast army began their complicated moves. Joseph noted how the Kaiser took command of the whole situation. The army was his plaything and the generals accountable only to him.

For four hours the observers stood on the hill and noted the progress of the manoeuvres. It was a vast, complicated system which Joseph Steiner could barely follow. Whole divisions advanced and retreated before his eyes. Cavalries charged with sabres drawn in colourful formations.

Then, on a distant hill there was a sudden explosion and panic seemed to take hold of the soldiers. Ten minutes later an officer, covered in blood, arrived at headquarters. An ammunition dump had been hit by accident and several men had been killed.

The Kaiser ordered the manoeuvres to continue. 'There are always casualties on manoeuvres such as these. It will test the medical corps. Let us see how they will act under such conditions.'

Soon, wounded soldiers began to arrive at the military hospital below them. Many hundreds of men had been wounded, but all over the hills the battles continued and at four o'clock when the trumpets sounded, the Kaiser was greeted by wild cheering.

He returned to the vantage point above the valley and watched as the battalions fell into line and commenced their march back to barracks.

Returning from the hill the crowds made their way to the small station and back to Berlin. Joseph Steiner was impressed by what he had observed. It was quite clear that the German army was furnished with the most modern artillery and guns. His practised eye quickly told him that this army could quickly move against France or Austria without much hindrance. He understood also why Prince Dmitri had been invited to the manoeuvres. Then, the Tsar would be personally informed of the strength of the German army.

The journalists, too, had been impressed by the demonstration. Clearly the Kaiser had built up a formidable force and he was now a central figure in European politics.

'Austria would stand little chance against the might of Germany. They are furnished with antique weaponry. Franz Joseph has lost the edge,' one of the Berlin journalists remarked. There was no one who could contradict him.

'If the peace holds, the Kaiser's forces can only grow. Soon he will be able to wage war on two fronts. He can split Europe in two,' he continued.

Joseph Steiner kept his counsel. It would not be wise to let people know what he thought of the manoeuvres. But as the train made its way back to Berlin, many of the journalists got drunk. They toasted the new Germany as they passed through the autumn countryside.

The previous evening Prince Dmitri, dressed informally, had met Baron Von Hertling in a shady suburb of the city. The recent attempt on his life had prompted Von Hertling to meet the Prince. He knew that Dmitri had important connections in Vienna.

They were polite to each other when they met. Von Hertling was formal and precise, with the measured gestures of the military academy. Prince Dmitri had the casual manner of an aristocrat.

'I was informed that you were invited to the manoeuvres. I thought perhaps we might have some mutual interests,' Von Hertling began. 'Let me be direct. Recently an attempt was made on my life by Austrian anarchists. I know that you are more than a diplomat at the Viennese court and I believe that it might be useful to keep each other informed about these groups.'

'Very good,' Prince Dmitri agreed. 'I do not think that it will interfere with our mutual fields of operation. In fact, we should keep ourselves well informed on revolutionaries of any nationality. They set out to destroy all our interests.'

This remark reassured Von Hertling. 'I have received information from Vienna that the generals are making plans to annex Bosnia Herzegovina. The plans are well advanced. It is something you might like to know. Perhaps later I can fill in some of the details for you.'

'That would be most helpful. What can I do for you?'

Von Hertling took a list from his pocket. 'If possible, I would like to have these people placed under surveillance. I ask as some of them are Russians and they frequently pass between empires. Where possible they should be imprisoned and interrogated. The underlined names are those of the people who should be eliminated.'

Prince Dimitri looked down through the lists. He recognised the name of Jacov Fieldmann.

When they said goodbye and Prince Dmitri left, he realised that he was shocked at the Balkan revelation. It was obvious that Von Hertling had an informant in the Austrian ministry of defence. He must alert his friends in the Balkans.

* * *

As Joseph Steiner and Sophie walked up the shallow steps to the Imperial Palace they were conscious of the military presence around them. The great entrance hall lacked the familiar frivolity of Vienna and the music was less light-hearted.

Sophie was dressed in a blue satin gown which set off her figure and she wore her most expensive jewellery. Her father was dressed in evening clothes suitable for the Kaiser's Ball.

When they entered the great hall they noted a preponderance of Imperial uniforms.

'Every military battalion must be represented here. It is like a fancy dress ball! Very few members of parliament are present,' Joseph Steiner noted.

'And what does that mean, Father?'

'It means that in the Kaiser's eyes they are of very little significance. The real power resides with the generals.'

They walked directly into the hall and were about to engage a colleague of Joseph's in conversation when an aide-de-camp took Joseph by the sleeve and led him into the presence of the Kaiser. Joseph noted that he had changed his blue uniform for a red one, even more ornate and heavily braided.

'Mister Joseph Steiner from Vienna and his daughter Sophie,' the aide-de-camp said by way of introduction. 'Mister Steiner attended the manoeuvres today.'

The Kaiser was immediately interested. 'And what did you think of my fine army? Did you not see how well drilled they were and how quickly they moved?'

'They were excellent, your Majesty, and armed with the most modern weapons. You have every reason to be proud of them.'

'Indeed I am. Indeed I am,' he laughed. 'But what brings you to Berlin?'

'I have old friends in the city and I would like to invest here. The markets are confident and society prospers.'

While the Emperor and Joseph Steiner were in conversation, Sophie noted that an officer nearby was staring at her. Her eyes lit up in recognition. She flashed a smile to Baron Von Hertling who acknowledged with a slight bow.

By now the guests had all assembled. On two oval balconies above the great hall the military bands began to play a Strauss waltz. It had a brassy, regimental tone to it. At that moment Sophie recognized the difference between Vienna and Berlin. In Vienna they would have played the waltz with strings.

She waited impassively as officers took their wives on to the floor, formal ladies without elegance. But they had the dutiful air cultivated by the Empress Dona, who rarely attended such gatherings.

She wondered how long she would have to stand in such a boring, statuesque position with her father deep in conversation. Another waltz was about to commence.

Baron Von Hertling approached her from across the floor. He bowed stiffly. 'May I have the pleasure of this dance?' he asked formally. She looked at her stepfather and he indicated that she could dance with the officer. Von Hertling moved quickly out into the middle of the dance floor, holding her firmly.

'It is wonderful to see you again. Our meeting in Leipzig was so brief,' he said, smiling warmly.

'Have you purchased an automobile?' she asked, returning his smile.

'Yes. It is a pleasure to drive. I overheard the Kaiser's conversation with your father. Very interesting.'

'And do you always listen in on the Kaiser's conversations?' she asked boldly.

'It is my business. Among other things it is my duty to protect him,' he replied in a firm tone which had a commanding quality.

'And what are your other duties?' she asked.

For a moment his face became taut, almost angry, then he relaxed. 'They are of a private nature. I do not discuss them,' he told her curtly.

It was at this moment she began to take an interest in Baron Von Hertling. In Vienna, men would have been only too willing to explain their positions at court. They would have flirted with her and she knew how easy it was to manipulate them. With Baron Von Hertling it was a different matter.

He smiled again. 'I believe that you are staying for some time. Would you like to see the sights of Berlin? Perhaps I could give you a tour of the city.'

'I have already had a guided tour,' she told him.

'You have seen what you are expected to see. I know parts of Berlin which no visitor ever sees. Perhaps that might interest you.'

'Perhaps,' she replied coquettishly.

As he led her back to her father he said, 'I shall contact you in the next few days.'

Her father was engaged in conversation with a banker when she returned. 'I notice that you have made the acquaintance of Baron Von Hertling,' he said.

'And what does Baron Von Hertling do?' she asked.

'Well, he is one of the most powerful men in Berlin.'

'And what makes him so powerful? Surely the generals and the politicians wield greater power.'

'He is in charge of the secret service. He is an ambitious man and feared by the officers and members of the Reichstag alike. They say that he possesses files on every important person in Berlin.'

Sophie looked about to see where he was. He had disappeared from the ballroom. He did not return.

She received several invitations to dance from young officers. They were all very polite and many expressed a wish to see her another time but she had no interest. Her mind was occupied with Baron Von Hertling.

* * *

Two days later, as she was entering a fashionable clothes shop on the Kurfürstendamm, an automobile drew up at the pavement. Before she could enter the shop, Baron Von Hertling was standing beside her.

'I promised to show you the city. Will you accept my offer? I have my automobile waiting for you,' he smiled.

She looked at the Mercedes. It was a beautiful machine painted white with all its brass fittings sparkling in the sun.

'What will my father say? I am to meet him in two hours' time.'

'I am sure that you can contact him by phone.'

She looked at the officer standing beside her. His eyes were determined and his character forceful. The sabre scar on his cheek added to his formidable presence.

'Very well. I will phone Father,' she said, eager to discover this new Berlin that he wished to show her.

Sophie telephoned Joseph from the shop to explain that she would be unable to meet him for lunch. Then she got into the automobile, the Baron revved the powerful engine and they rushed away.

As they moved towards the Tiergarten, she asked him several questions about his motorcar: its speed; its power and its petrol consumption.

Von Hertling smiled at her technical curiosity, then said, 'I shall show you the Reichstag, I think. It is an interesting place and, by seeing it, you will understand something of our parliamentary system. Not many women have ever entered its private chambers.'

They reached the Brandenburg Gate and turned left. The great sandstone building with its ornate façade stood before them. When they walked in they were immediately whisked through a series of corridors to a small doorway. It was opened and Sophie was ushered in. She found herself in a small space like an opera box concealed high above the Reichstag chamber, where she could look down on the assembled members.

'The Kaiser sometimes sits here and listens to the proceedings. They are never certain when he is present. When he is travelling abroad he appoints someone to keep him in constant touch with all that is going on,' Von Hertling explained.

'You are impressed by the Kaiser, I see.'

'He is the strongest leader in Europe. He has total control of the whole country, the army, the navy, even the electorate. He binds them together. Without him there would be absolute chaos. These gentlemen you see beneath you are of little importance. They can be manipulated, influenced. Power only appears to reside here.'

When they left, Sophie felt drawn towards him because of his secret power.

'And now let us visit the dark side of the city. It has a sinister side, you know,' Von Hertling said.

'I was not aware of the existence of such a place.' Sophie was taken aback.

'Perhaps we should not visit it, then.' The Baron was clearly amused.

'I am curious. I have strong tastes.'

They drove to the old area of the city, into narrow streets where the sun shone thinly. It was obvious that it was the brothel area. Prostitutes called to the baron and invited him inside.

'There is an area like this in every city. Tourists and pretty visitors rarely venture into these places. You would have your throat cut and your purse taken. But it is here that secrets are hatched, plans set afoot. If there is trouble in the city it is generated here and when revolutionaries and socialists arrive in Berlin they head for this area and disappear. It is difficult to trace them.'

'You have your spies here, I'm sure,' she commented icily.

'And do you object to spies? Do you not realise that without spies, secret services could not operate? Without informers placed in streets like this, the very fabric of society would be in danger.'

'I still think that this,' she indicated the squalor around her, 'is a despicable place.'

'Society at this level stinks. It always has. It only smells well in the wide streets, in middle- and upper-class society. But one must always watch the sewers. Here discontent breathes.'

She found it difficult to keep pace with him. He moved continually.

Finally, he said, 'And now it is time for lunch. Let us go to some pleasant place on the outskirts of the city where one can sit and eat.'

They drove through the Tiergarten and on to the Grünewald. Here the trees dominated the landscape, making it intimate and private. Finally they arrived at a small village close to a canal. Weeping willows grew close to the banks and white and red geraniums grew in flower boxes on the windows of the inn. It was midday and the sun was high in the sky beyond the trees. A barge moved past, smoke puffing from its stubby funnel.

The meal lacked subtlety but Sophie enjoyed the freedom of the place. The people were open and content and heartily enjoyed their food, appreciative of everything that was set before them.

She felt relaxed in the surroundings. The inn and the village had a rough, pastoral charm. Much later, when the sun began to sink in the sky, they returned through the woods, which were now filled with quiet mystery. Baron Von Hertling began to sing a sad German lullaby.

'Where did you learn such a gentle song?' she inquired.

'My mother often sang it to me. She was a very delicate and musical woman. She died when I was very young. I can still recall her light voice.'

'And did she teach you many such songs?'

'Several.' And with that he began to sing another for her.

His voice and the songs suited the woods through which they were passing.

They drove to the Brandenburg Gate and entered the old city. It was filled with bustle and excitement.

'Shall we have a final drink before I return you to your hotel?' he asked.

'Yes. But bring me to the district through which we passed today. I'm sure you know some interesting places,' Sophie smiled slyly.

'It is no place for a woman of good breeding,' he laughed.

'Nobody will know I am a lady of good breeding,' she laughed in response, stimulated by the sense of excitement.

'Very well. You may be offended by what you see. There is a side to Berlin which few ladies have ever seen.'

'Then let me see it.'

Soon they were passing through narrow streets bustling with rough life until they reached a square where they got out. Sophie studied her surroundings for a moment. There were several prostitutes standing at the doorways of bars and cheap cafés, inviting men in.

Von Hertling brought her through a doorway and up narrow stairs. He opened a door and they entered what seemed to be a small theatre and beer hall. It was dimly lit except for the stage, which was decorated with badly painted scenes of some rustic village in Germany. As she looked down at the tables she noted how many gentlemen in tall hats and in evening dress were sitting around the rough tables. Young women, highly rouged and with ample figures, sat with them.

'Where do the women come from?' she asked.

'Many are from the district. Some are young ladies brought from the countryside. It is a rough trade but they make a lot of money and some of them even return to their villages as rich women. Others remain in the district, grow old and take to the streets.'

The piano player began to play a polka and five dancers came on to the stage from the wings. They were dressed in flouncy gowns and they danced awkwardly on the stage. The men began to call to them. Then at the end they turned their backs to the audience and lifted their skirts. They had no underwear on underneath them and they wriggled their heavy buttocks. 'And that is how these women make their living,' Von Hertling said, turning to her. She was blushing. 'Shall we leave?' he asked, noting her embarrassment.

'No. I will not have this opportunity again.'

From the balcony she looked into the pit-like theatre beneath her. Periodically some of the young women drew the men away from the tables. They returned later and went to entertain other gentlemen. She was fascinated by the dark, rough and vulgar life beneath her, charged with cigar smoke and the smell of cheap perfume.

When they left later she carried the scent with her on her clothes.

He brought her to her hotel. As they parted at the great door she felt that she had betrayed some decency within her. She had permitted herself to be soiled. As she entered the foyer of the hotel she felt a thrill of decadent exhilaration pass through her body.

Chapter Fourteen

Alma had been making her way in Viennese society. Her visits to the Emperor continued and, like Franz Joseph, she loved this city.

'It is the centre of Empire. The greatest musicians of the age have lived here as well as some of the greatest writers.' It was a point he returned to again and again when they sat down to tea or walked in the ornamental park behind the palace.

But Alma wanted to travel a little further into Franz Joseph's empire. To satisfy her curiosity she announced one day that she intended to spend six months travelling through it. Franz Joseph was delighted. He unearthed large albums of photographs and had them sent to her. And with them he included several large maps over which she pored during the winter evenings when darkness was falling on the city.

In March of that year, a few days before she was due to leave, she went to visit the Emperor once more.

'Give me an account of what you see in my empire,' he instructed her. 'Tell me what my people are thinking. It is happy only on the surface and I fear a terrible cataclysm when I am gone. As you know, it is difficult to keep various people together. And this new nationalism is not a good thing. Not a good thing at all,' the Emperor sighed.

He also gave her several letters of introduction to governors in the various provinces. 'They will extend every courtesy to you,' he assured her 'And when you return I wish to have a good account of my empire. I wish to hear the opinions from the woods and the mountains and the small villages. The opinions of the great cities I know.

'I have also requested that Prince Eugene should travel with you. I can assure you that some of the roads are almost impassable and if you wish to travel into the mountains you will need the help of this young prince. He is well-acquainted with the eastern section of the empire. He was born there.'

'Yes, your Majesty, we have already met.' Alma's face was flushed with excitement.

He rang a bell and Prince Eugene appeared. He bowed stiffly from the waist. Tall, with wide shoulders, he had grown more handsome since their last meeting. His hair was dark and abundant and Alma was struck by his bright eyes.

'I am delighted to be your companion during the journey. I hope I can be of some assistance to you but do not expect the luxury of Vienna among the Carpathian mountains,' he told her, smiling.

'I have read extensively about the regions. I do not expect comfort,' Alma laughed. 'I wish to know what is happening in the real world of the Empire.'

'Then you will enjoy your experience.'

'I have no wish to see my daughter or hear her name mentioned. She has left this house. She has set herself up with some unwashed artist. Since the day she was born she has been a source of grief to me,' Margit Schmerling cried shrilly.

Before she left on her journey, Alma had heard of Marie's illness indirectly from an artist who had been commissioned to paint her portrait. For several years she had little wish to see her sister, but now she knew she must. If she left Vienna without finding out how ill Marie was, she might never see her again.

She wrote her a letter but there was no reply, and finally she hired a cab and set off for the Vienna hills.

Alma found the address and walked down the path to the studio. The place seemed empty. She went to the window and looked through the dusty glass. She could make out a chaotic studio with a large unfinished painting standing on an easel. She was about to go around to the back to see if anyone was about when a voice called out roughly:

'You are on private property. Who are you and what is your business?' She turned around and was confronted by a heavy-shouldered man with a scowling face and the swarthy appearance of gypsy. For a moment she thought that he might attack her.

'I have come to visit my sister. I believe that she is living here and that she has been ill.'

'She is better now. She has no wish to see you,' he said angrily.

'I will wait until she returns,' she replied forcefully.

For a moment anger flared in his face and she thought that he might assault her. 'If she had a wish to see you she would have replied to your letter. She no longer belongs to your society.'

'If that is so, I wish to hear it from her own lips.' Alma stood her ground.

The conversation would have continued in this fashion but the wooden gate opened and Marie came down the path, carrying a basket. Their eyes met in recognition. Alma was surprised at the change in her sister's appearance. She had lost weight and her hair was unkempt. She looked weak and tired. Alma was about to rush to her assistance but looking at the hostile expression on her sister's face, she stopped.

'What brings you here? Are you curious about my situation? Now you can rush back to Mother and tell her of my condition. Tell her that I wear a smock and sandals. Tell her also that I am happier here than living in the same great house with her.'

'But you look ill.'

'I have been ill. Now I am better. I do not need your help or your sympathy.'

'Can I not be of some assistance to you?'

'I do not wish to have your charity or your pity. Now, would you please leave this place. We have nothing to say to each other. Go to the Emperor and let him hump you. You have become a royal whore,' Marie said viciously.

Alma felt humiliated. She gathered her long skirt about her and walked up the garden path. As she closed the gate she looked at her sister. Marie had turned her back to her. It was both stooped and tired like that of some woman who had worked long hours in a field or in a factory. It had been a brief and bitter encounter.

On a warm March day, a carriage drove out of the main gates of the palace and headed for the Prater-Quai, laden down with luggage. As Alma took her last look at Vienna, she reflected that she felt secure in the company of Prince Eugene and his batman.

At the quay, they climbed aboard a river steamer and at midday they left the city on a firm flow of water and headed towards Pressburg. The Danube had already passed through a landscape of two thousand miles from its small beginnings at Berg. Eugene pointed out the long slender islands aligned to the flow of the river; wooded places haunted by birds. Here and there a fisherman had built a reed hut and tied his shallow boat to a mooring. Then on the left, hills with blue pines rose steeply from the river and a decaying castle stood on a flat ledge over the water.

At Pressburg the boat took on more passengers and Alma noted their faces and costumes. The faint presence of the east could be felt at this point.

For the next day, the journey took them through flat lands, where cattle grazed easily, and watermills turned their lazy wheels. Then at the foothills of the Carpathians the river turned south and moved towards Budapest amongst the grandeur of old mountains. Everywhere the evidence in stone could be seen of the civilisations which had left their mark upon the landscape during the centuries: Romans, Christians and Turks.

On the final morning of the journey, the boat passed Margaret Island, with its park and gardens the first sign that they were nearing Budapest. The city lay on either side of the river; Buda set high into the hills, Pest on the flat land of the opposite bank.

The boat moored at the quay below the suspension bridge, where a coach was waiting for Alma and Eugene. It took them directly across the river and up the slopes to a baroque castle. It was now dark and from the great shelf of land on which the palace was built she could look down on the magical city lit with a thousand lights.

Her father had often told her of the gypsy music of Budapest and that night Prince Eugene invited her to visit a tavern to listen to some. It was an intimate place and when they walked through the door they were greeted with the smell of local food. Soon a gypsy band began to play and Alma studied the sallow faces, wild and fine, their eyes blazing with passion.

Towards midnight Prince Eugene began to dance with one of the gypsy women. Alma looked at him intently. He had cast aside his heavy coat and now, dressed in a white shirt, pants and leather boots, he began to dance wildly.

'Perhaps I am beginning to understand what this empire is about,' she said when he returned.

'When the music is finished we grow melancholy. We swing from one mood to another. But tomorrow we will move into the heartland of the empire, towards the east. There two tides meet and mingle: the Christian and the Moslem. '

They rose early next day to begin the long journey on horseback through the wide Hungarian plains. The land stretched endlessly towards the east, filled with great wheat fields and prairies. She watched the dust rise and swirl on the even land where herdsmen followed their cattle. Small settlements rose from the buff, brittle reeds and clumps of willow.

At Mohacs they continued south and the landscape changed. To the right rose small hills covered in rows of vines and fruit trees. On the higher slopes dense woods grew.

When they stopped to rest in a small town set in a crescent of hills, Alma felt that she was floating through a new world. The sun seemed as though it would never set on the great Hungarian plains, endless and eternal. She climbed the hills behind the town and gazed eastward. No hill or village broke the evenness of the landscape.

'It ends only in the sweep of the Carpathian mountains. They run in a wide crescent from Budapest to Transylvania. They are endless,' Prince Eugene told her later.

'And have you travelled there?'

'Once. When I was a young soldier. We never left the mountains. We were mapping the area. It took us some nine months.'

'And what is life like in the mountains?' Alma was curious to know all she could about this strange country.

'Simple. I met men who had no nationality, who could not read or write and who spoke in dialects that not even the guides could understand. High in the mountains I entered chapels with old mosaics, like those of Constantinople. It is a world where the line between east and west becomes blurred.'

That night they rested in the inn. Over the next week, they made their way down the widening river to Belgrade. Set at the base of a limestone rock it was the city where the east began. The mosques with their slender minarets marked the presence of the Ottoman empire.

Prince Eugene took her through the city, filled with the

dense presence of history. 'Here you are on the very edge of Europe. It is an uncertain place. The Romans have been here, the Mongols, the Crusaders, the Turks and each one has left their mark. Minds and allegiances are uncertain, the power of Franz Joseph is at its weakest; it is here that his empire will begin to fall apart.' It was a gloomy prediction, but Eugene believed he was right.

'And what will happen to Transylvania?' Alma asked, thinking of his homeland.

'We will survive. Plains you can sweep through. The mountain regions are a different matter. There we can hold out forever, irrespective of what happens.'

They stayed in Belgrade for two days, before setting off on the final part of their journey east. Alma looked forward eagerly to the days ahead. She no longer belonged to the world of Vienna, the excitement of the east was growing in her mind.

When they reached the harbour town of Bazias she knew that they had come to the end of the Hungarian plains. The Carpathian range began in small hills, but the landscape soon became rugged and isolated. When they took a small boat they discovered that even the Danube had taken on a more eager, nervous temperament. Below Muldov it entered a narrow gorge where pinnacles of rock stood in the river like dangerous sentinels. At Drencoval the rapids began, the confined water rushing forward in confusion, threatening to overpower their small craft. At the gorge of Kazan the most imposing part of the passage began. The water, bottled into a narrow defile, carried them past vertical cliffs, then below them lay the Iron Gates, the last gorge on the Danube, and beyond that the calm, dangerous run to the Black Sea.

Perched high in the cliff-face was a small quay and Prince Eugene ordered his servant to moor there. Here tough donkeys were waiting to carry the passengers up a precipitous path to level ground.

With an easy sweep Prince Eugene lifted Alma on to a side saddle. She felt light in his hand. It was the first time he had touched her and she felt pleasure in his strength.

They began the steep climb up the narrow path. As they passed upwards she could look down towards the gorge at the Iron Gate and the river boiling in angry froth as it rushed between tall cliffs. Finally, they reached the top of the cliff and Alma could observe the countryside which surrounded her. Looking north she could see the rough, wooded hills building up into mountains. They shouldered out the horizon. She could see no town or village.

'We are home,' the servant told Prince Eugene excitedly as he breathed in the scented air.

'Yes, we are home. We will rest the night at my uncle's castle, then we will travel north.'

As they stood on the clifftop they heard the sound of horses coming towards them. A cavalcade of riders swept down the forest road, energetically and in apparent disorder. Alma thought that they might ride over the cliff so furious was their advance. But they reined in quickly, kicking up dust, and stopped in their tracks. They were rough bearded men, with rifles slung over their shoulders and they wore wide riding breeches and leather waistcoats.

Their leader advanced towards Prince Eugene and threw his arms about him. 'You are dressed like one of these civil servants from Vienna,' he laughed, looking at the Prince. 'Have you forgotten your native ways?'

'No, my friend. Soon I will dress as I should.' Immediately he ordered his servant to carry his chest into a cabin and when he emerged he was dressed like one of the riders.

Alma thought that Prince Eugene looked free and magnificent in his native dress. He was a young man filled with the vitality of the country. Now that he was relieved from the constraints of the court he seemed to belong to the landscape.

It was with growing excitement that Alma mounted one of the horses and they set forth into the mysterious land of Transylvania.

The land through which they travelled was very mountainous, but between the folds of the mountains stood fertile valleys, well-cultivated and tidy. There were few bridges along the road. Instead they passed across beds of pebbled stones through which streams moved in dubious channels.

'When there is a storm these streams become raging torrents. In spring and winter you pass them at your peril,' the Prince told her.

Alma looked in awe at the magnificent landscape about her, the great crevices gouged out by torrents, the forests stretching as far as the eye could see. She had read about the scenery but it was beyond all her expectations.

'Are you impressed?' he laughed.

'I am in awe. It is like a great fortress.'

'And that is what it is. No enemy can advance easily on this country. And if he does he can only have a toe-hold here. Time and again it has been conquered but only the Magyars have settled here in large numbers. It is a strange mixture of races. It the east you have the Szeklers who are descended from the Huns. My grandmother was a Szekler. You will find Rumanians here as well as Germans and ten more races if you search them out.'

'And will it hold together?'

'Yes. Transylvania will always be here. They may give it another name or annex it to another country but it has its own heart and the heart will keep it firm.'

There was pride in his voice as he spoke, a true prince, not only in name but in face.

Later they passed down into a long valley which led to a flat plain. Vines grew on the slopes of the lower hills and cattle grazed in wide fields. It was a controlled and measured landscape here, run on ordered lines.

'These farmers came from the lower Rhine many hundreds of years ago. We respect them. They husband the land well and belong here. This is their country.'

It was warmer in the valley. The roads were better and the villages gathered about chapels with their bulbous domes. It was a pastoral landscape with a controlled charm, contrasting sharply with the rugged mountains around it.

It was now late in the evening.

'You are tired and we will rest here for a meal,' Prince Eugene told her kindly. 'I will bring you to an inn. My men would prefer to drink at some tavern where the wine is cheap.'

They arrived at a small village, a quiet place of well-built houses. Carts drawn by slow oxen moved through the central street. Small gardens with wicker fences stood around the houses, filled with flowers which gave a soft gentle impression.

The inn-keeper recognised the prince and rushed forward to greet him.

Eugene ordered some light food and explained, 'Tonight we will have supper with my uncle. He is called Count Valkany. He is a true Magyar and he lives according to the old ways. So do not be surprised if the supper goes on for a night and a day. He has not seen me for two years and his welcome will be tearful and wild,' he laughed.

'You fit easily into both worlds,' Alma said.

'I appear to, but I always feel constrained in Vienna. The politeness of the court weighs upon me. Here I am at home.'

'Will you settle here?'

'I will inherit my father's title and his land when he dies. Like my uncle he belongs to the old world. He knows little of what is happening outside it. But I think it is better to be informed as to what is happening, then you can judge what the future will bring.' The Prince talked in a factual manner. His mind worked calmly and logically.

He continued, 'Germany is the danger. If trouble comes it will not come from Russia or the Turks but from the mad mind of Wilhelm II. He has no Bismarck to keep him in control and so the warlords who gather at the imperial court in Berlin are Junkers who are itching to test their arms against an enemy. Franz Joseph is no longer a powerful leader but when he dies then the whole empire could fall apart.'

Alma felt that she was being drawn more and more into the complex politics of Europe. She was anxious to know more, but their conversation was interrupted by the sound of gunfire in the main street.

'Ah. My men are ready,' Eugene smiled. 'We had better set out for my uncle's castle.' He helped her into the saddle and they set out.

Darkness fell and the men lit lanterns which they carried with them. The horses rode confidently through the dark, having an instinct for the terrain. They rode up out of the valley and into the forests until they saw the torches burning on the battlements of Ziben castle. When they entered the great courtyard Alma knew that she had arrived in a medieval world.

Chapter Fifteen

The small group was surrounded by a great circle of torchlight and dogs yelped in angry excitement at the horses until they were kicked aside. From the gate of the castle, Count Valkany emerged, dressed in ceremonial military dress with a large decorative sword dangling from his belt.

He went immediately to where Prince Eugene stood and threw his arms about him. Then he held him at arm's length and looked at him again.

'You have grown thin and pale in Vienna. That city does not suit you. It is a glasshouse for delicate plants. Tomorrow, we will hunt in the forest. That will put colour back into your cheeks.'

He turned to his servants. 'Tomorrow we hunt in the hills. Be prepared at dawn.'

'But I am expected in Kronstadt,' Eugene protested.

'I will send a rider to your father's castle. Time means nothing in Transylvania. You are not in Vienna now, waiting to catch a train to Paris.'

When he had made the gruff arrangements he turned his attention to Alma. He looked at her as he might look at a good animal.

'You are a well-bred woman. Good limbs and a strong body,' he commented as if he were studying a racehorse. 'But let us go inside,' he continued, before she could respond. 'We must welcome you in good fashion. We have waited with excitement for your arrival for some days now, ever since I received one of these marvellous telegrams from you. I have received one all the way from America, too. Very wonderful.'

They walked through a dark archway, up a wide flight of steps, then through another archway into a courtyard and finally, through the entrance to the great hall. It had few of the refinements or the luxury of the palaces in Vienna. The great walls were covered with heavy whitewash; rough oak beams supported the roof and on the walls hung shields, flags and stuffed animal heads in great profusion. The main table was set on a high daïs and beneath it sat another long table for Count Valkany's court.

People funnelled into the hall and took their places. When they were ready a gong sounded, trumpets were blown and the meal was served.

Alma noticed that the soup was served in tureens of gold. The prince saw her interest and said, 'This castle is filled with casual treasures. They belonged to the Turks. My ancestors raided their camps when they were withdrawing from the area. They also discovered hundreds of bags of coffee. That is why my uncle is an avid drinker of coffee. The story goes that there is a treasure chest embedded in the walls of the castle.'

Alma was also surprised at the food. It was well-served and tasty. Clearly, Count Valkany was not without elegance. But as the wine began to flow and more flagons were called for a general chaos crept into the gathering. Each time her goblet of wine was empty it was replenished. She was growing tired after her journey and she wanted to sleep. But the count insisted that she stay with them. 'Tomorrow, when we hunt you can sleep. Now, we celebrate the arrival of my nephew. Someday he will be king of Transylvania. We look to him to lead the next generation. So, you understand why we are excited at his return.'

It was towards three o'clock in the morning when the gypsies arrived from the village. They were dressed in their colourful costumes and the women had a wild and beautiful appearance. Immediately they began to play their music. It lacked the restraint of city and the women danced to its magic.

Later in the night the music changed. It became haunting and lonely and the mood of the guests changed with it. Alma realised that she was profoundly tired, but again Count Valkany would not hear her protests. Soon, her frustration overcame good manners: 'I am weary after my journey. I wish to sleep. I should have retired many hours ago but you insisted that I remain. Now, my patience is at an end.'

With that she stamped out of the room. Count Valkany laughed at his nephew's hot-tempered companion.

Alma reached her chamber and looked out of the window; dawn was breaking over the battlements and she stood and looked down over the countryside with the grey, narrow scarves of mist lying above the trees. In the half-dawn the air was filled with scent and somewhere in the woods an owl hooted. She could see the narrow, twisted streets of the village and the dense, red-tiled roofs. From some of the chimneys the smoke was rising lazily, filled with the smell of fresh timber.

All about her, stretching to the horizon, was the mysterious country of Transylvania.

A voice interrupted her thoughts: 'The bed is prepared for the lady,' she was told in simple German.

As Alma got into the huge bed, she remarked to the servant girl, 'I believe an army could sleep here,' but the humour was lost on her. She crawled into the deep comfort of the bed. Soon she was fast asleep.

She slept during that day and rose for a short time in the evening when the men had returned from the hunt. She looked down into the courtyard, where there was great excitement and confusion as the slaughtered animals were taken from the backs of the horses. Wine was brought to the men and they drank as they studied the fine stags and the massive boars they had hunted in the mountains.

Next morning Alma rose early, feeling fresh and excited. The castle was silent and seemed empty at that hour of the morning. She decided that she could now explore it at leisure.

A fortress set up as a defence, the castle was a confusion of styles and periods, perched on a ledge of rock to beat off the waves of enemies which had swept across the rough terrain of Transylvania.

Alma descended the stairs into a long corridor and followed it north. On either side were simple bedrooms with rough, basic comforts. She opened an arched door, which led into a small courtyard. It looked like the cloisters of a small monastery and it was very old. She decided to explore this intimate area and closed the door behind her. She felt she was entering a strange monastic world but without monks or nuns. She walked quietly along the corridor, studying the strange figures and ornaments on the cloister columns.

Suddenly, a noise startled her and she looked up. Before her stood a woman in simple white robes, her hands hidden in her sleeves.

They approached each other with apprehension. The older woman noted the fine satin clothes worn by Alma; it was clear to her that here was a woman of breeding.

'I am the Countess Valkany,' she stated simply.

'And I am Alma Schmerling. I have just arrived from Vienna,' she told the Countess.

'I am delighted to meet you. I do not meet many people from Vienna these days. You must tell me all the news from the very centre of the world. I knew Franz Joseph a long time ago. But come and let me show you where I have chosen to live.'

They passed through the cloister to a small church, the only light filtering through stained glass. As Alma entered the place it seemed dark and shadowy but as her eyes adjusted to the light it began to pulse and glow. She studied the stained-glass windows which illustrated a biblical world of great beauty.

'We do not know who created these masterpieces or from where they came. I have invited some scholars here to study them and they believe that they were brought here by a medieval Russian monk who had travelled in Europe. I do not know. However, the icons are Russian. They were brought here in the sixteenth century. I find my greatest happiness here. But you are a young woman and I will not burden you with theological talk. Let us go to my rooms.'

They left the church and entered the cloister again, climbing some stone steps to her apartments above, overlooking the hills and valleys of Transylvania.

The Countess rang a bell and a servant brought a tray of food.

'I had better explain my position,' she began as she poured out some coffee. 'I am a Hungarian princess. In fact if my children had lived they would be pretenders to the Hungarian throne. But that is another story. They died very young and we were left without issue. That is why my husband dotes on Prince Eugene. He believes that he will be king some day. He has Magyar blood in his veins.'

'And what of your husband?' Alma asked cautiously.

'My husband is a warlord. We have chosen to live separately. He brings his fancy women from the east to satisfy his passions. I buy up manuscripts and travel through Transylvania during the summertime gathering geological samples.'

For a moment Alma was confused. 'I gather rocks,' the Countess explained with an amused smile. 'I will show you my samples later. They may be of no interest to you but to me they are a boundless passion. Collecting them keeps my mind keen. In fact, I know more of the landscape now than the professors at the universities. They frequently write to me.'

Alma was impressed by the Countess's vigorous mind and, for the next hour, their conversation continued, ranging in every direction.

Alma was interested in hearing what the Countess thought of the Balkan situation. She sighed, 'I have been through the Balkans. The Croats and the Serbs will never be at peace. They are tribes, not nations. That is why my nephew is so important, here, to keep our nation together.'

'And what of Germany?' Alma asked.

'New and dangerous. I dislike Wilhelm intensely. He is to be watched and restrained. He possesses a great army and if it begins to move then nothing will restrain him. But, enough of political talk. Come, let me show you my collection of rocks.'

In another wing of the castle, laid out on great tables stood specimens of rock and on the walls photographs taken in remote areas of Transylvania, showing the countess in rough climbing costume.

'I look forward to these excursions after the winters here. Believe it or not, the information collected is worth a lot of money. I have discovered gold veins in the high mountains as well as seams of copper and iron. On our own estates I have discovered seams of coal,' she whispered excitedly. 'But I do not disclose my knowledge. I shall only let Prince Eugene know. It could be of great benefit to him.'

Alma was filled with admiration for the Countess. She was sharply intelligent and remarkably brave.

They walked into a library filled with manuscripts, ranged on shelves and in cases. It had a clean, intellectual smell which pleased Sophie.

'The history of Transylvania lies in these manuscripts. I have spent several years purchasing them. Had I not done so many of them would have disappeared into American collections and foreign libraries.'

'Joseph Steiner would love to visit this place,' Alma said to herself.

The Countess overheard. 'And who is he?'

'My stepfather. He collects art. He is also assembling a library of Jewish manuscripts. He is proud of his heritage, too.'

When Alma had exhausted her questioning, the Countess accompanied her to the door, saying, 'I shall not enter the castle proper. It is a rough world, more medieval than modern. Take care and may you prosper in your life and in your journey.'

As the door closed behind her, Alma reentered the world of the castle, feeling that she had met a truly extraordinary woman.

Two days later Prince Eugene set off for his father's castle, accompanied by Alma. As they passed through the hilly landscape, there seemed to be remnants of the stormy history of the country everywhere; ruined castles; fortified churches; walled towns.

The Prince rode beside her. 'I'm afraid I rather abandoned you for two days,' he smiled ruefully. 'My uncle lives for the hunt and the open life. I spent part of my childhood in the castle and when I return I revert to the old ways.'

'Do not worry. I met his wife. She is a most informed and interesting lady.'

'Yes, I spent some time with her yesterday. I never visit the castle without calling upon her. She is the most educated woman in Transylvania. Why she married my uncle I will never know. But they met in Hungary when he was a dashing soldier and she thought, perhaps, that he might become somebody of importance. But when he returned home he fell into his old habits. They live apart now. I have often gone to her for advice. Did she show you her geological specimens?'

'Oh yes.'

'She could be a very rich lady, you know. She told me yesterday that she knows where there are copper and lead veins in the mountains. Actually she owns two gold mines, which she discovered not far from the estate. So she has her own source of income.'

'It is an incredible story.'

'I admire her greatly. She knows what is happening around her and in the empire. My uncle still fears that the Turks will advance from Constantinople,' Eugene laughed.

Two days later they arrived at the castle. It was situated in one of the great valleys and built on an outcrop of rock. Like all the other castles it had a variety of mismatched features which she now began to recognise.

She became acquainted with Prince Eugene's father and his wife. They were people who lived quiet lives and the Prince ran his estates in an old-fashioned manner. Sophie was happy here. She spent time in the relaxing company of the prince and visited many places in the vast landscape, dressed in the rough riding costume of the country.

'Let me bring you to an enchanted island,' Prince Eugene suggested one day. 'It is situated in one of the Transylvanian lakes and we have a small Gothic cottage there. We could stay for a day and fish in the lake.'

Although knowing what it meant, it was an invitation she was willing to accept. She had spent several days with Prince Eugene, and despite her best efforts, she could not control her excitement when he came into her presence. In this strange and remote land, civilised control seemed to slip from her like silver chains.

Their day on the island lasted a week. A week that would haunt her until her final days.

One morning with two pack mules they set off for the hills.

The winding road led away from the newer one and Eugene explained that they were travelling into the most remote area of the country. As they rode up into the hills she noted the changes. The peasant costumes differed. The pace of life seemed slow and almost tedious. The village inns where they slept were noisy places where strangers rarely visited. But they knew the Prince. He had travelled there as a child and as a young man. He could speak the patois and dance with them.

Three days later they reached a great, narrow lake surrounded by hills. In the centre lay an island covered with trees which gave it a secretive charm. Eugene placed their bags in a boat and gave the horses to the old man who took care of the island. Then they set off across the tranquil lake. Only the dry sound of the oars in the oarlocks' gentle plash of water broke the silence. As she watched the Prince and the rhythm of his movements Alma noted how strong and fine his limbs were. As he rowed his body moved towards her and away from her again and she could smell the warm scent of his skin.

They arrived at a wooden jetty built of dry grey beams, moored the small boat, and walked up a covered path to the house. It was built of stone and timber and thatched with heavy reeds. Eugene lifted the latch and invited her in.

The small house had the same interior as the inns at which they had stayed on their journey there. Great rough beams supported the roof and the floor was planked with oak. The furniture was rural and strong.

Eugene built a fire with dried twigs then threw some logs upon it. Soon the interior glowed with the flames.

Alma and the Prince spent the day pleasantly on the island. They fished in the lake and caught several trout. They rowed to a remote part of the shore and climbed one of the hills. Eugene held her hand and drew her up the steep incline until they reached the summit. Everywhere they looked there were other ranges, wooded and distant.

When they reached the cabin, Alma exclaimed, 'I have never been so active in my life! I feel fresh and alive.'

'One forgets the countryside in Vienna. Here you feel that you are part of creation. But we must eat. Now let me show you how to cook a trout.'

She watched him as he cleaned out the fish and garnished them with herbs. Then he placed them on a pan and set them above the fire. Soon their natural aroma filled the room.

As darkness fell they sat at the table and ate the simple meal. Eugene had carried bread and cheese with him from his father's castle which they ate with their wine. The darkness and the silence about the island were intense.

When they had finished their meal they sat by the great fire and listened to the sound of the flames as the great logs burned.

And then at a certain point Alma looked at him. They rose from their seats and put their arms about each other. In a slow, warm rhythm the Prince undressed her before the fire and held her body from him, studying the perfection of breasts and buttocks and belly. He touched her skin lightly with his fingers as if it were fine velvet. She removed his clothes growing more excited as his body was revealed. It had perfect lines and rippled with strength.

Then her passion for him began to grow and rage. She kissed his body with a new hunger and drew him to the bed, where he moved down upon her.

Eugene did not rush her. Time and time again she cried out but he controlled his passion. Then, when she felt that she could endure no more pleasure, he came within her.

During the next few days the same pattern of pleasure was repeated again and again, every time more openly and brazenly on her part.

When they left the island she looked back longingly upon its gentle shape. Alma knew she would never visit it again. Her journey in Transylvania was now at an end. It was time to return to Vienna.

Passing across Transylvania, Alma continued to be fascinated and moved by the landscape and its strange beauty. As she neared the Hungarian border it became gentle and flat and when she looked at it, Alma realised that her happiness had come to an end.

In the plains, with their vast acres of wheat, she began to reflect on her stay with Prince Eugene at greater length. Perhaps she could have loved him and settled with him in the wild landscape of Transylvania, but she knew this was not to be the reality of her life. Her love for Prince Eugene had been passionate. She had enjoyed the ecstasy of romantic love. But in Vienna one could not trade with such currency.

All her life she had been fascinated by the Hapsburg dynasty. Now she would now fulfil her ambition to be a part of it. She was aware of the serious decision she had made and she would live with its consequences.

Chapter Sixteen

Margit Schmerling watched the relationship between Alma and Prince Karl develop and could not believe her own good fortune. Already, several well-connected ladies had invited her to their homes.

Joseph was relieved to see her keeping discreetly in the background and not intruding on them. But Margit did insist that her husband double her expense account: 'I cannot have my daughter attending the finest balls in Vienna dressed in rags. When she enters a ballroom she must catch the eyes of those in attendance. Very soon she may belong to the House of Hapsburg.'

Secretly she had her own plans for advancing the relationship. On one occasion she called Prince Karl aside and, with as much discretion as she could muster, she presented him with a large cheque, saying, 'My husband, of course, is a very wealthy man. Alma will always be independently rich. She is a clever woman, too, and would enhance any marriage.'

Karl accepted with good grace. 'My intentions towards your daughter are quite honourable. Soon we will announce our engagement and, later, the day for the marriage will be announced.'

Margit barely managed to suppress her delight. 'On the day of your engagement I shall present you with my own personal gift. It will far exceed my present paltry gestures of regard.'

An understanding had been born between them.

Now, Margit was well aware of the gossip in the city, because some of her friends whispered it in her ear. But she did not care. They were jealous both of her and of her daughter and soon she would be in a position far superior to theirs. 'They may say what they like of Prince Karl. I find him a gentleman. He is a Hapsburg. Perhaps he gambles and has had his little affairs, but what gentleman in Vienna has not had an affair? Their indiscretions are well known, and it makes no difference to their standing,' she argued when challenged.

Alma enjoyed the social life of the city as never before. She was acclaimed as a great beauty like the late Empress Elizabeth. She was invited everywhere and the months passed in a whirl. In late spring her engagement to Karl was announced. That evening Margit Schmerling presented him with a thousand English sovereigns, regal coinage suited to the occasion.

A week after his engagement Karl disappeared for three weeks. It was rumoured that he was living in the gambling houses on the islands to the south of the city.

It was Prince Dmitri who rescued him, drunk and in debt. He brought Karl to his villa and had him washed by Nikka. Then he strapped him to a bed for three days until he was sober.

A week later Karl reappeared in Vienna. 'I had important business to attend to in Italy,' he told Alma and refused to elaborate further.

She knew that he was telling her lies. His character was dark and there were times when he seemed a stranger to her. But Alma was willing to push these thoughts to the back of her mind. Life had never been so sweet. She was aware of her growing position in the city. The fact that she was now engaged to Prince Karl gave her power and enabled her almost to forget Eugene.

However, not everyone was happy. Some of Karl's family scorned her common status. Others disliked her because this upstart had the ear of the Emperor. 'She must be his mistress,' one of them argued. 'She is not visiting his private rooms for pretty conversations.'

Alma was well aware of the rumours and the scandals which could be attached to her name, but she refused to entertain them. She, too, was familiar with the liaisons of many of the royals. If necessary she could fight fire with fire.

Alma had also realised that old beauties were quickly pushed aside in Vienna and she had no desire to be relegated to some social corner. So, while most of the society women lived frivolous lives she read widely about political matters. She made it her business to talk with the generals and the politicians when they met socially. They were impressed by her knowledge.

'It is fresh blood the Hapsburgs need,' an old general told her. 'You have got it, but they take things for granted and believe that they have a divine right to the throne. That is a dangerous assumption.'

She reflected on what the general had said and realised that he was correct. The royal family had lost touch with reality and that could be their undoing.

June 1908 was a wonderful month in Vienna. The Emperor Franz Joseph celebrated his diamond jubilee and the city became joyful and nostalgic.

It was incredible to think that Franz Joseph had been so long upon the throne. The musicians who had made the capital waltz to their music had lived during his reign. He had presided over golden times, bringing stability to a troubled country and a divided empire.

For the occasion, Alma presented him with an ivory walking stick.

'Are you telling me that I am getting old?' he asked, smiling.

'No. It befits your noble stature,' she replied lightly.

On that summer morning, they left his apartments to

walk in the gardens and Alma summoned the courage to tell the Emperor about her betrothal. 'You know that I am engaged to Prince Karl,' she said hesitantly.

'It has come to my notice. He is a lucky man. He does not deserve such luck. Are you sure you are not making a mistake?'

'No,' she said firmly.

The Emperor sighed. 'I never interfere with these matters. The heart has its reasons and who am I to question them. By all means pursue your desires. But remain independent of him. If there is trouble, my door is always open.'

'I will always come to see you,' Alma replied gratefully.

They turned from that subject to discuss the jubilee celebrations. They were set to be a marvellous success. Telegrams were pouring in from all over the world. Visitors were coming from the very ends of the empire to wish him well.

'Will you be happy in this marriage?' Joseph Steiner asked Alma. They were sitting in an alcove in the library of the great house he had purchased for Margit. It was the first opportunity he had had to call Alma aside during the hectic week of preparations for this marriage of which he did not approve.

'You worry too much, Papa. Everything will be well. I will be as happy as one can expect to be. Are the other married ladies in Vienna truly happy?'

'Not many of them that I have observed. But you know that I wish you well and that I will always be here to give you advice.'

With that, Joseph left the room and began to walk thoughtfully in the garden. He could hear the sound of the light orchestra practising for the wedding in the blue salon. Their music filled the garden with charm and resonance.

He stopped and examined some roses. They were in fine heart and as he touched their soft petals with his fingers, they gave him a sense of delight. He walked into the glasshouse and looked up at the roof which arched above him in thin ribs of iron. He drifted through the palms reflecting on his good and his doubtful fortune.

Alma had a strong character and was ambitious like her mother. Marriage to Prince Karl ensured her a place in the royal circle. But, to Joseph, her future husband was a dubious character, arrogant and unpredictable with a quick temper. Furthermore, he had hired a detective to look into his affairs and a report now lay in a bank vault in Vienna. But, as he had warned Margit not to interfere in Alma's affairs, he was not in a position to do so himself. He could only watch over her from a distance and give her protection if it were necessary.

As Joseph was strolling thoughtfully through the garden, Prince Karl was lying unshaven on a mattress in a hunting lodge some distance from the city.

At the pounding on his door he dragged himself from his bed and slowly opened it. His aide-de-camp was standing stiffly to attention. Beside him stood the caretakers of the hunting lodge.

'Can I not sleep? I gave distinct orders that I should not be woken until evening,' he roared in a half-drunken voice. His face looked loose and foolish and his eyes rolled in his head.

'It *is* evening, Master,' his aide-de-camp replied urgently. 'We must hasten if you wish to reach the city in time. The Emperor expects you at the Schönbrunn.'

Karl quickly drew his mind into control. 'Prepare a bath of warm water and set out my uniform,' he instructed the caretaker. 'And you, come with me.' He drew his aide-de-camp into the room.

Prince Karl sat down on the bed and looked at him. 'How much did I lose?'

'Five thousand florins. You signed several promissory notes. I tried to restrain you but you ordered me to be silent. I believe that you were cheated. Czernin uses sleight of hand.'

'And the others?'

'They were ranged against you.'

The hunting lodge was now empty, filled with the smell of stale smoke and wine. For four days Karl and his friends had gambled in the large trophy room. The curtains had been drawn so that they could not distinguish day from night. On the second day the prostitutes had been sent away as the games became more serious. On one occasion the Prince had challenged Czernin to a duel but he had refused.

'That damn Jew, Steiner, is rich. He will underwrite all my debts. But I feel soiled in his company. I wonder if his Alma Schmerling has tainted blood in her veins.'

'No,' his aide told him. 'It has been checked out. With a little straining of the truth it could even be argued that there is a certain amount of noble blood in her veins.'

Karl smiled, examining himself in the mirror. Despite the years of debauchery his skin was still white and fine, his hair remained blond.

Two hours later he was ready to depart.

In the coach Karl opened a cabinet and took out a bottle of brandy.

'Let us drink to this farce of a marriage,' he toasted as they passed through the hilly countryside. He was broke and this was the only manner in which he could become solvent.

Four hours later they rode through the main gates of the Schönbrunn.

When Karl was shown into the Emperor's study, his aide-de-camp remained outside the door. The prince saw Franz Joseph sitting at his desk which was covered with papers and letters. He was wearing glasses and was bent over some parchment or other. He signed his name to it then pushed it aside.

He did not invite Prince Karl to sit down, but opened a red file with a crest on the cover and examined it. 'You know what this is?' he asked.

'No, your Majesty.'

'It is your dossier, kept in the files of the secret police. I have access to all such documents. This is how I am familiar with all that is happening. The reports in this document do not flatter you. But soon you will get married and I will wipe out your debts as a marriage gift. I do it for the lady you marry, not for you. I expect you to behave like a gentleman towards her, and remember, the file will remain open.'

Beneath his calm exterior, Prince Karl was furious. This Emperor, with his bald, domed head, controlled his future. The old man was more interested in the commoner he was about to marry.

Nonetheless, he appeared humbled. 'I shall do everything to please your Majesty. I am most grateful for your gift. I can assure you that I shall not fall into debt again.'

'Of that I am most sceptical. I cannot see you changing your ways. Soon, our ambassador to Russia retires. I am sending you and your wife to St Petersburg. I expect that you will acquit yourself there with some dignity.'

'I shall do my best to live up to the expectations you have for me.'

'Good. Do not disappoint me as you have in the past.'

The Emperor did not rise to wish him goodbye. He took up the large parchment sheet he had abandoned and continued to read it. The Prince clicked his heels, turned and made his way out of the room.

He moved through the beautiful palace from which he had once been banished, his mind racing with plans. He had been given a second chance.

* * *

Franz Joseph looked blankly at the parchment in front of him. Perhaps he should have advised Alma more strongly against the marriage. There were other more reliable gentlemen in Vienna. He then took a velvet case from his desk and snapped it open. It contained a gold necklace encrusted with jewels. He gazed at it for a while. It had once belonged to his wife Elizabeth. The velvet still seemed to carry the scent of her perfume.

He took some paper and, pausing for a moment to compose his thoughts, began to write in a strong, deliberate hand.

When he had finished, he studied what he had written. When the ink was dry he folded the letter, secured it in a strong envelope and placed it in the case. He phoned one of the servants and ordered him to have it delivered to Alma Schmerling.

Franz Joseph got up from his desk, went to the window and looked down on the courtyard. It seemed empty and remote from Vienna. He returned to his desk, pinched the tiredness from his eyes and continued to work well into the night.

It was late when the news arrived at the Russian Embassy. Prince Karl would soon be appointed ambassador to Russia.

'Are you quite certain of this?' Prince Dmitri asked.

'Quite certain,' his informant replied.

'It will give us time to make arrangements in St Petersburg.'

When the man had gone, Prince Dmitri sat at his desk and considered the situation. His stay had ended in Vienna. He had been ordered to return to Saint Petersburg by the Tsar to take charge of one of the Russian military departments. But the contacts he had made in Vienna would continue to serve him.

* * *

The late summer morning broke over Vienna. It was a radiant day with the great buildings along the Ringstrasse looking imposing and imperial.

Margit Schmerling had woken early. She now looked out of the window of her room. The scent of roses from the garden filled the air with rare perfume. As she listened to the birdsong, it reminded her of her youth in the Imperial city. It seemed a long time ago.

Now, she was filled with joy. Her dreams had been realised. A daughter of hers would finally marry legitimately into the royal family. Any child born to her would carry the royal blood in its veins.

They had once called Margit a royal whore in Vienna. She had been indiscreet in her youth and had taken many lovers. And for these indiscretions the Viennese had despised her. Now they would have to recognise her presence amongst them. Many of the nobles at St Stephen's cathedral would wonder if they were father of the bride.

She returned to her room and called her maid. She began to prepare for the wedding. In the other rooms servants were busy preparing the bride and her sister.

At ten o'clock the gilded coach arrived, flanked by guardsmen from the Imperial regiment. They were dressed in the colourful uniforms of the Hussars. They waited attentively for the bride and Joseph Steiner to descend the steps and enter the carriage. Then, as the bells of St Stephen's rang out, they set out on the short journey to the medieval cathedral.

The city was aware that a Hapsburg Prince was getting married. The crowds lined the route from the Stadtpark along the Kärntner Strasse to the Cathedral. Alma looked out at the great crowds. Joseph Steiner sat quietly beside her. It was her moment of glory and honour. They waved to her as she passed down the most imposing street in the wide empire.

'Are you happy?' her stepfather asked.

'Yes. At this moment I'm happy.'

It was an unsatisfactory answer and, taking her hand in his, Joseph said, 'Remember that I am always at hand if anything should happen. We never know what course our lives will take.'

'I shall do my best to make this man happy. He will settle down in St Petersburg. The Emperor believes that it will direct his energies into something of significance.'

As they neared the medieval cathedral the crowds grew larger and more ecstatic. They watched as Alma, in her voluminous silk dress, descended from the coach. Immediately the imperial guards stood to attention. The young pages gathered her train and as the great organ pealed out and echoed from the high and massive vaulted roof of the cathedral they entered the church.

Joseph Steiner felt overawed as he entered the ancient church. All his life he had lived in private places, out of the public eye. Now, as he moved nervously past the great decorated pillars reaching up towards the roof like the trunks of noble trees and looked up towards the altar lit with hundreds of candles, he knew that this would be the greatest moment of his life.

Finally they reached the altar rails. He stopped and the bride went forward to where Prince Karl was waiting for her.

For Margit, kneeling beside her husband, the ceremony marked her return to her rightful position in Viennese society.

Beside her knelt her daughter Sophie. She had driven from Berlin for the occasion. Margit knew she was mistress to that German spy, Baron Von Hertling, and her interests now lay in Germany. She presided over her father's business in Berlin, where Ernst Fischer had built his modern factory, to produce trucks. Margit could hardly believe that Sophie had driven them and tested them outside Berlin.

Despite Margit's best arguments that Von Hertling was dangerous, her daughter refused to listen. They had gone for a coach drive through the Vienna woods before the wedding to discuss the matter and Sophie had been full of chatter about new methods of warfare and the strength of the German empire. Her daughter would not countenance her advice for caution.

As Alma recited the marriage vows and the ring was placed on her finger by Prince Karl, Margit wondered where her eldest daughter was at that particular moment. Despite Marie's lowly birth, Margit had placed her greatest hopes in her intelligence and beauty, but she had betrayed the trust. Once Margit had seen her from her coach passing down the Ring Strasse. She was dressed in long common clothes and in the company of the disreputable artist with whom she was living. She had heard that Marie was now a member of the Communist Party.

And then the ceremony was over. The trumpets blared out from the galleries. The couple signed the great register of the cathedral and then they moved down the aisle slowly and with dignity. The great bells rang out in the tall tower and sent the pigeons fluttering above the square. Guardsmen formed a wide and colourful quadrangle outside the great church.

The married couple entered the gilded carriage and set out for the Belvedere-Schlösser which had been placed at their disposal for the occasion. The carriages passed through the city while the bells in the church towers rang out. They continued ringing until the wedding party entered the Belvedere.

The wedding feast was an occasion which would be remembered for many years in Vienna. Joseph Steiner had made certain that no expense was spared for his step-daughter. The most expensive wines had been purchased in France and Germany and the city orchestra had been hired for the great ball.

As the guests sat down to a sumptuous meal prepared by chefs from Paris, Joseph Steiner looked at the table. Although a man with a modest appetite he appreciated what had been set before his guests.

When the meal was finished, Joseph tried to retire quietly to an ante chamber but Alma insisted that he should meet the ambassadors and princes who had come to wish the couple well. He bowed quietly as he shook their hands. So, it was late that evening when Prince Karl had the opportunity to call Joseph Steiner aside.

Karl detested this unobtrusive Jew who seemed to inhabit the shadows. But he needed to speak to him. They went into a small office and locked the door. Prince Karl felt uncomfortable in the confined space.

'As agreed,' Joseph Steiner began, 'I would like to present you with a cheque for one hundred thousand florins. I make only one stipulation. Treat Alma well. If I hear that you abuse her in any way I will have you assassinated.' He spoke in a quiet, controlled voice.

'You threaten a prince of the House of Hapsburg,' Prince Karl laughed nervously.

'Yes,' Steiner replied grimly. 'I have the contacts and they stretch out across the empire. They extend even as far as Saint Petersburg.' With this he handed Karl a sealed envelope.

The prince snapped it from his hand and put it in his pocket.

As they left the small office Joseph reminded him, 'I have kept my part of the bargain. Now you keep yours.'

As soon as they reached the corridor they parted.

While Karl went in search of champagne and his friends a coach pulled up outside the palace. A distinguished and handsome gentleman mounted the steps and entered the great hall. He passed quickly through the crowd. Alma was talking to her sister, but gazed open mouthed as he approached. She had not realised that Prince Eugene was in Vienna.

'May I have the pleasure of this dance,' he said directly. Before she could answer him he had taken her by the waist and waltzed her out into the centre of the floor.

'I informed you by letter that I had made my decision. I cannot meet you again. The whole affair is over,' Alma protested.

'I have travelled night and day to get here. Had I known this earlier I would have come to Vienna and asked you to marry me. I would have pleaded with you. I know this man's character. He is dangerous.'

'I am a married woman and I will not let you talk in such a manner of my husband. I have made my decision.' Yet as she waltzed she was aware of his strong hand splayed on her back, the presence of his lithe body close to hers. Despite her best effort to suppress the memories she recalled the idyllic days they had spent on the island, and the delightful wild landscape of Transylvania.

But she had chosen this centre of power and excitement. 'I must not see you again,' she said anxiously. 'Return to your country. Its destiny lies in your hands. Can we not be simply good friends?'

'That is impossible. I can be friends with other women but not with you. You know that quite well.'

'When the waltz ends, please leave the palace and save me this embarrassment.'

'Very well. But I believe that we shall meet again. Some day our paths will cross.'

Then the waltz ended and the great, moving crowd retired to various parts of the great hall. The Prince bowed and moved away from her. Shaken, Alma watched him as he passed through the crowd and strode out through the great, glass-panelled doors.

She tried to brush the memory of their encounter from her mind, when Joseph asked her to dance with him.

'Who was the gentleman?' he enquired.

'Somebody I knew a long time ago in a distant place,' she said mysteriously, refusing to look into her stepfather's eyes.

It was a splendid occasion. Joseph Steiner could not entertain dark suspicions on such a night.

Early next morning a carriage drew up in front of the Belvedere-Schlösser, flanked by ten outriders.

When Franz Joseph descended and entered the ballroom the guests looked in awe at the old man who so rarely made public appearances.

He came forward to Prince Karl and Alma and wished them a happy life together.

Then he directed the orchestra to play the 'Emperor' waltz.

'May I have the pleasure of this dance,' he said to Alma.

Her eyes filled with pleasure.

The old man took her in his arms and they began to dance.

'All your ambitions have been fulfilled, my dear,' Joseph Steiner smiled at his wife.

She did not answer. She was weeping.

But even as Alma waltzed about the floor in the arms of the old Emperor she recalled the days she had spent with Prince Eugene. They flashed past her: the trip through the wild mountains, the lake, the lonely island, the hunting lodge.

It seemed like something from a light opera. Life was now a serious matter and she was member of the Hapsburg dynasty.

She was at the centre of the Empire and dancing with the Emperor.

She would forge happiness from this life.

Chapter Seventeen

Like the Emperor, Matthias Eisenerz, the head of Vienna's secret police, wore large handlebar moustaches. He was a small, heavy-shouldered man with Asiatic eyes. His voice was rough and peasant-like and when he spoke, people shuddered.

He was sitting at his desk working, when the telephone rang. 'Who is speaking? This is a private telephone,' he roared.

'Franz Joseph. Come immediately to the Schönbrunn. It is a matter of urgency.'

'Yes your Majesty,' Eisenerz stuttered. He was surprised at the directness of the Emperor's command. He wondered what file or information had arrived on his desk. Despite his age Franz Joseph kept a constant eye on all that was happening in the empire. He was known to examine documents so thoroughly that he corrected their punctuation and spelling.

Worried, Eisenertz thundered out of the building and called a cab. He face wore a tight, pensive expression. Outside he pulled on his leather gloves and placed his bowler hat on his head. He wished to remain as unobtrusive as possible. Very few people in the city knew his precise occupation.

Eisenertz lived an ordered life with a beautiful wife and four children. His only recreation was mountain climbing. Each year he set out for Innsbruck and spent three weeks climbing the mountains. He loved the Tyrol with its open spaces, its forests and its steep mountains. Someday he hoped to retire to one of the villages in the region.

Now, on his way north through Mariahilfer Strasse, he puzzled to know why he had been summoned to the palace. He looked vaguely through the window as he passed through the streets. It was an old habit. He looked at people intently. They were all potential criminals.

The cab drove into the great yard of the Schönbrunn. The palace always filled his mind with a sense of awe. The massive facade, the great stairs with their shallow steps, and the Schlosspark itself, impressed his village mind. He looked up towards Neptune Fountain and the Gloriette. Once every six months he walked with the Emperor though these gardens as he gave the old man an account of the secret life of his empire.

He was brought hurriedly into the presence of the Emperor. His secretary quickly retired.

The Emperor, his face suffused with anger, threw a bundle of postcards on the desk in front of Eisenerz. 'Examine them closely,' Franz Joseph ordered him.

Eisenerz looked at the set of prints. They were obscene caricatures, showing the Emperor in various sexual positions with Alma Schmerling.

Horrified, he said hastily, 'I can assure your Majesty that I have alerted my men to be on the look out for lascivious material such as this.'

'Then they are looking in the wrong places,' the Emperor growled. 'These are being sold in the low clubs of Vienna right under your nose. Caricatures I can tolerate but not obscenities.'

'I will put my very best men on the task. I can assure you that this purveyor of filth will be brought to justice.'

'I want him in jail within a week. You are losing touch with what is going on in the city. Subversive forces are at work, Eisenerz.'

'I will attend to it directly. May I have a copy of the cards?'

The Emperor handed him the series of cards with disgust.

Eisenerz bowed to the old man and left the room. He felt diminished by the old man's anger. He vowed that he would comb the city until the artist was discovered.

When he returned to his office, night was falling in Vienna. Coaches were on their way to various coffee houses or to the opera. The lights were burning firmly in the streets. Eisenerz looked down from his window at the scene below. Then he pulled down the blind and sat in his armchair, his forehead knitted in thought.

After some time, he got up and took down a file on the printers of Vienna from the bookshelves above his desk. He studied them carefully. He would begin here. Next he phoned a man called Von Hensil and ordered him to come to his office. He had consulted this printer before on such matters.

When he arrived Eisenerz handed him one of the cards. 'Well, have you any ideas on the matter?' he asked.

Von Hensil studied it carefully through a magnifying glass. 'This is the work of some hand press or other. Most likely it is owned by the artist and hidden in the city. No reputable printer would print such a crude card.'

'Good. Now tell me about the artist. I am not an art connoisseur,' Eisenerz told him.

Von Hensil looked at it again and studied each line with his magnifying glass. 'The artist has a firm, fluid hand. He can balance his spaces well on a page.'

He continued to explain the aesthetic values of the postcard, until Eisenerz interrupted. 'What are you trying to say?'

'This man is not an amateur. He is a professional draftsman or artist. I am sure that there are several artists in Vienna who could identify him.'

'That is what I need to know. Goodnight,' Eisenerz said curtly, dismissing the man.

He sat back in his armchair. Now, his task would be an easy one.

Eisenerz took up his telephone and made several calls. At two o'clock that morning his men began to converge on the building. Their instructions were short and gruff. Eisenerz had made out a list of six graphic artists. He wished them to be picked up and brought to prison.

When his men streamed out of his office he put through several other telephone calls. Then he too left the office, for the city prison. He would know the artist before dawn.

His men moved through the city in a thorough fashion. They knocked upon garret doors, entered dark, smoke-filled clubs where artists gathered or called at discreet private addresses. They took the artists quietly and bundled them into cabs. They were immediately brought to the city prison.

Matthias Eisenerz wished to break them quickly. The artists were dragged underground and thrown into padded cells. Then two secret service men entered each cell, showing one of the drawings to each suspect and asking him to identify the artist. At first some of the artists refused to talk. The secret service men began to torture them, a precise, clinical procedure. Their screams were absorbed by the padded cells. The agents were familiar with the techniques and felt no compassion towards their victims. They were obviously enemies of the state otherwise they would not be there.

At four o'clock in the morning they began to break. Each one submitted names, which were taken to Matthias Eisenerz at his office. He examined the lists. One name occurred in all the lists, that of Jakov Fieldmann.

'Very well. You can release these suspects. Tomorrow we have more work to do.'

Eisenerz had his chauffeur drive him home. He was pleased with his night's work.

The light in his study was burning when he entered the small garden in front of his house. He felt serene as he walked up the path. His wife heard his footsteps and immediately came to the door. She was a tall, beautiful woman from the provinces.

'I worried about you. You should have sent some message to me.'

'I was called to the palace by the Emperor. I had some official business to attend to.'

His wife had never met the Emperor. In fact the court seemed like some palace from a fairytale to her. Eisenerz sat quietly with her and gave her all the details. She was eager to know the colour of the walls, the shape and age of the furniture and the contents of the great paintings. He took delight in her simplicity and managed to answer all her questions without giving any details of his business.

She looked at him with her large, lustrous eyes. 'I have only one desire,' she said.

'I know. You wish to meet the Emperor. But that is impossible. However, if there is ever an opportunity I shall see that you have an audience with Franz Joseph.'

They talked for an hour, then, arm in arm, they went up the stairs to bed.

Matthias Eisenerz had five days left to play with before he presented his findings to the Emperor. He had been humiliated by Jakov Fieldmann. Now, he wished to have further information on him.

Two days later one of his men discovered a file in the basement of the building, giving details of Fieldmann's life and his opinions, his travels abroad and his affairs. Even some of his letters had been intercepted and copied.

Eisenerz had his men visit Fieldmann's house that same afternoon, when both himself and the woman he was living with were in Vienna. They moved through the rooms and quickly discovered the hidden printing press. In a small, timber chest they found the stained copper plates of the postcards. The agents examined them and returned them to their positions. Then they left the building as silently as they entered it.

'We will make our raid before daylight,' Eisenerz said. 'It will not give them time to destroy any of the evidence.'

That night they moved out of Vienna under the cover of darkness and made their way up into the hills. They travelled in two fiachres, all closely wedged together in the frail vehicles. They were dressed in black coats and bowler hats, and in their pockets they carried loaded revolvers. At six o'clock, as the dawn broke faintly in the east, they surrounded the building. Then at a signal they broke down the door and entered. One rushed up to the loft and as the artist jumped from the bed he shared with his lover, he saw a gun trained on him.

Fieldmann cursed their presence. 'Who are you and what right have you to enter this house?' he roared.

'We are the police,' Eisenerz responded. 'We believe that you are the purveyor of pornography.'

'We have our rights,' Marie called from behind him.

'You have no rights,' Eisenerz responded curtly.

'Then may I have permission to get dressed?' she asked.

Eisenerz turned his back. She quickly put on her clothes. Jacov Fieldmann, restrained by two detectives, watched as they drew aside the dresser and exposed the printing press. They knew precisely what they were looking for.

Matthias Eisenerz opened the small chest and drew out the copper plates. 'I believe that this is your work?' he asked.

Fieldmann did not answer.

Suddenly Eisenerz saw his revenge. He took one of the heavy hammers Fieldmann used to beat metal, and began to move towards the great plaster work which stood in the centre of the floor.

'No. That is a lifetime's work. It is one of the finest art pieces in Vienna,' Marie cried, throwing herself in front of him. There were tears in her eyes.

'This, too, is an obscenity,' he said as he smashed the hammer into the great work. It crumbled easily, revealing the skeletal ribs of wire beneath the plaster.

Jacov Fieldmann's eyes bulged. He could not speak. He watched the great piece crumble into lifeless lumps of clay. Something broke inside his mind.

Soon the whole structure was a shapeless mass of plaster. Out of the mass rose the lifeless ribs of wire, bent and twisted out of shape.

The detectives continued to examine the small concealed room behind the dresser thoroughly. They confiscated several offensive posters and copper plates.

They were about to leave when Matthias Eisenerz happened upon a sheet of clear copper set against the wall. He held it up to the light. It caught the fine scored line of images which had not been cut by acid. They were clearly a new series of erotic postcards.

'I believe we have unearthed more filth,' he said as he scrutinised the figures on the copper. 'We have enough evidence to prosecute Fieldmann for obscenity and treason. Take him to the prison.'

'And the lady?'

'She has committed no offence. She is free.'

They gave Fieldmann some time to wash and put on some clothes. But his spirit was broken and he followed their directions obediently. They placed handcuffs about his wrists and led him away.

Marie watched her lover depart and at that point she began to understand the great power of the state which was vested in obedient barbarians. She had witnessed them destroy a great masterpiece with the indifference of fools.

With her arms wrapped about her she looked hopelessly on as Fieldmann was bundled into the carriage and taken away. She felt isolated and alone. There was nothing she could do and nowhere to turn.

Marie returned to the studio. She sat on a stool and looked at the heap of dry and brittle plaster on the floor. For six years she had searched for a patron who would have the group cast in bronze. Now, the masterpiece was lost.

She did not leave the house that day.

Fieldmann recognised the city prison as they approached. He had met prisoners who had spent time there. The sight of the honey-coloured stones, the black gates swinging open to consume him, charged his mind with fire. He began to cry out and tear at his handcuffs. One of the detectives smashed his fist into his face. The blow cut his lips and broke one of his teeth. He spat out the bloody mucus on the floor as the gates closed behind him.

He was dragged immediately to a large office, where his handcuffs were removed. An officer asked him several questions and took down his personal details on a large sheet. Then his humiliation began. He was brought to a dark wing of the prison, where he was stripped naked and searched. A baton was pushed up his rectum and twisted. His testicles and penis were examined for venereal disease. Any identifying scar in his body was noted and entered on a file. Then he was dragged to an ice-cold bath which had clearly been used by other prisoners, covered with a film of grey scum. Fieldmann was pushed into the cold water and held there until his teeth began to chatter.

'It is in the general interests of hygiene. Never know what disease the criminal classes carry,' one of the warders said.

Next, Fieldmann was taken from the bath and marched through a dark corridor, dripping wet. They passed down some steps to the basement. Here, the arched corridors were low and unplastered. Naked bulbs burned at long intervals in the gloom. The place was like a labyrinth and he quickly lost his direction. Finally, he was thrown into a dark cell and the door was banged shut. Fieldmann stumbled about in the darkness. Finally he discovered a damp mattress and a bucket. Shivering and still wet, he felt he was about to scream. No. Don't scream. That is what the bastards expect. Control your anger, he told himself.

He stood in the centre of the dark floor and with a sheet he dried himself. Then he began to exercise to bring back heat to his body. He must not let his spirit be destroyed.

Matthias Eisenerz returned to his office, having left firm instructions at the prison regarding the treatment of the prisoner, Fieldmann. He was to be humiliated and tortured but not broken. Otherwise he could not be brought to justice.

Eisenerz was a cautious man but he believed that he could now perhaps make a request from the Emperor Joseph. He phoned the Schönnbrun. The Emperor's secretary made arrangements for Eisenerz to visit and he set off immediately.

When he arrived at the palace he was ushered directly into the presence of the Emperor. 'Well, what have you discovered? Has the culprit been brought to justice?' the Emperor asked gruffly.

'Not only has he been brought to justice, your Majesty, but a further plot to offend you has been foiled. Let me show you.' With this Eisenerz took the copper plates from his leather case and laid them on the Emperor's desk.

The old man looked at the inky plates. 'And what are these, may I ask?'

'They are the mother plates from which the cards were printed in a secret printing works here in Vienna. They now belong to your Majesty.'

The Emperor looked at them without touching them. 'Take them and throw them in the fire,' he ordered. Eisenerz took the plates, went to the large fireplace and threw them in.

As the flames crackled and licked at the plates, the Emperor said, 'You have done excellent work. I applaud the speed at which you brought this dreadful incident to a conclusion.'

'But that is not all, your Majesty,' Eisenerz said. 'As I examined the printing room I discovered this simple plate of copper. At least it looks simple. But when held at an angle one can see lightly etched lines. They would have been a second set of more vile and indecent postcards.'

The Emperor held the copper plate at an angle to the light coming through the window. It took him sometime to make out the slight lines. 'Quite shocking. Quite shocking. The man has a diseased mind,' he muttered.

'Insane, I might add. If it is your Majesty's wish, he can always be confined to a lunatic asylum.'

The Emperor considered the case for a moment. 'I will leave it in your hands. Be discreet. I do not wish this to be known abroad. I want to hear no more of the matter. It is now in your most capable hands. You have done well.'

This was the opening which Eisenerz was waiting for. 'I have a wife, your Majesty. A most pleasant and charming woman. She would be greatly honoured if she could have an audience with you.'

The Emperor looked at him sharply. 'See my secretary. He deals with such matters. Good day.' There was a frigid note to his voice.

Eisenerz bowed and left the room. He felt humiliated. He had misjudged the situation. He did not even consult with the Emperor's secretary. He knew that he would be refused.

Suddenly he hated the old man living alone in the great palace.

When he returned to the office he discovered that in his confusion he had forgotten to hand the remaining copper plate to the Emperor. He studied it carefully. Perhaps the artist was correct. Perhaps the Emperor was a filthy old man. Then he suppressed his anger, hid the plate at the bottom of his cabinet and placed the files on top of it.

Eisenerz looked out of the window at the grey roofs of Vienna. Here and there a spire or cupola broke the skyline.

He did not love the city as others loved it. He knew the human filth which inhabited both the palaces and the back alleys. Cities corrupted human beings.

Some day he would leave and live out his days in a Bavarian village in sight of the eternal mountains.

For now, he would have his revenge.

Chapter Eighteen

Marie stood at the centre of the studio where she had lived with Fieldmann for several years. It was in this cold and huge barn-like building that she had been poor but happy.

She went to the tin biscuit box in which they kept their money, emptied the coins onto the table and placed them in columns of ten. She had enough money to last for a week.

Marie left the columns of coins on the table and went to the range, where she poured out a cup of strong, black coffee. She sat at the table and looked out of the window at the garden, with its green shrubs and bushes. It was a chaotic, joyful place where she had spent many summer days lying naked under the sun, her body filled with a sense of natural pleasure.

Finally she made the decision. She took several canvases, wrapped them into a cylindrical shape, eased them into a leather tube and left the studio.

She met a carter on his way to the city and he drew her up to sit beside him. It was a pleasant morning and they spoke of the vines and the harvest.

When she reached the market place she said goodbye to the carter and made her way to Tienfelt Strasse. Fieldmann had sold some of his work to Franz Matsch, a dealer who had confidence in the new painters.

There was a customer in the shop when she entered. While she waited she studied the paintings on the walls. She was impressed by some but none had the fire or the originality of Fieldmann.

'Can I interest Madame in one of the paintings? They

represent the best work of our young artists in Vienna,' Matsch asked as he approached her. When he studied her clothes more carefully he knew that she was not there to purchase anything he had on offer.

'I have something to sell,' she told him, drawing the canvases from the leather tube. She rolled them out, and Matsch's eyes lit up.

'Ah, the work of Jakov Fieldmann,' he commented with admiration. He studied them carefully and then examined the date at the corner. They had been painted ten years previously when Fieldmann had made his first break with the academicians, a series of nudes, highly coloured and brash in their presentation.

'How much will you offer for them?' Marie asked directly.

'I am a poor art dealer,' he began, 'and there is no immediate sale for work such as this. People wish to be reassured. They like comfortable images.'

She listened to the mean tone of his voice and grew angry. 'You know that the man is a genius! He is as great as Manet and Monet. The nudes of Renoir lack conviction compared with these. Look at the realism of the figures. They are erotic and human. No one has painted the nude in this fashion before.'

'I note that Madame is well informed in these matters. But my buyers are not as well versed in the new trends in painting.'

'Then you have no wish to purchase the paintings?'

'I did not say that I was not interested. Of course I'm interested, but there is a narrow market for them.'

'If I brought them to Paris they would be three times more valuable than they are in this stuffy city. Make an offer,' Marie retorted.

'Let me consider for a moment. Perhaps I have a buyer for them. I take a chance when I buy from Jacov Fieldmann. I will offer you five thousand florins for the paintings.'

It was a paltry offer and Marie began to roll up the paintings. 'Good day, sir. You insult the artist.'

Matsch immediately stayed her hand. 'Would nine thousand florins be sufficient?'

'At twenty thousand florins you would be getting them at half their worth.'

'Perhaps so, Madame, but I cannot purchase paintings which will not sell. This is a gallery, not a museum.'

Finally they fixed on a price of fifteen thousand florins. Matsch went to the back of his gallery, carefully opened a safe and with his back to Marie counted out the money. He handed it to her reluctantly.

'Good day,' she said brusquely and turned on her heel.

'If Madame would care to sell other paintings by the same artist I would be only too willing to purchase them,' Matsch said, as Marie walked briskly to the door.

'I needed the money. You have robbed me but you will never have the opportunity to do so again.'

When she left Matsch spread the paintings out on a table, studying them carefully. Each one was worth forty thousand florins. He had buyers for such work all over Europe.

Marie felt secure for the moment with the money safely tucked away in her purse. Now she had further and more serious business to attend to. She headed for the old quarter of the city beside Saint Stephen's cathedral, having always felt secure among its narrow, conspiratorial streets. She made her way into a courtyard, where daylight fell thinly. From the top balcony of the old building it looked like a huge well with a few potted plants growing in the corners. Marie knocked at one of the doors and entered.

'Were you followed?' Pieter, Fieldmann's friend, asked when she entered.

'Not that I am aware of.'

'One cannot be too careful. You have heard what happened?'

'No.'

'Several artists were picked up by the police before Jackov. They were held at the prison for a few days. Then they were released.'

'Have you any further news?'

'It is difficult to find out but we do have friends amongst the guards. One or two believe in our cause. I have arranged to meet one of them tonight, so perhaps then I will have more information as to what is happening. But I fear for Fieldmann's life. Others have been known to disappear. Some have even been declared insane and locked up in mental hospitals. Someday the whole of society will rebel against that doddering Emperor up at the Schönbrunn.' He paused and looked at Marie closely. 'You know that you will have to leave Austria, and soon.' Then he smiled, 'But have some food, now, you look perished.'

In a small kitchen into which they could barely fit he prepared goulash for her. Pieter was a large man, an artist and silversmith by trade, who lived the intense life of an intellectual in his garret.

They left when darkness was falling. They slipped into the dark shadows of the buckled streets and walked until they reached the café. It was a drab place, with little of interest apart from a large barrel from which the new red wine was drawn. It was partitioned by rough timber. Working men from the brick factory came there after a day's work. They all wore the same dull overalls coated with red dust. They talked in a tired manner over glasses of cheap wine, their conversation limited to the day's events at the kilns.

Pieter ordered two glasses of the raw wine and some brown bread. They sipped the wine and talked quietly. They looked up when a stranger, a plump, heavy man, with an expression of resentment in his face, entered. He sat heavily down beside them.

They talked of the weather in Vienna for some time, then Pieter quietly changed the subject. 'What is the news from the prison?' he asked.

'Fieldmann is confined to the cellars. He has been isolated from the other prisoners. This is an attempt to break him down. Later, they will bring him to the office and have him sign some bogus confession. Or they may leave him long enough in the cells to go insane. Then they can commit him to a lunatic asylum. It is very convenient.'

'Do such things happen in Vienna?' Marie asked. Pieter noticed that this was the first time she had looked frightened.

'They happen everywhere,' the stranger said bleakly.

'Then what shall we do?' asked Marie.

'There is little you can do. He is now in the hands of the secret police. The prison has its own laws. Eisenerz has the cold heart of a fish.'

Suddenly, Marie felt that there was no way out of the situation. She handed the man some money. He looked around suspiciously, placed it in his pocket, slid from the seat and left the café.

'There is no way out,' Pieter sighed.

'There is always a way out,' Marie answered firmly. 'If Fieldmann is confined to some dark cellar he will not go mad. He loves life too much.'

They continued to drink the harsh wine. Marie knew that she was getting drunk, but she did not care. She thought only of Fieldmann, confined in the damp cells beneath the prison. Finally she hit upon a plan. It was her only card and she decided to play it.

'They have tried to suppress the cards which have given offence to the Emperor. Perhaps we could have them reprinted in some underground paper and post them on the walls of Vienna. I took some copies with me from the studio.'

Pieter considered the idea for a moment. 'That would be too dangerous. Let us threaten Eisenerz with the publication of a whole series of posters. You can visit him and show him what you intend to do. It might frighten him. Obviously he would have no wish to be drawn into public controversy.'

It was a bright suggestion. 'Very well,' Marie agreed. 'Let us take the chance. We have nothing to lose.'

Matthias Eisenerz took no pleasure in breaking a human being. It was part of the process of destroying a disease which attacked the political body. And this criminal had almost brought about his humiliation at the hands of the Emperor. However, Fieldmann was holding out in isolation. He had not succumbed to the darkness and the cold. Eisenerz considered his position. Perhaps now Fieldmann would have to be tortured. It was obvious that he was part of a net of anarchists. They were dangerous. They were cancerous cells in all the great organs of the empire.

Vienna slept. Eisenerz called his cab and prepared to leave the house, with its clean, washed smell which gave Matthias a sense of order. Before he put on his overcoat he went to see his wife and children. He tiptoed into the bedrooms, where they were all asleep.

Outside, the streets were dark and empty. Eisenerz reflected that while the people slept peacefully in their beds he was defending them against a disorder which could throw the realm into chaos.

The vast doors of the prison creaked open on their heavy hinges and he entered the courtyard. The place was in darkness except for lights in the governor's office.

The governor was waiting for him and handed him a file. Matthias took it and looked down through it. 'The prisoner has not talked, obviously.'

'He has been kept awake for four days. He cries out for sleep but he is woken each half hour. I believe that he is almost ready to talk.'

In the dank cell Jakov Fieldmann was beginning to hallucinate. He had tried to keep hold of his sanity, drawing imaginary pictures in his mind. But the cold began to numb his sense of purpose. His body grew chill and a cough began to rake his chest. It tore at him every time he tried to rid himself of phlegm. The hunger was gnawing at his guts as he defecated into the bucket. Soon there was a stench in the cell. He grew accustomed to the smell of his own filth.

At each hour the door was thrown open and he was made to stand against the wall. Now the lids of his eyes were growing heavy. They seemed to be made of lead. He lost track of time. Twice he fainted. When he did, a bucket of cold water was thrown over him by the warders before the door was banged shut again.

'You must live,' he muttered to himself. 'Don't let the bastards destroy you.'

He could not tell how many days he had been kept awake when the doors were thrown open and two warders entered. They took him by the arms, dragged him to a shower and washed the filth from his body. Then they threw him a rough towel. He rubbed it hard to bring some warmth to his skin. Then they ordered him to put on prison garb.

Despite his fatigue the few minutes in the shower had given him some time to draw his hazy thoughts into order.

'Where am I going?' he asked as they marched him along the dim corridor.

'You will soon find out. No more questions,' they replied.

He was brought up from the basement to the first floor which was open and bright. The sense of space gave him a renewed sense of confidence in himself. He began to sing off key.

'Stop singing, you fool,' one of the warders said.

He began to recite a nursery rhyme. He was singing when he entered the interrogation room.

Eisenerz looked quizzically at the governor. 'I thought you said that the man had his wits about him.'

'He had this morning,' the governor replied.

'We shall see.'

Fieldmann looked at Eisenerz. He smiled at him, then cocked his fingers at him.

'Stop this fooling. Do you know who I am?'

'You are a king, a king in a black coat. Do you sing?' Fieldmann began to sing again. One of the warders hit him on the mouth. He pretended that he did not feel the pain and continued.

'And I can dance. I will dance for the king who is dressed in a black coat.'

Eisenerz looked at him intently. He had seen the lunatic leer before. He wondered.

'For a florin I'll show you my prick,' Fieldmann said and giggled.

The warder hit him on the side of the face and he fell on the floor. 'Then you do not wish to see my prick? So sad. So sad.'

'Take the fool back to his cell,' Eisenerz barked. 'You can wait for further instructions from me. I am sceptical about his condition. I will have a doctor examine him. He will not trick me.'

Fieldmann was carried back to the dark cell. They let him retain his prison clothes. When they banged the door he began to feel warm. He fell on the mattress and began to sleep.

A day later Marie received information about what had occurred in the cell. That night, when Eisenerz returned home from his office, she was waiting at the opposite side of the street in a darkened alleyway. When he went in she waited for half an hour, then she approached the door and knocked. It was opened by a young and pleasant-faced woman.

'I have an urgent message for your husband. I possess some document which he might wish to see.'

The woman was about to shut the door when Eisenerz approached. 'Well, young woman. Why do you come knocking on my door at this hour of the night? Do you know who I am?'

'You are Herr Eisenerz, head of the secret service. That is why I came. I have some documents to show you. They will be of interest to you.'

'I will see the lady in my office. Follow me.'

Marie was filled with fear as she followed him into a pleasant office with a large roll top desk by the wall.

Eisenerz offered her a chair. Then he studied her carefully. 'You are that woman who lives with Fieldmann. By right you should be in prison with him. We have nothing to discuss.'

She plucked up her courage. 'Yes we have. I have brought some drawings in which you might be interested. You failed to secure them when you raided the studio. Perhaps you might like to examine them.'

He took the drawings and studied them with disdain. They offended his sense of propriety, particularly in his own home. He looked at her with narrowed eyes. 'And what do you intend to do with these drawings?'

'What do you intend to do with Fieldmann?'

'He has insulted the Emperor and members of his court. He deserves to be prosecuted. He is a dangerous man.'

'He may deserve to be prosecuted but he hardly deserves to be tortured,' Marie glared at him.

'We do not torture people in Vienna. This is a civilised country.'

'I am not a fool. I know what goes on in the dungeon of the prison. I came to make a deal with you.'

'Are you in any condition to make a deal? I could have you thrown into a police cell and, my dear lady, you would not see the light of day for years. You would emerge a broken woman,' Eisenerz grew angry at the woman's impertinence.

'I am not afraid of your threats. Find some way to release Fieldmann, otherwise these postcards will appear as posters all over the city. They will even be posted on the doors of the Schönbrunn palace.'

'You threaten me.'

'I play my best hand.'

Eisenerz considered his position for some time. He had no wish to have another encounter with the Emperor. The fact that the postcards were on sale in the underworld of Vienna had caused enough trouble. If they appeared on the walls of the city it would cause a scandal all over the Empire. He thought of the copper plate hidden in his desk. Someday he might use it against the Emperor. For the moment, it would be better to rid Vienna of the artist.

He sighed. 'You are a woman of some courage. I am sure you are aware of my reputation.

'Very much so.'

'Then let this be the bargain. I want both you and that filthy minded artist to leave not only the city but the Empire. Go to France or to Russia but do not remain on Imperial soil.'

'I will consider the offer.'

'There is nothing to be considered. I will make arrangements that Fieldmann leave the prison some night soon. You will take the last train that evening out of Vienna. Let it take you wherever you wish. You will hand over the original drawings and plates at the border. Understood?'

'Yes, I understand.'

'Then goodnight. Be at the prison on Thursday night.

And take these filthy drawings with you. They defile my house.'

He pushed the sheaf of drawings into her hand. She took them and left the house.

It was only when she was some hundred yards away that she paused for breath.

It took Marie the rest of the week to place her affairs in order. Some of Jakov's paintings were placed in crates and sent to Paris. Others she removed from the frames and placed the canvases in her suitcase. Then, on Thursday when it was dark, she hired a cab and drove to the gates of the prison.

At ten o'clock the Judas gate opened and Fieldmann was thrown on to the street. He was dazed and confused. Marie directed him to the cab and they set out immediately for the great railway station on the far side of the Donau Canal. Here some detectives were waiting. They were directed into a private compartment. The detectives were to accompany them to the border.

Fieldmann was in a confused state. His face was haggard and his beard ragged and long. He lay on the seat and fell asleep. All through the night the train journeyed to the border.

Marie carried very little with her. Some clothes, the paintings, and some letters she had received from Lenin as well as a signed copy of one his books. She vowed that, like him, she would work to bring down the tyrants who sat on the thrones of Europe.

Chapter Nineteen

The Danube flowed pleasantly past the lawn. Beyond the river were small rolling hills, wooded and mysterious, over which a small summer mist lay each morning. From the balcony of the small palace, Alma watched this mist melt under the dawn light to reveal the trees and the rich, dewy grass. She wished she could dress in a heavy cloak and walk in bare feet on it, the sensation filling her body with a fresh sense of life.

Now, her thoughts turned to her husband. In the six months of their marriage, Prince Karl had not changed his ways. On formal occasions at the palace he behaved attentively but this was only a pretence. At home it was a different matter.

The domestics were beginning to notice that all was not well with the newly married couple. From behind locked doors they heard the long arguments, the beatings and the voice of the woman calling out for pity.

Word swiftly carried beyond the private walls of the palace, the news filtering up through the middle classes into royal circles.

Before her marriage Alma had dismissed all gossip about Karl's behaviour, but now she began to see his true character.

Sometimes after a bout of heavy drinking his whole body shook and his mouth foamed like that of a rabid dog. He lived for the darkness of the city, and the delights of Verna island, where he would spend the night gambling, returning in the early morning. Sometimes he stayed there for several days.

Alma looked sadly towards the far side of the river. Then she turned and went back to her room, with its bright walls, ornamental ceiling, and gilded mirrors which should have reflected the light brightness of the place. She caught a glimpse of herself in one of the great mirrors, now cracked into a thousand sharp triangles. It carried her image in many distorted fragments.

The carriage wheels sounded on the cobbled yard and then there was silence for some moments. A door was thrown open and she could hear steps in the corridor. She knew that the coachman, Bukin, was helping her husband up the stairs. 'Enough. I will walk the rest of the way,' Prince Karl was telling him in an ungrateful voice.

'Are you certain my lord?'

'Do you question me? Does a lackey question me? You have not been hired to ask questions,' he roared.

He then opened the door and fell into the room. Even from a distance she could smell the stench of urine on his body. His face was drawn and unshaven. Blood vessels ran like red nets through the whites of his eyes. He looked at her with a loose, hateful expression. 'And how is the virtuous Jewish maiden this summer's morning?' he began sarcastically.

'I am not Jewish,' Alma insisted.

'You are tainted. The gypsy women have better blood than you. At least they know where they came from, not from a family of dubious title seekers from America. I should have married into one of the European royal families and not some bastard woman with money.' He continued to ramble, 'Well, my dear, we are in debt, up to our necks in debt. Last night I lost what remaining money we had. We are royal but we are poor. What does the aspiring Empress think of this?' he asked speaking in a stumbling voice.

'You are a disgrace to your family and to the Emperor. You are not fit to represent him at St Petersburg.'

'No one,' he roared 'speaks to me in a voice like that! I am Prince Karl.' He staggered towards her, drew his hand back and hit her on the side of the face. She felt the blow cut the inner skin of her lip as she fell to the floor.

'How dare a commoner talk to me in this manner.' She felt the blow of his boot to her ribs. She rose from the floor and suddenly her resolve was firm. She had taken too much. She would never be beaten again.

She stood erect and looked at the man she had married. It had been a mistake but there was nothing she could do to change matters now. So, she took the pistol from her pocket and aimed it at his forehead.

His eyes bulged in disbelief. 'Would you dare raise a pistol to your husband?'

She aimed a little past his head and fired. A china vase on the mantelpiece splintered into fine pieces.

'I have practised my shot carefully. I know how to handle a pistol. Now, if you ever lay a hand upon me again I will kill you. I will not tolerate this abuse for the rest of my life. Listen to me carefully. You will never enter my bedroom again. You can sleep with the gypsy women and all the whores in Vienna; you can gamble the rest of your inheritance but do not come to me to underwrite your debts. Now, I will pay off what you owe and that is my final gesture. Never again abuse or touch me. I have had enough.'

He gazed at her in disbelief. 'I do not have to listen to such talk. Nobody has ever spoken to me in this manner before. I am a prince of the royal house of Hapsburg,' he began and moved towards her, his fingers open to claw at her. She fired the pistol again. The shot tore skin from the edge of his ear. He howled in pain.

He rushed to the mirror and looked at his ear and the blood flowing down into the pink lobe. When he looked at her again she still had the pistol pointed at his forehead. 'You could have killed me.'

'I could have, but I did not. You are not worth killing for the moment. Tonight you move into other apartments. I will deal with the final debts on the island. Then you fend for yourself. Now good day.'

She left the room and banged the door. Prince Karl began to tremble involuntarily, too drunk to control himself. He rushed to the balcony and vomited on to the patio below. Then he returned to bed and fell into a stupid sleep.

Alma dressed herself and ordered her breakfast in the small office where she kept her correspondence and records. When she had finished writing a letter she called Bukin, the coachman.

He knocked on the door and she bade him enter.

'Sit down, Bukin,' she directed.

'Thank you, madame,' he replied politely. He admired Alma. She treated him like a human being.

'Tell me what went on at the island. You were there and you know.'

'Shall I tell you everything or will I leave out the parts which are distasteful?'

'Tell me everything.'

In a sad confessional voice he described to her the prince's days and nights on the island. 'It is a den of iniquity, madame. Not only are women involved but also young men for the pleasure of the Prince and other gentlemen. Then there is the gambling. Prince Karl has been cheated out of a fortune by the owner, Czernin. I have noted cards being drawn from under the pack. Some of the decks are marked. Even the dice which they throw is loaded. I have eaten with some of the servants. They tell me these things.'

'Thank you, Bukin. Today I am going to visit the island. I will put an end to my husband's gambling.'

'But that is dangerous, madame.'

'Everything is dangerous,' Alma replied firmly. 'I am not afraid of these criminals. I will deal with them in my own way. Prepare the coach.'

They left the palace at noon. An hour later they were on the outskirts of Vienna moving down a narrow road, before turning right towards the river. They drove through a copse of trees and arrived at a small jetty. At a hundred yards distant stood the island, gentle, set in the centre of the Danube, the roof of the casino just visible among the trees. Bukin untied a boat and they moved out into the river. He rowed upstream for a little. Then when he was above the island he changed direction. The current swept the boat towards the wooden jetty set on piles sunk in the river.

Their approach was noted. As soon as they reached the pier a man with a shotgun approached. 'You cannot land here. This is private property,' he called to them.

'I wish to see Czernin,' Alma told him bluntly. 'I am the wife of Prince Karl.'

The man was taken aback. He disappeared into a tunnel of trees and Alma followed directly behind him. The tunnel opened onto a large, wooden building, with delicate, almost feminine lines. A veranda surrounded it and the door was ornamented with stained glass.

Alma walked smartly into the building. It carried the heavy scent of cheap perfume. In a large room, curtained with heavy brocade and made dim by the stained glass windows, a game of cards was in progress. A naked woman played the piano close to the fire.

No one seemed to notice Alma's appearance for a moment. She recognised several of the gentlemen sitting about the table. Then one of them saw her and rushed to the door, bundling her into the hallway.

'Who are you?' he hissed.

'I am the wife of Prince Karl. I presume that you are Czernin.'

'That is correct,' he seemed uncomfortable in her presence.

'Then I would like to speak to you privately.'

He hastened down a corridor, took some keys out of his pocket and fumbled with the lock. While Alma stood beside him the German ambassador to the Viennese court came down the stairs wearing only a shirt. He was helped by a gypsy woman with her breasts bared. He immediately recognised her and hastened back up.

In his office Czernin asked, 'Well. What can I do for you? You have no reason to come here. This is not a place for women.'

'Unless they are prostitutes,' she shot back at him.

'Let me know your business and leave immediately. Your husband has created enough trouble here during the last week. He is a most undesirable man.'

'The devil in hell preaches virtue,' she replied. 'I will not sit here and listen to you talk to me in that fashion. I have evidence about this place which could have you thrown in prison for twenty years. I have interviewed young men from Vienna who have been buggered here.'

Czernin swallowed his spittle.

'You have cheated my husband out of large sums of money,' Alma continued. 'Your dice are loaded, your cards are marked and you cheat people when they are drunk. I demand that you return my husband's losses for the last year.'

'But that is impossible, madame,' Czernin stuttered.

'Nothing is impossible. I will remain here for a week if necessary until the money is returned. If not, I shall go immediately to the Emperor and tell him how young men are debauched here. That is the only offer I will make.'

'How can I tell how much your husband lost, madame? We do not keep accounts here.'

'I can tell you precisely,' she told him. She took a piece of paper from the table and wrote it down.

'But this is a vast sum of money!'

'I know,' Alma replied stolidly. She studied his face, which was weak from self indulgence. His skin was white and sunless.

Czernin went to a safe and unlocked it. He took out a large wad of money and placed it in front of her.

Alma undid the cord which bound it and counted it. 'This is not enough,' she said.

'But I have no more on the premises,' he complained.

'Then find it,' she directed.

He left the room and returned later with gold coins. They made up the deficit.

Alma took the money and bundled it into a bag. 'I will now leave. I have received what I came for.'

'Your husband is not welcome here anymore.'

'He was never welcome. And if a word of what has happened here reaches his ears I will have the place closed down.'

Alma left the building, hastened to the boat and ordered Bukin to row her ashore.

Karl could not understand why he was refused entrance to the island and the other gambling houses in the city. Even the fashionable brothels were suddenly closed to him. He became morose. For days he shuffled about the palace. He even tried to distract himself in the library but his attention began to wander.

In the autumn he left for Italy for some months. The winter passed quietly for Alma. She spent as much time as possible reading books on Russia and trying to learn the rudiments of the language.

At the end of that winter Prince Karl returned and some weeks later they set out for Saint Petersburg.

Chapter Twenty

Sophie Schmerling had now lived for several years in Berlin. She believed in the young empire, in its vigour, in its military power. Baron Von Hertling had been correct in all his predictions.

The north of Germany was the locomotive which ran Europe. It was a vast pulsating giant. Everywhere new factories were being built. They were modern in their construction, bright places where great machines were turning out the objects which made life easy.

There were now more of Sophie's beloved automobiles on the streets of Berlin than horse-drawn cabs and Joseph Steiner's factory in the eastern section of the city had expanded rapidly.

Steiner had invested his money well. Ernst Fischer was now director of one of the most modern factories in Berlin. Also, through the patronage of Baron Von Hertling, he was now producing motor vehicles for the army.

Sophie had followed her father's advice on all financial matters. The investments he had made for her had made her a woman of independent means; she could read a balance sheet as well as she could read her German poets and philosophers and the blueprints of some new machine were as familiar to her as road maps. Every day there was some new challenge for her in Berlin.

Her former lover, the baron, had by now established a reliable network of spies right across Europe. He had retained his quarters in a featureless building which looked over one of the new modern factories which were being built to the west of the city. It was set amongst trees, which he had ordered to be planted when he first took charge. Now other buildings had been constructed close by. They formed the centre of a spy ring for which he had recruited men and women from every profession and trade.

'Only with the best can I obtain the best results,' he had argued with the ministry of defence when he had asked for further finance.

'But we do not know what is going on,' some of the ministers at the Reichstag had complained.

'Just as well, just as well,' the Kaiser had told the baron when they met together for a private briefing. The baron had been wise to establish a direct line of access to the Kaiser. He gave Wilhelm secret documents which were of minor importance but which gave the Kaiser a sense of being master of a private and powerful kingdom which belonged to the shadows of the night, secret meetings, sinister alleyways and exotic countries.

Sophie and Von Hertling met for coffee each week at the Café Metropole close to Unter den Linden. She was a familiar figure there and it was rumoured that she was mistress to Wilhelm, something which gave her an air of mystery.

The Baron and Sophie had been lovers for some years. Then they had drifted apart. She had taken other lovers. She had rough tastes which were satisfied by the military elite. Her mother said that there was a coarse grain in her nature. In Berlin she could satisfy this inclination.

Baron Von Hertling had brought his wife from the south and was now a model husband. His German children were growing up about him. Each year his wife presented him another and he felt proud that they were all boys.

They had a familiar corner in the café, surrounded by potted palms which concealed them. From there they could look onto the wide thoroughfare and observe the traffic passing by.

They swapped the gossip of the city. Sophie was party to more of its secrets than the Kaiser himself.

'I have some information which you might like to read,' the baron told her. 'It comes from one of our men in Vienna. It will keep you up to date with your family.'

Sophie read through the typed notes with growing interest. 'You are quite an amazing man. Here we sit at a café in Berlin and you can tell me what is happening in the bedroom of my sister's house?' She smiled. 'I can imagine her in Saint Petersburg. She will create quite a dash there. She had ambitions for herself and now they are fulfilled.'

'Her husband is a libertine and a gambler. You can see how she dealt with him. That took some courage.'

Sophie read on carefully. The notes on her sister Marie were more interesting. 'Where is she now?'

'She is somewhere in Russia with her revolutionary, Jakov Fieldmann. I have a score to settle with him.'

'What has he done? Surely he is only a wild artist with mad ideas.'

'He was instrumental in sending some fools to try to kill me in Berlin. I barely escaped with my life. But he will not escape my net. I am still on his trail.'

'Even in Russia?'

'I have friends there. You remember Prince Dmitri, the Russian envoy to Vienna?'

'Yes.'

'He is more than just an elegant figure. He is high up in the secret service. We keep in contact through various channels. I have not told you of our mutual Russian friend, the Armenian?'

'No.'

'He is an expert. His methods are subtle and he is now on Fieldmann's trail.'

'Will he kill him?'

'No. That is too easy a solution. If we are lucky, Fieldmann will end up in Siberia. At least that is the plan. At this very moment the net is being drawn about him.'

'You have subtle ways,' she told him.

'Our best spies are those you do not notice.'

'You have agents everywhere.'

'That is why I know where to expect trouble. However, I would like to know more of what is happening in the capital, Saint Petersburg. Would you like to visit? You could serve Germany well in that city.'

She looked at him closely. He was gazing into the middle distance.

'Are you inviting me to become a spy?' she asked.

'I would not call you a spy. But you could bring your bright mind to bear on what is happening in the salons of Saint Petersburg.'

'I prefer the life of Berlin. It is more exciting. Russia is such a barbarous place.'

The baron laughed. 'You underestimate Russia. Some of the most intellectual and artistic society in Europe lives there. Someday, when they reorganise their economy, they will be as European as the French and the Germans. But at present it is a dangerous place. I can assure you that it will be worth a visit.'

He sipped his cognac and looked at her. A smile played on his lips. He knew her sense of adventure.

'I shall think about it. I must reflect on the matter.'

'Very well. In the meantime, let me give you the current gossip. I am sure that you are interested in gossip?'

'It is the very elixir of civilised living.'

Von Hertling looked at her for a moment. He wondered if he should tell her what he knew. He decided that he had known her for many years. She was a shrewd woman and she kept her mind to herself.

He explained that an article had appeared in a Bavarian paper which had exposed one of the Kaiser's close associates. The man had been caught engaging in unnatural acts with a sailor and some young men.

'Will it be reported in the papers in Berlin?'

'Of course it will. It is my business to make certain that no scandal is attached to the Kaiser himself. They were very good friends and our friend belonged to the intimate circle of the court. I will have to distort the truth. One has often to bend the truth a little in the interest of the greater good.'

'But is the Kaiser implicated? Of course there is no direct evidence for anything, but rumour feeds upon rumour.'

'He has been known to pat young men on the backside. This has been observed. But there is no direct evidence.'

'Perhaps you have information on your files,' Sophie suggested slyly.

For a moment anger flared in his eyes. She knew that she had gone too far. 'I am sorry. I should not have asked such a question.'

'Or made such a suggestion. The Empire must be protected and it is my business to protect it. I can assure you that nothing will besmirch the Emperor's name.'

Von Hertling turned and ordered more cognac. Both stared at the traffic on Unter den Linden.

'When I look at these automobiles I am aware that some day similar vehicles will transport soldiers to war.'

'Will there be a war?' Sophie asked.

'Who can say. There will be no war in the immediate future. But the British are building up their fleet and we are following them. Better guns are being built. Even this new flying machine I have heard tell of could have a military purpose. Every invention is eventually used for the purposes of war. At present the dogs of war are on the leash but some day these dogs will be set free and then the world could fall into chaos.'

Sophie was surprised at the baron's pessimism. 'You take too grim a view of things. Surely people will not permit this life which they now enjoy to be taken from them. They will not permit their leaders to go to war.'

'People's minds can be controlled,' he countered. 'The very people who pass by in these cars may be marching tomorrow to some front or other. Give them a cause and an enemy and a flag and you can send them marching in any direction you wish. But when the war comes we will be prepared. We will march to the gates of Paris if necessary. And we will do so with speed.'

Von Hertling was too proud of the Empire, too caught up in its destiny, Sophie thought. His body was always controlled, his thoughts hidden. Sometimes she did not know what was passing through his mind.

He quickly changed the subject. 'You have asked me for some information which might be of value to you. This, of course, is secret information. No one else in the city is aware of it. But a new factory is about to be built, backed by Krupps and others. They have discovered a new way to roll steel. In a month's time the company will be floated on the stock exchange. I believe that within three months the share will treble, particularly when the names of the directors are disclosed. Here is the information. I trust that you will destroy it, when you have read it. And for this you owe me a favour,' he smiled.

Sophie took the paper and glanced through it. It was a succinct document, but she was aware of the implications of the development. 'I am interested. I wish to obtain a house in the city and with this information perhaps I might be able to buy it.'

'I ask only one favour. Go to Saint Petersburg in the autumn. Find out what is happening there, particularly at the court. Russia is a threat to us. If there is a revolution, then we must be prepared for it. Find out the state of the Emperor's relationship with his people. Above all, find out if he has lost contact with what is going on in the intellectual circles and in the factories. I have other people working in these fields, but your opinion would be welcomed.'

'Very well. If this deal works I will visit Saint Petersburg.'

'I can assure you that you will be a rich woman. It is secret information and very few are party to it.'

Sophie took the document and placed it in her handbag. They sat gossiping for a little longer. Then she left.

She drove straight away to the Mitte district of the city. Twice during the last month she had visited the mansion she dreamed of buying. A high wall ran about it and gave it a sense of complete seclusion.

At a leisurely pace Sophie entered the grounds of the old house. The avenue was choked with weed and the shrubs on either side had become overgrown. Above them stood firm trees, old and well-rooted. She walked up the avenue to where the shrubs gave way to an overgrown lawn.

Her first view of the house made her catch her breath. It had been built in the eighteenth century and was firm and old. Finely cut pillars carried a classical pediment at the front entrance. Above it stood a Venetian window.

Sophie took the key from her pocket and opened the dry oak door which led to the great hallway. Dust lay like a protective patina on pictures, tables and on the delicate plasterwork.

She walked up the sweeping staircase with its marble-wrought banisters, surrounded by the Italian charm of the interior. The lines of the plasterwork were fine and exuberant. In the great dining room she walked to the window and looked out onto the tangled garden. She could make out its general plan – the steps descending to a round pool with floating water lilies.

Sophie looked down at the garden for a long time. 'I must possess this house,' she decided. In her life she had lived in many places. This house would give her security and a feeling of rootedness. But her stepfather had always told her that she should hedge her bets. She should never invest all her money in one single venture. Now, she intended to play a dangerous game. If she won, she would be a rich woman. If not, she would return to Vienna penniless.

By the time she reached the gate she had made up her mind.

That night she invited Levi Belkind to dinner. She was aware of his reputation. He was a partner of her stepfather and had a deep respect for privacy and secrecy where investments were concerned. However, she had her maid and footman remain on at her apartments, as at a certain point in such evenings Levi Belkind often got amorous and might make advances to her.

Towards the end of the meal, Sophie told him her business.

'You wish to invest your money in a new company about to be floated on the market?' Levi Belkind did not disguise his surprise. 'Do you know how many of such companies fail? Some of these people are swindlers. Your father would not approve of such recklessness.'

'It is my decision and I wish to abide by it. Will you deal for me or should I seek out somebody else?' she asked him bluntly.

'I will deal. But I assure you that you could be making a great mistake,' he sighed. 'That remains to be seen.' He studied her closely. Clearly she must be in possession of some firm information.

Sophie directed Levi Belkind to sell off all her other shares, even those that had firm promise. Having finished his meal and the discussion he set off for the red-light district of Berlin.

It was a Monday like any other July Monday in Berlin. It was cool in the woods, but the great city was beginning to stir; trains from the suburbs carried the workforce to the factories; the great thoroughfares were already filled with vehicles; in the fashionable shops the shop assistants were dressing the mannequins in the latest fashions.

At ten o'clock Levi Belkind left his house for the Berlin stock exchange, the Börsengebäude. He invariably carried a gold-tipped cane and wore a gold watchchain across his waistcoat. His shoes were of the softest leather. Everything about him had a luxurious quality. He felt comfortable in his light suit and reflected that he liked this city more than any other in Europe.

He reached Hardenbergstrasse, the home of the exchange, at half past eleven. It was a grey-stoned, rectangular building close to the River Spree. As he approached it Belkind felt that he was entering an arena as vicious in its savagery as the Coliseum. He had destroyed competitors in the three-storeyed building. Here he had bought and sold currencies in minutes while others hesitated. But he never made rash speculations. Like Joseph Steiner he had his informants in every capital of the world. He lived at the centre of an international web of intrigue.

At noon the stock exchange began trading. On Mondays it lacked excitement. There was only cautious buying of solid stock.

At half past twelve a new company was floated on the market as Sophie had predicted. There was only a mild interest shown in the flotation. Quietly Belkind began to buy all available shares.

The conversation between the brokers always turned to the same topics. They discussed the stock exchanges of Wall Street and Paris. Now, a whisper began to pass through the dealing booths. Krupps were backing the new company. At a quarter past two they began to speculate.

That evening the value of the shares had doubled.

Levi Belkind was visibly shaken when he entered the coffee house. Sophie sat quietly in the corner sipping coffee, an innocent look on her face.

'Did you purchase the stocks?' she asked.

He handed her a folder. There was anger in his eyes. 'You knew that they were a subsidiary of the Krupps Company. You could have let me in on a secret.'

'I thought you knew all the secrets. How was I to know that the company had the backing of the Krupps foundation,' she smiled.

He looked at her intently. Her expression remained bland. 'You will be a rich woman if the shares continue to climb,' he told her.

'We will watch closely. I expect that they will peak next month. When they have reached their full value I will sell them. I am anxious to lay my hands on a large amount of money.'

'Joseph Steiner would be very proud of you. I have been fooled by a young woman. I have only one request to make. Do not let it be known. The news would pass quickly through the city. I can hear the gossip: that wily fox, Belkind, has been outwitted by a slip of a girl.'

'I can assure you that it will not occur again. I have no intention of playing the stock exchange. From now on I will take Joseph Steiner's advice and diversify.' They remained in conversation for half an hour, then Sophie took her leave. She wished to be alone.

The next few weeks were the most anxious and exciting that she ever had in her life. Every day the shares moved higher in value. After three weeks she was tempted to sell but she held out. At the end of the month she was certain that they would rise no higher. She asked Levi Belkind who advised her to sell. She followed his advice. However, the shares continued to move upwards. The rise continued for seven weeks. Had she retained her stocks Sophie would have made an even more immense profit.

She was never to know that Levi Belkind had purchased them.

Two months later Sophie moved into the house in the Mitte district. Immediately she set about restoring it to its former grandeur. She felt that she belonged in Berlin as she belonged in no other city.

Chapter Twenty-one

St Petersburg stood on the banks of the Neva River in all its summer magnificence. Prince Karl had chosen to travel to the city of the Tsar during the warm months as the prospect of a freezing journey appalled him. 'I will not freeze at the very edge of the civilised world during the winter! Nothing will convince me that the Russians are other than barbarians. Mongolian hordes who threaten the empire.'

At first Karl had shown interest in his new appointment. Now, it was more like a sentence of banishment. Paris and Rome would have suited his tastes better. On their way to St Petersburg he had sat sullenly in the railway carriage drinking his way through central Russia, taking no interest in the landscape through which they passed. It seemed bleak and barren to him.

He made only one comment, an astute one. 'The land has no frontiers. A well-equipped army could sweep through the plains without any fear of encountering obstacles. Had Napoleon a good rail system at his disposal, Russia would now be an organised society and not a country of serfs.'

Unlike her husband, Alma looked forward to her life in St Petersburg. She did not possess a closed mind on the matter and had taken the trouble to inform herself about the history of the capital. She was also aware of the city's strategic importance. When Peter the Great had built his log cabin on the muddy delta in order to supervise the erection of his magnificent city he had removed himself from the centre of a great continent to a corner of the Baltic in order to have a window on Europe.

Once the names of the railway stations began to appear in the Russian alphabet Alma knew that they had passed into a new country. She grew excited. Instantly she took her pencil and copied the Russian letters on to a notepad; then she tried to pronounce them. She did so with some ease. Karl was peeved at his wife's rudimentary Russian, reminding her that the language of the court was French.

As finally they approached the great city, Alma sat by the window and looked at the landscape. Silver birch woods gave way to wooden houses and soon she could see the great city itself, built from millions of tons of red granite, carried to this marshland to set the foundations and define the banks of the river.

When they arrived at the station Prince Karl was slightly drunk. He had consumed a bottle of brandy during the last few hours in order to dull his spirits, as he said. Now he emerged from his carriage and attempted to straighten himself. Several members of the embassy staff were waiting for him. He looked around, surprised by the modernity of the station and of the people.

'Take me through this city,' he ordered his driver, when they had been settled in the waiting automobile. 'Seeing as I will be incarcerated here for the next few years, I might as well see what my prison looks like.'

'Very well sir,' the driver said cautiously.

The started off from the Moskovski station down through Nevsky Prospekt. Alma was amazed at the spacious loveliness of Peter the Great's city. In high summer it was a place of shimmering beauty and the light falling on the streets seemed to have the sharp quality of the Mediterranean. They drove directly through the heart of the city, past the Pushkin Theatre, the Karansky Cathedral, towards Dvortsovaya Square where, before them, stood the vast Winter Palace. It was a long, immense building which impressed even Prince Karl with its proportions and colour.

From this square Russia was governed.

St Petersburg had the stamp of a European city on every street and every building. Wherever Prince Karl turned a building stood which was impressive by the best Viennese standards. However, the palaces built along the canals had an intimate charm which Vienna lacked.

Nonetheless, he refused to admit that he was impressed. 'I've seen enough. Let us go directly to the embassy.'

On their way Alma continued to look at the enchanting city. She would never forget her first day there. It seemed never to end as the light held in the sky.

The embassy was situated on the banks of the Neva and a private garden planted with trees and shrubs led directly to the river. Here a boathouse had been built which contained a motor launch. The trees and shrubs were in bloom and the flowerbeds were rich with brightly coloured flowers.

From her balcony Alma gazed over the enchanting city. The windows had been thrown open and the air was light and fresh. A gentle summer breeze cooled the great rooms. Her eyes travelled along the skyline. Everywhere there were golden church domes, a mass of roofs, and in the distance the tall chimney stacks of the factories to the north-east, sending out slow plumes of smoke into a blue sky.

Prince Karl insisted on meeting his staff together in the main hallway of the house.

He walked past them in his imperious manner, looking disdainfully at each one. He did not say a single word to any of them. Then he picked out the oldest serving member of the embassy staff.

'You. What is your name?'

'Von Schoon, sir.'

'How long have you been in St Petersburg?'

'Twenty years.'

'Then twenty years is too long a time to spend here. You look like one of the Asiatic hordes. Your clothes are creased, your hair is unkempt, even your shoes need a bright shine. Have you gone native?'

'My wife died some time ago. I am afraid I depended a lot upon her.' Von Schoon looked anxious.

'I am not interested in the personal details of your life! I believe that you should be pensioned off and return to Vienna. We need new men here.' His voice was cold and superior. It was obvious to the staff that the ambassador regarded them as of inferior rank.

Karl did not dismiss them. Instead he walked into his office and banged the door shut. They stood awkwardly in line for a moment, too confused to speak. Then they broke into small groups.

'This is terrible, terrible,' they murmured to each other. Von Schoon had been well regarded by all the civil servants in the city. He had given advice to several ambassadors and had written their correspondence for them. He also knew more about the intrigues of the city than anyone in the Viennese court. To address him in such a fashion was a mistake, they agreed. This new ambassador would make many enemies and many mistakes.

The news of what had happened soon reached the kitchen. There too, there was mild panic. Perhaps the new ambassador would not like the cuisine and have them all dismissed. Prince Karl, in one half hour, had given them much to worry about.

Alma was removed from all this emotional turmoil. She visited the garden and stood at the very edge of the river. She noted how pure and clear the water appeared. The river breeze was fresh and invigorating.

That night they had supper in the Italian dining room. It was a lonely occasion. They sat at distant ends of the table and the servants served their meals, seeming hesitant and nervous. However, Prince Karl had to admit that the food was excellent and the embassy cellar well stocked.

When the meal was finished he received a phone call from Prince Dmitri Shestov and without giving any excuse, left the embassy.

Alma returned to her rooms and stood on the balcony. By eleven o'clock the colours of the day had faded into a cave of pearl. Light lingered on the edge of the city never departing, bathed in mystical twilight. At one o'clock, before she retired to bed, Alma looked eastward. A new day was breaking on the unspoiled horizon.

Prince Karl took a carriage to Kotin island. It lay to the north of the city. There Prince Dmitri was waiting for him.

'At this time of year the sun never sets. Of course, in winter it seems to set as soon as it rises. The summer is good for roaming through the city. I am sure you have not lost your taste for the good life now that you have been made ambassador,' Dmitri chuckled, 'We will have to sweeten your life here, I think.'

Prince Karl was only too well aware that Prince Dmitri knew all the strange haunts of the city.

'I have been expecting you for a week. Have you been reluctant to come to Saint Petersburg? Do you not know that this is the most European and intellectual of cities? Here, all your wishes are catered for. Once you get the taste for this city you will never want to leave it.'

They walked along the shore of the flat island. There was a mute glow of light about them. The aspen and the silver birch were in leaf and, close by, the silent waters of the Neva flowed towards the Baltic. The air carried the salt tang of the sea.

Prince Dmitri walked with him for some time talking at some length about affairs of state. For Dmitri, the Tsar's failure to respond to the events of 1905 was directly responsible for the current shambolic state of affairs: the disastrous naval battle in the Straits of Tsushima still troubled his mind. The thought of the defeat rankled. He recalled the events again and again. The fleet, having been sent from the Baltic, had spent seven months travelling down the Atlantic and across the Indian Ocean to engage the enemy. It had been ill-prepared for the engagement with Admiral Togo and the whole Russian fleet had been wiped out. The consequences for the country would be far-reaching.

'It was a stupid mistake,' Dmitri said. 'The Tsar underestimated the enemy. Time and again he had been advised against such an action. Had he read the reports on the Japanese navy he would have had more respect for them. Even now he is ill advised by his uncles and has no mind of his own. He is too weak to take control.'

Prince Karl found the conversation strange. Normally Prince Dmitri would have whisked him away to some casino or other but obviously Dmitri wished to talk to him. 'Surely he has some command over the situation.'

'It is more apparent than real. He is weak in the east. He should leave the Chinese to sort out their own problems. Five years ago in Odessa the sailors seized the battleship *Potemkin*. Even some of the officers joined! Then in October the country was paralysed by strikes. Over a million workers stopped working. Now, despite Stolypin's efforts, Trotsky has urged the workers' councils to arm themselves in preparation for another revolution. People will never forget Bloody Sunday when the Cossacks shot down innocent protesters in front of the Winter Palace.'

He continued to list out the problems which confronted Russia in a serious voice, something which surprised Prince Karl. 'And what are your answers to the problems?'

'Another Tsar perhaps? Or a palace coup. Get rid of the old men and surround the Tsar with men of determination. I would fill the prison camps with the revolutionaries. Some, I would hang. I would smash the Soviets. If the centre of their power is destroyed, then we can have a sane society.'

Karl listened intently to all that had been said. It was something he could report back to Vienna. The old Emperor would be delighted with such reports.

And then, as if realising his indiscretion, Prince Dmitri suddenly turned from the subject. He began talking of racehorses. He had some in training on one of his estates and expressed the wish that Karl join him for a weekend in the country.

'But first let me bring you to the Casino. It is at the centre of the island.'

At some distance they had been followed by the silent figure of Nikka, with his narrow, Siberian eyes. He now helped the men to mount their waiting horses. They rode through a narrow track to the Casino. It was a large-timbered building, with elegant ironwork in the balcony. Electric light burned in all the rooms and as they approached they could hear the sounds of music and laughter.

They dismounted and Nikka led the horses away. When they entered the building Prince Karl was surprised at the luxury and the elegance of the place. A great chandelier, with a thousand blue tiers, hung over the roulette table. In the corners lamps covered with blue shades glowed filling the place with lights and half-light. Elegant prostitutes mingled with the guests.

Immediately a servant dressed like a Parisian waiter advanced with a tray of drinks. 'Surprised?' Prince Dmitri asked Karl.

'Overwhelmed. It reminds me of haunts of mine on the Riviera and in Paris.'

'We are as decadent and civilised here in St Petersburg as they are in the great cities. I can assure you that every delight awaits you here.'

Prince Karl walked towards the roulette. He was always

fascinated by this game of chance. He studied the wheel as it flashed about and the white ivory ball flicked restlessly from number to number. Then it quickly came to rest on a black number. He began to calculate the odds. All his life he had calculated the odds at the wheel.

Very soon he began to bet. At first it was a few gold coins but as he got caught up in the motions of the spinning wheel, he began to double his bets. Then, when he had lost almost all his money, his fortune turned. He won on four consecutive occasions. He had not been so fortunate before. At the end of the night he had doubled his money.

When he checked his watch he realised that he had spent three hours at the table.

Prince Dmitri noticed and said, 'Let us retire upstairs. I am sure that you are hungry. I have prepared something for you.'

He followed Prince Dmitri up the carpeted stairs. On the walls hung paintings of large reclining nudes, well-executed but vapid. They entered a private room. A table was set out with silver ware. Candles burned in the centre. Prince Dmitri locked the door and clapped his hands. Immediately, a naked woman appeared and prepared to serve them. She was a tall Norwegian, with longs limbs and fine breasts. As she poured the wine Prince Karl put out his hands and stroked her buttocks. She smiled pleasantly at him. He found his passion for her mounting. He wished to take her as she stood pouring the wine.

Prince Dmitri noted his lust. 'Let us eat. Then other pleasures await us. I have hired some more of these women to please us. I can assure you that you will be quite surprised by our decadence. It is exquisitely refined.'

Reassured, Prince Karl settled into his meal.

When he left the island early in the morning all his tastes had been satisfied. He felt sated. Dmitri, who had left at the end of the meal, had returned to collect him. 'Let's hope that there will many such pleasurable evenings,' he said as they parted on Dvortsovy bridge close to the stock exchange.

Prince Karl hastened home to bed.

Prince Dmitri, however, had other business to attend to. He returned to his offices overlooking the Moyka Canal. He opened a diary and accurately entered all that had happened during the night. It was obvious to him that Prince Karl had not changed his ways.

Chapter Twenty-two

The small town of Loslov lay to the east of Odessa on the Black Sea. It was set on a hillside which overlooked an ancient harbour. The houses were set in tiers on the hillside and surrounded by luxuriant trees and plants. On the higher slopes vineyards flourished in the rich, red soil. The older village, where the fishermen and vineyard workers lived, surrounded the harbour. It was an ancient place of narrow streets and small houses. The deep scent of flowers mixed with the salt smell of the sea hung over it. Flowers and shrubs cascaded over fences, softening rock and slope and wall.

Loslov was a town almost as old as history. Fieldmann, who had travelled through Eastern Europe and all of Russia, noted the remnants of old civilisations there: Greek, Roman, Byzantine and Russian. He saw that they surrounded him in profusion in every building, chapel and mosque.

When Jakov and Marie had arrived they had seen, far out to sea, a ship with great sails passing along the horizon. It could have belonged to ancient Arabian traders. Close by, fishermen were playing out their nets in quieter waters. The sky was blue and the great eye of the sun poured heat and warmth on the landscape and the village. The air shimmered with heat.

They arrived in Loslov two years after their exile from Austria. They had travelled through Russia, never remaining long in any one place. They had rested in villages where the peasants shared their food with them, dull places, set in featureless landscapes. No hill or mountain marked the rim of the horizon. Their world was a limited place.

Sometimes they had stayed at the house of a landowner who was caught up in the new intellectual ferment. At night, on lonely estates, they argued in some library or drawing room about the future.

Fieldmann quickly saw that thought was most vibrant in the cities and in the towns. Here the plans for a revolution were exercising the minds of young men from the middle and upper classes.

From his journeys he realised that if a revolution would take place it would happen in the cities and the universities.

Loslov was a perfect place in which to settle down, far from their previous home of Simbirsk on the Volga. Simbirsk had been a harsh town, gripped by ice in winter and whipped by Arctic winds. It seemed, during these harsh months, lost in the wastes of Russia.

Their flight from the city had been in winter. They had travelled in a troika through a snowstorm in order to evade the police. They had hidden in a village, fearing that they might be captured and brought to trial.

'The Armenian is a double agent,' Marie had often argued during that cold month.

'Impossible. He was also captured.'

Marie had suspected the Armenian the first moment she had met him with the other young revolutionaries. He had suggested that they assassinate one the Romanov cousins. He had provided arms and plans.

The young men were fired by his talk. 'It could bring about a general revolution,' he argued. 'Think of all your comrades imprisoned in Siberia. Many have been sent there without trial. They depend upon you to carry the flame of revolution.'

Even Fieldmann had believed his words.

The attack had been a disaster.

As soon as they had approached the house they were fired upon. Two young men died in the snow crying out for help. The rest escaped through alleyways.

Fieldmann had been lucky. He had avoided the cordon set up about the square by escaping along the roofs.

The rest were captured and brought to trial. Many of them were sent to Siberia. The Armenian had not been seen since.

Fieldmann and Marie had often argued about the Armenian as they made their way south.

They arrived at the town in early Spring 1912. It was already warm on the edge of the Black Sea. In the hinterland, on the vast plains, the wheat had begun to show in fresh, green blades.

As they made their way up through the old part of the town in the early morning they felt at ease. They stopped at a granite wall and looked down at the harbour.

'This is where we will remain. We have travelled great distances and it is time to have a settled life. You need time to rest and recover your strength. I like the smell of the earth and the sea. The light is vibrant and the colours possess contrast and strength. I will work well here,' Fieldmann told Marie.

She locked her arm in his and they both stood for a long time gazing at the flat sea, green and translucent, stretching towards a wide horizon. Both were aware of its great antiquity. The *Argos* had sailed across these azure waters in search of the Golden Fleece.

Close to the pier the markets had opened. People were moving around the stalls. Peasant women in their coloured shawls and domestics from the great houses built higher up the hill. The boats had returned from their morning fishing and were unloading their catch onto the quay. Nets were drawn from the decks and stretched to dry on the pier, the pace and movement slow and harmonious. Fieldmann looked on the scene with an artist's eye. There was enough subject matter lying before him to occupy him for a lifetime. Their friend, Mentov, had directed them to the right place.

'Let us go to this Ibram's tavern,' Fieldmann advised. 'It will give us time to set our thoughts in order and perhaps find some place we might rent for two or three seasons.' He led the horse and cart, upon which were bundled all their possessions, and they moved further into the heart of the old town. After some directions they reached a small square with a fountain. The water splashed unevenly from a central stem of pipe into a basin, but it was cool and clear and must have come from the very heart of the hills.

Fieldmann untackled the horse and tied him to the spoke of the cartwheel. He left some dry hay for him to eat and then entered the only tavern in the square. It was a place of half light with a flagged floor and a ceiling supported by solid beams. The man Mentov had told them about, Ibram, was talking to some men and looked at them suspiciously. He did not immediately come to their table. Then after a while he moved towards them. He was a heavy man with olive skin who wore a Fez and could have been a Turk.

'You are strangers here?' he asked.

'Yes.'

'We do not have many strangers passing through.'

'A friend, Mentov, sent us. He told us that we would find hospitality here.'

Ibram's eyes brightened when he heard the name. He brought over a pitcher of local wine and sat at the table with them.

'Mentov is my friend. An important man no doubt in the city. He played here in the square with me and then went to the Lycée in Odessa. He was the very brightest in the class. What does he teach?'

'Philosophy and political science.'

'Philosophy is good. Plenty of talk, plenty of ideas and no action. Political science is dangerous. It stirs up men's minds. Leave well alone I say. Allah will take care.'

'Then perhaps Allah will take care of us,' Fieldmann smiled. 'We need a small house where I can work. I am an artist. And my wife would like a small vegetable garden and a room where she can write and study.'

'Let me think. Let me think.' He reflected for some time. 'I will make a bargain with you. My young children are growing up. I hope my young son, Pascha, will go to the Lycée, like Mentov, and for this he needs someone to teach him. Could you teach him?' He looked at Marie. 'He is a very bright child. I am a busy man and I do not have time to attend to such matters. My wife cannot read. It is a real problem. You teach Pascha and you can have the house rent free.'

Mentov had been correct. He had told them that Ibram could arrange everything for them.

'You paint pictures?' Ibram turned to Fieldmann.

'Yes.'

'Then you can paint me and my family. I have noted that in the houses of the rich they pay artists to paint their pictures. They pay much money for this. But I am not a wealthy man and I cannot afford such things. We could make a deal.'

'I like deals. I prefer deals rather than money,' laughed Fieldmann.

They spent some more time talking and Ibram introduced them to his wife and his family of one boy and three girls. They were children with a happy disposition, smiling eyes and gentle temperaments.

Marie looked at the girls. They possessed gentle, supine natures. 'I will prepare Pascha for the Lycée entrance examination. But I will teach them to read and write, too,' she announced. 'It is a very good thing and you will be proud of them.'

The idea that the girls should be educated had not entered the tavern keeper's mind.

Now he looked at his three daughters with their soft skin and bright eyes. 'Yes that would be a good thing. That would be valuable to them. Things are changing a lot. I would like to see them read and write. For this I will give you food. It is a good deal.'

'A very good deal,' Marie replied happily.

Ibram turned to his wife and explained the contents of the conversation. She joined her hands and showed her delight by looking towards the roof.

They stayed in the tavern for two hours. Fieldmann sent one of the girls to fetch a suitcase from the cart, he opened it and took out his pad and pencil. Very quickly he drew the young girls. The men at the end of the tavern came and watched as he quickly outlined the figures. They were greatly amazed at his skill. He handed them to Ibram.

He was obviously proud of the result. 'He is a great artist from Austria,' he explained to his friends. 'He has painted a portrait of the Emperor.'

The portrait generated much excitement in the tavern and others who lived in the square quickly heard about the artist who was a friend of Ibram. They gathered in to see him at work. Fieldmann felt able to relax. The spontaneous nature of the place, the genuine response to his work and the pleasure they derived from his sketch brought out the best side of his mind. Marie looked on, happy to be in such a secure and contented place. She had not eaten so well in a week and the local wine was heavy and dark and induced sleep.

Three hours later Marie and Jakov left the tavern, with the four children. They directed them up several small cobblestoned streets to a small house set on a ledge above the village and the sea. A French window opened on to a small garden at the front, with trellis fencing, brown and weather-beaten, and tangled with exuberant vegetation.

Two orange trees grew in one corner of the garden close to some vines.

'It belonged to a Jewish Rabbi,' Pascha explained. 'He died a year ago and my father bought it at a public auction. It is filled with old books which we do not understand. But we have left them there. My father said that they should rest there until someone came along who understood such matters. He respects books.'

They entered the house. The walls were lime-washed. The furniture was simple. In the bedroom there was a deep bed with a down mattress. Sheets and blankets were folded in a neat pile by the window. Only the study remained intact with its rows of books lining the walls. Some were printed on cheap paper, others were bound in leather and some others, too long to place on shelves, lay piled in neat order. There was an atmosphere of austere intellectuality about the place.

Fieldmann and Marie stood at the centre of the room, placing their hands on the large table, and looked about them at the books. For years they had travelled from town to town with only a few books in their luggage. They had read with the aid of candlelight in lofts and garrets. There was never a time when they could sit down in an armchair and spend a whole day reading a book in security and comfort. Here, at last, above the shores of the Black Sea, they could find time to rest and think.

Marie opened the French windows. A light wind, carrying the scent of flowers through the house, filled every room with its freshness.

With the aid of the children they carried their few possessions into the house. Sometime later when the children left they stood alone in their room above the sea. They placed their arms about each other and remained silent. The journeys through Russia, the nights they had spent in rough shelters, the lack of good food had taken their toll upon their bodies and minds.

'This is the first time we have been lucky in a long time,' Marie said wearily. 'I will sleep for a whole week and I will lie in the sun until my body is bronzed and I will swim in the sea again,' she promised.

The children had carried fruit, cheese and bread to the house. Sitting in the garden, with the breeze blowing up from the sea, they ate a pleasant meal slowly and with joy.

'I must sleep now,' Marie said later. She removed her clothes and let them fall onto the floor. Fieldmann looked at her tall body. It was still beautiful and perfect. But the skin was white and anaemic and her ribs showed when she stretched herself. The raw food of the steppes had not suited her. She needed rest now. He watched her walk from the room, her movements graceful and assured.

When she reached the bedroom she felt the comfortable down mattress. It was like velvet to the touch. She lay down on it, feeling its smoothness against her body. She drew a coverlet over her and fell soundly asleep.

For some reason or other she dreamt of her stepfather. He was dressed like a rabbi, making his way furtively through a dark ghetto.

Jakov Fieldmann looked towards the sea. Its eternal quality filled his mind. He, too, felt tired. He had abandoned his art for too long. He had spent useless years in exile from his friends, a nomad passing across great spaces of land with no roots set in any place.

Now, he felt that he was at home. The beauty of the area, its soft climate and luxuriant vegetation, was like some narcotic substance, working in his mind. Sleep seemed to fill the air. He looked down upon the emerald sea, the even waves moving towards the shore, the opaque haze which erased the horizon. He fell asleep in the armchair.

Their days at Loslov soon fell into a pattern. Each morning at ten o'clock the children arrived for their lessons. They were eager to learn and advanced quickly, particularly the young girl, Amina, who learned how to read and write. Sometimes their mother came with them and sat down at the table. She had a soft olive face and a patient expression. Her life had imposed limits on her which she accepted.

But soon she began to make the letters of the Russian alphabet with her small plump hand and her face filled with pleasure when Marie praised her. She was very excited on the day she wrote her first word. The simple woman had been give a new power and a new vision. She began to smile. Later she would read her first book purchased from an elementary school in Odessa.

Ibram was pleased at the progress of his children and his wife. She began to grow in his estimation. No woman in her village which lay to the east of the town had ever learned to read.

Fieldmann did not begin to paint immediately. He preferred to walk in the hills and observe nature in its luxury. Never in his life had he been exposed to such colours and to such a variety of vegetation. Sometimes he took handfuls of the free fertile earth and let it slip through his fingers, feeling its cool luxury.

He looked at the scope of the blue sky and the purple mountains running away in the distance. The intensity of the colours almost frightened him. He knew that he would have to change his palette; if he were to paint this landscape he would have to use vermilion, bright yellow, bright green, wine red and violet – all the rich colours. And beneath all this must lie heat and intensity.

The astounding gaiety of the landscape entered Jakov's mind. Sometimes he failed to return in the evenings, but went up into the mountains and lay on a blanket under the stars, drawing in the night scents, and waking in the morning to the sound of insects and birds. He would return next day filled with ideas for paintings. But he never touched his easel and canvas which stood in the room facing the sea. Instead he rested in his wicker armchair and looked at the magnificent scenery which lay before him.

'Do you not feel the urge to paint in such pleasant surroundings?' Marie asked him one night as they looked down at the small lights of the harbour village.

'Do not ask me such questions,' he replied angrily 'I will begin when the time is right. Someday I will begin. I do not know when but it cannot be hurried. I wish only to walk in the hills and the mountains, to visit the orchards and the vineyards and look closely at all that is happening.'

What he saw in the villages and in the hills was as eternal and elemental as the sea; men working the earth as they had since settled times; vines being tended on the slopes; fishermen casting their nets into the sea. Jakov passed from village to village and looked at the shapes and mass of the houses, the onion domes of Orthodox churches, the minarets of the Muslim world. He noted the dresses of the women as they went about their work in the fields and in the streets.

He began slowly to forget the masterpiece he had once created in Vienna and which had been destroyed by the secret police. Perhaps they had destroyed his artistic interest in the west. Now he studied the Byzantine saints with their austere faces, the luxury of their robes done in mosaic. He began to see composition in terms of fragments of light, strong, square brushstrokes which captured the luminosity of life.

Then one day Jakov began to read the rabbinical literature in the library. He was surprised at the breadth of its vision. Not only were there books on the Old Testament, but there were histories of the Jews after the Diaspora. He read avidly for many weeks, lighting an oil lamp at night and reading in the soft glow of the light. Colours and shapes and themes began to form in his mind.

Despite all that he felt that there was something missing. He had not discovered the vital colour to carry his paintings beyond shape and weight and give them mysterious substance. Then, one evening, as he was looking towards the old village, he discovered what he had been lacking. It had been staring him in the face for so long he had failed to recognise it. As the sun caught the golden cross above the onion dome, it shone in full lustre above the village. He would use gold in his paintings, as the old craftsmen had used gold in their mosaics. He had discovered the mystical colour.

One morning he went to the cabin at the side of the house. It was cluttered with simple objects he had purchased in the bazaars at Odessa: icons, vases, copper urns. He took the charcoal in his hand and knew that he had picked the correct time to begin. Quickly, he drew remembered shapes of minarets and domes, the old streets of the village, and above them he placed a figure of a Rabbi, brooding over the village scape and the rich vegetation. It was the picture which he found most joy in creating and he painted in a single day. Twice Marie had come to the door to offer him some food but he told her to go away. Instead he drank the red wine of the locality as he stood back from the painting and appraised it. It was a new vision and it had not been attempted before. Even Klimt had not been so adventurous in the use of shape and colour.

It was evening when it was finished. Jakov sat down on his stool, exhausted, and looked at the painting. He was proud of his work and more proud of his courage. His art had an eastern quality now and his style did not belong to any jaded western school. The colours, still wet, glowed with power and mystery. He finished his wine and stumbled from the small shed.

Marie was reading by the globed light in the front room. She looked up at his exhausted face. 'I will eat now,' he told her simply.

It was only later that she plucked up the courage to ask him how his work had progressed.

'I have finished a painting. If you wish you can take the light out to my studio and examine it,' Jakov told her.

She was excited and afraid as she entered the garden and made her way towards the shed. Below her the lights of the village burned and further down the coast she could see the small lights of other villages. The garden was filled with the rich scents of late autumn.

She walked into the studio and the lamp flickered for a moment and she thought that it might go out. Standing before the painting, Marie was amazed at its quality and at how much had been compressed into one canvas. It glowed with the colour and the mystery of the area. It had taken its inspiration from all the icons and primitive paintings they had seen in Russia, gathering all the elements into a powerful painting.

She closed the shed door and returned to the house. Fieldmann was nowhere to be seen. Then she heard him snoring in the bedroom. She did not wake him. She returned to the room and sitting on the chair looked out into the darkness and at the stars above the sea. She felt in harmony with the beauty about her.

Chapter Twenty-three

The next two years at Loslov proved to be the happiest in their lives. Marie recovered her strength and an old brightness returned to her eyes. She looked forward eagerly to the morning visits from the children, when they made their way up the steep path, chattering. They were making progress and were eager to learn from their new mistress.

The day before Pascha sat his examinations for the Lycée at Odessa she visited Ibram's tavern. The family were anxious. Ibram wanted his son to be a professional man as it would give him status in the town. He was always concerned about his status.

'I am very nervous, very nervous,' Ibram told her when she came in. She sat in a corner and he brought her wine. Then he sat down beside her.

'I watch him study day and night. There is no end to the books. I counted them – ten. He is growing tired and I wonder if his memory will work. Perhaps it will seize up.'

She reassured him. 'I have taught Pascha how to remember things. He knows several tricks for recalling what he has learned.'

'But this examination is not a game. They come from all over the province to compete. Some of these children are very clever, very clever,' Ibram frowned.

'I can assure you that we have studied all the examination papers. I have tested him against all the old questions. I have been to Odessa and asked for advice.' Marie continued, smiling, 'You should take a holiday. If your son catches your anxiety it will be like a disease and it will work against him. Go to the country and make one of these deals with farmers.'

'And leave my boy?'

'Yes. Leave your boy. He can get along well without you.'

Ibram played nervously with his worry beads for some time. 'Perhaps he needs me?'

'I can assure you it would be better if you left the place. It will be here when you return,' she laughed.

He called his wife from the kitchen and they whispered together. Then he returned to where she sat.

'She agrees with you. She says I make my son nervous. I worry too much. So I have decided to leave the place and do some business. Will you bring him to the examination hall and make certain that he is there before time?'

'I promise.'

He took a bundle of notes from his robe and handed them to her. Marie refused to accept them. 'You have been more than generous to me, Ibram. I cannot accept your money. We have become good friends and this is unnecessary.' Her voice was firm.

He replaced the roll of money in a pocket of his robe. 'I will leave without delay.'

Ibram said goodbye to his son and called one of his workmen to harness two mules for the journey. He set off in the evening time when the sun was passing down the western sky and a cooling breeze was coming in off the sea. They watched him ride down the street, a large Muslim man on a small sturdy mule with his old workman riding beside him.

'Will you eat with us this evening, Marie?' Ibram's wife asked.

'Yes. Fieldmann has gone up into the hills to paint and I do not expect him to return for a few days. He wishes to be alone.'

They ate their meal in an enclosed courtyard which was

filled with potted plants and trailing vines. The air carried the heavy scent of flowers and small candles burned in lanterns in the corners. By now it was dark and the sounds of night filled the place. They sat around the table and talked of village life. Marie had become acquainted with the people of the locality and took an interest in the gossip.

She was very content in this enclosed place and at the warm simplicity which surrounded her. It was at moments like this that she doubted her revolutionary enthusiasm. Why was it necessary to engage in some abstract class struggle? The world had always been an unequal place to live in and she doubted if her voice and actions carried any weight. Perhaps Ibram and his family had the answer to most of the problems which were agitating the great cities across Europe.

Marie did not remain too late in the house, but said goodbye and promised to be ready early for the journey to Odessa. As she walked up the path to her house she felt a wave of great calm take possession of her. The stars were glowing in the sky like lanterns and she looked at them in awe. Mariners had passed across the sea beneath her with only these stars to guide them. They were pointers to unknown destinations.

The town was now asleep. Here and there a light showed and she could hear the faint pulse of the sea as the waves washed up on the pebbled beach. Marie felt drugged by the scents and the joy of the night.

She slept soundly and awoke early as the light poured into the eastern sky. She dressed quickly in a neat dress and made her way down to the tavern. There was great excitement in the courtyard. Pascha was dressed in his best western clothes and carried a small travelling bag.

They set off for Odessa by train. Pascha sat at the window, his face filled with wonder as the train followed the shore, never out of view of the sea.

They reached the great city later in the day. Odessa was a strongly fortified sea port, which gave Russia access to the Mediterranean. In its great warehouses were stored the harvests of the south which were exported throughout the southern countries. The Empress Catherine who founded it had chosen her site well. The bay was extensive and the anchorage good and above it the delightful city sloped gently towards the harbour.

Following the directions given by Ibram, Marie and Pascha reached the Muslim quarter. Close to a mosque whose walls were decorated with bright blue ceramic tiles, they found the address of Imar who was a merchant.

They entered a small courtyard, covered with a trellis-work of vines, where the sun broke through in mottled light.

A woman, her face concealed by a veil, came out when they rang the bell and invited them into the house. It was filled with oriental carpets, stretched on the timber floors or hanging on the walls. They gave the interiors a sense of lightness and colour.

There was a babble of voices from somewhere in the house and soon a whole group of women poured into the hall. They talked incessantly and gathered around their guests. They looked at the western woman with her neat clothes, her white open features and the sandals on her feet and they made a great fuss of Pascha who stood in their midst quite amazed at the attention he was receiving.

When they had been shown to their attic rooms, Marie remained with Pascha for some time. She set out his books on a small table and directed him to go over certain pages in preparation for his examination. He was quiet and obedient and a little in awe of the immense city. She told him that she would leave him for some time and then return to see how his work was progressing.

Marie left the house and set off to explore the city. It was now warm and she kept to the cool side of the street. She was looking in a shop window when she heard a familiar voice beside her. For a moment she could not believe her ears. She turned quickly and faced the chubby features of the Armenian. She barely recognised him. His hair had been cut and he had grown a large moustache. His body had become corpulent.

'When were you released?' she asked, looking nervously up and down the street. She knew that the secret service had agents everywhere, particularly in Odessa, which was the Western Gate of Russia. With the variety of accents and cultures in the city it was easy for an agent to disappear into a crowd or hide in the catacombs which ran for a hundred miles under the city and the surrounding area. To have a knowledge of the catacombs was to have a key to the secrets of the city.

'I escaped. I could not endure the snows and the ice and the winter any longer. So I am here now with a new identity. As you see I have put on a lot of weight. I have hidden my old self inside this comfortable flesh. I have been here with some friends for many months,' he told her.

'And have you found work?' she asked.

'I write for a newspaper. I can assure you I do not write about political matters. I have a social column and it gains me access to the best places. I never realised how vain the aristocracy were. They cultivate me and even confide in me. If there is a whisper of gossip in the city I am the first to hear about it. With my press card I can move about the area. It suits my intentions very well.'

Had she not known his previous life she would have believed that he was a man about town. He carried his cane with confidence and he wore his white hat at a cocky angle. She found it difficult to reconcile the fanatic she had known at Simbirsk with the corpulent dandy who stood before her now.

'May I invite you for a cup of coffee, or perhaps something stronger? I frequent the most fashionable places, I can assure you.' His smile did not reach his eyes.

'I would like a cup of coffee. It is rather warm standing in the street.'

The literary café to which he brought her was panelled in dark brown timber. Great potted plants in burnished urns were scattered about the place in profusion.

'It is like a botanical garden. However, I prefer to call it a jungle, for the finest female predators in Odessa move between its fronds.'

The head waiter, immaculate in his dress suit, arrived at the table and bowed courteously.

'I shall have some cognac. The lady, I believe, would like some coffee. Could we have a tray of confectionery, too, please.'

'Very well, sir. Countess Olga Kurlov was inquiring for you today. She was quite angry that you did not mention her in your social column. It took me some time to restrain her temper.'

The Armenian frowned. 'She is a faded rose. There are younger beauties who have taken her place.'

The waiter left, very much impressed by what he had heard.

'Always treat a lady like a kitchen maid and a kitchen maid like a lady. It works wonders.'

Marie could not understand the changes which had taken place in the Armenian. He had never lacked confidence and he had been a master of disguise. His only weakness was that he was too sure of himself. It had been his downfall before.

When the cognac and the coffee had been served and Marie had been persuaded to have some of the pastries they settled down to a pleasant conversation.

After a while the Armenian reached into his pocket and took out an ornate envelope. 'You may, perhaps, be interested in this,' he said handing it to her.

The first thing which struck Marie was that it bore the imperial seal of the Tsar. She took out the card – an invitation – and studied it. Then she looked up at him and realised the implications of what she held in her hand. His eyes were cool and searching. 'You have penetrated the police ring around the Tsar in a most subtle way,' she told him.

'When I was in the prison camp I realised what we were doing wrong. We were dressed like revolutionaries. We were obvious targets for the police. We could easily be identified. Now, I can walk past the secret service on the arm of some notable and charming woman.' He paused, then continued, 'I believe I should see Fieldmann. I think that he might be interested in a proposition I would like to make.'

It was at this point that Marie realised she had made a mistake. The Armenian had been dangerous in the past. Now he was more dangerous. His mind and manner had grown subtle.

'I don't believe he would be interested in any plans for the moment. He is growing stronger each day and his health is returning. And he is painting again. He has not painted for several years. I believe that his work at present is more important than any revolution.'

'I am not speaking of revolution. I would like to meet him for old times' sake. Perhaps I could visit him, in secret. I have no intention of preaching revolution. I am a gossip columnist. I have lost the taste for the harsh life of the camps I can assure you.'

Marie noted how quickly his manner had changed. He knew precisely what he was implying when he showed her the invitation card. Now he was retreating from his position.

'I think it is better if you do not meet,' she insisted. 'His mind remains tired. He needs rest and he needs to paint.'

'Very well. It was a pleasure meeting you after the intervening years. Perhaps we will meet again on some social occasion. I take an interest in all my friends.'

Marie excused herself and left the café, her mind in

turmoil. The Armenian was the most dangerous man she had encountered in Russia. She still believed in her instincts. She believed that he was a double agent.

She continued to walk along the Primrose Boulevard, but the beauty of the promenade with its magnificent architectural front, the great steps which led down to the harbour in a generous sweep, could not distract her from her encounter with the Armenian. He was dangerous. Everyone who had been drawn into his circle three years ago had been destroyed. Only Marie was immune to his poison. However, Fieldmann might be seduced away from his work, perhaps drawn into some mad scheme to assassinate the Tsar. Marie shuddered at the idea as she made her way back to the Muslim quarter of the city.

She was delighted to sit down with the women, enjoy their simple food and the local conversation. Their minds did not range beyond the quarter, but they were filled with wonder and small gossip satisfied them.

Marie's sleep that night was troubled by images of the Armenian, but next day, the excitement of the examinations engaged her interests. She was as anxious as any parent she realised as she accompanied Pascha to the examination hall.

At midday she was waiting for him at the entrance. There was a pleased look on his face. The questions which they had prepared had turned up. On the small green in front of the college they sat under a tree and had a small picnic. Marie insisted that he would eat only fine morsels as too much food would make him drowsy during the warm afternoon. Before Pascha returned to the hall they prepared the questions in Geography, rhyming off the couplets she had composed to help him remember facts. She left him at the door and watched him walk to his desk in the great hall, a small, neat, figure lost in the vastness of the place.

That evening there was an occasion to celebrate at the Imar's home. Pascha was happy with his performance, telling the women how easily he had recalled the towns of

Russia and the rivers which flow into the Baltic as well as the imports and exports of the vast empire. The simple women were greatly impressed. They could not understand how such a small and young mind could carry such an amount of knowledge. Some wondered if it were a bad thing to have so much wisdom stored in a young head. Perhaps it might being on a fever.

Two days later the examinations were over and it was time to return home. The family accompanied Marie and Pascha to the station and waved to them until they turned a bend and were out of view.

When they returned to Ibram's tavern there was great excitement. There were a thousand questions to be answered. Late that evening Marie said goodnight to the family and walked up the hill towards the house. She had a sense that she belonged to this landscape more than any other.

There was light burning in the front room of the house when Marie entered. Fieldmann was sitting in an armchair, reading from one of the Jewish books. She placed her hands on his shoulders and bending down, kissed him on the cheek.

'I have something to show you,' he told her.

They went outside and walked across the path to the studio. He opened the door and showed her in. She gazed at the canvas he had finished in wonder. It was a stylised landscape of the harbour and above it her nude figure floated, ethereal and translucent. In the painting, she had become part of the place and the feelings she had experienced as she walked up the hill were expressed in a warm visual form.

She would never feel quite as happy and fulfilled again. She turned to Jakov and put her arms around him and held his tough body close to hers. Then she undressed him and looked at the craggy roughness of his body. She drew off her dress and they lay naked in the grass. They made love under the stars and surrounded by green, growing things.

Chapter Twenty-four

There was great excitement when the results of Pascha's examination arrived. Ibram rushed up the hill, breathless with excitement, shaking the paper in his hands. He tried to talk when Marie opened the door. He placed his hand on his heart and tried to catch his breath. 'Pascha has passed. My son has passed. Next year he will attend the Lycée. I am a very proud man this day. You come immediately to the house and celebrate with us. We must all celebrate.'

Fieldmann and Marie hurried down the path to the square. Already news had spread and as they entered the crowded tavern and the courtyard, the women were quickly preparing plates of food and the men were drinking.

'We owe our success to Marie,' Ibram told his neighbours. 'She is a very intelligent woman. She knew what questions were on the papers even before Pascha entered the great examination hall at Odessa.' He continued emotionally, 'Others come here on holidays from the cold centre of Russia. But you have come here and given us your help. We are grateful to you. You stay as long as you wish.'

As Marie looked at the great crowd in the courtyard, she felt that she now belonged in this corner of the Crimea. She had proven her worth to the people. Many now asked her to educate their children so that they, too, could go to the Lycée and make something of their lives. They would not always stay in the village and look up at the slopes on which were built the houses of the wealthy who worked in Odessa.

It was during the celebrations that Fieldmann told Marie that he must leave immediately for Odessa. He did not explain the nature of his business. He simply said that he might be away for a few days.

It was only when he left the party that she began to have doubts. Perhaps the Armenian had discovered their address. He was a persistent man who stopped at nothing to achieve his aims. However, not wanting to spoil the day she dismissed the thought from her mind and remained on with Ibram and his family. It was a most pleasant day and she was tired and slightly drunk as she made her way up the path. She had achieved something which had given her great satisfaction.

Two days before the celebrations, Fieldmann had received a letter from the Armenian. He had studied the stamp mark and wondered who could be writing to him from Odessa or who knew his address. When he opened it he discovered that it was a typed letter which was unusual. He studied the signature at the bottom. It was a name once used by the Armenian.

For a moment his heart missed a beat. He was about to tear the letter up but some fatal fascination prompted him to read it again. He recognised all the code words in the bland letter and recalled the activities of the Armenian in Simbirsk. He had drawn him into an almost-fatal plot. As a result of his association with the Armenian he had been forced to leave the town in a hurry.

For two days Jakov pondered the Armenian's invitation. Then, curiosity and the memory of old times settled the question. Jakov decided to meet him, but even as the train sped towards Odessa he was still in two minds. He looked out at the tranquil sea, green and turquoise, and reflected on the peaceful life he now led. There was so much work to do, so many paintings he had planned to paint. He knew that because of his decision, he might never enjoy the opportunity again. This life which had been so tranquil had been disturbed by his revolutionary past.

Jakov got off the train at Odessa and made his way to the offices of the *Centurion* newspaper. He walked through the door of the imposing building with its old frontage and frosted windows. Inside, the place smelled of cigar smoke and paper. He discovered the Armenian in one of the spacious cubicles, dressed in a white suit with a blue velvet waistcoat, and a white hat with a black band. He was sitting on a leather chair, his hands on the knob of a silver cane, dictating his social column to an intense young lady. Jakov barely recognised him.

'Ah, my good friend Fieldmann. How charming of you to come and visit me at my office. 'Marta,' he looked at the young woman, 'Let me introduce Vienna's greatest artist. Some of his works hang in the finest homes in Paris.'

Waving Jakov to the door he continued, 'We are going to dinner at my club. I believe that I have given you enough titbits to write up a most flattering column. And if Countess Anna phones please tell her I am engaged. I shall not be able to attend her party tonight. Tell her I am horribly disappointed. I have already accepted another invitation.'

Fieldmann studied the Armenian. He had put on at least three stone, possessed heavy jowls and pudgy fingers. He had lost his nervous habits and spoke with a slow sophisticated accent. Even his conversation had changed. It seemed trivial and frivolous.

They left the building together, the Armenian walking with a slow elegance, raising his hat to anyone he recognised and giving a slight bow. Fieldmann felt scruffy walking beside him.

As if sensing his thoughts, the Armenian said, 'If you are to dine with me at my club, then you will have to look more like an artist. They have a certain conception of an artist in the social circles in Odessa. Let us humour it. We shall go to my barber and while you are being shaved I will send for something more appropriate to your high calling. Leave it to me. I know exactly what I am doing.'

It never struck Fieldmann that he should object. He was being sucked into this man's net.

When they reached the barber shop he had Fieldmann sit down on a luxurious armchair in front of a sink framed in chintz and a bevelled mirror. The Armenian studied the craggy bearded face for some time. 'Keep the rugged appearance, but trim back the beard. The face looks too thick. Remove some of the hair from the side of his face.'

The Armenian continued to watch as the barber followed his instructions. 'Is the gentleman pleased?' the barber asked obsequiously when he had finished.

'Very satisfactory. Now have the tailor bring some velvet jackets and a choice of cravats here. The trousers will do. They have that worn appearance which we associate with artists.'

One hour later Fieldmann was transformed. The Armenian paid the bills and gave a handsome tip to the barber.

When they left the shop, Fieldmann said brusquely, 'I have gone along with your little scheme for the moment, but you are up to your old tricks. Tell me what is going on.'

'I am up to my new tricks and I will tell you precisely what is on my mind during our meal. As you see, I have changed my guise somewhat. Time spent in a labour camp sharpens a man's mind very finely. You remember once that we worked on the edge of things? We never knew what was going on in the inner circles. Well, I decided to make myself welcome in these circles and no place is better than Odessa. Even the police chief welcomes me here as a friend.'

'You go too far.'

'Yes, I go too far and that is why I am not recognised. I possess excellently forged papers. I have an impeccable past and some of my phrases, many of them borrowed from Oscar Wilde, are widely quoted in Odessa.'

The arrogance of the Armenian amazed Jakov. He caught him by the sleeve and stopped him. 'There is no offer which you can make that I will accept. I came here on a social visit.'

'Then a social visit it will remain,' the Armenian smiled.

They reached the club, a large room with panelled walls and paintings of generals and high government officials. The Armenian bowed regally to the guests at the tables as he made his way down to a window which overlooked the seafront.

He ordered a sumptuous meal. Fieldmann had enjoyed plain food for so long that he could only eat small morsels of the exotic food. Looking at the Armenian he could understand why he had put on so much weight in these surroundings. He tucked into his food and spoke glowingly of its texture and flavour. When he was finished and in a relaxed mood he took the same ornamented invitation that he had shown to Marie from his pocket.

'You have seen the Tsar then?'

'Seen him? I have spoken to him. Quite an offensive gentleman and almost plebeian in his choice of clothes. His wife, the German woman, is overbearing, quite impossible to talk to. I believe that she does her crochet even while they are taking the sun in the south. The courts flock about them; ministers come and go from Saint Petersburg for them and generals and admirals are two a penny. Such then are the Tsar and Tsarina of Russia.'

Fieldmann looked at the card. He knew the Armenian's tactics. 'This could be a forgery,' he snapped back.

'Forgery, my dear friend? I can assure you I was at the palace. Here, read this.' He drew a page of a magazine from his pocket. It gave a list of the guests at the Tsar's garden party. The Armenian's name was amongst them.

Jakov looked at the heavy face and the sensual lips, the large blue eyes staring at him. He knew precisely what was going on in his comrade's devious mind.

It struck him for the moment that the man might be a double agent. Perhaps he was drawing him into a position where the secret police could throw him in prison. On the other hand if the Armenian still retained his revolutionary beliefs he was now in a position where he could assassinate the Tsar and his family and many members of the court. Fieldmann started. The idea was beyond belief. He could throw all of Russia into turmoil. A bloodbath would follow, equal in savagery to that of the French Revolution.

The Armenian broke into his thoughts, 'There have been many revolutionaries who would have given their lives to be in my position. But we must be careful with our words.'

He paid the bill and they left the club.

'It is my custom to sleep for a period after such an excellent meal. It is a habit I have developed since I arrived at Odessa. It grows intensely warm at three. So let me take you to my apartment. I have arranged a bed for you to rest. My man is expecting you.'

His apartment was as exotic as his way of life. It was decorated in oriental fashion: red wallpaper covered the walls, persian carpets were spread across the floor, lights glowed in corners and the heavy tasselled curtains were drawn halfway across the windows to keep out the light. There was a heavy scent of opium in the air. The 'man' the Armenian had mentioned was a youth of about twenty with Turkish features. He was dressed in light silk clothes and was effeminate in his gestures.

'Permit me to introduce Mohammed. He's my pet. We shall retire to the bedroom for a siesta. You may stay across the corridor from us. In fact, I would prefer if you did. I shall see you at five o'clock.'

Fieldmann found the whole atmosphere of the place cloying. He wished that he was walking in the hills outside the village, or working with the peasants in a local vineyard. He retired to the room, took a book from a small library and began to read.

The Armenian appeared at five o'clock. He had changed into more formal attire, but it still had a faintly decadent look about it. His olive skin possessed a sheen like that of a seal. His man fussed about him arranging his wide, red cravat, brushing imaginary dust from his lapels and arranging a flower in his buttonhole. Standing in front of the large mirror he looked at himself, swivelling his large head to obtain the best view of his features. He patted his stomach with satisfaction. Then he turned to Mohammed and asked him to pour some white wine.

As Fieldmann studied each languid gesture he began to have increasing doubts about the Armenian. His luck had been too good and his fortune too easily acquired. He did not believe that he still possessed the fiery ambition which had once burned in his mind. The thought that perhaps he was a double agent began again to tease the edge of his mind.

He accepted a glass of wine. It had a fine quality and was fruity to the palate. But like everything else in the place it seemed tinged with decadence.

Lying on a chaise longue the Armenian discussed the present state of art and literature in Russia. He believed that it was the harbinger of social chaos. 'Of course we must have social chaos. It is as necessary as the chaos in Genesis out of which the world was created. How many years this chaos will reign is another thing. Certainly all the old remnants of the nineteenth century must be swept away. Finally we may create the new Utopia,' he concluded.

Fieldmann had heard the argument a thousand times before. In every literary club in every city and town in Russia the same phrases were used. 'There is chaos already. What we need is a new order. We need a parliament which will take over the running of the country. The civil service must be kept in place and we must have a plan. At present Russia is without a plan,' Fieldmann told him firmly.

'You are becoming an economist,' the Armenian replied.

'I am practical. If there is chaos then the poor will suffer.'

'They always suffer. Those at the base of the social heap will go under. It is a necessary consequence of evolution. Then a finer type will emerge.'

It was a futile conversation and one without conviction on the Armenian's part. Fieldmann felt that he was probing his ideas, finding some avenue by which to draw him into some vague plan that was forming in his mind. The Armenian never spoke without some purpose.

Nevertheless he continued, 'I have lived with them and I know their defects. They need land. It is in their blood and must be vested in them. Landless liberation is useless. And then they must be educated in the use of land. Communes will not work. Give every man a parcel of land and let him work it. It will give him a purpose. At present he is the plaything of social planners and legalists.'

This was too practical for the Armenian. He had never followed a plough, never dressed a vine, or spent a long winter with the peasants. 'It could be an endless subject for conversation, but we must call a cab. We are expected at the Postmaster General's house at eight. Like his letters, he is a punctual man and believes in promptness.'

They set off in the cab for the Postmaster General's estate on the outskirts of Odessa. It was summer and the sky was still light. The landscape was delicate under a smoky haze. The scents of the Crimea were in the air.

Electric lanterns lit the long avenue to the white mansion of the Postmaster General, and through the windows, they could see the figures of the ladies in their long flowing dresses in the great gallery which ran along the left wing.

Tall windows had been opened to catch the summer air and as they descended from the cab, Fieldmann and his companion could hear the graceful music of a waltz floating out into the garden.

When they entered the great hall Fieldmann was overcome by the opulent splendour of the mansion. The floor was of white marble, grey-veined and polished. A great crystal chandelier hung from a ceiling, splintering the light into blues and silvers. Statues stood in white ochre alcoves and everywhere flowers were packed into tall Chinese vases.

The Armenian led Jakov across the hall, passing impeccably dressed men and women, drinking champagne from long-stemmed glasses, their conversation tailored for these occasions. Even the laughter of the women was light and musical and of little substance.

Fieldmann felt awkward in his artist's clothes. He stood for a moment and took in the whole scene. He had not seen such elegance in Vienna. He wished for a moment that he could escape from his condition but immediately the Armenian called out to someone and two ladies approached him. They were very charming and possessed fine skin. Their flesh was pampered and opulent like the mansion itself. Their conversation, their dress, their movements were in harmony with the place.

The Armenian introduced Jakov as a portrait artist from Vienna and his acquaintances were immediately interested in what went on at the court of the Imperial city. Jakov explained that he had not visited the city for some time but it amused him to give them the impression that he was acquainted with court circles. The Armenian explained to them that several of his paintings had been purchased by discriminating buyers in Paris.

Gradually Jakov began to fit in with the crowd.

Their food was carried to them on porcelain plates. They ate small morsels and as soon as they had finished a servant discreetly carried away the plate. The whole occasion moved at an elegant pace. The gauze curtains billowed slightly in the wind like a magical backdrop.

Much later the Armenian led him to a small man with a

bald head and a heavy moustache. He wore several medals on his velvet frock coat.

'Let me introduce you to our Postmaster General, Nikolai Shulgin. Without him the whole train system of the Crimea would grind to a halt.'

'You flatter me,' Shulgin smiled. It was obvious that he liked to be flattered.

'I was suggesting earlier to the Postmaster General that you would be interested in painting his family's portrait. They do, of course, possess the work of several reputable artists but I think one by Fieldmann would add to his fine collection.'

'Indeed. If it could be fitted in. I am, of course, a very busy man,' Shulgin said self importantly.

'I am sure you can draw yourself away from a busy schedule for a sitting. Perhaps Jakov could visit your office in Odessa.

'Perhaps.'

The conversation might have flagged had not the Armenian observed that the Postmaster General was wearing a new insignia. He examined it.

'An honour from our Tsar,' Shulgin told them proudly.

'And most worthy. I believe that you keep the train lines free when he is visiting the Crimea?'

'Yes. It is most essential. I receive prior notice from Saint Petersburg. All very secret of course. There is always the danger of assassination from revolutionaries. That is why we have to have two trains ready. In that we way we throw the would be assassins. And only an hour before they pass through the stations are the stationmasters told which one is the real royal train.

'I believe the Tsar and his family come only in spring. The rest of the year is spent at Tsarskoe Selo, is it not?' the Armenian asked innocently.

'That is not strictly correct. At any moment I may receive a telegram from the Palace. We have to be on constant alert.'

Fieldmann watched closely as the Armenian extracted information from the pompous little figure. It was the purpose of his visit to the villa. Everything the Armenian did had some purpose or other.

The rest of the evening passed pleasantly. Fieldmann turned down several offers to paint family portraits. It was something which he detested when he had no feeling for his subjects.

That night as they returned through the darkness to Odessa he reflected on all that had happened.

Mohammed was waiting on their return, and the Armenian lay on the chaise longue and smoked opium while they talked.

'If you can find out the times when the trains pass through the Crimea then we can change the present order of things. I have some young men prepared to assassinate the royal family,' he told Jakov.

'I do not think I wish to have any part in this. It is too dangerous.'

'Sleep on it. This will be your one chance to put an end to the old order.'

That night Fieldmann tossed and turned in his bed. He was a revolutionary, but this plot was a foolish and a dangerous one, with only a slim chance of success. However, it might be better than no chance at all.

The next day he had still not made up his mind. He went for a long walk in the hills, considering the matter. When he returned that evening he decided to go along with the Armenian's plans.

Chapter Twenty-five

Two weeks later Fieldmann began to make general sketches of the Shulgin family. They were innocuous people: a small, plump man, a wife, much taller, with sharp features and a scrawny neck, two plain daughters. His subjects were boring and of little interest. Fieldmann would have preferred to have painted the servants or the stable boys. The world at the mansion was far removed from normal reality.

However, his close relationship with the Shulgin family gave him free access to the house. Sometimes, when he worked late, he stayed there the night. He often sat in the kitchen with the servants and sketched them at work or sat in the yard and observed the ritual of life. He also discovered that there was a switchboard in the house, manned by a young man with intelligent features, who sat for hours waiting for calls which he would put through to Odessa. Fieldmann had noticed that the young man's reading was often of a revolutionary nature so he often sat and talked with him and asked him about his work.

'It is often tedious. The girls use the telephone a lot and call their friends. However, just once a week there may be a phone call from Moscow or St Petersburg which is of national importance. They may ask me to arrange that one of the train lines be closed to let troop trains pass through. Then I have to alert every station along the way. See, these are all the stations. I tap out instructions to them. It can become very involved.' He showed him a map which carried all the codes to the stations. Beneath the black codes lay others in red.

'Are the codes in red for special emergencies?' Fieldmann asked.

'When the Tsar is travelling by train then I use the red codes; the black are for the troops. Of course, you know, two trains always travel when the Tsar makes a journey to the Crimea. In that way assassins are never sure which one carries the Imperial family.'

'And have you any way of knowing which one carries the Tsar?' Fieldmann continued probing.

'No. I have never broken the code. Only the Postmaster General knows which train is a decoy.'

It was information which Fieldmann delivered to the Armenian.

'Good. At least we know the line of communications. I always believed that it was through the office in Odessa. There are certain groups which will be very interested in this. If we break the codes then perhaps we might work out some plan or other.'

Fieldmann was not to know that he was a pawn in a much larger game.

Prince Dmitri's web of intrigue spread across the great empire. He was aware of what was happening in the Crimea and he felt pleased that Fieldmann had so easily fallen into his trap. The Armenian, during the year, had made contact with many of the revolutionary groups in the Crimea. He had even financed the purchase of weapons for many of them, telling them that he would provide information on the movements of the Tsar in the south.

'This is the point in the annual calendar of events when the Tsar is at his weakest,' the Armenian would tell meetings of his groups. 'At other times there is a ring of iron about him. He is flanked by an army. But you cannot flank a railway line. It is exposed for a thousand miles. Pick your correct spot and the assassination can be easily carried out. I know. I was party to a failed assassination attempt. For my troubles I spent two years in Siberia and would still be there had I not escaped,' he had explained to the young revolutionaries.

To prove his point, he would produce documentation. He would place old newspapers articles on the failed plot in front of them and his identification papers, soiled and creased.

Every revolutionary who wished to assassinate the Tsar was drawn towards these groups. They were set up in towns close to the railway line running through the Crimea.

It was a tightly knit organisation, composed of young men and intellectuals.

'Remember, he is the figure which sustains this antique system. Destroy the Tsar and watch the edifice come tumbling down. Only then will we have a representative parliament and a democracy,' the Armenian would preach.

It was on the final day when Fieldmann was putting the finishing touches to the Shulgin family portrait that the young man rushed into the family salon and handed the Postmaster General a telegram. It had just arrived from St Petersburg.

Shulgin studied it carefully. 'But this is extraordinary. The Tsar never visits the Crimea at this time of year. How many trains did you say?'

'One.'

'There is normally two. Are you certain?'

'Yes.'

'Then alert all the stations. Tell them to reschedule all the trains on Tuesday.'

Fieldmann could not believe his good fortune. It seemed as if the fates were on the side of the revolutionaries. Perhaps this might mark the end of the monarchies and the empires. If one fell then the others would fall. Franz Joseph, the Kaiser and all the others.

Then he restrained himself. He quickly worked on the final details, deciding to remain for a further day at the mansion and make certain of the details.

'That is the final sitting,' Fieldmann told his clients. 'Tomorrow I will not require you any more, but I will need work on the finer points of the portrait. I wonder if I could spend the night in the house?' he asked.

'Certainly. I will have the servants prepare the usual bed,' the Postmaster General replied as he studied the family portrait. It was exceptional work, better than all the other portraits which hung in the various rooms. It caught the colour of the Crimea, bright and sparkling and the family looked suitably imperial.

That night Jakov left his room and made his way quietly to the exchange at the back of the house. He drew the railway map from the desk. In red circles stood the codes for the times at which the imperial train would pass through each station. Fieldmann decoded them as the Armenian had instructed. The Tsar and his family were doomed.

Fieldmann was paid well for his portrait and for the next week returned to Loslov and walked the hills, troubled by what lay ahead. At nighttime he turned and twisted in his sleep, unable to shake off the sense that a nightmare was about to happen. He never confided in Marie. She had settled into work at the small school she had founded. Each morning several children trekked up the path to the classroom, where she sat with them, content with her new-found occupation.

Then, the night before the attempt, he turned to her in bed and said directly. 'The Tsar will be assassinated tomorrow.'

She sprang up in the bed. 'What did you say?'

'The Tsar will be assassinated tomorrow. The Armenian has laid the plans. The Imperial train is coming through to Odessa and we know the times at which it will pass through the stations.'

'*We*? Are you implicated?'

He confessed to his part in the plot.

'You fool,' she told him angrily. 'I met the Armenian some months ago. I did not tell you because I knew that he would draw you into his net. I do not trust him. He is up to no good. You remember the last time, when he organised the assassination of a provincial governor? All the others in the group are either dead or in Siberia. He alone struts about Odessa with an obvious fortune at his disposal. What if he is a double agent?'

'It is impossible. If he is then we are all doomed.'

Marie controlled her anger. 'For the first time in many years I have been happy. I have found joy here and I thought perhaps I might settle down. Tomorrow we may be on our travels again. That is if you do not end up in jail.'

'We must prepare our things in case we have to leave quickly in the morning,' Jakov said anxiously.

'I am returning to sleep. Prepare for flight if you wish.'

All that night Fieldmann gathered his paintings and stacked them neatly in a large box. He packed his paints and paintbrushes together with his clothes. In the morning he was ready to depart if the coup failed.

He spoke with Ibram, who understood the situation. 'I have a cellar where you can hide for a few days. It is very old and only I know where it is. You can leave your paintings with me. They will be stored safely.'

Jakov returned to the house and waited.

Prince Dmitri walked through the imperial train checking security arrangements for the next day.

He spoke to the captain. He explained precisely what he expected of him. 'Shoot to kill. We are dealing with revolutionaries. Then use the cavalry to mop up the operation.'

He then went to dinner with a landowner who was an old friend of his family. They sat and talked well into the night. It was a pleasant occasion when he could relax and discuss the petty gossip of the noble families in the area.

He left the house very early on Tuesday morning and boarded the train.

Early that day several groups waited for their final orders from the Armenian. They had been supplied with dynamite and guns. Each group was given a specific point along the track to cover. They were anxious, conscious of the possibly fatal undertaking. Again and again they checked their fuses and their guns. Then at three o'clock in the morning they set out from the towns and the cities and found their exact locations along the track. They set the dynamite and waited for the imperial train.

At twelve o'clock the Imperial train passed the first group and headed for the hilly countryside. They watched it as it made its way towards the assassination point. The gleaming black locomotive drew royal-blue saloon cars, bearing the imperial crest.

As it approached a bend in the track, one of the assassins pushed the plunger. They waited for the dynamite to explode. Nothing happened. Again and again he pushed down the plunger.

The assassins opened fire with their rifles and the train stopped. Immediately the windows of the royal carriages were thrown open and the surrounding area raked with gunfire. The doors of another carriage flew open and mounted Cossacks with swords drawn urged their horses forward. They poured out of the carriage and immediately drove forwards towards the assassins' positions in the shallow hills.

It was soon over. Most of the revolutionaries lay dead. The rest were rounded up and brought to the train. As they approached it they realised that they had been duped. It was an armoured train. A cynical captain, smoking a cigarette, watched the captives as they were kicked aboard.

Immediately the train set out on its journey. By the time it had reached Sebastopol, five young men were confined to one carriage along with thirteen dead. The assassination attempt had been a disastrous failure.

In a cellar beneath a grain store Jacov Fieldmann read the papers Ibram had brought him. He cried when he realised that he had been party to the deaths of so many young men. In one single and well-organised plan the Armenian had wiped out all the revolutionaries in the Crimea.

That day the police arrived at Loslov. They questioned Ibram and his family and ransacked his tavern in search of incriminating evidence.

Two weeks later, when the excitement had died down, Fieldmann and Marie slipped away. It was dark and there was a sailing boat waiting for them in the harbour. It would take them east where they could safely enter the empire again. As they sailed through the dark waters of the Black Sea Fieldmann resolved to track down the Armenian and murder him.

Chapter Twenty-six

'If there is going to be a war it will begin in a Russian protectorate,' Von Hertling told Joseph Steiner as they sat at dinner at his club in Berlin.

'You believe that?'

'Of course I do. Naturally, the diplomats and the press believe that there will be no war, that we are all now civilised people. But let me assure you that this is not so,' the baron said cynically. During the years his hair had turned grey and his skin was creased with thought and intrigue.

Joseph Steiner was dressed in a neat black suit and looked like a government bureaucrat. He had a lonely expression on his face, as if his heart was empty of feeling.

Von Hertling had come to trust the older man's opinions over the years since Sophie had introduced her stepfather to him. Quietly, he had followed Steiner's advice and had invested in several companies in Germany. They were all steel and chemical based.

Now he had a proposal for Joseph Steiner. The baron told him that there was a warehouse, filled with arms, to the north of Berlin and that he would like him to do some business for him in Russia.

'Arms to Russia? What if we are discovered? This could be treasonable!' Joseph exclaimed.

'I can assure you that there is no treason involved. It is a clean deal. Come with me.'

When the meal was finished they left the restaurant. Von Hertling's Daimler was waiting for them. It was a large, comfortable automobile which sped quickly through the boulevards of Berlin.

They drove through the woods which flourished on the great plains around Berlin, until finally they came to a clearing in a forest. They approached a small hillock. It concealed the vast armoury underneath. Several impassive soldiers stood guard in front of the entrance.

The great doors were slipped aside and they drove directly into the centre of the building. Timber crates stood in tall columns along its whole length.

'You could wage a war with the amount of weapons stored here. And I can assure you that this is only part of the arsenal. However, we must clear out the warehouses. These guns return to the smelters or they can be sold. I am offering you twenty per cent on every box you sell. The Russians are eager to buy. You are a broker. Make the deal and we will ship them through Denmark.'

Joseph Steiner opened several cases of guns and examined them. He looked at their markings. They had been erased. 'Good to fight a war in Africa, but not in Europe. They are out of date,' he said.

'You must convince the Russians that this is a good deal. The Russian army is ill-equipped. Some of the officers still believe that they should go to war with swords and horses. I fear that American dealers might sell them modern weapons which would have a longer range than these. We do the Russians a service and we do them a disservice, you understand.'

Joseph Steiner considered the offer. Twenty per cent was generous and it was possible he might find a buyer in Russia. It was worth a try, but he would not commit himself just yet.

As they left the hangar the baron turned to him and said, 'You asked me to trace some Jewish immigrants in Cologne. You will find the information you want in this letter.' He handed it to Steiner.

'Thank you,' Joseph said.

With that they left the warehouse. The great doors were closed.

* * *

Later, in his hotel, Joseph Steiner considered the arms deal. For him it was neither moral nor immoral. Somebody had to provide arms for the warlords. It had the taste of danger about it which he relished. Life could be too safe at times and intrigue always stimulated his mind.

Furthermore, he could find his way through the complex web of officialdom in St Petersburg. He had known arms dealers to spend a small fortune trying to persuade officials in the arms department to purchase arms. They were given vague promises, spent six months in Petersburg hotels and returned to America and Britain with empty hands.

He would be more subtle.

Besides, Sophie and Alma were already in the Russian capital. One representing the Austrian Empire and another the interests of Germany.

Joseph was particularly proud of Sophie. She was an independent woman and he enjoyed her company. Her mind was sharp and active and she could turn a deal as well as any man.

For a moment he wondered if he should involve her in the arms deal. Then he decided against it. In the event of a war she might be thrown in prison.

He would do the deal alone.

While he considered the moves he would make in St Petersburg he visited Cologne. The baron had been correct. A family of Steiners did exist in the city. They could trace their line back to Russia.

The Steiners dealt in precious stones. In a small factory, hidden from the eye, they worked quietly at their benches cutting diamonds. Joseph stood with them while they considered the rough stones and the angles and planes within the ungainly crystal. With fine accuracy they brought out symmetrical diamonds which sparkled in the light.

'It is a valuable art,' Abraham, the old man, told him. 'In a small leather bag we can carry our expertise across Europe and across the Atlantic if necessary. I say to my sons, cut diamonds or specialise in theoretical physics or mathematics. They cannot open your brain at a customs post and remove your ideas.'

He laughed when he spoke. He was small and rotund with a large hooked nose.

Abraham was cynical about the Germans and the Russians. 'Do not trust them. They will make us scapegoats. When there is a boom they will use our expertise. But when the people cry out for bread or there is a financial crisis, they will call for the blood of the Jews. One must be mobile and always ready to leave. I do not know why you wish to trace the Steiners to some Russian village. We belong nowhere; perhaps in Jerusalem. I do not know. I have peace in Cologne. But peace in Cologne will not last for ever.'

'Do you believe that Jews will return to the Promised Land?' Joseph asked.

'There are those who do. One of my sons has returned there. The conditions are primitive. He works from morning until night on land he has purchased. But he is happy there and master of his own faith.'

Joseph Steiner had been giving some thought to the Promised Land. He had read about the new pioneers who had settled there.

Would the Jews return to their old lands? Would the wandering come to an end? These were questions which often entered his mind.

In the meantime the old man had given him the information he needed. If he were to discover his roots they would be in Russia.

Two months later Joseph set off for St Petersburg. He brought with him two trunks containing arms taken from the warehouse outside Berlin.

He had no wish to contact his daughters immediately. His methods would be subtle and devious.

He booked into an hotel on the Nevsky Prospekt. The foyer of the hotel was teeming with arms dealers. Several of them were puffing on large cigars and drinking vodka. Their conversations were always the same. They were making some contacts which would generate millions for their firms in New York or London. If they were not talking of such matters the subject would turn to Rasputin, the wily monk from central Russia who held the Tsar and the Tsarina in the palm of his hand. He was an unwashed lout who seemed to exercise some mesmerical power over the royal household. The wealthiest women in St Petersburg flocked to listen to him. He had slept with most of them. They seemed to be attracted by the scents of holy oil and incenses combined with the peasant stench of his body.

Two days after his arrival Steiner met Ivan Katovitch, a senior civil servant in the arms ministry. He was a plump man with snuff stains on his waistcoat, a pompous official with an inflated sense of his own importance. Katovitch invited him to dinner at one of the best restaurants in St Petersburg, frequented by the nobility and many English factory owners and merchants. Joseph watched him as he drank heavily. Every time he enquired about the minister for Defence, the Grand Duke Cyril, he received the same reply.

'It is impossible to meet him. Every arms dealer in the city seeks to make contact with him but it is quite out of the question. He is connected with the royal family and cannot be approached or bought.'

'Then he possesses everything.'

'Not even the Tsar possesses everything. The Grand Duke's collection of Fabergé Easter eggs is almost equal to that of the Tsar. They may not be quite as expensive but they are all exceptional.'

Joseph Steiner had got what he was looking for.

He might have found the rest of the meal boring except for the entrance of a strange figure into the restaurant. The stranger's faces was pockmarked, his nose flat and Mongolian, his black hair and beard unkempt. Despite his rich clothes he had the gait and the gestures of a peasant. He was surrounded by several well-dressed women.

Immediately the atmosphere in the restaurant became electric. All eyes turned to the strange figure

'That is the renegade monk Rasputin. You have obviously heard about him. Everyone has. He rules Russia,' Katovitch whispered, in awe of the monk who had the ear of the Empress and the Emperor.

Joseph Steiner looked at Rasputin: his eyes glowed with some inner power; his manners were appalling. The wild man called for vodka and poured himself a large glass of it. He gulped it back and called for food.

'Fish soup. Bring me fish soup,' he ordered. They rushed to serve him. When it was placed before him, he picked out the morsels of fish with his filthy hands and ate them. The juice poured down him beard. In fascination the women looked on in awe at his behaviour.

With his hand still sticky with soup he caressed one of the women's breasts. 'My lovely mare,' he called her. There was casual lust in his eyes.

Joseph witnessed all this with a feeling of nausea. He had read about the monk's behaviour. Now he was observing it at close hand. Their eyes met for a moment. They held each other's gaze. Then Joseph Steiner looked away.

The official was nervous. He was eager to leave the restaurant.

'Let me give you some advice,' Joseph Steiner told the pompous man. 'Pretend that you have not noticed that he has arrived. Have some cognac. When he is drunk and he soon will be, then we will leave. If he rules Russia then he can have you dismissed if you displease him.'

He noted how the official's appearance had crumbled. He felt a slight sympathy for him. Meanwhile the people in the restaurant returned to their normal conversation.

'He is filthy. You should hear the rumours that circulate

through our offices. The noblest ladies in the city have slept with him. He rarely washes himself. How can such a ragged *moujik* exert power over them?' Katovitch asked.

'He is a Russian phenomenon. Where else would a monk hold power over the ruler of a country,' Joseph Steiner said.

'He should be assassinated,' Katovitch said rashly. 'Then we would be rid of him. He is a devil. He holds a hypnotic power over people. And he has the gift of healing. I know it from well-documented cases. He is unnatural, filled with lust and spirituality. In Rasputin, the demon lives with the saint.'

Joseph Steiner was fascinated by this peasant who carried such power. He was attracted to the man's eyes which seemed to change colour with his mood. When a roast duck was carried to him he quickly tore it asunder and gnawed the flesh from the bone. Then he drank large tumblers of vodka to wash the food down.

'The powerful flock to him at his apartment. All you need from Rasputin is a note and you are secure. His notes are the hard currency of advancement,' the official told him.

For a moment Joseph Steiner considered that a visit to Rasputin might secure an arms deal. However, on reflection, he felt that he would be quickly dismissed by this peasant. And he did not want to be tainted by him.

When Rasputin became drunk Joseph Steiner called the waiter, paid him discreetly, and left the restaurant with Katovich. He ordered a cab for the official and decided to walk home through the wide streets of the city. There were always moments in the day when he wished to be alone and place his affairs in order. He failed to notice that he was being followed.

It was a pleasant night. Light summer winds filled the city and the light in the sky was pink and fragile. The outlines of the city had the delicacy of a great watercolour.

Joseph's affairs had prospered. He had moved to the rhythm of the times and he had caught the changing tides. But now his thoughts centred on other issues. He knew he must travel to a small village to the east of St Petersburg. It would give him great tranquillity of mind to look upon his family's landscape, to pray for them at some Jewish cemetery. He would feel part of Russia, part of Europe.

The spy who had followed him so closely departed when Steiner entered the hotel.

Two arms dealers were playing cards in the foyer of the Hotel de l'Europe. They were men who had made their fortunes dealing with the Russians. One was Goldmann, a Jew from France the other an American from New York, Peters. They had brought arms and vehicles in through the port of Archangel and sold them through the offices of the war department. They had large suites at the hotel and the most beautiful coquettes in the world frequented the foyer. When they had heard that Joseph Steiner was in St Petersburg they grew suspicious. They had hired a detective to follow him and to note his movements.

'Well, what have you discovered concerning Steiner. He is bound to be up to some of his old tricks,' Goldmann said.

'He had supper with an official from the war department,' the detective replied.

'I was right. My instincts told me that he was here on business. Steiner is always on business. What has he to sell. Is he acting as middle man for some agent?'

'I do not know. He returned to his hotel and retired.'

'And you overheard nothing at the restaurant.'

'No. The conversation was rather dull. Rasputin arrived and all their attention was directed towards him.'

The two dealers considered Katovitch's position. He was without influence. If Joseph Steiner was well informed he would seek a contact elsewhere.

'He is out of his league in St Petersburg. There is little he can do to harm us,' the American told his friend.

'That is the mistake they all make with Steiner. They underestimate him. He is devious. He was born devious.'

But Peters was barely listening. He had noted the presence of a coquette in the foyer. She was a young Cossack girl. She looked fresh and her skin was perfect. She had a high cheek-boned face, heavy-set features and a firm neck. She sat at a table and looked overawed at the rich hangings of the foyer. The American excused himself and left the company. Soon he was talking to the young woman.

Goldmann continued his conversation with the detective. 'My American partner does not understand what is going on in Steiner's mind. I do. If necessary, employ two more detectives. I want him followed day and night. I wish to know everything he does and everybody he meets no matter how insignificant. He has a plan.'

When the detective left Goldmann sat morosely looking at his toast and caviar. Twice Steiner had outwitted him. Now, secure in St Petersburg, Steiner had to arrive on the scene again and disturb his life.

'He must have a plan. He must have a plan. Steiner is never without a plan,' was all he could repeat to himself as he looked out at the vast space of the foyer where everyone of any importance in the city met.

The detective was surprised at how little sleep was required by Joseph Steiner. When he checked the hotel next morning he discovered that Steiner had already eaten a light breakfast and departed.

Joseph Steiner's plans were simple. He left the hotel and set off for the Nevsky Prospekt. He was impressed by the grandeur of the great street leading to the admiralty and the Winter Palace and marvelled that a barbarian like Peter the Great could have built such a place. He turned into Boulevard Morskaya and kept walking until he arrived at number twenty-four. He would wait for Fabergé in his office.

Steiner had always noted that business was best carried out in the early morning when the mind was fresh and not cluttered up with accumulated details. As he arrived, a shop assistant was already removing the wooden shutters from the windows. He glanced in and even the cursory glance convinced him that Fabergé was the greatest of jewellers. His creations possessed restraint and elegance.

The assistant was important and fussy. 'You must meet Monsieur Fabergé by appointment. I have turned away the crown princes of Europe from this very door. He is a busy man,' he told Steiner.

'Perhaps the princes of Europe did not offer you a week's salary,' Joseph Steiner replied and with that he took several notes from his pocket and handed them to the man.

'Follow me, sir. Perhaps Monsieur Fabergé might give you some of his time. He arrives punctually at nine o'clock. I will show you to his secretary's office.'

'No, I will browse here, I think. I wish to examine these magnificent works of art.'

Joseph walked amongst the tall, slender glass cases examining the works of the craftsman. Fabergé's use of translucent blue, red and rose enamel as a primary material gave clear restraint to his work. The unobtrusive positioning of lines of small diamonds on the edges of cigarette cases and ornamental boxes gave pleasure to the eye. His work was tranquil and spare.

At half-past eight most of his assistants were at their places behind counters waiting for the business of the day to begin.

At five minutes to nine the assistant directed Joseph to Monsieur Fabergé's office. He sat in a stiff chair outside the door.

'The master will be along almost immediately.'

At one minute to nine Monsieur Fabergé entered the building and was surprised to see Joseph Steiner sitting outside his office. He looked at his assistant.

'He was most insistent that you should see him,' the assistant said in an apologetic voice.

'Very well, but only for five minutes. I will ring the bell when I am ready to see him.'

Five minutes later the bell rang and Joseph Steiner entered the office. He wondered if he was playing for stakes that were too high. However, when he entered the room and gazed at the paintings hanging on the wall he believed that he might have a trump card.

Carl Fabergé was a stolid man with heavy features and a grey beard. He tapped his fingers on his desk as if he were playing a piano. He looked quizzically at Steiner.

'I admire your jewellery,' Steiner began blandly.

'Everyone does but not everyone can afford it,' Fabergé commented caustically. 'What can I do for you?'

'I wish to purchase one of your Easter eggs,' Steiner told him bluntly.

Carl Fabergé was taken by surprise. Then he began to laugh.

'Sir, you possess immense gall. Do you believe that I can ring a bell and a work of art will appear from nowhere. Besides, you could not pay for one of my eggs. In the morning I can call up fifty clients in St Petersburg and they would make me offers you could never match.'

Joseph Steiner was not angry at the arrogance of the man. He deserved to be arrogant. He possessed immense power and privilege. He enjoyed playing with an opponent, particularly when he possessed what he believed was a better card.

'How many of your clients possess *Madame Morphy* by Fragonard?' Joseph asked, looking at him intently. The eyes held all the secrets. They flickered.

'You possess a Fragonard?' Fabergé asked in disbelief.

'Yes and like your jewellery, it is priceless. I could contact a hundred clients all over Europe and they would pay more for it than you could ever afford. My name is Joseph Steiner. You may not have heard of me but among other things I collect art. I possess a Fragonard.' For the next five minutes Joseph Steiner spoke of the painting, its previous owners, the year of its creation and many other details in which the jeweller was interested.

'Let me think. You say that this painting is in Vienna and you could have it here in six days?'

'If necessary it could be hanging on your wall within five.'

'It is unbelievable,' he said and he looked around at his wall and the collection of Fragonards. 'I never believed that I could possess such a fine painting.'

'As yet you do not possess it.'

'You are willing to do a deal?'

'Yes, when I see the merchandise.'

'Then I will show you.'

Fabergé stood up and took a small key from his pocket. He opened a walnut door in the wall to reveal a series of documents and papers. On the top shelf of the safe stood a velvet box. He took it down and placed it on the table. Joseph Steiner watched as he reverently opened it. Inside stood one of the fabled eggs.

The golden shell was surrounded by a band of crusted diamonds and precious stones. Joseph took it in his hand and opened it. Within was a miniature hunting scene, each figure carefully worked in gold, each with a delicate proportion.

Joseph Steiner held it in his hands. It was a beautiful object.

'I always keep it, just in case an egg is not ready for Easter to present to the Tsar. Nothing like it exists in the world.'

The egg was returned to the safe. 'It is a bargain then,' Fabergé said.

'Consider the Fragonard yours. If you could send a man

to Vienna I will have it removed from a bank vault there. I will give him some letters to carry back with him for identification.'

Joseph sat at the desk and wrote several letters on Carl Fabergé's headed notepaper. These he sealed in an envelope and handed to the jeweller. They shook hands and he left the office.

Two days later he left Saint Petersburg by train and travelled east. The carriage was first class, with luxurious drapes on the windows. Joseph appreciated comfort and now sat back and contemplated the flat landscape passing by. Russia seemed to be an endless vast tract of forests and wheatlands. Here and there a village stood surrounded by trees and presided over by the onion-shaped dome of its church.

On that particular day the cast of Joseph's mind was melancholic. As he considered the achievements of his life he felt hollow. He belonged in no particular place, even Vienna. After Paris it was the most charming city in the world, luxurious and modern, but he did not feel at home there.

Towards midday the porter served him a light meal. As he sipped some after-lunch cognac he continued to observe the landscape. In the fields the peasants were working to a rhythm that seemed as old as Russia. Dressed in belted smocks and loose trousers and wearing heavy leather boots they laboured with bent backs, unaware of the events of the world. They were shackled to the land, many of them still serfs. Sometimes they straightened and waved to the train.

Evening came gradually and it was already dark when he arrived at a drab town set in a wide plain. The streets were dry and dusty. The hotel was a two-storeyed house with primitive accommodation. After he had left his luggage in a white-washed room, with a heavy wardrobe, a washstand

and an icon above the brass bed, Joseph sat in the front room, where a young woman played Chopin on the piano. He studied her face. It had a transparent quality about it which attracted him. She played for two hours, then she closed the piano lid and slipped out of the hotel. As he watched her pass down the street, Joseph wondered who she was and what had brought her to this backwater, a mere pin prick on the map of Russia.

At eleven o' clock, with the evening light still holding in the sky, he retired.

Next morning, very early, Joseph caught the train and left the town, continuing eastward through the flat steppes.

At noon the train arrived at Venkov.

Joseph stood on the platform and contemplated the place. It had a dejected appearance about it. The houses were set a little back from a main street which consisted of hard mud. On the edge of the street a filthy stream ran and across this were laid single planks which led to the timber houses. A few old people moved about the village in an aimless fashion. Pigs roamed freely amongst the houses and hens picked at the hard earth.

'Can I be of some assistance to you?' the station master asked from behind Joseph. He was an old man with one arm, perhaps a war veteran, and he smoked a pipe.

'Yes. I wonder if I could meet the local schoolmaster or the priest?' Joseph asked.

'You must meet Father Andrei. He teaches the children when he is not drunk. But many of them see no purpose to education. Every hand must work in the fields.'

'Then I will see Father Andrei. May I leave my luggage at your office?' Joseph left his trunk in a small office and set off through the village towards the church. As he walked along the rutted surface of the road he was conscious of eyes peering at him from dark doorways. Few strangers alighted at Venkov.

The church was perched on a small hill surrounded by a wall. Close by stood the priest's house. Joseph made his way along the path towards the house, his heart pounding. He did not expect that he would be so moved and wondered if perhaps the priest would resent his presence in the place.

He knocked on the door and waited. After a long time he heard steps inside. The door creaked open and a small priest in his robes and carrying a metal cross on his breast looked at him quizzically. He seemed very old. He looked up at Joseph over the tops of his glasses.

'Whom do you seek?'

'I seek Father Andrei.'

'I am Father Andrei. Come in. The place is in some confusion. It has been in confusion ever since my housekeeper died.' The old man with his bent back shuffled forwards, bringing Joseph into a room filled with books and papers. He directed that the younger man sit down.

'I shall fetch some vodka,' he said and went off into another room. He appeared with a bottle and two glasses. With trembling hands he poured out the drink.

'To your good health. Rarely does a stranger call here. It is a backward place and I have only my books for company. I am writing a book on the natural history of the place but it will never be finished. I am old now and I cannot travel about as much as I used to. But tell me what brings you here?'

He had already finished the glass of vodka and poured himself another. Joseph Steiner refused a second glass.

'As you see, I drink. Well, there is nothing else to do here. I tried to save their souls but I should have tried to save their bodies. If your belly is empty you cannot listen to the sacred words. Are you a believer?'

'I am a Jew.'

'From where?'

'New York.'

'In America?'

'Yes, in America.'

'A fine country. I would have liked to travel to America and start a new life there. But you did not come to listen to me ramble on.'

Joseph hesitated. 'Perhaps I am following a false trail but I am trying to trace my ancestors. My family, the Bikels, are said to have originated in this village.'

'I see. I see. Yes, the Bikels did live here. I know it because I have the records. In fact I was going to burn them because I could see no use for them.'

Joseph Steiner controlled his excitement. 'What records?'

'They were written down a hundred years ago by people who are long vanished. Some rest in the old Jewish graveyard. It is now covered with weeds and the graves have almost disappeared in the undergrowth but in winter time you can still make out the humps on the earth and the writing on some of the stones. It is a sad story.'

The old man's mind was clear as he told Joseph of the history of the area. A hundred years ago there was a Jewish settlement in the area. Then the Cossack soldiers descended upon the place and burned the village and put most of the inhabitants to death. The rest made their way west across the plains. Nobody was certain where they disappeared to.

'Whenever there is trouble in Russia, the Jews are always blamed. Whenever there is trouble anywhere the Jews are to blame. I have read their history. They carry a heavy burden.' By now, Father Andrei had drunk half a bottle of vodka and his speech was slurred.

'But the records. You spoke of records, Father Andrei.'

'Let me see where they are. This place is so cluttered that I lose things and find them a year later. There are not great records. Just lists of names and occupations.'

He began searching through the heaps of notes on the floor. Joseph Steiner looked on anxiously as the old man sought the records. Perhaps they did not exist.

'I am certain that it is here somewhere,' Father Andrei said, rummaging through the piles of faded paper, casting them carelessly aside. 'Ah, here we are.' He took the battered Manuscript and handed it to Joseph.

Joseph opened the first page. It looked like a merchant's account book. Anxiously, he scanned the list of names; 'Bikel' did not appear.

It was only when he turned the second page that Joseph saw the name of his great grandfather.

He began to weep.

Chapter Twenty-seven

The club was situated along the canal close to the Nevsky Prospekt, frequented by the aristocracy from St Petersburg. It was a sleepy place where men sat and read their papers and talked quietly with each other. The membership was limited and one could be invited there by a friend.

Joseph Steiner had done his research well. If there was one place where he might meet Grand Duke Cyril it was at his club. The secretary was only too willing to exchange the membership list for a handful of roubles. As Joseph Steiner looked through it he discovered one name he knew. Kukov and he had traded together many years ago in iron. Joseph phoned him and suggested that they might meet at his club.

The club was plush and comfortable. Joseph noted the quality of the gentlemen sitting about reading papers or having their drinks. It was the type of place in which one could do business quietly and without undue fuss, as he had been doing for much of his life.

He sat with his former associate. They discussed the possibility of importing coils of wiring into Russia. It was obvious that they would require copper cabling for the installation of new electricity generators in the northern section of the city. Joseph explained that he had contacts in Berlin and in the great industrial cities of Germany. It would be an easy matter to transport material directly into Russia.

'Of course certain officials will require bribes,' Kukov explained.

'And what official does not require bribes in Russia?

Steiner laughed. 'The whole organisation of government depends upon bribes. We could operate a margin of five to ten percent. That would give us a substantial profit.'

'It can be arranged.'

While they were talking, Joseph noticed that there were several rooms into which gentlemen disappeared. They emerged later having attended to some business or other. He continued to talk with his former colleague concerning shipments of copper wiring from Germany.

They had been talking for some two hours when the Grand Duke Cyril appeared. He was a tall, thin man with aristocratic features. He wore formal clothes and it was obvious that those present held him in awe.

'Is it possible to have a few words with the Duke?' Joseph asked Kukov. 'I believe that we have a common interest.'

'I have rarely spoken to the man. In fact very few members of the club ever talk to him. They play cards in the evening with some friends and keep very much to themselves.' Joseph Steiner continued to stare at the Duke, as he ordered some brandy and the waiter lit his cigar.

'He follows the same ritual each day. He is never disturbed,' Kukov whispered.

Joseph called the waiter. 'Could I have some club paper and an envelope, and bring me a pen and some ink.'

When the stationery arrived he quickly penned a short note, folded it and placed it in the cream envelope provided. He gave the waiter a handsome tip and asked him to deliver it to the Grand Duke. He watched as the other man opened it and examined the contents. For a moment Joseph wondered if he had been too bold to make such a direct approach.

The Grand Duke beckoned to the waiter. He asked him a question and the waiter pointed to Joseph.

After a moment, the waiter walked over. 'The Grand Duke Cyril would like to see you in one of the private rooms,' he told Joseph.

When he entered the room, the tall aristocrat was standing with his back to the fire, still puffing his cigar. A glass of brandy stood on the mantelpiece behind him.

'I am not in the habit of being interrupted at my club but you seem to be an astute observer of human frailty. Who are you and where do you come from and tell me how you came into the possession of a Fabergé Imperial egg? Even I cannot acquire such a masterpiece.'

Joseph understood that he had discovered the man's weakness and he intended to play upon it. He disclosed as little as he could about himself. He explained that he was a businessman with several interests in Europe and he had come to Russia to sell arms.

'As to how I came into the possession of the Imperial Egg. That must remain a mystery,' he smiled.

'I see. I would like to examine this fabulous egg. It could be a fake.'

'I know your taste and your expertise in these matters and I would not attempt to deceive you.'

The Grand Duke sipped his brandy. 'And the price for such a precious gift?'

'I believe that I have a consignment of arms in which your government might be interested.'

'Yes, we are always interested in arms, but where is their country of origin?'

'Germany. But the markings have been removed. They are good, reliable weapons.'

'And so say all the arms dealers, until we test them. What is their range and capacity?'

Joseph explained to him the best qualities of the rifle.

The Grand Duke listened intently. 'I am acquainted with them. Adequate but old fashioned. And why are the Germans disposing of these rifles?'

'I did not inquire. I came into possession of a warehouse filled with such guns. I am trying to dispose of them.'

Joseph realised that the Grand Duke was no fool. He understood the business of armaments.

'And ammunition?'

'Ten thousand rounds for every gun.'

The Duke considered the position for some time. 'When can I examine the Fabergé egg?'

'Tomorrow morning if necessary.'

'Then bring it to my office and we may work something out.' He checked his watch. 'Now, I must meet some of my friends. You are aware that several other dealers have tried to contact me? I admire the manner in which you dealt with the situation. I shall see you tomorrow. Now, good evening.'

As Joseph Steiner left the club with his colleague he felt that he had already secured the contract.

The detective was waiting outside the club. He followed Steiner and Kukov until they parted and Joseph Steiner returned to his hotel.

'How did he gain entrance to such an place?' Goldmann asked when the detective reported to him.

'He was with a member, Kukov. They have dealt together before. He is in the export and import business.'

'And of course it is no coincidence that the Grand Duke Cyril is also a member of the club. Bribe one of the waiters to find out what went on. Did he make contact with him? He would have the gall to go directly to such a man, something nobody else in St Petersburg would dream of doing.'

That night the detective returned to Goldmann and explained what had happened in the club. He even carried with him the torn pieces of paper which Steiner had thrown in the ashtray.

Goldmann pieced them together and examined the letter, intrigued by its contents. 'Are you sure this is the correct note?' he asked.

'Very certain, sir,' the detective replied.

Goldmann studied it again. Perhaps it was in code. Steiner had a devious mind.

'Why should the Grand Duke be interested in eggs? Do the royalty eat special eggs of which we have heard nothing?'

'I don't know. It beats me,' Peters appeared, puffing on a large cigar.

'Turkeys I know something about. Eggs no. Must be an egg from France judging by the name. Could be a chocolate Easter egg.'

Goldmann laid the note on the table and examined it. He could not break the code. Something told him that Steiner was ahead of every arms dealer in the room with this Fabergé egg.

'Drink your champagne,' Peters said. But for Goldmann the champagne was insipid. He had invested heavily in his consignment of guns and he expected to sell them to the Russians. They were quality pieces.

After a while he noticed his old friend from Paris, a jeweller who had come to St Petersburg to open a shop for the middle classes, sitting in a corner, smoking.

'Fourchet,' he called across the room, 'You know something about French eggs?'

'Not a lot. I eat them. My wife makes omelettes from them.'

'Well did she ever make an omelettes with a Fabergé egg?'

Fourchet was very amused. He began to laugh. 'You have a wry sense of humour, Mr Goldmann. I must tell this story to my colleagues. An omelette from Fabergé eggs? Do you know what a Fabergé egg is?'

'Never heard of it in my life.'

'Well they are the most precious objects in the world. Fabergé is the court jeweller to the Tsar. Each year the Tsar commissions two eggs from him; one for his wife and one for his mother. Have you one to sell?' Fourchet asked.

'No, but I know someone who has.' Goldmann looked blankly ahead, then, talking to himself, he said, 'He has beaten me at my own game. I believe that he has discovered the one weakness in the man. He could always play on the weakness of others. It is his trademark.'

Later that night he paced his room trying to figure out the terms of the deal.

All night the detective sat in the foyer of the hotel and waited for Joseph Steiner to appear. Next morning when the place was almost empty Joseph Steiner walked into the dining room. He ate a light breakfast and then ordered a cab, which set off along the Nevsky Prospekt.

'Ah, Monsieur Steiner,' Carl Fabergé said when he entered the office. 'You are a most reliable man. Two days ago I received the Fragonard. It is beautiful beyond words. What magnificent sensuality. It glows. Look how it fits into my collection.'

They studied the jewellers collection of Fragonards on the wall. Joseph admired them but he preferred paintings from the Sienese school. The Fragonards were beautiful but carried no substance.

Nevertheless he said, 'They are beautiful. They glow.'

'And now to the egg.' Fabergé went to his safe, opened it and presented him with the box containing the egg.

Joseph studied the precious object, so finely crafted, closed the small box and placed the object in a leather bag.

Then he left the shop, followed by the detective.

He made his way to the Grand Duke's club. The detective stood across the street and waited.

An hour later an automobile brought Count Cyril to the club. The chauffeur remained in the car.

The detective walked over and studied the face of the

driver. He decided to approach him. 'A beautiful piece of workmanship,' he said, touching the car.

The chauffeur looked at him sourly. 'Don't you dare touch it. I have spent many hours polishing it. Once I drove coaches. Now I drive a Mercedes.'

'You are an important man, then.'

'Anyone who drives Count Cyril is an important man.'

'Then you are not a man who would accept a bribe.'

The chauffeur looked at him directly. 'No.'

'Not even a hundred roubles to know his business in the club?' the detective said, taking the roubles from his pocket and flashing them in front of the chauffeur.

'What information do you require.'

'What is the business of the Count with this arms dealer?'

'I do not know. We are leaving for the rifle range to the south of the city. They are testing a new rifle. That is all I am willing to tell you.'

The detective handed the driver a hundred roubles and hurried back to Hotel Astoria.

When he delivered the news to Goldmann he turned pale. 'Steiner is the very devil. He has tricked me again. Why does he always appear during happy times and poison them. Make no mistake. He has already swung the deal in his own favour. But who is he acting for and how great is the consignment of arms?' He stared out the window at the traffic on the Nevsky Prospekt. His mind was churning with anger.

While Joseph Steiner waited for Count Cyril to appear, he took some of the headed notepaper and wrote down the amount of arms at his disposal together with the ammunition, as well the ports through which they would pass before they reached Archangel.

Count Cyril arrived at precisely eleven o' clock. He was eager to see the golden egg.

Joseph followed him to a private room, where he placed the ornate box on a table and watched Count Cyril open it and take out the delicate egg.

The Grand Duke held it in his large palm and caressed its surface with his fingers. 'I have longed for such a precious object. It is as delicate as gossamer or fine silk.' Then he opened it and looked at the perfect figures in gold, each tooled until they were flawless. He studied the precious egg for five minutes. Then he closed it and placed it in the box.

He looked at Steiner. 'How did you obtain it? I have made Carl Fabergé fabulous offers yet I could not persuade him to sell one to me.'

'It was very simple in the end. I discovered his weakness. I did not play on it but I offered him a painting by Fragonard which he could never otherwise have had. That is how the egg came into my possession.'

'You are a clever man. Then you discovered my weakness and you play upon that.'

'That is true. When I came to Saint Petersburg I took stock of the situation. I have a good product to sell but so have several others. I could not break through the intrigue or the petty officials at the War Ministry. I took a more direct route.' Joseph said simply.

'Then let us go and test the rifles,' The Grand Duke said, handing Joseph Steiner the egg. .

'Keep it. It belongs to you.'

'And what if we do not seal the deal? What if I do not buy the weapons?'

'Accept it as a gift.'

It was an astute and delicate gesture.

'Very well.'

The chauffeur took them through the city and ten miles south to the rifle range. Two boxes of rifles had been sent ahead.

They were tested for an hour and it was concluded that

they were serviceable weapons, as good as anything in the Russian arsenal.

'Yes. We can use them,' Prince Cyril said. 'You are certain that they can be delivered on time?'

'As soon as the deal is signed, the first delivery will be shipped from Holland.'

'Good. I am satisfied.'

They left the rifle range and returned to the War Ministry offices beside the Winter Palace. By three o'clock the necessary papers had been drawn up.

'Perhaps we might do business again,' the Prince said as Joseph took his leave.

'Perhaps. And I shall bring another egg,' he smiled.

Joseph slipped out into the square. The documents had been signed and he had acquired a small fortune.

Later in his hotel, he allowed the doubts to creep in. Why had the Germans sold arms to the Russians. In a war they would be used against German soldiers. But he quickly dismissed such thoughts. Business, not politics, was his province.

That evening from the German embassy, Joseph sent a coded message to Berlin in which he told Von Hertling that the deal had been signed and that the first shipment of arms was expected through Archangel port during the next month.

Von Hertling read the message with some relief. His plan had succeeded.

One of his spies had informed him that Peters, the American, had planned to supply the Russians with new rifles which had a longer range than those sold by Steiner. The baron had used Steiner to circumvent their plans.

Two days later Goldmann heard of the deal through one of his sources at the ministry. He packed his bags in fury and left St Petersburg.

Chapter Twenty-eight

In the pit of the Mariinsky Theatre, the members of the orchestra tuned their instruments. They sounded cantankerous and querulous as they were drawn into concordance, gradually finding their pitch.

The crowds began to fill into the main body of the theatre and into the gilded boxes. The chandelier, suspended from the ornate ceiling gave off a brilliant light. There was a babble of conversation as people sat or stood in the aisle before the ballet performance of *Swan Lake*. Then, by some instinct, they took their places and the great theatre fell silent. The lights dimmed and the overture to the ballet commenced.

Prince Karl had only a slight interest in ballet. To him it was a trivial pursuit. He preferred the opera.

It was only when the *corps de ballet* appeared that his interest was stimulated. He took his opera glasses and looked at one of the ballerinas, a young woman who had recently made her debut with the company. He could not take his eyes off her.

Beside him sat Prince Dmitri, with Nikka behind. The prince was a ballet enthusiast who knew all the steps and applauded every excellence with the rest of the audience.

At the interval he turned to Karl. 'And how does *Swan Lake* agree with you? Can we convert you to the finer points of ballet? Remember that this is the greatest troupe in the world, better than anything they can offer at Moscow.'

Prince Karl's mind was still filled with the beauty of the young woman he had seen dancing. She seemed to stand out from the other dancers. Her youth and charm, the cast of her head, her fragile neck filled him with the desire to possess her.

'Who is the young woman dancing in the third row?'

'I do not know,' Dmitri looked amused. 'Perhaps one of the young women from the academy. Each year they introduce new talents into the troupe. We can always meet her later. I can make inquiries about the party she will attend. The ballerinas are always invited to parties.'

Karl was jaded with the gypsy women of the islands. They were wild and unpredictable. He had seen them fight over a man, tearing at each other's eyes, screaming in savage anger. He had drunk with them and made love with them. He had paid them well for their passion. But the young ballerina had the breath of spring about her and revived early memories of Vienna when the world was fresh and cavalier. Perhaps she could stir some youthful passion in him.

The second act began. He continued to gaze at the young woman through his opera glasses. He felt that he must have her no matter how much it cost him.

Prince Dmitri was conscious of his friend's intense interest in the young dancer. He called Nikka and sent him to inquire after the young woman.

When he returned, Nikka whispered to his master, 'She intends to have supper tonight at the Cubah restaurant. Then she will play cards at the Casino.

'Then we shall be there. Have a bouquet of flowers sent to her dressing room and another to present to her during her meal,' Prince Dmitri said.

Finally the curtain fell and people began to move out of the great theatre. As they passed down the shallow stairs to the main foyer, surrounded by the nobility and beauties of St Petersburg, Prince Karl's mind was captivated by the young woman he had been watching all night.

As they set out for the Cubah restaurant, the evening

light still held in the summer sky. The air had the tang of salt carried down from the Baltic sea. They drove across the Venetian canals and Prince Karl realised that he had made a mistake when he had remarked that the Russians were barbarians. St Petersburg was one of the most beautiful capitals in the world and never more so than on this evening when he was about to meet the young woman he had studied with mounting passion at the Mariinsky Theatre.

When they entered the large restaurant many people from the theatre had gathered there and were sitting around their tables drinking champagne and eating caviar. Waiters dressed like those in the finest restaurants of Paris flitted about taking orders. At one of the tables sat the young dancer, who Dmitri had discovered was called Lydia Savina, with other members of the corps de ballet surrounded by admirers. Prince Karl's party took a table close by. The place was filled with laughter and talk, trivial in content and concerned mostly with the quality of the performance of *Swan Lake*.

When their meal was in progress Nikka entered and presented Lydia Savina with a bouquet of flowers. There was much excitement as she took the small envelope which accompanied them and read the card inside. Then Nikka pointed to Prince Karl. Lydia Savina looked at him with her limpid eyes and smiled. Then she blew him a light kiss and began to giggle.

'Well, you have made an impression on the young woman,' Prince Dmitri laughed. 'But for goodness' sake don't make it so obvious that you are interested in her. People will begin to talk. You know how gossip travels in St Petersburg.'

But Prince Karl could not take his eyes off the young woman. She looked innocent and vulnerable. Beside her sat an old man, Prince Alexander Federov, who owned vast estates in central Russia. His St Petersburg palace stood on the edge of one of the canals and had been built by Rastrelli. He had a reputation in the city as even at seventy he fascinated women. He had great charm and his strong, leonine head, his grey, pointed beard, his deep baritone laugh filled the restaurant. On several occasions he took the young girl's hand and covered it with light kisses.

'You have a rival in old Federov. Do not underestimate him. He is a powerful figure in the city and has many friends. He is still potent if the rumours are true and has several mistresses in apartments in the city,' Dmitri said quietly.

Prince Karl looked carefully at Federov. His passions were irrational and immediate and now he decided he hated this old man. Periodically he tried to catch the attention of the young girl but she seemed to be absorbed by Federov who was paying her such flattering attention.

'You should not be surprised. You do not know the politics of the ballet world. It is as intricate as life at the imperial palace. She might remain in the corps de ballet until she retires. Fedorov has the power to make her with a word in the right ear. And of course, the newspapers can play their part. A good notice could bring her forward into a solo role. Then the crowd in the galleries can be bought. They have been known to make or break the reputation of a ballerina.'

'How sordid that a delightful art form should be subject to such intrigue.'

'It makes life at St Petersburg interesting. It enlivens the conversations at the salons and the dinner parties.'

Prince Karl felt like leaving the table in disgust. He was about to cast his serviette aside when Lydia Savina looked at him when Fedorov was paying attention to another young lady. She gave him a delicate wave with her fingers. He smiled. She was aware of his existence. He decided to remain.

The meal continued into the late evening. Then when the company was tired of eating and the conversation was growing dull, Count Federov called out. 'Let us go to the gaming tables at the island. I feel that fortune favours me this evening.'

The dancers' eyes began to sparkle at the thought of the famous gaming tables where fortunes had been lost and won in a single evening. They gathered their furs around their shoulders and moved out of the restaurant, chattering like exotic creatures, untouched by life. Alexander Federov took a handful of gold roubles from his pocket and scattered them on the table. He did not bother to count them. They were more than adequate to pay for the meal.

Later, both Prince Karl and Prince Dmitri left the restaurant. Prince Karl said goodnight to his companion and set out for the casino on the island.

He found no difficulty in gaining admission. His diplomatic position and his title were sufficient. He had little interest in gambling at a roulette wheel, preferring the subtler pleasures of cards, but the prospect of seeing Lydia Savina had swayed him.

The baize tables had been set out in the former ballroom. Great chandeliers hung from rococo ceilings decorated with mythological figures tumbling in abandon across the great space above the gamblers.

The casino was filled with the cream of St Petersburg society along with wives and mistresses. They stood around the tables, their conversation reduced to a whisper as they looked at the spinning wheel and the ball which bounced from number to number before it finally came to rest. The croupiers then called out the numbers and drew in the bets in gold which had been placed on the table. It was a smooth operation, religious in its serious intent.

Several people tried to engage the handsome Karl in

conversation but his mind was occupied by Lydia Savina. He wondered if she had come with Count Federov to the casino. He pushed through the crowd, looking at each table. Finally he saw the leonine head of Federov, sitting at a table, surrounded by his entourage.

Prince Karl pushed through the crowds until he was close to his rival. On the green table Federov had set out stacks of gold coins. He placed his bet and then looked at the spin of the wheel. He was unlucky on that particular night. The great columns of gold coins seemed to be melting until finally, only ten remained.

Federov asked Lydia Savina to sit on his chair while he went in search of further money. Her eyes were bright with excitement as she tried to decide on a number. Others called out to her. 'You confuse me,' she laughed.

When there was break in the talk Prince Karl called out, 'Place it on number twenty-two. It will bring you luck.'

He could not say why he picked out the number. It sounded correct but later he would often wish that he had not chosen it.

'Very well,' she said. 'I will place it on number twenty-two.'

The croupier spun the ivory ball. It kicked from number to number. Then as the wheel began to slow down, it became erratic, jumping and finally rolling from slot to slot. It hesitated and finally fell into the slot marked number twenty-two. The young ballerina screamed with delight. 'The gentleman has brought me luck. The gentleman has brought me luck.' She drew the gold coins towards her with both hands and piled them neatly before her.

By now Federov had returned. 'You have been lucky,' he told her. 'The money is yours.'

Eagerly she put it in the silk bag which hung from her wrist. While Federov returned to the game she looked coyly at Prince Karl. He smiled at her and bowed. He felt that he had made his first impression on her. He would not press his chances.

He left the casino and took an automobile back to St Petersburg. He did not immediately return to the embassy, but walked along the canal banks and gazed at the great palaces that had been built by the emperors of Russia and the nobles during St Petersburg's two hundred years of history. His heart was light. He felt that love had returned to his life. He hoped that he would be lucky in his pursuit of Lydia Savina.

Later that evening at the casino, the same young woman watched Federov lose a small fortune. Finally she begged him to let her sit in his seat and try her luck. The crowd stood around her and advised her on the numbers. But fortune did not favour her and she quickly lost her gold roubles.

She eagerly pulled off a diamond ring and offered it as a bet but the croupier refused it. 'You do not give me a chance to win back my money,' she said angrily.

'Sorry, Madame, I cannot accept jewellery,' the croupier told her. 'Please make way for the gentleman behind you.'

It was late and Federov wished to return to Saint Petersburg. He had lost interest in the casino. 'If only the gentleman had remained. If only the gentleman had remained. He would have brought me luck,' she complained as she reluctantly left the table.

She returned with Federov to his palace. After he had made love to her she lay awake and recalled her luck at the table. Again and again she remembered the numbers upon which she had bet and the final position of the ball on the wheel. She had lost a small fortune. But she promised that she would regain it at the gambling tables. If luck ran with her she would not only win it back but perhaps double it. But she must discover who the gentleman was who had called out the lucky number to her.

* * *

Prince Karl found that he could not stay away from the theatre. Each night he sat in the box and looked at the young woman in the *corps de ballet*. He followed her every movement through his opera glasses. He felt that he knew every part of her body. He held his glasses on the expression of her face, cast down so innocently.

'She is dangerous,' a diplomat friend told him. 'Choose any other ballerina, choose one of the gypsy women, but for goodness' sake do not become obsessed with this woman. She will poison your life.'

But Karl would not heed the advice. Each night he sent her a bouquet of flowers but she failed to respond to his gifts. Then one night in his box he received a card. She would see him after the ballet.

He waited in an automobile outside the stage door. When she appeared she looked anxiously up and down the street. He sent the chauffeur to escort her to the car. Her eyes were bright when she sat beside him. She bent over and gave him a slight peck on the cheek.

'Alexander Federov is so possessive. But he is out of town for a week and I feel free. I knew that you were in the audience every night but I did not dare contact you. You are my lucky gentleman. Had you remained at the table on the night we first met, I would have won a hundred golden roubles. Instead, I lost every coin. And I have been back again to the tables and my luck seems to have abandoned me. I must win. I am due a lucky break,' she chattered on.

Prince Karl had planned that they should go to some intimate restaurant where they could dine together and talk. Perhaps his witty conversation, his connection to the Emperor Joseph might impress her. He would promise her an important position in Vienna. He would promise her anything in order to be in her company and to possess her.

As they drove along the banks of the canals he felt like putting out his arms and crushing her fragile body to him but he knew that such a rough gesture might destroy his chances with Lydia Savina.

'I have arranged for a private meal,' he told her.

'I am not hungry tonight. I crave excitement. I wish to return with you to the tables. I know we will be lucky. You are a rich man and you can indulge a young girl's wish,' she smiled at him and kissed him lightly on the mouth. Her lips were as soft as velvet and the kiss broke any fortitude which he possessed.

'Very well then. Let us go to the casino. But first I must call at the embassy.'

Karl entered through the side door, went directly to the safe and took two hundred sovereigns from the tray inside. The money had been set aside to pay the embassy staff, but Karl blinded his mind to the consequences of his actions. He had two weeks to replace it and something would turn up.

Soon they were on their way to the casino. Lydia Savina's eyes were bright with anticipation. 'I know we will win. In fact, I am certain.'

When they reached the casino she rushed to one of the tables. She took a seat and watched the ball whirl about the glittering wheel. Her eyes were wide with interest as she watched the ball bounce from number to number and fall into a slot.

Prince Karl placed five hundred roubles in front of her. Lydia Savina set them out in columns of ten, composed herself for some time and set down her winning numbers on a slip of paper. Then when she was satisfied, she placed four bets on the table. She won her first at eight to one. She gave a small scream of delight. 'I told you that you were my lucky gentleman.'

She placed more columns of money on the table and played again. Three times she lost and then she won. The sequence of losing and winning continued and she became desperate.

'I know I am going to be lucky,' she told Karl as she took a desperate chance on a single number. Her body shook with excitement as she followed the ball. It came to rest in her number and she was about to cry out in delight when it slipped into the next slot.

'I could have won a fortune. Please get some more money. I know I shall be lucky. I know it. I hear a voice at the back of my mind urging me to continue to bet,' she begged.

At this many of the crowd now gathered around the couple looked at Prince Karl. All the money which he had taken from the safe had been frittered away. He left the table and talked with the manager of the casino. After some time he convinced the man that he could honour his debts. He borrowed a further five hundred gold roubles and returned to the table.

It took a little longer to lose the money. But by early morning Lydia Savina had lost a small fortune.

They were almost the last to leave the casino. Already a grey light was beginning to show in the east and the roofs and domes of St Petersburg were emerging from the darkness. There was a delicate wind from the sea filled with the fresh smell of salt.

As they drove home through the empty city Prince Karl thought that the young woman might invite him to her flat.

'I am so tired,' she said in a pouting voice, 'and I know you will understand that I must sleep if I am to appear fresh and bright at the Mariinsky tonight. Perhaps tomorrow I will invite you up to my apartment.' She directed the driver to halt the car, gave him a light kiss on the lips and climbed out. He watched her disappear through the ornate door of one of the apartment buildings.

He was in a cold sweat when he reached the embassy. Caution prompted him to sell some valuable jewellery which he possessed and cut his losses, but the memory of the young woman haunted him through the day. He only wished to be with her, to smell her perfume, to feel her arm in his. He slept very little.

At three o'clock that afternoon he went to a pawn shop and obtained five hundred roubles for a gold cigarette holder. When he received the money he knew that he could please Lydia Savina for another night.

That night they went again to the casino. Lydia Savina lost all his money and for the second time he had to borrow from the manager. He began to feel that fate was drawing him into a dark trap.

The same pattern of events continued for a week. Night after night they left the theatre and went directly to the casino. The place became hateful to Karl. He was in debt to the manager and he had already pawned all his private valuables and the money in the embassy safe had to be returned. But when he sat beside Lydia Savina, and smelt the scent of her hair, and felt her soft arm and looked into her eyes, he wished to possess her. Had he power and influence enough to challenge Federov he would have taken her away from St Petersburg and secured her in some country dacha where he could live with her.

Then one night at the casino when she requested more money, he had to refuse.

She jumped up from her armchair and stared at him. 'Get more money from somewhere. I know I will be lucky. I must have more money. The manager of the casino will extend your credit. You are an ambassador and related to Franz Joseph,' she mocked.

There was a moment of embarrassed silence, before Karl said firmly, 'I have over-extended my credit and you are not on, and will never be on, a lucky streak. I have watched you let money slip through your fingers like sand for the last week. I cannot afford to lose at this rate.'

She lifted her hand and slapped him viciously across the

face. 'Then I will find someone who can afford my tastes.' With that she swept out of the casino.

Prince Karl stood awkwardly beside the table, stunned by the immediacy of her action. People were beginning to talk. There was a whisper of conversation about the room as the gossip spread.

Prince Karl had always hated the place. Now he quickly turned on his heel, walked swiftly across the floor, mounted the few steps to the hall and was about to pass through the doors when a voice called out to him, 'Just a moment, Ambassador. I believe that we have some debts to settle. It is quite obvious that the young woman has lost a considerable amount of money which has been borrowed from the casino. When can we expect the debt to be honoured?'

The manager spoke with a French accent. Beside him stood two men who were obviously armed. These people's methods of extracting money could be very direct.

Prince Karl felt humiliated that he had been so directly addressed by a commoner. 'The debt will be honoured.'

'We hope so. We believe that monsieur is also in debt to others. We would regret to have to take steps which might be a source of embarrassment to your wife.' He spoke in a low-key voice and retained a sweet smile.

Prince Karl could scent the perfume from his body. 'As I said, the debt will be honoured.' And with that, he hurried from the room.

Outside, he drew in the fresh air. It was bracing and seemed to clear his mind for a moment. He tried to think. If only he could be free of the debt. If he could borrow money from the Jew, Steiner, it would lift the strain that was bearing down on his mind.

And then the face of Lydia Savina in anger filled his memory and imagination. His humiliation had made him more determined than ever to possess her.

He wondered where she was. Had she returned to the

home of some old lover. It made him jealous to think of her in the arms and in the bed of another man. He could see some imagined rival making love to her in a large, comfortable bed. He could hear her cries of pleasure as she abandoned herself to the joys of her flesh. He stamped his feet on the ground and tried to drive her image from his mind.

He decided to walk to the embassy, setting out at a fast pace. Soon he was surrounded by darkness. Only a few lights burned in peasants' cottages. In the distance he could see the lights of St Petersburg.

The pace of his walking and the scent of the sea was setting up an old rhythm in his mind. He reflected on his youth in Vienna, riding through the woods to the south of the city, drinking young wine in the villages and singing songs from light operas.

Perhaps all was not lost. Perhaps there was some way of saving the situation.

Karl's obsession for the ballerina had not gone unnoticed in the city. Despite the aristocrats' belief that their nocturnal visits to the islands went unnoticed, their scandals and indiscretions were known to the diplomatic corps.

The old diplomat, Von Schoon, had received confirmation that the gossip concerning Prince Karl and Lydia Savina was correct.

He frequently recalled the public humiliation he had received on Prince Karl's arrival in St Petersburg. He had been dressed down in front of the servants. He might have been dismissed from his post and have had to return to Vienna had not Alma defended his fine record.

Von Schoon's devotion to Alma was profound. He had schooled her in the diplomatic intrigue of the city and had advised her on delicate problems.

Now he decided to approach her on the subject of her husband.

They met in Alma's office to discuss the correspondence of the day.

'You have been of great service to me since my arrival in the city. I appreciate it greatly,' she said, smiling at him. 'If you ever wish to return to some high office in Vienna I can make whatever arrangements will be necessary.'

'I have spent most of my diplomatic life in St Petersburg. I will retire here and write my memoirs. It is my life's ambition.'

'Very well.'

Von Schoon was about to leave when he turned to her nervously. 'I have some information which perhaps might be of interest to you. However, I feel that I may be presumptuous in bringing it to your attention.'

Alma knew from the tone of his voice that it pertained to a personal matter. 'Sit down and let us talk.'

For the next hour she listened to what he had to tell her. She did not betray any emotion.

When Von Schoon had left and she reflected on the matter she felt a failure.

But then she considered her position in a logical manner. Her husband would never change his ways. He had fallen back into his old habits. There was nothing she could do about it. But some day she would have her revenge on him. The revenge would be subtle.

Chapter Twenty-nine

Sophie settled in St Petersburg in a small villa situated on one of the canals, close to the Admiralty district.

Two days after her arrival a steel box was delivered to her by a member of the German embassy. In her room she opened it with a key which had been given to her in Berlin. It contained several documents. She read them carefully. They dealt chiefly with contacts and spies in the city who were sympathetic to the German cause.

She spent the first few weeks making herself familiar with the city. It was indeed beautiful in every respect and she felt in awe at the magnificence of some of the buildings.

Her escort on her journeys was Pieter Blum, a young attaché from the German embassy. He was a man of medium build with strong shoulders and he could speak Russian with confidence. He brought her to places she would not have visited and explained to her the qualities of the architecture and the history attached to them.

'Are you becoming seduced by the Russian way of life?' she laughed one day as they sat and listened to some musicians playing peasant songs in a small park.

'I am interested in all cultures. But I find myself in Russia and I wish to know the Russian mind. It is Asiatic in part and in part European. Even the nobles who speak French and discuss the latest novels from Paris will weep at the old songs. It is a mystical place.'

'And if we should go to war with these mystical people what would happen?' she asked sharply.

'They would follow the orders of the Tsar, particularly the peasants.'

'Despite the fact that the poor were slaughtered in front of the Winter Palace in the winter of 1905?'

'Despite that fact.'

'And what about the intellectuals?'

'They could bring down the whole system in the end. Many of them are in exile, others are in Siberia and others are here in Russia making their plans. Many believe that the assassination of the Tsar would solve all the problems.'

'And what do you think of the Tsar?'

'A simple-minded man, full of goodwill towards all and dominated by his uncles and his wife. He would make a good schoolteacher perhaps but he was never born to rule. A weak and vacillating man. He lives only for his children.'

They held many conversations on these matters as they walked through St Petersburg and studied the architecture of the city. Pieter also shared her interest in business, eager to know of every transaction. She instructed her broker to buy stocks in a new industry which had just floated its shares on the market, having been advised by Baron Von Hertling. The secret negotiations had been agreed with the army. When it became public it would guarantee a rise in prices. Her fortune was rising on the back of the great industrial surge passing through the German economy.

Sophie was also aware of Pieter's social connections. 'I should begin to make my way in St Petersburg society,' she told her young escort one day. 'I believe you can arrange such matters?'

'The French embassy is giving a party on Friday night,' Pieter smiled. 'You will receive an invitation.'

'Two. I wish you to accompany me.'

'It would be my pleasure,' he smiled.

Sophie realized that she felt attracted to this young man.

The soirée at the French embassy was a glittering affair. The French had a taste for fine evenings. The intellectuals of the city as well as some foreign ministers were invited. An orchestra played some light music from an Offenbach opera which added a frivolous enchantment to the occasion.

When Sophie appeared with the young man she made an instant impression. She was wearing her most expensive diamonds and she noted the manner in which men scrutinised her. She was well-practised in such occasions and mingled easily with the guests.

The conversation followed the usual formal pattern. It was always so at the beginning of one of these evenings. It was only later after wine and food that people began to talk. Sophie mingled easily in the company. She had been to Paris and was familiar with the latest exhibitions and had read some of the books which had caused a stir in the city. At least once a month some book or other caused a stir in that artistic city.

The Dreyfus affair still hung in the air. The army captain had been vindicated after spending several years on Devil's Island and now the establishment in France was reeling from the after effects. It had divided the country for many years. The radicals were in power and the monarchists were in retreat.

The French ambassador had been newly appointed to his position and was voluble in his praise for the new secular state. 'The whole affair festered for too long. It was a disgrace that a man should be used as a scapegoat for the army,' he told those about him.

'And what of the monarchists? Will they not rally around a new pretender?'

'Not in my lifetime. At last we have a secular state as we had in the days of Napoleon. Perhaps we might now be able to build a decent state.'

'And will another Napoleon emerge from the ranks of the generals?' someone incautiously asked.

'I believe not. Europe is safe and so is Russia. I do not think that any country in Europe will ever be strong enough again to dominate the rest. Surely we have learned lessons from the past.'

'If the past teaches us anything,' Sophie interjected, 'It is that we never learn from the past.'

The ambassador was surprised to hear a woman make such a strong statement. He looked at her with a certain amount of disdain. 'Madame, this is an enlightened age. I can assure you that all problems can be solved by diplomatic means.'

'I am not so sure,' she replied, refusing to be dismissed by such generalities.

The ambassador was about to reply when he was called to one side. It was obvious that such indelicate situations were to be avoided and an aide-de-camp had intervened.

'What a dreadful woman,' she heard him say when he thought he was out of hearing.

'I detest the arrogance of the French,' she replied loudly.

Pieter was at her side and noted the turn the conversation had taken. The orchestra had begun to play and taking her by the hand the young attaché led her on to the floor. He swept her into the easy rhythm of the waltz.

'You are a wonderful dancer as well as a diplomat,' she told him.

'One has to be on these occasions. We always stir up the worst possible emotions in the French. They are the victims of their own logic. This logic will be their downfall.'

'Then I have made a fool of myself.'

'Not at all. You were splendid. Tomorrow you will be the source of gossip in all the salons. Indeed, you will find invitations pouring in your letterbox. The French are not very popular at present. The Germans are more popular in this city. You have helped the cause.'

Later they sat down. Beside them were several embassy wives. She listened to their conversation, not surprised to hear they were speaking of Prince Karl. His reputation was well-known in St Petersburg.

'I can assure you that he is head over heels in love with her. It is the gossip of the city. She slapped his face in front of several of my friends at the casino and walked out like a spoilt and brazen hussy.'

'And has his wife heard of all this?'

'The wife is the last to hear of any such scandal. It is said that they sleep apart. She has taken over the affairs of the embassy. And if you note he is not here tonight. He is at the ballet, gazing at her from his box. They say that he is smitten.'

They did not realise that they were speaking of Sophie's sister. She continued to listen intently.

'And he is up to his neck in debt. Some say that he owes the casino five thousand roubles. Others say that his debt is much larger than that. The banks refuse to give him a loan. He is quite desperate at the moment.'

Sophie had discovered a piece of information which she could use to her advantage. She decided to try to discover more details about Karl. She had detested him from their first encounter and she still resented him. He had been arrogant and dismissive of Joseph Steiner. He had used the old man in order to borrow large sums of money to service his debts. Now perhaps it was a moment to settle old scores.

That night she invited the young attaché to return to her villa with her. She called the servant to serve champagne. Pieter sat at the piano and played for her. She looked at his well-bred features as he played.

She was falling in love with this young man, several years younger than her.

Pieter was not aware of her intense desire to make love to him. 'Shall I play another piece?' he asked.

'No, come and sit in the armchair opposite me,' she smiled.

He sat in the armchair. There was a fire burning in the

marble fireplace, which threw out wavering light. Sophie looked deep into the flames.

'Did you enjoy your evening at the French embassy?' Pieter asked.

'It was interesting to a certain degree. But I find such occasions tedious, particularly the gossip of the ladies. Embassy wives are inclined to indulge in the lightest gossip but you do discover what is going on the upper circles of society.' She paused. 'In fact, I would like to you to find out exactly what Prince Karl owes at this casino he visits. I believe that he is infatuated by a ballerina. Men can be such fools where younger women are concerned. Tell the casino manager that if he were to pay me a visit, I would make it worth his while. I have some business I would like to discuss with him.'

'I will attend to it tomorrow. But I believe that it is time for me to retire. It is late and you must be fatigued after the evening.'

Pieter rose to go and Sophie put down her glass and walked towards him. She put her arms about him and smiled. Then she kissed him and held him close to her body. At that moment she could have invited him to sleep with her but there would be a more charming occasion, when her mind was not bent on settling old scores.

'Goodnight,' she said as she released him from her arms.

Next day the casino manager arrived by cab. He was a dapper man, neatly dressed and smelling of perfume. He sat formally on the edge of his seat when she invited him into her writing bureau.

He was of indeterminate nationality. 'I believe that you wish to speak to me concerning certain matters,' he said in a formal, accentless voice.

'I believe that you have served the Imperial cause well and your services are valued not only here in St Petersburg but in Berlin.'

'Although my accent may belie the fact, I am German. I have from time to time passed on information which I thought might be of interest to the secret service in Berlin,' he said proudly.

'Then you can be of further service to us. I believe that Prince Karl has run up a heavy debt at the casino and that he had been refused further loans?'

'That is correct. He may be related to the Emperor Franz Joseph but that is no guarantee of limitless borrowings. As it is and from the general gossip I hear he will not be able to meet his debts.'

She listened to him as he explained in detail how the debts had mounted at the casino. He mentioned a large sum of money. 'I cannot see any way around the problem. And I will have to account to my employers. They have permitted me to make prudent loans but in this case I have been imprudent,' he now looked nervous and worried.

'Tell me precisely how much he owes,' she said.

He mentioned a large figure.

She opened a drawer and took out a large bundle of notes. 'This is double what he owes you. Let him know that his credit is extended. When he has exhausted this credit let me know. I believe that I will have words with him. Now I wish you to sign a note which makes me liable for the debts.'

'Very well, Madame. It takes a great burden off my shoulders. If I can be of any service to you feel free to call upon me at any time.'

The meeting was over. She rang a bell and a servant escorted him to his cab.

Two days later Prince Karl received a note at the embassy. He could not believe his good luck. Not only was the manager willing to extend his credit but his letter was filled with base apologies. His relationship with Franz Joseph carried weight in St Petersburg.

His thoughts brightened. Perhaps Lydia Savina could be induced to spend another night at the roulette wheel.

Karl had flowers sent to her flat with a note and that night he attended the ballet, sitting close to her in his favourite box. His infatuation for the young woman had become intense and painful.

'I was so cruel to you,' she pouted later as they were driven to the casino. 'You are so good and understanding. And tonight we will surely win. Fate has been against us but I know we will win. I have been to a fortune teller and she has predicted that fortune will favour us.'

But that night fortune did not favour either of them. When they left the casino, Lydia Savina was in tears that could not be controlled. Twice that evening she regained the fortune she had lost and Karl had advised her to leave with her winnings but she could not be moved from the table. The winnings melted before their eyes.

'I am too exhausted to invite you to my apartment,' she whined. 'But another night I will invite you to supper. We will have the whole evening to ourselves.'

His mind was in torment. He loved this young woman and her heart seemed as cold as ice. She behaved like a spiteful child encouraging him and then pushing him away.

The next morning, he sat in his office refusing to deal with his correspondence. He had not spoken to his wife for several weeks.

In her first winter in St Petersburg, Alma had caught pneumonia which had left her weak and depressed. Her determination had been sapped and she had no interest in matters of state.

Her thoughts turned towards Vienna. She had often studied the map and traced the railway line through Russia and Austria to the capital. She was eager to return to her favoured city and regain her strength.

It was obvious that her husband was spending nights out at the islands gambling and with gypsy women. Her servant had often described the islands to her.

'Places where no respectable woman should be seen or a gentleman for that. Of course the landowners and the nobility obey their own law. But a good Christian should not be seen there.' The servant crossed herself many times when she spoke of the island.

On several occasions Alma had seen Karl return from the islands just as other people were going to work. His face was haggard and there was despair in his eyes.

One morning she confronted him as he came up the central stairs. His eyes were sunk in their sockets and there was a suggestion of black stubble on his face.

'Could I discuss a private matter with you?' she asked formally.

'Not at this hour of the morning. Is it not obvious to you that I am tired and that I need a wash and a shave?'

'Then I will discuss it here. I will be brief. I intend to return to Vienna for a short break. I need to recover my strength.'

'And discuss my affairs with the Emperor?'

'I am sure that the Emperor is better informed of your affairs than I am,' she replied testily.

'Very well, return to Vienna. It is of no great interest to me.' He walked past her, entered his room and banged the door. The sound echoed through the corridors.

Alma returned to her rooms and called the maid. The months of inactivity were at an end. She felt excited at her decision. Soon she would return to a city that was filled with light hearted charm.

Two days later, with her cases packed and attended by one of the embassy staff, she made her journey to Vienna.

Prince Karl was delighted to be rid of his wife. Now if he wished he could openly invite Lydia to the embassy.

Fortune, too, began to favour him at the tables. Lydia Savina won a great amount of money one night, and as they left in the morning she linked his hand in hers.

'I knew our luck would change. I told you that you were my lucky gentleman.' She threw her arms about him before they parted and kissed him passionately, probing his mouth with her tongue and setting his passion on fire.

'Can I not visit your apartment? I have never been there since we first met,' Karl grew excited.

'Not tonight. There will be other nights. I believe I will soon grow tired of the casino. Just a few more evenings and I will recoup my losses. Then we will have an evening at my flat.'

Karl's patience was wearing thin and he could barely restrain his sexual excitement and his open passion.

The luck did not last. They had a disastrous run when he was plunged further into debt by this young woman who betted recklessly on improbable odds. One night he could no longer raise further money. His debts were staggering.

Before he left, the manager called him to his office. 'A gentleman honours his debts. I have allowed you almost unlimited credit in the hope that you might recoup some of your losses. I no longer hold your promissory notes. They have been bought by an interested party. I believe that you should call this number. You may be able to raise further credit. I believe that it would be in your interest in order to avoid a certain scandal.'

Karl took the address and put it in his pocket. Then he left the casino. Lydia Savina was nowhere to be found. He looked about. Then he asked the doorman if he had seen her.

'Alexander Federov asked her to return to the casino. He has just returned from the Crimea.'

Karl felt humiliated. For a moment he felt like rushing back into the casino and challenging Federov to a duel. But better counsel prevailed. He returned to the embassy and spent the rest of the night drinking. Next morning the servant found him in a stupor, wandering the corridors.

Two days later he decided to find out who had purchased his promissory notes. He drove to the address, sounded the bell and waited. Very soon a servant in livery appeared.

'Are you expected?' the servant asked.

'Tell the owner that I would like to see him. Tell him the Austrian ambassador wishes to have a few words with him.'

'The present occupant is a lady. If the gentleman would be kind enough to follow me I will announce him. I believe that she is expecting you.'

The servant knocked at a door and announced that the Austrian Ambassador wished to speak with the lady.

Prince Karl went forward and stood at the door. His face turned pale when he recognised Sophie Schmerling. For a moment he hesitated.

'Be seated,' she told him directly, her face without emotion.

He closed the door and, still staring at her, moved forward to an ornate armchair before her desk. Time had changed her very little. She was still beautiful and her brown hair had not grown grey. Her body had grown plump; the shoulders were firmer and on her neck were the first wrinkles.

She did not refer to the fact that they had known each other in Vienna and that Karl had insulted her in front of so many people at one of the city's grandest balls. Sophie was direct.

'I have come into possession of your promissory notes. Now, I can foreclose upon them but I believe that at this present moment you are without any collateral.' At her brother-in-law's incredulous expression Sophie smiled. 'You do not have to be amazed. I am informed of your position. And you do have a liaison with a pretty ballerina called Lydia Savina. Now, it all costs money which you have not got. All your sources have dried up. So I will cancel all your debts. In fact, I can provide you with further money if necessary. But there is a price to be paid for everything.'

'And what is your price?' Karl rasped.

'I seek information. You are ambassador and you have access to all the files in the embassy. You possess privileged information. I would like to purchase it.'

'I will not betray my country,' he said haughtily.

'Then our meeting is at an end. I expect that you will honour your debts to the German people. I bought your promissory notes with government money. These notes will leave for Berlin in the next train if necessary.'

Karl began to perspire. 'Perhaps we can do a deal,' he told her.

'Very well. I wish to know the names of all the Austrian agents operating in Russia. You can provide a list for us. Furthermore, I would like to have copies of certain letters which pass through your embassy concerning troop movements. I will indicate the ones I require. In anticipation of your service, I am authorised to advance you further money.' Sophie opened her desk and took out a large wad of soiled Russian notes.

He looked at them intently.

'Take them. They are not tainted,' she told him.

He gathered the notes and put them in his pocket. They would buy a week's gambling at the casino.

'Our business is at an end. You can show yourself to the door,' she said coldly.

Karl rose from the chair, turned briskly and let himself out. He felt humiliated as he entered his automobile. But he put his humiliation to the back of his mind. He was in possession of necessary money and he could satisfy his desires.

* * *

For a whole week he indulged Lydia Savina. As always she was unlucky. At the end of the week he was broke.

In order to raise more money he made out a list of all the spies in Russia and handed them to Sophie. He knew that he had betrayed the empire and the thought of what he had done began to prey on his mind. Perhaps the secret service had already discovered that he was giving information to another country which could be used against the state. He had become a traitor to his emperor.

But as he watched Lydia Savina dance on the stage of the Mariinsky theatre he thought only of the immediate moment.

Then one night after they had lost a vast amount of money at the casino she invited him to her apartments. They were on the third storey and overlooked the river. He remained with her for two hours. Several times he tried to draw her into the bedroom but she sat on his knee and kissed him.

'There will be another night when we can enjoy our pleasure. But I am tired. I must have my beauty sleep. If I cannot sleep I cannot dance.'

He felt her warm firm breasts beneath the silk dress she wore and it set his desires on fire. Would he ever possess this wayward young woman, he thought to himself. And what of his rival, returned from the Crimea?

He was growing nervous and his treason began to haunt him. He could not sleep at nighttime. Instead he drank heavily, paced the floor and only slept when he was drunk.

The information sent by Sophie to Berlin was impressive. Von Hertling studied the list of spies operating in St Petersburg against his own lists. At least a quarter of the names were new. Several could be used against the Russians and the Austrians as they were in vulnerable positions in the government. He immediately wired Sophie and placed further money at her disposal.

But Sophie was not interested in the money. She was interested only in drawing a noose about Prince Karl's neck and hanging him if possible. Furthermore, she would do it in the most public way.

Like her sister, who had returned to Vienna to recuperate, she was a power broker in St Petersburg. It gave her a deep sense of pleasure that she could manipulate people's lives, perhaps change the course of history. Also, young Pieter had proven an adequate lover. He possessed a raw Germanic power which satisfied her.

Von Hertling had been correct in sending her to St Petersburg. It had sparked off political ambitions within her.

The great city, beautiful as Paris, on the banks of the Neva, was working its fascination upon her.

Chapter Thirty

The autumn came quietly to Vienna. The leaves in the woods turned to gold; the Danube passing through the capital seemed to catch the gentle melancholy of the city; in the outlying villages people were enjoying the new wine and the gypsy music. Life seemed fluent and content but beneath this surface, and all through the Austro-Hungarian empire, tensions were growing. The Balkans were a cause for concern to the east. In the north the Germans were preparing for war.

Margit Schmerling was not interested in any of these things. 'These matters are no concern of mine,' she told Alma when she came to visit her in the villa Joseph Steiner had purchased for her. 'Since you left Vienna, my social standing has fallen. I blame Joseph Steiner and Marie. I have given up on that man. Had he pushed my case and used his power I would now be a countess. And I have heard strange gossip concerning Marie. It is said that both herself and that artist Fieldmann tried to assassinate the Tsar.'

'You have high social standing in Vienna, Mother,' Alma reassured her.

'Not as high as it should be. They still have not fully accepted me. And what of Sophie? She never writes to me. I am told that she drives lorries! There was always a coarse streak in her nature. I am disappointed in my daughters.'

She gave Alma little time to reply to her complaints. Talk poured from her in torrents. Finally, she turned to her daughter and said, 'I will leave you now. You look drawn and tired. Take care of yourself.'

With that she left.

She has learned nothing from her experiences in Vienna, Alma thought when her mother had left. She decided to distract herself by taking a walk along the path which led to the small boathouse on the river's edge.

In the garden the final flowers were in full bloom and there was the heavy smell of autumn in the air.

Alma sat down in a wicker chair and drew a rug around herself. She felt tired and lonely. The pneumonia had sapped her strength and her mental energy.

She continued to visit the garden every day for the next week. One evening she was sitting in her armchair, watching the sun set, when she received her first visitor. The muted light of evening was falling on the pathways and on the woods on the far side of the river. Only the birdsong or the blast of a barge horn broke the tranquillity of the place. Suddenly there was a flurry behind her and Countess Dona swept down the garden path.

'I had to come,' she said as she breezed along. She looked at Alma. 'You could catch cold sitting here,' she began in her fussy way. She might have ordered the servant to carry the armchair indoors and help Alma to her room had she not restrained her.

'No. I am happy here, but a quilt would keep me warm. I will wait until darkness falls. There is no need to fuss. I can take good care of myself.'

Countess Dona arranged to have a quilt brought from the house which she arranged about Alma. 'You should have phoned me,' she began briskly. 'There is so much I have to tell you. Vienna is never without a scandal, you know. It is so difficult to follow all that is happening. Count Francis has fallen in love with a young actress. He has left his wife and children and gone to live with her.'

'But he is seventy years of age,' Alma gasped.

'I know, and the father of six grown children. In fact, he is a grandfather several times over.'

'And what age is this actress?'

'Scarcely a woman. Just twenty and completely frivolous. You will see them at Landtmann's café every day. He dotes on her and has asked her to marry him.'

'And can he still perform?'

'Of course he can. Of course he can. As rabid as an old goat. He was always one for the women. I recall him in my youth chasing the maidservants about his estate. Got several of them with child.'

'And what does the Emperor think of all this?'

'I doubt if the Emperor knows what is happening. He spends most of his time at the Schönbrunn, meeting delegations, writing endless letters. He lives the life of a hermit. You must visit him.'

'When my strength returns, but for the moment I rest. The Vienna air is good for me.'

'And how is Prince Karl?' Dona asked pointedly.

'Very well,' Alma replied and left it at that. Had she given her friend the least morsel of gossip about St Petersburg it would be common knowledge next morning in the cafés of Vienna. She quickly changed the subject. 'But tell me all the news about Franz Ferdinand. Has the animosity between himself and the Emperor softened?'

'No, they remain on speaking terms and he turns up at the court but there is always suspicion and animosity between them. He knows that if Franz Joseph could chose another heir he would. But I do admire the man. He is no coward and is determined to assume the title of Emperor when Franz Joseph dies.'

'I remember when he chose Countess Sophia Chotek to be his wife the Emperor lost his temper,' Dona continued. 'He was given the choice of the crown or the Bohemian countess. Everyone tried to change his mind, even the Archbishop of Vienna but to no avail. Finally, they settled on a morganatic marriage. I can assure you that the best legal brains in the empire were occupied with this affair for a year and a half. It provided us with no end of gossip.' Countess Dona knew the intricate details of the marriage.

'And is Franz Ferdinand still mean and rude to his servants?'

'A leopard does not change his spots. But I admire the way he preserves the old architecture. He has been ruthless with those who would change the old churches and buildings. But with his wife he is an angel. The marriage has worked, despite those who were against it.'

'And the Hungarians? Has his attitude changed towards them?' Alma was interested in more than the court gossip.

'He still hates them. He believes that they are destroying the empire. They demand too much and are too vocal in these demands. He believes that too much power rests in Budapest. His feelings are well known.'

'And the Emperor is aware of all this?'

'The Emperor is isolated. Perhaps he is too old to rule the empire and he wants no more change. He wants to leave well enough alone.'

Alma realized that when Countess Dona was not engaged in gossip she could be quite intelligent. She belonged to one of the best families in the empire and knew more than most about the confused issue of the Balkans. In her youth she had lived in Belgrade and Bucharest and she was familiar with the languages and customs of the eastern empire.

However, their conversation turned to more frivolous topics. They barely noticed the night fall. Darkness quietly fell on the great river and on the hills on the southern bank. Lights came on in the houses which ran along the riverbank and made paths of gold on the water. The air was filled with the rich, narcotic scents of autumn. In the small palace the servants had turned on the new electric lights which transformed the place into a fairy world, the windows open to catch the autumn air.

'But it is time for us to go indoors,' Dona exclaimed. 'I have kept you too long here with all my gossip.'

'But I like gossip and I need to know everything which is going on in the city.'

'Well, I will call tomorrow and bring some of the other ladies with me. What I have forgotten they will remember and we will bring you up to date on all that has happened in your absence.' She helped Alma out of her wicker chair.

She stretched herself and taking the arm of Countess Dona made her way up the garden path.

Later, she slowly climbed the marble stairs to her room. The maid was waiting for her and helped her undress.

'You may leave now. I wish to sit at the window and look at the houses on the far bank of the river.'

'Very well, your ladyship,' her maid said, bowing.

With one small light glowing behind her she sat at the open window and enjoyed the great peace of the place.

As Alma sat by her window Prince Eugene was making his way to Vienna.

He was anxious to meet Franz Ferdinand, the future emperor. He had spent the last months in Galacia studying the political situation on the borders of the Empire with Russia. He had concluded that if the Balkans were to survive then the maps must be re drawn. Races and religions straddled too many borders.

'Will Franz Joseph listen to your advice?' his aide had asked before he set out.

'No. But Franz Ferdinand will. He is interested in retaining the empire. He has a bright mind and he is open to suggestions.'

'The changes are too far reaching,' his aide argued. 'The western European mind cannot grasp such ideas. They have never even seen a mosque or an orthodox church. They have romantic notions of the Balkans. They do not understand that, sooner or later, there will be civil wars right across these lands from Slovakia to Greece.'

For weeks they had prepared their proposals. They were familiar with the mixture of races and religions which made up the area and they knew the historical forces which had formed them.

Now, Prince Eugene looked weary. He decided to sleep while the train moved towards Vienna, leaving his aide to roll up the maps and rearrange the documents they had been studying. He retired to the end of the coach and drew the curtains in his compartment. As he lay in bed and listened to the monotonous sound of the wheels he began to think of the future. The burden of history weighed heavily on his shoulders.

Next morning when Eugene awoke they had passed across the border and were approaching Vienna. The morning light was flooding the countryside. He looked nostalgically at the villages set out in the flat countryside and at the bare wheatfields which ran to the end of the horizon. He had a great affection for the creaking empire. He had been educated in Vienna and he had enjoyed the culture of the great city. Once it had seemed to be as gay and sparkling as a waltz by Strauss. But he had heard the newer music and he had studied the new artists and he knew that men's minds were changing, even though they were not aware of it.

The train arrived at the station at noon. An automobile was waiting to take him directly to the Belvedere Palace. As he passed through the city he realised how much he had missed its buildings, its cafés and the general atmosphere of the place.

When he alighted a young soldier rushed down and carried his papers and documents into the palace. As he waited to be called into the presence of Franz Ferdinand he gazed at the ornate ceilings, the heavy furniture.

'Franz Ferdinand will see you,' a civil servant interrupted his thoughts. He followed the man dressed in coattails through a series of corridors until he was ushered into the presence of Archduke Ferdinand.

The Emperor's son was standing at a window looking down across the lawns of the Palace towards old Vienna. Franz Ferdinand's hair was closely cropped and his head was solid and square. There was little humour in his face. He wore a light military jacket with several decorations on the left shoulder.

He continued to gaze out the window in a imperious manner. Then he turned to the young man standing in front of him. 'I received your letter from the Carpathians. I hunted in the mountains and I am familiar with the terrain. Not an easy place to conquer. It is never easy to storm a mountainous country and it is a barrier against Russia. I fear the Russians. But show me your maps. I am interested in the suggestions you made.'

Prince Eugene set out the maps on the table. Franz Ferdinand considered them closely. Prince Eugene explained to him the meaning of the various symbols.

'I agree with you. The borders should be re drawn. Look at Hungary for instance. It belongs properly with Romania. Even part of Galacia should be brought into a new country. It is my wish to preserve the Empire but I fear its eastern borders. I know that even at this moment there are men who would wish me dead. I feel it in my bones that one day I will die by an assassin's hand.'

'But you are well protected.' Prince Eugene was taken aback at the Archduke's frankness.

'One is never well protected. There is always some chink in our secret service armour. Every year some political figure has been assassinated either here or in America. No monarch is safe on his throne. Unless the Empire is held together there will be chaos and chaos will start here,' he said pointing to Serbia.

'We should not have extended our empire into Bosnia and Herzegovina,' he continued. 'Your charts demonstrate this quite clearly.' His mind was alert and his hand moved rapidly across the maps. 'There is nothing I can do at the moment but bide my time. When I am Emperor I will give consideration to all these matters. I believe that I have your support.'

'Yes you can expect that, your Highness.'

That evening Eugene received an invitation to a soirée at the Russian Embassy.

He felt that there was always something stirring beneath the surface at these gatherings. Low conversations in corners might decide the fate of a state.

When he reached the embassy the lights were burning in the ornate building and as he mounted the steps he could hear the light sound of a waltz coming from within. In Vienna one was never far from the sound of a waltz.

It was an intimate occasion and about thirty people were gathered in the salon. They were familiar with each other and stood in small groups waiting to be called to dinner.

'Ah, Prince Eugene, glad to see you have returned from the borders of the Empire,' the ambassador said to him as he entered the room.

'And I am delighted to be given the opportunity to meet some old friends,' he replied in his easy manner.

'And how did your day pass with Franz Ferdinand?' the French ambassador asked slyly.

It was a pertinent remark and Prince Eugene avoided a serious reply. 'Quickly. But I'm sure that you are well informed on the matter,' he smiled.

'We do have our informants in the city.'

'I am sure that many others pay visits to the Belvedere besides a simple attaché. Even the French have already taken the precaution to ensure that they are favoured by Franz Ferdinand. Someday he will be Emperor and it would do well to court his friendship.' It was a light touch but it did indicate how every movement was watched in Vienna.

Eugene moved into another circle. They were talking excitedly about an air display they had witnessed that day. A plane had taken off from a field on the outskirts of Vienna and had flown over the city.

Prince Eugene was excited at the prospect of aviation. Over the past two years he had followed the development of the aeroplane. Every day there was something new. Men were pushing the new machines to their limits. Since Louis Blériot had crossed the channel Eugene knew that the oceans were no longer a barrier to warfare.

He was eager to purchase such a plane and he wanted to discover all he could about the machine in Vienna.

'I would not trust my life to such a fragile craft. If man were meant to fly he would have been born with wings,' a retired general said.

Eugene interjected, 'He may not have been born with wings but he has now grown a pair for himself. It was a dream held by Daedalus and Leonardo Da Vinci.'

'Yes,' another military man agreed. 'They are developing at a rapid pace. Their structure will grow stronger and the engines more powerful.'

'And what will the outcome of all this effort be?' the general asked.

'Is it not obvious?' the military man responded. 'This new and fragile machine will be used in war. It can fly above the enemy lines and detect the movement of troops. Photographs can be taken from the air and carried back to headquarters. I am sure that most countries have already recognised the military possibilities of these machines. I believe that bombs have been already dropped from them.'

'Wars will always be won by good cavalry charges. Nothing to replace a good horse,' the general remarked.

Prince Eugene knew that the old man was wrong. He had secret information about the French and German plans for aerial warfare. He wondered if the old Emperor was aware of this new development and if so, if he realised its potential.

The major domo announced that dinner was served and the guests filed into the dining room. Candles were lit on the tables interspersed with low bowls of flowers. Now that the women had joined the men the conversation tended to be lighter. It always turned to court matters. Vienna was never without court gossip and the royal family were always touched by some scandal or other.

Eugene listened to the conversation as it passed over and back across the table. It was of marginal interest to him, until he heard the mention of Alma Schmerling's name. He could not believe that he was so stirred by pleasant memories of their days spent together.

'She has just returned to Vienna alone. There is much rumour in St Petersburg about the marriage. They rarely see each other it seems, and he has been caught up in the dubious nightlife of the city. He has fallen head over heels in love with some ballerina or other who treats him like dirt. Alma has been quite ill.'

The chatter continued. 'Karl is a sybarite like Prince Rudolph. There is an odd strain in the line. Even the Empress Elizabeth was strange towards the end of her days. Following the hounds in Ireland while Franz Joseph pined for her in Vienna.'

'And he is in debt.'

'Then old Steiner will have to come to his rescue. I believe that he paid the prince's debts after he married his daughter.'

'Of course she was eager to marry into the royal family. Steiner was pleased with the arrangement. It gave the old Jew a certain respectability. Did you know that they were called the Three Disgraces by certain people in the city?

Sophie took off with her German count and the other is living somewhere in Russia with Fieldmann, the artist.'

Soon the subject changed to horses and everyone was on familiar ground.

It was late in the night when Eugene left the embassy. It was warm and the lights of Vienna glowed over empty streets. As he was driven across the river he decided that, despite the late hour, he would pay a visit to Alma. He felt that he must be with her again, see her face, recall their trip down the Danube and across the mountainous region of Transylvania. Perhaps she had forgotten the occasion.

When he found Alma's villa, he walked up the front path, sounded the bell and waited. After some time an elderly servant appeared and looked at him.

'I am Prince Eugene. I would like to call upon Alma Schmerling.'

The servant looked at him quizzically. 'Is the young man drunk? No one calls upon a lady at this hour of the night and Madame requires sleep on account of her recent illness.'

'I am a very old friend.'

'Then as a very old friend you should have more respect for her.'

'Yes, perhaps I should have shown more consideration. Tell her that Prince Eugene called and will call at a more appropriate moment.'

He was about to leave when he heard a voice from the balcony. He looked up at Alma. Her figure was caught in the soft luxuriant light of her bedroom.

'You may show the gentleman to my room,' she called.

Mumbling to himself the old servant, querulous and a little unsteady on his feet, put on the lights and led the way up the stairs. He knocked on Alma's door and when he heard the order to enter he nodded and left.

Alma was sitting in a pink armchair, a warm gown drawn about her. Her face was radiant. Her eyes sparkled when she looked at him.

She was about to rise and come to greet him but he rushed to her and gently pushed her back into the armchair. She threw her arms about him and he kissed her.

'I have missed you very much, Prince Eugene. Why did you not write to me?'

'I thought of you many times. But we had said our farewells when I last danced with you. But when I arrived in Vienna I heard that you had recently been ill. I decided to call.'

Alma held his face in her hands and looked at him. 'How handsome you look. Where have you been?'

He explained that he had just ended a year's visit to the Balkans.

'The outdoor life suits you. You have a healthy colour in your cheeks. You were not meant to work in some embassy office.'

Then she stopped talking. She placed her finger on his eyebrows and on his cheeks, tracing the fine, well-bred lines of his face.

He looked down on the creamy flesh of the woman he loved, at the rich, luxuriant hair, at the heavy, sensual lips.

'Have I disturbed you?' he asked.

'No, I was lonely. At nighttime I sit and watch the lights of the ships and barges as they move up and down the great river.' There was a note of despair in her voice.

'Are you not happy?' he asked anxiously.

'Remember, romance is for the Viennese light operas. Where royalty is concerned there is little time for love. In fact the only one in this capital who is deeply in love is Franz Ferdinand, and he is hated.'

'Will you come with me to Transylvania? You will be welcome there,' he told her, taking her hand.

'And create a scandal? I have no intention of causing a scandal. I have made my own bed and I must lie in it. I have made the choice,' Alma said firmly.

'Despite all that, I love you and I will continue to love you.'

'Even when you get married?'

'Yes, even when I get married.'

'You are an incurable romantic.'

'And I have no wish to be cured.'

They began to laugh.

'I am delighted that you are here. I returned to Vienna because I am weary. Seeing you, my strength returns. My husband wished to stay in St Petersburg. He has not mended his old ways. He gambles and from what I know he is making a fool of himself with a young ballerina. I am not supposed to know any of this but there are ways of finding out and I am a realist. But bring me some wine. This is a special occasion and I wish to celebrate it close to the Danube.'

The sun was rising over the autumn woods when Prince Eugene left the villa. All night they had talked, of many things and the time seemed to fly past. Towards morning, they made love to the sound of birdsong.

As he made his way home through the dawn streets he felt elated. He could think only of Alma.

Chapter Thirty-one

Fieldmann and Marie had spent migrant days in Russia since leaving Loslov. They travelled from village to village and town to town, never settling in any particular place for more than a month. They purchased a horse and a covered cart and with their few possessions they led nomadic lives. They passed through plains of waving wheat, broken only by forests and lakes. They moved along the banks of the great rivers cutting through the plains and camped under the spread of stars which stretched from end to end of the sky.

Sometimes they stopped at small huddles of villages, with wooden houses and muddy streets where the hens picked on the road and the pigs ran freely around.

When they were invited to stay in one of the small houses, Fieldmann entertained their hosts by playing his guitar or drawing portraits of the children. They were amazed at his great skill and looked over his shoulder as he sketched out their features.

There were times when they spent weeks in a village during the harvest. Fieldmann would go to the wheat fields and with a sharp scythe join the long line of peasants and spend the day moving forward, cutting the firm stalks. Behind the line of men would come the women binding the wheat into buff stooks. It was pleasant, rhythmic work. Fieldmann would soak in the sun and his face grew tanned. At midday he would sit with the others in the fields and drink milk and eat the dark brown bread. It was sweet on his palate.

The farmers' conversation was always simple and limited

to the landscape in which they lived. They had simple and miraculous beliefs that the Tsar was their father and protector and that heaven was about them and not very far away. Their history was that of their ancestors, some of whom had gone to battle and never returned, of great-grandfathers and great-grandmothers who had come to the place and settled down. They were buried in the cemetery, their graves marked by plain crosses.

In the late evening when the sun was descending beyond the great plains, Jakov would troop home with the others, tired after the day's work. His muscles would ache but his mind would move to the great rhythm of nature. He no longer wished to burden his mind with thought. The simple philosophy of the peasants, their songs and recitations were food enough for his mind. He would sit at their tables and eat with them and then, smoking his pipe, sit on a chair in the veranda and look at the ending of the day.

Such a village was Tanzov.

'Why should I try and change all this?' he argued with Marie, after they had settled there for the summer months.

'This is an ideal. There are villages where men and women are broken by work, where they are tied to their masters. They are still serfs. Education is never lost on these people. Teach them to read and teach them to think.'

'And look what thinking has done to western man. He no longer lives by his heart and his instincts.'

'We have been to the cities and the towns and you have met serfs who are chained to their master's will. They have never had a free thought in their lives. They live like swine and they die like swine. They are bound by a limited horizon. The fight must go on to free them from oppression. These days of ease under a warm sun are rare,' she argued.

'Perhaps that is true but these days also give us a view into a simple world which has its own harmony and that is a good thing. I would willingly remain here and forget what Europe has learned over the centuries. Of what use is the Sistine chapel and the works of art at the Louvre? We can live without them.'

'And so you argue now. But when winter comes and the cold winds whip down from Siberia and the villages become quagmires you will wish for the civilised life of the town. You will stretch your hand out for some book or other and you will ache for the sight of a painting by Rembrandt or an *étude* by Chopin.'

It was an argument they often engaged in during the warm summer months when the sun beat down upon them in simple surroundings.

When the harvest was finished in Tanzov they looked at the fields of stubble where they had cut the wheat, stretching evenly away from the village. A merchant came from the city and they sold him the great bags of wheat they had gathered into the barns. For five days the great carts came and went across the plains carrying the grain to the stations.

Then the place was quiet again. Men began to prepare for winter. They went to the woods and cut trees and carried them to the village and piled them beside their houses. The days grew short and migrating birds began to pass across the sky.

'It is time for us to leave,' Marie said one day. 'You have enjoyed the long and pleasant days here. We have even earned some money which will keep us for a few months. But we must move on. If we remain, the dream will be destroyed.'

Fieldmann walked through the fields towards the woods, deep in thought. His gait was that of a peasant. He wore a smock and loose trousers and a peasant's peaked cap covered his head. He smoked a large, bent pipe which he gripped firmly between his teeth.

It was late when he returned. 'You are correct,' he told her. 'It is time to move on. I know I could not live here. We will say our goodbyes.'

Tanzov was one of the peaceful interludes in their lives. Now in autumn they announced to the village that they must depart. The people begged them to remain and share their winter with them. It would be a peaceful time with the barns filled and the spectre of famine kept at bay. But both refused the kind offers.

'The geese are wheeling down from Siberia and it is time for us to depart,' Marie told them.

Before they left they held a feast in the garden of the house they had lived in. All the village turned out for the occasion, dressing in bright embroidered clothes which they had secreted in chests and which they took out only for important occasions. On long trestle tables covered in white linen they placed their best ware, filled with flowers, bread and fruit. A calf had been slaughtered for the occasion and the roasting carcass was turned slowly over a fire. After the priest had blessed the food they began to drink. Great kegs of beer which they had brewed during the summer were tapped and the men and women began to eat the food and drink.

It was a warm autumn day with a slight cooling wind blowing in across the steppes.

After the meal, three old men brought out their balalaikas and began to play traditional music. They invited Marie to join them as over the summer and autumn she had learned to play the instrument and now had some mastery over it. Together they played the fast airs full of gaiety and the slow airs, full of the tears and the tribulations of the whole Russian nation, spread out across the vast plains which stretched to the very borders of China.

Later, when their spirits were high they danced to the music. Fieldmann joined in the dancing. He had a natural ability in picking up rhythms and as Marie watched him move free and easily, she knew the source from which his artistic power derived. He was as much part of the earth and the air of the place as the peasants who danced with him.

Evening spread in from the east across the stubble plains, broken here and there by a solitary tree. Soon darkness began to fall and the villagers gathered logs and branches and made a great bonfire. Now they began to drink vodka, passing the green bottles between them. Fieldmann noted the strong, spare faces caught by the flames particularly those of the old men who had weathered all the exigencies of life. He wanted to take some charcoal from the fire and draw their expressions on a sheet of paper.

Later, they became sombre in their talk and the spirits made them sentimental. Some wept at memories of events which had happened in the village many years ago. Gradually the flame turned to a steady glow of burning logs. Periodically the logs collapsed and a galaxy of sparks shot up into the sky.

Very late in the night they said their goodbyes to Fieldmann and Marie, then they drifted drunkenly down the village street to their homes. Finally, an old man came to say goodbye. He was too old to work in the fields and spent his days carving timber.

He presented Marie with a balalaika he had made. It was painted black with simple red motifs running along the edges of the timber and down the back. 'It is for you,' he told her simply. 'Bring it with you through Russia. You will never want for a meal while you have this balalaika. I once tramped through Russia with my instrument. I saw great places and huge cities. I never became rich but I never starved.'

He smiled a toothless grin.

'I will bring it with me and I will play it each evening and I will always remember you,' Marie said affectionately.

In the end only the two of them were left by the dying fire. They were content. They did not realise now that they would never be content again.

'Play for me,' he said. 'Play one of the old, slow airs which disturbs and heals the mind.'

Marie began to play a mournful tune. When she was finished he took the instrument from her and laid it aside. He gripped her in his arms and kissed her on the mouth. 'You have come with me through all this. You should have stayed in Vienna and led a soft life.'

'I regret nothing. I would make the same choice again.'

Jakov made love to her by the dying embers of the fire. Beneath him she cried out, long groans that came from deep in her throat. The earth was soft on her back and the scent of the fire was in her nostrils.

Just as he was about to fall away from her she viced him to her body with her legs and held him close to her. 'Not yet, Fieldmann,' she called. They lay locked for a time. Then they fell apart.

Two days later they left the village, their cart laden with food for the journey.

They waved to the villagers who had gathered to say goodbye, their throats dry with emotion.

He continued to drive the horse forward until the village had disappeared beyond the horizon.

Towards the end of October they reached the industrial town of Kotlas. It was situated on the banks of a sluggish river which ran towards the Barents Sea. From tall brick stacks, grey smoke moved eastward and there seemed to be the permanent smell of sulphur and coal dust in the air.

'It is a grim place,' Fieldmann commented as he looked at the city from the crest of a hill. 'But I'm sure that we will find warm lodgings there and perhaps I can paint and sell some of my paintings.'

'Do you regret that we left the village now?' Marie asked.

'I have no strong thoughts on the matter. We had a simple life there but perhaps we are not made for the simple life. The intellectual life of a city attracts me.'

They moved down the hill towards the city. Being an industrial town, Kotlas followed the pattern of all such places. On the outskirts were the houses of the merchants and the industrialists, well-built and ornate, distempered in rich colours. They were isolated behind high walls, surrounded by mature trees. In the heart of the city lay the old quarters, built of stone and set in narrow, twisted streets. Marie reflected that they always seemed to be attracted to such places.

It was late that night when they finally found a place to lodge. They stabled their horse in the yard and secured their belongings in the barn. Their lodging place was damp and roughly plastered and only a gas lamp, hissing in a sprocket in the wall, gave them half-light.

Fieldmann studied their surroundings. 'All over the world, in France and Germany and America people are condemned to live their lives in places such as these. That is why the world must change.'

They put out the gas lamp and went to bed. The mattress was damp and stale and even when their bodies warmed the sheets and the blankets they felt that they were still damp. Finally they fell asleep.

Next morning they set out to walk through the city in daylight. The factories stood close to the river, great hillocks of coal standing beside them and long wagons of iron ore from the Ural Mountains ranged outside the wide doors, to be drawn to the blast furnaces.

They looked into the vast and half-dark interiors where bare-backed men fed the furnaces. Great cauldrons of molten ore were poured into moulds to form long oblong blocks. Jakov and Marie watched the livid metal in awe.

At midday they ate at a soup kitchen close to the factory. Some of the miners, with grime on their faces, sat at the tables and ate great bowls of meat and vegetables, too tired to talk. They had tired, humourless faces.

There was one millworker who sat alone. Propped up

before him he had a newspaper which he read as he ate his food. He continued to read when the others left the canteen.

Fieldmann and Marie went over to him and introduced themselves. The mill worker looked at him with a suspicious eye. He did not welcome strangers, particularly when they were dressed in clean clothes and smelt of soap.

'I am new to the area. Could you tell me who owns the factory?' Fieldmann asked.

'It is written over the main gate, if you wish to look. Where are you from? I have not seen you before.'

'We are from Vienna but I have spent the last few years travelling through Russia. I have worked with the peasants on the land and my wife has taught children.'

'It is an easy life, teaching. I would have been a teacher but my parents were too poor to send me to college. That is why I read. Every night I read. I have read all the Russian authors.' His face was tired but his eyes had a deep, penetrating quality about them which impressed Fieldmann.

'Have you read Hertzen and Chernyshevsky?' Marie asked.

'I have read them all.'

'But they are dangerous authors.'

'They free men's minds.'

'From what?'

'Tyranny.'

'And you agree with their thoughts and aims?'

He looked at them intently. 'What I believe is my own business. I have the freedom to think and my thoughts are my own private possessions. The Tsar's secret police cannot pry into my head.'

He turned away continued to read the papers.

'That is a matter of debate,' Fieldmann continued. 'They have their means and methods of knowing what a man thinks. If you go to jail and are isolated from your peers then they can quickly discover your thoughts.'

'Are you one of them or one of their agents?'

'I have been subjected to their methods. I believed once that I could hold out against them. They broke me.'

'The Tsar's secret police?'

'Franz Joseph's secret police.'

'They have such men in Vienna?'

'They are in every city of every Empire in the world. They know their trade, let me tell you.'

They would have continued to talk in this manner, exploring each other's position, but a man entered the canteen and sat down close to them.

'Is he one of them?' Fieldmann whispered.

'Look at his hands, they are smooth. Look at his eyes. They are suspicious. Of course he is one of them. I have not seen him before, though. Let us walk by the river bank. At least we will have some privacy there. My name is Mikhail Kedrov.'

'Jakov Fieldmann and Marie Schmerling,' Jakov introduced them.

They left the canteen and walked through some squalid streets, close to the great chimney stacks, where the coal grime had blackened the birches until they were drab and without lustre. Thin children with rickets played on the cobbled stones. Their skin had an unhealthy white pallor and there was no musical ring to their voices.

'Many of them will never reach adulthood,' Kedrov told them. 'They will be carried away with the white scourge, tuberculosis. What they need is fresh air and fields to play in.'

'Have you no sanatorium in the district?' Marie asked.

'It is understaffed and too close to the city. It is always crowded. Perhaps you may meet Dr Volodin. He is a socialist and has written several pamphlets on the subject.'

They continued to talk until they reached the bank of the river. Here, the water was grey and sluggish and a cold wind sharpened on its surface.

'It is straight from Siberia,' Kedrov explained. 'Soon, it will bring the snow. But the snow here is never white. It is pitted with coal flecks. Even nature is tainted. And look at the trees. Many of them are stunted. Others wither. They grow for several years, then the tops turn brown and dry. They shed their leaves and finally the whole tree fails,' he said sadly.

Fieldmann began to describe their vagrant life of the previous two years, of their time in Loslov and how the Armenian had led them into a trap, leaving many young men dead in an attempt to assassinate the Tsar.

Kedrov walked with them to their lodgings. Then he said goodbye and left them. He said that he would contact them later.

'Have we told him too much?' Marie asked anxiously.

'No. I looked deep into his eyes. I studied his face. He is a revolutionary.'

'We will see,' she replied.

The next few days passed quickly. There was much to attend to. They hired a small cottage with a garden on the west of the city. The air was clear and the small plot of land gave them some sense of freedom.

Immediately, Marie placed a notice in the local paper advertising private lessons in German. Several pupils from the upper class, who were preparing to take state examinations, answered the notice. 'At least we will not starve,' she told Fieldmann after the first week.

'And I had better become an artistic prostitute for the moment. I have been to an art gallery and I have noted that Romantic scenes sell very well.'

Jakov set up his easel in a small room and with great facility began to paint from some pretty postcards he had purchased. Smoking his great pipe which had been given him by a peasant farmer, he hummed contentedly as he drew sketches of flowers from Italy and Switzerland.

Over the next few weeks, as his name became better

known, he painted the buildings of Moscow and St Petersburg from photographs. With the money they both earned, they prepared for winter. They purchased logs and set them in a great angular pile at the gable end of the house. They bought pork and fish and salted them in barrels which they placed in an outhouse.

After a month, they had almost forgotten that they had met the factory worker and talked with him. Then one night when they were asleep there was a tapping at the back window. Fieldmann sprung awake, pulled on his trousers and went to the door. 'Who comes bothering us at this time of night? Can people not have their night's sleep?' he asked the dark figure crossly.

'It is Kedrov. We have checked out your story. What you said was correct. You have been in jail in Vienna and secret police have a file on you in Odessa. We have also been in contact with Lenin in Switzerland.'

It did not seem to enter his mind that he had disturbed Fieldmann. He was so immersed in his revolutionary ideals that time or inconvenience meant nothing to him.

'Will you come in and have a glass of vodka. It is a chilly night.'

'No. I must be on my way. I am certain I was not followed. I will contact you again and you will meet the others. Goodnight.'

With that he disappeared into the darkness.

'Who was that?' Marie asked.

'Kedrov, from the iron works.'

'What a strange hour to come and knock on our door.'

'He is a strange man. Those deep-set eyes of his are disturbing.'

'Let us sleep,' Marie said tiredly, turning from him.

The meeting with the group took place at the sanatorium some distance from the city. It was set amongst birch woods. The trees were bare and the slanting sun turned their barks to burnished silver as they stood, mysterious and beautiful.

Dr Volodin, who had quarters in the grounds, looked tired and exhausted when he came to the door. Fieldmann wondered if he had picked up the deadly tuberculosis from one of his patients. He smoked cigarettes continually and had a dry cough.

There were three others in the room. One had written some short stories for a Moscow journal and was engaged in writing a short provincial novel; the others were engineering students studying in St Petersburg. For a while, they discussed the political topics of the day, until eventually Dr Volodin came to the purpose of the meeting. He drew a large sheet of paper from his pocket. It had been neatly folded and he opened it carefully. Then he pinned it to the wall. It was a large map of St Petersburg and its environs. It had been hand copied in an exact hand and certain buildings had been highlighted in heavy ink. There were several green and yellow lines leading from the outskirts of the city to the Church of St Isaac.

'These are the routes the Tsar will take,' Volodin began. 'There are several points along the route where his carriage will slow down. If one wished to begin a revolution it could be along this route,' he said in a clinical voice.

'But would a revolution begin? The peasants are not going to rise up. They are spread across Russia and they know little of what is going on. Besides, many of them are quite happy with their lot,' Fieldmann told them.

'And how can you speak for the peasants? You are a stranger in Russia,' the young writer commented.

'I worked in the fields with them. I shared their evening meals. I sang their songs and I listened to their stories. We imagine that they have a political sophistication which they have not got.'

There was tension in the room. There was a curl of disdain on the young writer's lips. He began to quote political theories which were nebulous.

The doctor, who had been smoking a cigarette, looked at the map.

'It is the only way to rid the country of the disease. The aristocrats are a disease. Things have gone on for long enough. If a revolution must begin it must begin in St Petersburg.'

'Even to utter words like these is to condemn yourself to Siberia and to attempt such a deed is to condemn yourself to death,' Fieldmann told him.

'Disease has already condemned me to death. The fetid slums of the mining towns have shortened my days. I do not fear what they can do to me. Let us make the plan. Give me the bombs and I will make sure that the Tsar dies. I have nothing to lose.'

The conversation had moved too rapidly for Fieldmann. 'One must consider these matters carefully,' he said. 'I would like to weigh up our chances. Besides, I am only new to your circle and you draw me too quickly into the plot.'

'The time for theorizing is over,' the doctor told them bluntly.

One of the engineers, Yuri Akimov, broke in on the conversation. 'This is the best time to attack, when the Tsar is attending a religious festival. People would not be prepared for such a move. The bombs and the pistols are ready. I have them hidden away in the city. In the meantime, let each one consider if he is willing to be part of the attempt on the Tsar's life.'

The meeting broke up late in the evening. It was dark and cold outside and snow was beginning to fall. Winter was isolating the villages and the towns. As Fieldmann rode home he considered the implications of what had been said. If a revolution was to take place it would have to be gradual and general. Perhaps Russia was not ready for a revolution.

Besides, he had to consider his position. He had already been drawn into two abortive plots by the Armenian. Why should he trust the present group. There was always an infiltrator in such plots. How could he be certain that somebody had not reported them to the police.

The following morning, he explained his fears to Kedrov.

'We did have a spy in our ranks two years ago.'

'What happened?'

'I shot him,' he explained simply.

'Then you believe that your plans are secure?'

'Yes.'

'I must consider all of this. I am not certain what I should do. Assassinating the Tsar is an extreme measure.'

'I will leave you to consider it,' Kedrov said and left.

Soon events would make up Jakov Fieldmann's mind for him.

Chapter Thirty-two

Throughout the winter the group met weekly at the sanatorium. They described it publicly as a literary club and it was always held in Dr Volodin's library, at a birch table piled with books.

The doctor continued to grow weaker. His long hours at the hospital were taking their toll on his health. Now he began to spit blood. It was clear that he was dying of tuberculosis.

Fieldmann was never certain of his position in the group. Despite their arguments he believed that change should be gradual and through the new parliament called the Duma.

'It lacks power,' the doctor told him irritably.

'It is now in place and will take power to itself,' Fieldmann replied.

'Not while Nicholas is on the throne and the ministers remain responsible to him. I tell you that if the Tsar goes then the whole rotten edifice will crumble; the estates; the church; the secret police.'

'It will engender chaos,' Fieldmann cried.

'We need chaos,' Kedrov replied. 'A new order will come out of chaos. There will be new life and new blood.'

The group might have come to blows but Dr Volodin began to cough again. A raw rasp tore through his body. Before he could draw a handkerchief from his pocket he spat onto a sheet of paper in front of him. The sputum was stained with blood.

They ceased to argue.

After the meeting Kedrov took Fieldmann aside. 'I have

certain information for you. You asked me to trace a gentleman from Odessa. He is now in St Petersburg.'

'Is it the Armenian?'

'Yes. He is in the service of Prince Dmitri.'

'So he does belong to the secret service.'

'Yes. It has been confirmed.'

Fieldmann recalled the manner in which he wiped out so many young men. It was at that moment he decided to assassinate the Armenian.

It was in midwinter that Fieldmann's mind was changed dramatically about the revolution.

He had decided to take Marie to the central square of Kotlas for a meal and to buy some clothes. He felt financially secure. He had sold his paintings as soon as they were finished and Marie's small school had attracted several pupils from the middle classes.

On that day revolution was far from his mind.

As they drove through the northern section in a tram where the great chimney stacks poured acrid smoke into the sky, they noted small groups of people moving along the road. They carried banners with badly painted slogans on them.

'You should be painting proper banners for the revolutionaries, Fieldmann,' Marie told him, a smile on her face.

'Yes. Art for the people,' he replied, chuckling.

As they neared the central square of the city they noticed the confluence of small groups there, becoming a mass of marching people. They were singing a revolutionary song.

Fieldmann's face grew dark. 'I do not like this at all,' he said. 'They are fools. They carry no weapons. A Cossack regiment could wipe them out.'

'It is only a peaceful protest in front of the government ministry. Nothing will come of it. Surely they have learned from Bloody Sunday,' Marie tried to reassure him.

'They never learn,' he told her.

They continued on their journey and found that the square in front of the ministry buildings was almost empty. A light wind whipped up a mist of snow from the surface of the square. Now and then a troika passed, bells tinkling, and disappeared through an archway. Most of the buildings were empty that Sunday morning. The civil servants were at home or in church.

The governor's residence stood at the centre of a crescent at the far side of the square. A few guards, in heavy overcoats, stood in sentry boxes outside.

The square was a place which Fieldmann particularly liked on a Sunday. The great space relaxed his mind. He sat with Marie in a café set behind one of the arcades. The great tiled stove which ran the length of the far wall kept the café warm.

Jakov had painted the portrait of the owner along with his family. The owner was very pleased with the painting which hung in his drawing room above the café.

Jakov liked the owner who had lived in Paris for many years and tried to emulate what he had seen there in his own establishment.

'Ah, Mr Fieldmann. You must begin with some vodka. We will toast the New Year.' He fussed about as he brought them two glasses of vodka.

'Your husband is a true artist, Mrs Fieldmann. I have been to Paris and seen his great works there,' he boasted. He was very proud of his patron.

'May we all drink vodka and eat caviar when the revolution comes,' Fieldmann toasted humorously.

'Do not speak of revolution. What is to be achieved by revolution? Things are bad but they could be worse. This march will not help things. Last night the Cossacks arrived at the barracks.'

Suddenly Fieldmann became apprehensive. 'What Cossacks?'

'I do not know what Cossacks. Last night they rode

across the square and disappeared through the ministry gates. The governor is in residence.'

Marie looked at Fieldmann.

He groaned, 'There is nothing we can do. It is too late. They will be trapped.'

And as he spoke they heard the sound of the brass band from one of the steelworks that they had seen earlier. They heard the fatal sound of the large drum before they heard the music of the instruments. Then they watched the band march into the square followed by a long, ragged line of men and women. From the far corner another group appeared.

'I think it would be better for me to close the shutters Mr Fieldmann,' the owner said, rushing out to the colonnade and drawing closed the timber shutters. The gas lamps burned inside the café and people spoke in whispers.

Fieldmann and Marie rushed up the stairs and entered the drawing room. From here they had a complete view of the square.

The crowds stood in the centre in long lines, facing the residence of the Governor. Someone began to address them.

Then it happened.

Two great gates swung open. Out of the haze the Cossacks rode forward. They swung to the right and the left and formed an iron line between the people and the palace. Suddenly the speaker fell silent. Marie and Jakov watched the movements of the Cossacks, as if they were on military drill. The two grey lines met and turned forward into formation. They drew their swords, pointed them in the air and then forward. The horses began to move. At first they rode at a canter then it developed into a charge.

Suddenly the dense group of people panicked. They screamed and ran towards the great arches at the edge of the square. Some stumbled on the snow and were trampled upon.

Fieldmann and Marie looked in horror at the spectacle. The Cossacks thundered forward, trampling on the crowd, slashing left and right with their swords, splitting heads, trampling on the unfortunates who stumbled before them.

Many of the band members lay dead, still clutching their instruments. The drummer, with his great drum still strapped to his chest, lay across the top of a heap of bodies.

And then it was over. Like mechanical soldiers they drew into a line in front of the palace. At an order they turned and marched back through the great gates which were drawn behind them. Only the dead and the dying remained.

'The Tsar must die,' Fieldmann said simply to Marie.

They made their way down to the café. 'You can open the shutters now, you fools,' Fieldmann called. 'You are still alive and your miserable bellies are filled.'

'But Mr Fieldmann, I had to protect my property. I have put all I earned in Paris into this café.'

'Then invest all you can get for this café in good coffins both for you and your family, because you will need them,' Jakov said, drawing open the door and rushing into the square.

Both he and Marie helped as best they could. The dead were piled up into carts; the wounded were taken to a nearby hospital. As dusk fell the square lay empty. Only the bloodstains on the snow bore witness to what had happened.

The events in the square cleared any doubts from Jakov's mind. He would join the assassins.

Some weeks later, the group waited at the station for the train to St Petersburg. They stood at a distance from each other, stamping their feet in the snow or clapping their gloved hands to bring some warmth to their bodies. Jakov stood in cold isolation, looking down the narrow expanse of tracks, waiting for the train to emerge from the morning haze.

He looked around anxiously to see if they were being observed. There was always the danger that they were being followed by a member of the secret police.

The train arrived. They boarded it and took their seats in various carriages. Fieldmann looked stolidly out of the window. It was fogged and periodically he cleared it with the warm palm of his hand. There was nothing to see; vague outlines of silver birch woods sped past. But it gave him time to place his thoughts in order.

He had discovered the address of the Armenian from Kedrov.

He had gone into the woods each evening and practised with the revolver.

Now his hands were beginning to tremble. He took out his pipe, filled it with tobacco and began to smoke. He listened to the sounds of the wheels turning and the monotonous hum settled his mind.

The train reached St Petersburg that evening. It was the first time that Fieldmann had visited the city. As he passed through streets on the way to his lodgings he was struck by the architectural beauty of the place.

Eventually he found his way to the lodging house, concealed behind a coal yard. The others arrived later. They assured him that they had not been followed.

'Very well. Let us go over the plans again,' Dr Volodin said. 'If any of you feel that you do not have the nerve to go through with our plans, now is the time to say so. We must have nerves of steel,' he ordered.

Nobody said a word. They looked at each other. Their expressions were taut and strained. 'I have brought a bottle of vodka for the occasion,' the doctor told them, taking a bottle and some glasses from his case.

'Let us drink to our plans,' Kedrov said. They sat around

the table and drank from the bottle, toasting a a new society.

'Tomorrow we will spend the day examining the locations and finding out the best methods of escape. Make sure that you can run up some alleyway or other in the confusion following the attack. Once the revolver is fired and the bomb detonates, leave as quickly as possible. The city will be crawling with police and soldiers.'

That night they slept in bunk beds. In the morning they ate dry bread and water. Then at intervals they made their way across the coal yard and into the city.

Jakov waited some distance from the hotel. At eleven o'clock the Armenian emerged. He was dressed in a long fur coat, with a wide collar and he had a fur hat on his head. He was still portly. Jakov watched him disappear into an automobile and drive into the Nevsky Prospekt. According to the information Jakov had received, he would return at six for his dinner.

During the day Jakov wandered through the city. The central part was opulent and charming, more western than any other city in Russia. He crossed the Neva and looked at the formidable fortress of Peter and Paul. He was only too well aware of its bleak history.

He ate at a working man's café. He drank a large bowl of soup, ate a loaf of dark brown bread and listened to the talk of the working men. It was heavy and limited.

He smoked his pipe beside a billy stove. To pass the time he borrowed several newspapers from the owner and began to read them. As he was reading the social columns two names caught his attention, those of Alma Schmerling, the wife of Prince Karl, and Sophie Schmerling.

He must tell Marie that both her sisters were in St Petersburg. It was strange that the three should be so close to each other.

Darkness began to fall early. The streets were gloomy and introspective when he left the café and the heat had made him sluggish. A wind from the north cut through his clothes and he felt cold to the bone.

He hastened to the hotel and stood in the shadows and waited. The Armenian was on time. As he had been informed he returned at six o'clock.

Jakov made his decision instantly. He walked forward. The Armenian was not aware of his approach as he was escorting a young woman out of the automobile.

Fieldmann drew his collar up about him and pulled his cap down over his eyes.

When he was three yards from the Armenian he drew his revolver. He shot directly at the heavy figure. The young woman screamed and rushed back into the automobile. The Armenian charged at him. Their eyes met. Coldly, Jakov pulled the trigger twice more. Blood splurted from the Armenian's eye. The second shot made a neat hole in his forehead.

Then he rushed from the scene. He ran down an alley, through a courtyard and out the far side. As he passed a wide canal he threw the revolver in. In the half-light it slid across the ice and into the dark, flowing water beyond. Jakov quickly doubled back to the Nevsky Prospekt and mixed with the crowd.

His hands were trembling. He recalled the final moments when he had shot the Armenian at point-blank range. He would never forget the expression on the man's sallow face.

But he suppressed his compassion for the spy, remembering that he had caused the deaths of many young men.

He did not return directly to the coal yard, but continued to walk through the streets, burning off his nervous excitement. When he was exhausted he returned to the confined quarters.

'These were not our plans,' Dr Volodin cried when Jakov explained that he had shot the Armenian. 'We have come to assassinate the Tsar. Perhaps you have been identified. The secret police will question the bystanders, you realise.'

'I can assure you that I was not seen. I took precautions,' Jakov said.

'You are a fool, Fieldmann. You acted out of passion, not logic.'

'He deserved what he got. He destroyed my friends.'

'We are not here to settle old scores. We are here to kill the Tsar.'

They might have lost their tempers but the young engineer calmed them down.

'Return to Kotlas on the early train. Leave the rest to us,' the doctor ordered.

Early the next morning Fieldmann left his friends and took the train east.

He wondered if it would be a day of vital importance in the history of Russia.

Next morning the Tsar left his palace at Tsarskoe Selo for Saint Isaac's Cathedral. The magnificent church had been built in the nineteenth century. Its great dome resembled that of Saint Peter's in Rome. Thousands gathered in the square to watch Nicholas and his wife Alexandra pass up the steps to the cathedral. They stood in the snow, dark masses of people against the white. After the service the automobile moved across the square, flanked by Cossacks with sabres drawn, and the crowd began to call out to the Tsar.

'They still think that he is father to them, the fools,' Dr Volodin told his friends as the automobile drove towards them.

He took the bomb from his coat pocket and lit the ten-second fuse. The other two covered him as the fuse began to sparkle. The automobile moved towards them.

'Now,' Kedrov called out.

Dr Volodin lifted the bomb to lob it onto the Tsar's

automobile. Suddenly the great crowd about him heaved and the bomb fell from his hand to the ground. They looked at the spluttering fuse. The doctor rushed to take it in his hands and throw it again at the automobile. As he bent down, it exploded. The shrapnel tore into his body and shredded his torso and face. Blood sprayed onto the snow.

Immediately, the Tsar's automobile accelerated. The cavalcade thundered past the dying man.

Several people had been injured and others began to scream. Some in the vast crowd broke out in panic and began to rush across the great square to get away from the danger. Others fled down the various side streets or along the canals. Only the doctor and some of the wounded remained.

The assassination attempt had failed.

In Kotlas, Fieldmann was waiting for some of the group to return from St Petersburg. When they did not he began to worry.

'Something must have gone wrong,' he told Marie. But they agreed to continue as if everything was normal, until they heard further news.

Two days later there was a report in the local newspaper that an attempt on the Tsar's life had failed. It gave few details about the incident.

Then three days later, as Fieldmann sat down to work at his easel, the house was quickly surrounded. He did not have time to escape.

'Pack some of your belongings and come with us,' he was ordered bluntly by a gentleman in a dark coat and a fur hat.

'Where are you taking me and what have I done?' he asked.

'You will find out when you get to St Petersburg,' he was told.

Before he left he wrote a brief note for Marie.

Then, surrounded by four secret service agents, he was bundled into an automobile and taken directly to the railway station.

Eight hours later he was driven through St Petersburg to the Fortress of Peter and Paul. Six days previously he had studied its bastions, thick and formidable. Now he passed through the Ivan gate and the grim, imposing place sent a cold shiver through him. Soon he would be in the power of the secret police. In this prison Peter the Great had beaten his son to death; the Decembrists had been imprisoned here as well as Dostoyevsky and others.

Jakov was brought through a maze of buildings. Finally he entered a bleak room where a gas light burned. He was ordered to sit down in front of a bare table. Two guards stood by. They remained silent. Fieldmann's mind was gripped by fear. He remembered the days he had spent in the cell in Vienna.

The only sound in the room was that of a cheap clock. After a while, its ticking became hypnotic.

Finally the door opened and an officer entered. He had a heavy face. He looked at Jakov. 'I believe that you know something, Fieldmann, of this attempt to assassinate the Tsar,' he said directly.

'What attempt?' he asked.

The officer lifted his eyes to the soldier. The man raised the butt of his rifle and brought it heavily down on Fieldmann's head. He fell to the floor, blood flowing from his ears. He feared that his eardrums had been burst.

He dragged himself back onto the chair and the heavy-faced man stared at him. There was no emotion in his eyes. He had been through the procedures of interrogation before.

'I believe that you know something, Fieldmann, of this attempt to assassinate the Tsar,' he stated again as if nothing had happened.

Fieldmann's head began to throb. 'Yes, I have heard of the attempt.'

'Good. Now we can proceed .'

Fieldmann was frightened by the officer's manner. His mind was distant and he had no interest in his prisoner. If necessary, he would beat Jakov's face to a pulp in order to extract information.

'Did you know Dr Volodin?'

'Yes.'

The guard raised the butt of his gun to bring it down on the side of Fieldmann's head.

'I visited his clinic very frequently. We had literary gatherings there.'

'Which turned into political gatherings and at which it was eventually decided to assassinate the Tsar,' the officer continued.

'It was Dr Volodin who decided to assassinate the Tsar,' Fieldmann told him.

'He will never be able to tell us. But we have captured the others. They are only too willing to talk about each other. They are locked away in cells where no one will hear their screams. And we have a photograph of your group, supplied by the police at Kotlas. Dangerous things, photographs. Now, let me ask you some simple questions.'

He took out a typed sheet of paper and proceeded to question Fieldmann. He asked short questions about his life, his movements, his friends and his political beliefs.

When he was finished he closed the file and looked at him with cold eyes. 'I believe that you knew the Armenian. I cannot prove that you killed him, yet I know you did. But you did us a favour. He had outlived his usefulness and he cost us too much. If you had not killed him then some other group would have. Good day'

He left the room.

Fieldmann felt frightened. He had never met anyone as efficient as the officer in his life.

One of the soldiers butted him in the side and ordered him to rise. He was marched out of the drab room, down a long corridor and down again to a lower level. He was pushed into a cell and the door was locked behind him. A small, barred window close to the ceiling let in some grey light. The cell was furnished with a camp bed with some thin blankets thrown on top of it. They were unwashed and smelt of urine.

Jakov sat on the bed and gazed at the wall.

His prospects were grim.

For this, he would surely hang.

Chapter Thirty-three

Prince Karl was now in the pay of the German Secret Service. While Alma recuperated in Vienna, he continued to visit the ballet.

When the lights dimmed at the Mariinsky theatre and the curtains were drawn back to reveal some fairy scene or other, his opera glasses would range through the *corps de ballet*.

Every night he would send extravagant bouquets of flowers to Lydia Savina's dressing room. She continued to treat him like a plaything. Sometimes she would throw her arms about him. At other times she pouted and would not speak to him.

When Federov was in the city Lydia Savina could not resist the count. After a meal at Restaurant Cubah he would invite her to the Casino. There she would fritter away the roubles he gave her.

When she returned to her apartment after each night of gambling on the island, Prince Karl would be hiding furtively in the shadows outside. Alexander Federov would often remain with her until dawn. It was clear that she was the mistress of Federov and that she was more attracted to the old man than to Prince Karl.

'I am a Hapsburg,' he often argued to himself. 'She is perhaps the daughter of a peasant and Federov is a Tartar. She has no right to reject me.'

By now Prince Karl had neglected his office of ambassador. He ignored his appointments and spent long hours drinking in his rooms, arguing with himself.

Sometimes in a drunken stupor he imagined grandiose

schemes to win the heart of the ballerina; he would challenge Federov to a duel and kill his rival. In darker moments he considered how he would murder Lydia Savina. He had spent enormous sums of money upon her. She belonged to him as a serf belonged to a landowner.

Before Alma's return to St Petersburg, Franz Joseph sent a letter to her, inviting her to the Schönbrunn.

When she walked into his private rooms and saw him standing by the window, she noticed that he had grown more feeble during the past year.

He invited her to sit by the great fire. Outside, snow lay on the great courtyard and on the gardens.

'The stillness of beauty and the stillness of death,' he said returning from the window and taking a seat opposite her.

'I will not begin with trivialities,' he said. 'We have known each other too long for such things. I have good reason to believe that Prince Karl is neglecting his duties in St Petersburg and this at a time when Russia could be thrown into revolution.' He paused. 'I need not go into further details. I could recall him, but that would be humiliating.'

'You are disappointed then,' she said.

'With him, yes. Not with you. Look to the history of France. The French Revolution swept away the monarchy. The same thing could happen both here and in Russia. I need a trustworthy presence in St Petersburg, therefore, I am now giving you signed instructions to take over the post of ambassador there. Prince Karl will remain on as a figurehead,' he said grimly, handing her an envelope bearing the imperial seal.

Alma had many things to consider. The Emperor had placed a heavy burden upon her, but it did make her independent of Prince Karl. She felt that she now had a part to play in the destiny of the empire.

They spoke of less formal matters for an hour. Then it was time for her to leave. Several other ambassadors were waiting to meet him.

She returned to St Petersburg with confidence and enthusiasm. As the train made its way through the endless snow towards the capital on the Neva River she recalled her weeks with Prince Eugene. They had been happy together in the small villa on the banks of the Danube.

Sophie Schmerling waited for Joseph Steiner. He had returned from Berlin and as usual was spending the night in a small hotel. Despite his vast wealth he could never feel comfortable at a palace. 'I have the mind of those born in ghettos and small rooms,' he often told her.

'But you have more wealth than the Kaiser,' she would laugh.

'I may have. But I have known Jews who have been richer than the Kaiser one week and as poor as church, or should I say synagogue, mice the following day. I never flaunt my wealth. I never keep it in one place.'

As Sophie waited for him now she studied some papers on her desk. Her position in St Petersburg drew her more and more into the political turmoil of the city. At the same time, she watched the German empire grow both powerful and wealthy. Its brash youth lay in its favour.

Finally her stepfather arrived, dressed in a dark fur coat which her servant removed.

She placed her arms about him and kissed him on the cheeks. 'You will have some vodka? It will warm you.'

Joseph drank the glass of Russian vodka swiftly, feeling it reheat his body.

'Why do you not come and stay with me, when you are in St Petersburg?' she said. 'I have a wing where you can do your business.'

'I have always run my business from my coat pocket,' he laughed.

'From your two black notebooks,' she remarked dryly.

'From my two black notebooks which even the secret police cannot read.' He took the two notebooks from his pocket and showed them to her like a child sharing a toy. However, he knew that Sophie called him because she had some serious matter to discuss with him.

When he was seated she handed him a typed sheet of paper, containing information on the recent attempt on the life of the Tsar. Towards the end of the report the name Fieldmann caught his eye.

'Not the artist from Vienna?' he asked.

'Yes. He has lived with Marie for some years. Now he is imprisoned in St Peter and Paul's.'

'That means that Marie is still in Kotlas. Is she implicated in all of this?'

'I do not know and I do not care. I am sure she is. Fieldmann is a maniac.'

'But what if she is sent to Siberia?'

'Then it is too bad. We all choose our own paths. She chose the one of revolution. You see where it has got her. Let her rot in Siberia. She would bring down not only the Tsar but the whole structure of government in this country.'

'You have no wish to see her?' Joseph asked.

'No. I know that Fieldmann was once involved in an attempt on the life of Baron Von Hertling,' she said in a hard voice. 'He has directed young men to their deaths. He spreads the poison of his doctrine in every place through which he travels. Marie is a revolutionary and she, too, would destroy the very society in which I believe. No, I will not see her.'

Her stepfather was wise enough not to pursue the matter.

After a conversation in which Marie's name was not mentioned they entered the dining room. It was a lavish place decorated with paintings depicting scenes from

Switzerland and northern Italy. The ceiling was ornamented with rococo shells and leafy tendrils.

Joseph Steiner had a small but delicate appetite. He enjoyed a glass of champagne with some cold sturgeon and caviar.

Sophie had arranged the meal and the conversation to suit his tastes. When they began to discuss his collection of paintings, he became excited. 'I am most anxious to purchase some works by Joseph de la Tour. They found their way to Russia after the French Revolution. It is amazing how many works of art found their way to Russia at the end of the eighteenth century. He is a marvellous artist, completely undervalued.'

'And where are these paintings?'

'I am not at liberty to tell you. But I know I can purchase them.'

'But why keep on collecting such masterpieces? You keep them in storage in Vienna!'

'That is only a temporary measure. Some day they will hang in all their glory in the city art gallery,' he said proudly.

'Have you seen the room in which they will hang?'

'No, but the curator is preparing one for me. I look forward to the day when I will walk through the Joseph Steiner Room. People will realise that this Jew has taste and that he has made a bequest to a great empire.'

Sophie looked at her stepfather. One had only to tell him that a painting existed somewhere in an obscure village in the heart of Russia and he would abandon all his business and set out to purchase it.

'I have a proposition to make,' she began. 'Berlin would appreciate your collection. If you made a bequest to the museum the paintings would be hanging in a Joseph Steiner Room in six months. They have the space for them. And I can arrange that you will be raised to the position of Baron. I can make you an aristocrat. They have made no such offers in Vienna.'

Joseph looked at his stepdaughter. He could not believe the proposition she had made. 'Is it possible?' he asked.

'Not only possible but most probable.'

'Baron Von Steiner,' he said testing the title on his palate. 'No. I cannot accept it. I have never aspired to such a position. I thought I might have received some honour in Vienna. Nothing great but something which would acknowledge my gift to the city.'

'You will never be honoured in Vienna, Papa. Berlin will honour you. The title is a protection which will bring you into the ranks of the gentiles. You will belong in Berlin. You will travel through Europe and your title will earn you respect. You will no longer be a wandering Jew.'

Sophie realized that she loved this small man who had secured her position and happiness. Now, after months working through her sources in Berlin, she could present him with this honour. And his collection would enhance the city.

He was visibly shaken. 'I am overcome,' he said. 'I must think about it. I must consult your mother.'

'Do not consult Mother. Take your own decision. Vienna will neither accept you nor her. Germany will. She will scream a little and protest, then she will accept it.

'I will let you consider the matter. But remember, money and wealth need respectability and Jewish money doubly so. You have uneasy feet. This will give you roots in a landscape,' Sophie said firmly.

Joseph admired his stepdaughter. She had a strong mind, almost masculine in its purpose. She was a political woman with whom he could have lively discussions. She knew his mind better than any person alive.

Joseph left Sophie's palace and walked along the Neva River, his mind on fire. Would his journey in search of roots and acceptance end in Germany?

He recalled the Diaspora. He had set out the maps in his home in Vienna, following their lonely journey through history.

He must accept the title. He would accept it for them. Perhaps it would give them a voice and every voice which spoke for the Jews was necessary. Too many spoke against them.

From where he stood Joseph could see the grim fortress of Peter and Paul on the northern bank of the river where Fieldmann was now imprisoned. He knew its bleak history. It was the harshest prison in the world. The revolutionary Nechaev had been incarcerated in the Alexei Ravelin bastion and starved to death.

Why did Fieldmann not stay with his painting, Joseph wondered. Revolution is a dangerous game. He could have been one of the greatest painters of his era. A talent wasting away in a cell. How terrible.

Having walked through St Petersburg, he returned to his hotel, where he phoned a private detective whose services he had often used.

When he arrived late that night, Joseph outlined to him the line of inquiries he was to make. Above all, he was to find out about Fieldmann's jailers. Were they corruptible? Could they be bribed?

That night he slept erratically. Several times he snapped awake and walked the room, looking down on a gloomy street lit by few lights.

Early next morning he had an automobile take him to the station, where he set out for the city of Kotlas.

Marie Schmerling felt isolated and alone. There was nowhere she could turn for help. The whole revolutionary group had been captured. Fieldmann would be hanged for his part in the affair. She fretted about the house expecting the secret police to arrive at any minute and whisk her along to some prison for interrogation.

An automobile drew up in the small street in Kotlas, and children crowded around the vehicle. Marie peered at the figure emerging from the back seat in disbelief.

She wondered how Joseph Steiner had obtained her address.

She did not know how to greet him.

There was a knock on the door and her heart missed a beat. She was shabbily dressed and her hair was in disorder. She combed it quickly and looked at herself in the mirror, knowing that her stepfather would be shocked at her appearance. They had not met for several years.

Then she walked calmly to the door and opened it. Joseph stared up at her. His eyes were still sad.

Suddenly she rushed to him and put her arms about him. 'You know about Jakov,' she said.

'I hear everything,' he replied, as they entered the timber house. The cold had gripped it and Marie was wearing mittens on her chapped fingers.

'I must fetch some wood and light the stove. Since Jakov was taken to prison I have neglected the place.'

She brought some small dry branches from the back yard and placed them on a stove. Soon a fire was blazing.

Joseph looked at Marie. Her skin had coarsened during the years. Her hair was unkempt. There was the suggestion of a stoop in her posture, which came from the hardship of the years.

'You always came when I needed you,' she said, looking at him.

'I happen to turn up. No more.'

'You did not have to come from St Petersburg. I turned my back on you a long time ago. I still believe in my principles,' she told him defensively.

'I believe in principles. But who will listen to my principles,' he said in a lonely voice. 'You believe you can change the world. I believe that you cannot. You believe in the distribution of wealth. I know that is a foolish ideal.

Distribute it today and tomorrow some Joseph Steiner will set up a stall somewhere in Prague or Vienna and within ten years he will be a wealthy man. When you take Joseph Steiner's money from him, spread it about and in ten more years Joseph Steiner will still be a wealthy man.' He threw his hands in the air. 'But I have come about other things. I know where Fieldmann is.'

'Where?'

'In Peter and Paul prison. You will never get to see him.'

'What will happen?'

'At worst he will be hanged. At best he will be sent into exile in Siberia.' Joseph said, although he did not believe it.

'I will follow him to the ends of the earth,' Marie said firmly.

'I have begun to work behind the scenes. I am not certain what I can achieve, but I will do my best,' Joseph said.

'And why should you care for Fieldmann?'

'I care for his art. I believe that he could have been one of the greatest painters of the century. Perhaps he is. I purchased the paintings you sold in Vienna.' He spoke in a quiet voice.

'My sisters are in St Petersburg, I believe. It is strange that we should all end up in Russia.'

'They are quite important there now,' Joseph smiled. 'Sophie is independently rich.'

'Could they help Fieldmann?'

'They have no wish to be associated with you.'

'And so I am alone. They must laugh at my straitened circumstances.'

'Perhaps they do.'

'What steps can I take?'

Joseph told her of his intentions.

'You think that you can save his life then?'

'I believe that I can save it. But he will spend a long time in some backwater in Siberia. But pack your things and come with me to St Petersburg. I must hire an advocate.'

Joseph Steiner remained until the evening discussing matters with Marie. Then he left for one of the small hotels he favoured when travelling.

Next morning, with a small suitcase between them, Marie and Joseph Steiner set off for St Petersburg.

As the train passed through the great plains of Russia Alma considered her future in St Petersburg. Her affair with Prince Eugene had been passionate and had helped her regain her strength and confidence. Now she was pregnant. She would confront Prince Karl with the news on her arrival, and she would be direct and to the point.

Three days after setting out from Vienna, she entered the embassy offices, which occupied the west wing of the palace. She called the staff together and told them that they were now responsible to her.

'But Prince Karl,' one said. 'He will be furious.'

'Let him be furious. There are complaints from Vienna. Letters receive no reply. Reports do not arrive on time. We have lost contact with several embassies. All this must change. I will give you a week to get all your affairs in order. If necessary, work through the night.'

Two days later, returned from the islands, Prince Karl burst into her private office. She was sitting behind the desk writing a financial report.

His face was purple with fury. In his anger he had struck one of the servants and knocked him to the floor.

He did not speak to her. Instead, he rushed across the room, his hand raised to strike her.

Alma had expected such an outburst and had prepared for the event. She drew a pistol from a drawer and pointed it at him. 'Sit down,' she said, 'or I will shoot you. I am only seeking a good reason to do so.' There was firm anger in her voice.

He sat down, stunned.

'Read this,' she said, pushing the letter she had received from Franz Joseph across the table.

He read the letter in disbelief. 'This is humiliating. I will not tolerate it,' he said, not taking his eyes off the letter.

'I have more humiliating news for you. I am pregnant,' she said not taking her eyes off him.

He did not grow angry. 'So someone has finally humped the Jewess,' he said. 'I will file for divorce. You will be disgraced. You will return to Vienna as an untitled woman.'

'I have considered such an option. However, in evidence I will state that you are syphilitic, which can be easily proved, that you carry the madness which drove Prince Rudolf to suicide and that you corrupt young boys as well as dote over young ballerinas. I have all the evidence secured in a safe in Vienna. So, let us do some horse trading.'

For the next hour they argued violently together. Finally they came to an arrangement.

Karl left the room. He spent the next three days drinking.

Prince Dmitri soon received news from the embassy of all that had transpired. He noted it in his diary.

It was clear that Prince Karl was becoming an undesirable acquaintance.

Chapter Thirty-four

It was intensely cold when the carriages and automobiles pulled up in front of the Winter Palace. It was the most magnificent building in the city, stretching along the south bank of the Neva.

The three blocks of the building were flooded with light. Braziers burned around the immense Alexander column, a granite monolith, topped with a delicate archangel, which stood at the centre of the great square in front of the palace. The winter season, which began on New Year's Day and ended at Lent, was now at its mid point.

All day the servants had been preparing the great palace for the arrival of the guests for the Winter Ball. Now they were ranged along the great corridors and galleries with their trays of champagne or standing behind tables, observing the nobility.

Two thousand guests moved easily around the gigantic galleries supported by columns of jasper marble and malachite.

At half past eight the ball began. The grand master of ceremonies emerged, tapped loudly on the floor with his staff and cried out 'Their Imperial Majesties.'

Tsar Nicholas and the Empress Alexandra appeared, Nicholas dressed in his red jacket and black trousers, a blue sash running across his chest and medals pinned to his left shoulder. Alexandra was dressed in a silver brocade gown sewn with diamonds and pearls.

Their expressions were tense and the Tsar stared forward into the middle distance as if the whole evening would be a burden to him. It was obvious that both were under some strain.

The orchestra broke into a polonaise and the royal couple led the dance. It was clear that both were still very much in love with each other, but those who knew the intimate details of the court felt that the Tsar was weak and dominated by his wife and family. He did not compare well with his father, Tsar Alexander II who had been of magnificent stature.

The ball continued until midnight. Outside snow was falling on the domes and roofs of St Petersburg, covering up the coach and automobile ruts on the roads and squares. Light from the great windows of the palace fell on the square, giving it a fairytale quality. At some distance from the palace, soldiers dressed in heavy grey coats threw a cordon around the place, to protect the aristocracy from the assassin's bomb or bullet.

It was late in the evening when Alma and Sophie met in the Rastrelli Gallery. Alma was with her husband, Prince Karl, Sophie with her young German aide de camp. Prince Karl had grown noticeably older and there was an unstable glint in his eye.

The sisters had met at a number of banquets during the season and they had been formal with each other. Now, while the men were engaged in conversation, the two sisters retired to an alcove. They wanted to speak privately.

'No doubt you are as well informed as I am about Fieldmann,' Sophie began.

'Yes. I had a visit from our stepfather. He is trying to save Fieldmann's skin. Can you believe this? Of course he is implicated. Up to his neck in it. I would have them all hanged without a trial,' Alma replied.

'As long as it is done quickly and without undue fuss by the newspapers. I cannot afford to be linked to either Fieldmann or Marie,' Sophie said. 'It would do my reputation in this city little good.'

'The papers have been warned.'

'I will ensure that it is more than a warning they get,' Sophie told her in a sinister voice. 'I have some influence in the city and I intend to use it. Let them report the case, as long as they keep our names out of it. And remember that Marie is illegitimate.'

'Would you use that against her?' Alma was a little shocked.

'If necessary,' Sophie said. Sophie spoke in a menacing tone. Clearly, her nature had not changed during the years in Berlin. 'She should be with that anarchist in Saint Peter and Paul's. She was always bent on pulling down the whole structure of law and order.'

'Then we are decided that we should not meet her and that our names should be suppressed from any reports,' Alma said.

'Yes. I will use my influence and you have contacts in the highest places. Use them.'

'If anything further arises I will be in contact with you.'

Having discussed their business they returned to their partners. They conversed together for a short time, then moved away from each other.

While the orchestra was playing and the aristocracy of the capital was moving through the rooms and corridors of the Winter Palace, Joseph Steiner was busy with the Fieldmann affair. His methods were never direct. He remained out of sight, like a puppeteer. When a string needed pulling it was pulled, when a character was needed, he drew him out of a box and brought him to the centre stage.

Four days remained to him to save the life of Fieldmann.

He had invited an advocate to dinner, to a discreet place where they could talk.

'I wish to employ you to defend an artist,' he explained during the meal. 'I know your legal fee. I am willing to double it. If there is a successful outcome to the trial, then I will be very munificent. Money is of no account in this particular case.'

The advocate looked at the small man sitting opposite him. He knew that he was Jewish and very rich. 'Of course, I accept. Explain the case to me.'

'You have heard of Fieldmann?'

He tried to recall the name. He must be of no importance in the city.

'Fieldmann is an artist. He is a prisoner at the St Peter and Paul Fortress. In four days' time he will be tried with others for the attempted assassination of the Tsar.'

The advocate turned pale.

'No, I am afraid I could not accept the brief.'

Joseph Steiner had anticipated his reply. 'I am not asking you to act directly. You must know a bright young lawyer who can act for you. With your experience he should be able to defend my client.'

'As long as my name is not associated with this Fieldmann. It would not do my practice any good, you know.'

'I am well aware of your position,' Joseph replied.

'Then let me explain to you what problems you face. By now they will have beaten a confession out of him which, no doubt, he has signed. He will have confessed to his knowledge of the plot. That is enough to convict him. You must provide witnesses to swear that he was nowhere near St Petersburg when the incident occurred.'

'I already have a list of witnesses who were in the carriage with him on his way to Kotlas when the attempt was made. They can be produced on the day of the trial.'

'Very good. Now, one impossible task remains,' the advocate explained. 'You will have to have Fieldmann's statement at the Fort altered.'

'That will be done,' Steiner said in a matter-of-fact voice.

The advocate was taken aback. This small Jew who only nibbled at his food and was abstemious with his wine seemed to possess extraordinary power in the city.

'How can that be done? Do you know someone in high office?' he asked.

'Oh, I know many people in high office. But to achieve something like this you need somebody in a low office,' Joseph said mysteriously.

They did not dwell on the subject further. Their meeting had come to a conclusion. Before they left the restaurant Joseph presented the advocate with an envelope. It contained a large sum of money.

Stanislav Kopylov lived in the northern district of St Petersburg. Every morning he took the bus to work, at the Fortress of Saint Peter and Paul.

His business was to interrogate prisoners. This he did with efficiency. His methods were simple. Torture men until they were so desperate they would sign any sheet of paper placed before them.

As soon as a man was set before him he could gauge his mental strength. He knew how much force was necessary with each individual.

In the evening he would return to his apartment. During the summer months he would dig in his small plot, encouraging flowers and plants to grow in the short months of light and heat. His small apartment was filled with potted plants which he tended with care. His library contained only books on gardening and farming.

Stanislav's father had been a serf. As a child he had watched him work from morning until night for a landlord for little reward. He had been only a beast of burden.

The army had been a way of escape for him from the tedium of life in a small village. He was assured a small salary and he lived in frugal comfort.

Now, in wintertime, when the frost gripped the earth, he would read farming books and hope that the temperature would not injure his plants. During the long nights of winter he would drink cheap vodka and think of the small plot of land he wished to purchase in the Ukraine.

The detective followed him from the station along the street which led to his apartment. He stood outside for some time. Then when he was satisfied that Kopylov had settled in, he approached his room.

'Who is there?' a gruff voice asked.

'A friend,' the detective answered.

'I have no friends,' came the answer.

'Are you certain?'

The door opened. The detective was confronted by the dull face of Kopylov. He held a watering can in his hand.

'What do you want? Have you been followed?'

'No. I checked several times.'

'Come in then. State your business.'

'I come on behalf of an interested party. You could do them a small favour. For this, you would be well paid.'

Kopylov felt that he was being led into a trap. 'Nobody has ever come to my apartment and offered me a large sum of money. I will complain to my superiors.'

'Very well. I will leave, and you will never know what the offer is. You may regret it until the day you die. You might have had time to live with your plants, perhaps buy some place where you could watch crops grow.' The detective had been quick to study the apartment. It was filled with plants. He was surprised that such a brutal-looking man could lavish such care on plants.

Kopylov looked at him. His mind was racing. He was surrounded by enemies; there were many who would like his job at the fortress. One slip and he could find himself in the very cell to which he had committed some prisoner.

His thoughts were interrupted when the detective noticed an exotic plant from the Ukraine. 'I did not believe that such a plant could flourish in Petersburg,' he said.

'And no other one does, not even at the botanical gardens. It is very delicate. I must keep it in the correct temperature at all times. It flowers in winter and reminds me of home.'

The wild Ukrainian flower had sparked an idea in the detective's mind. 'Would you like to possess a small farm in the Ukraine?' he asked.

'Of course I would. There the earth is warm and fertile. Here the earth is frozen. It is like the womb of a barren woman. Why do you ask?'

'I could introduce you to somebody who would make all this possible. Think about it. Tomorrow, as you enter the fortress of St Peter and Paul, stop at the gate. Take off your cap and wipe your forehead. Then I will know that you are willing to meet the third party.'

With that he left.

That night Kopylov did not sleep. He paced the room. Only one question occupied his mind: was he being drawn into a trap by the secret police? He knew their methods. He had witnessed them in action.

It was early in the morning when he decided to take a chance. His life in St Petersburg was featureless. It would drag on until he retired on a miserable pension. Perhaps fate was on his side.

Next morning, as he was about to enter the fortress, he doffed his cap and wiped his forehead.

That night Joseph Steiner visited him.

Kopylov was hesitant when Joseph entered his apartment. There was the danger of being caught. Perhaps Joseph Steiner was an agent and the farm in the Ukraine was only a mirage.

'I cannot make up my mind,' Kopylov told Joseph.

'Do you fear that you fail in your sense of duty, that you dishonour the trust the Tsar has placed in you? I can assure you that the Tsar is enjoying one of the season's balls tonight, unaware that you exist; he would not particularly worry if you died.'

'It is not that,' Kopylov retorted. 'I owe no allegiance to the Tsar. But his secret agents are everywhere. They play all sorts of tricks on people. I have condemned men to death. I know how easy it is to beat false statements out of them. I have seen prisoners disappear into Siberia never to appear again. So, I fear the secret police. Perhaps you are one of them. Convince me that you are not.'

'I will,' Joseph told him. He took a large bundle of notes from his pocket, placed them in front of Kopylov and piled them on top of one another.

'These are old notes. I always take that precaution when I am doing deals. Now, examine them. Tell me if they are genuine.' He pushed the notes slowly towards Kopylov.

The man had never seen such an amount of money before. He took a bundle in his hand. It sent tremors through his body. He went through the notes. They were creased and filthy and possessed a used beauty.

He pushed them back to Joseph Steiner, realising that the price of his farm land in the Ukraine was being given to him.

Joseph broke the paper band on one of the bundles. He took some of the money and tore it down the centre. 'I will keep half of the money. You keep the other half. It is useless to both of us.'

It was at that point that Kopylov knew that Joseph Steiner was not an agent. The secret police would not have torn up genuine money.

'Stop. Do not tear any further money. What do you want me to do?'

'Alter the confession of Jakov Fieldmann,' Joseph said bluntly.

Kopylov blinked. If he was caught, he, too would die. And then he thought of his beloved Ukraine.

'I will change the files. I cannot dissociate him from the group; they were stupid enough to have a photograph taken of themselves and that links them all. But it can be proved that he was not at the scene of the crime. I will change the confession he made.' He continued, 'Remember, he was part of the plot. Have no doubt about that. You purchase his life with this money. I purchase my farm.'

Joseph took a bundle of money and handed to him. 'I trust you. That is part payment on your farm. The rest you will receive when I hear the evidence.'

He wished the officer goodnight. Then he slipped into the shadows and disappeared.

Two days later the trials began, attracting considerable interest in the press. The reporters sat in the gallery taking notes, expecting a verdict of guilty. The three accused would be hanged for their attempt on the life of the Tsar.

Joseph sat with Marie and others who had come to witness the proceedings. Marie was taut and nervous. She did not believe that her stepfather would be able to change the evidence. In these cases, it was impossible to determine the outcome.

She watched the doorway through which the prisoners would enter the dock, hoping to see Jakov.

At eleven o'clock the judge entered the court. At ten minutes past eleven the door to the dock opened, but only two of the accused entered. She recognised them. One was Kedrov, the engineer. He had been wounded in the blast and the side of his face was bandaged. Both prisoners looked exhausted. They stood in the dock while the accusations were read out against them.

'Where is Fieldmann?' Marie asked.

'He will be tried by himself.'

'What does that mean?'

'He will not be accused of an assassination attempt. However, as he was part of the group, he will receive a sentence.'

'Are you sure?'

'Yes.'

They fell silent.

It took the court two hours to arrive at a decision. Both men were found guilty. They were sentenced to be hanged. They were led away to their cells to await execution.

The cold formality of the court frightened Marie. She remembered the passion which had set Kedrov's mind on fire; she recalled the scenes in the square where innocent protesters were cut down by Cossacks.

Now, she held her breath as Fieldmann entered the courtroom in handcuffs. His beard and hair were wild and ragged. He stared about him as if unused to the harsh light. Then his eyes focused on Marie and Joseph Steiner.

Only the young advocate had been able to see him in prison. He had explained to Fieldmann that they would make the case that he was not party to the plot.

'You have come too late,' Fieldmann had replied. 'They have beaten the confession out of me. I will hang like the others.'

'But we have witnesses who will state that you were in the carriage with them when the Tsar was assassinated,' he argued.

'Let the justice of the Tsar have its day,' Fieldmann had sighed.

Now, as he stood in the court, he knew that he would be condemned to be hanged. The evidence had mounted against him. As he looked from the dock, he wondered why Joseph Steiner was with Marie. How had he contacted her? How had he discovered where she lived?

The evidence for the state was presented. Photographs were shown to the judge, implicating Fieldmann. It was only when the confession he had given at the Fortress of St Peter and Paul was read out that Fieldmann sharpened his mind. It had been altered.

He listened incredulously. He then knew why Joseph Steiner was in the court. His financial power had penetrated the grimmest prison in Russia. He would live. He would be sent to an isolated spot in Siberia but at least he would have the gift of life.

At five o' clock Jakov Fieldmann was sentenced to ten years' exile in Siberia.

He was taken back to his cell.

As he sat in the semi-darkness in disbelief, he realised that soon he would be making his way across the bleak, featureless tracts of Siberia. It would be a living death, but there was always the hope of a resurrection.

Marie walked away from the courtroom with Joseph. They went to a small restaurant where he bought her a basic meal of vegetables and meat.

She was hungry and she ate the food with appreciation. 'You saved his life,' she said simply.

'Yes.'

'So I owe you a life in return?'

'Can you give me such a life?'

'I do not know. Look at me. I have grown old in the cause of revolution. I teach to eke out a living. The future looks bleak.'

'And what will you do with yourself?'

'I will go into exile with Jakov.'

'Then here is some money. Take it. You will need it.'

She took the bundle of notes and put them in her pocket.

They parted outside the restaurant and Joseph made his way back towards his hotel.

Chapter Thirty-five

That summer of 1913, St Petersburg was at its most beautiful. It was the season of the white nights, when the light never left the sky. The air was heavy with the scent of honeysuckle and the heavy fragrance of lilacs. The gardens of the Winter Palace were in bloom and the Neva flowed evenly through the city towards the Gulf of Finland.

The ice which had bound the city had long since melted. The snows had disappeared and the forests of birch and pine were filled with warm scents. The salt tang of the sea filled the air. Yachts and sailing boats under full sail made their way out into the Gulf. They sailed past the wooded islands, filled with summer mystery.

Even in the industrial districts the workers threw open the great doors of the factories and let the breath of summer pass through the great buildings.

The talk of revolution, which always lay beneath the surface of men's thoughts seemed to have eased.

Alma Schmerling felt fulfilled. Her child had been born, a healthy boy whom she had called Joseph, after her stepfather and the Emperor. As she looked down on him in his cradle she recognised the features of Prince Eugene in his tiny face.

The christening had been a magnificent occasion. Prince Karl had been present at the great cathedral of St Isaac, together with her sister Sophie and many of the Russian nobility.

Now she had settled back to her work in the embassy and Prince Karl had resumed his wasteful ways. She paid little attention to his behaviour. She was too involved in the business of the embassy and the heavy correspondence with which she now had to deal.

Before she opened the letters on her desk she went to the window of the embassy and looked across the city at the Fortress of St Peter and Paul with its red granite walls and its spire of gold leaf, rising needle sharp into the sky, the highest steeple in the city. To the west lay the great Rostal Columns and the Exchange. At that time of year the city looked more magnificent than any other city in Europe.

A slight breeze blew through the windows of the ornate room as Alma opened the large envelope with the Viennese postmark.

She set the contents on her desk. When she read the first line her forehead tightened. She could not believe it. She read it again and quickly read the following pages.

Set clearly in type-written columns were the days and dates when her husband had visited her sister Sophie, along with details of the information which had been passed to her: troop movements in Austria and Russia; details of military plans; the capabilities of factories to produce arms in the event of war.

Her husband was in the pay of the Germans.

She left her desk and returned to the window.

For more than a year she had supervised the affairs of the embassy while her husband lived his own wayward life. Twice she had to ask her father to underwrite his debts. Prince Karl had been subservient for a week after each debt had been paid, then, following some wild instinct, he left the embassy and disappeared into the luxurious world of St Petersburg.

As she gazed out of the window at the clear waters of the Neva she tried to come to terms with what she had read.

She could accept his gambling and the nights he spent at the casino or with prostitutes. She could not forgive him for betraying his own country. He deserved to be executed by a firing squad.

Had she the power at the moment she would order him to be arrested. But she had to think in a cold and political fashion. A disclosure of his actions at this time could create a diplomatic incident.

Then Alma wondered how she would deal with her sister Sophie. It was clear that she had not come to St Petersburg to enjoy the social life of the city. She now knew from some of the correspondence on her desk that Sophie was dedicated to the military might of Germany. She possessed a Prussian mind as extreme as that of Baron Von Hertling.

To distract herself from these thoughts, she returned to her desk and continued to work on other documents which her husband would later sign. Some of them were of a sensitive nature and she was certain that the information would be passed on to Sophie.

That afternoon as she was walking along one of the city's canals, she decided upon a plan.

She quickly returned to the embassy and called Von Schoon, whom she trusted beyond anyone else in St Petersburg.

When he arrived, Alma came quickly to the point. 'I believe that some of our confidential documents are finding their way to Berlin. They are in the hands of the secret service. Where is the leak in the embassy?'

'Prince Dmitri has an informant here. We use him sometimes to feed false information to the Russians. Sometimes he does receive genuine facts and would be happy to pass them to Germany as well as Russia, for a price. He is most likely the source.'

'How dangerous is Prince Dmitri?'

'He may appear to be a libertine, but I can assure you he is both devious and dangerous.'

'And he informed Vienna?'

'I believe so. The whole business has his mark upon it. I am sure he has set someone to spy on Prince Karl.'

She looked out the window and thought for some time. Then she turned to Von Schoon. 'Let us first deal with Berlin. We will feed them some information which will cause Baron Von Hertling a mild panic. Also, it will remove my sister from the scene. She is working against us.'

'You have some scheme in mind?'

'Yes. We know that several German agents are working in the city. The lists have been supplied to us. Let us make out a document which suggests that they are double agents, in the pay of Vienna. That should lead them on a wild goose chase.'

Von Schoon did not bat an eyelid. He was delighted to be given an opportunity to settle a score with Prince Karl, who he detested. 'Should this list come to us from Vienna with the official stamp? I can have it delivered to the embassy during the next few days.'

'Excellent. I will leave it in your hands.'

Three days later the document arrived from Vienna, carrying the stamp of the secret service. Alma had one of the secretaries leave it on her husband's desk, along with other documents and letters.

The trap was set.

Prince Karl detested the very presence of his hated wife. Since the birth of her son she seemed to have grown in stature. Now, she had complete power over him. Not only was he indebted to Joseph Steiner, who had twice paid his gambling debts, but he had been ordered by Franz Joseph to let her run the affairs of the embassy. All confidential documents passed through her hands, rendering him ineffective.

He had tried to restrain his passion for Lydia Savina. He had spent nights in the best brothels of the capital; he had indulged in all his jaded tastes; he had slept with young men and smoked opium, but he could not erase her memory from his mind.

He must possess her. She was an affront to his self-esteem. Whenever Count Federov returned to the capital from his estates or from Europe, she rushed to him. His wealth seemed endless and he could indulge her passion for gambling. She would disappear for weeks, joining Federov in his luxurious carriage, which was said to have been better appointed than that of the Tsar, to go to one of his estates in the South. On one occasion he had taken her to Monte Carlo where she had lost a fortune in the casino.

It was only when Federov was out of town that she turned to Prince Karl and despite his best resolve, he rushed to her side. Their meetings always followed the same pattern. They always ended up at one of the casinos where she lost a small fortune.

Now he was growing desperate. He had visited Sophie on several occasions and had begged for more money. But she turned on him and with a vicious voice said, 'Money for information. You bring me valuable information and you will be well paid.'

'But I need the money,' he had cried.

'Then earn it.'

Now, Lydia Savina had returned to St Petersburg from the south as Count Federov was spending a month on his estates with his family.

She immediately phoned Prince Karl. When he heard her voice his heart missed a beat. It was filled with a sweet innocence which seduced him.

He was desperate for money. All his sources had run dry. Then fortune favoured him. On his desk lay information from Vienna which was of great value. The secret service had sent a list of their double agents to the embassy.

Karl went down through the list. There were fifteen names in all. He took a pen and two sheets. On the first he wrote eight names and on the second seven.

'I'll make the German bitch pay heavily for this information,' he told himself.

That evening he set off to meet Sophie. The light was bright in the sky and the air was balmy. The day would last forever. The sun would no sooner set than it would rise again in the east.

When he was issued into her drawing room which overlooked the canal, he decided he despised her as much as he did his wife. He was anxious to make a deal quickly and leave the house.

The door opened and Sophie swept in, dressed in an expensive gown and obviously ready to leave for some party or other.

'I hope that you have something of value for me. For the last six weeks you have brought me little more than court gossip.' Her voice and bearing were dismissive.

'I believe that I carry information which will greatly interest Berlin. In my pocket I have a list of counter agents in the pay of Vienna.'

He took a folded page from his coat and handed it to her. She looked down at the list. She suppressed her surprise. Some of the best agents working in St Petersburg and Moscow were on it. She would have to send a ciphered message immediately to Berlin.

She opened her safe and offered him five hundred roubles.

'Surely my information is worth more than five hundred roubles,' he said as she placed the money on the ormolu table in front of him.

'That is all I am willing to pay you,' she told him dismissively. 'I have the list of names in my head. Take it or leave it.'

'Then you can go to hell. I have retained part of the list. Your superior will be no doubt most anxious to get his hands on it. I will leave you the unenviable task of telling him that there are other agents you do not know about, working against Germany.' There was venom in his voice. It was the first time that he felt in a superior position for many months.

'Perhaps I have underpaid you,' she began retracting her position. 'How much do you require?'

'Ten times the amount on offer.'

She did not betray any emotion. She opened the safe and took out a large bundle of money. 'There is no need to check. It is correct.'

He took out the second list and handed it to her. Then he took the bundle of money, put it in his pocket and left the room.

Sophie was overwhelmed by the information which lay on her desk. It was quite evident that their spy system was riddled with informers. It threw the whole operation in Russia into doubt. She wondered how much false information had been sent to Berlin.

She called her secretary, explaining that the information on her desk must be ciphered and sent immediately to Berlin.

She was uneasy. She understood the gravity of the situation. Perhaps her days in St Petersburg were at an end. She would be recalled to Berlin in disgrace.

At his office in Berlin Baron Von Hertling received the information as it came through. It took an hour to decode the message. He watched anxiously as the list grew longer.

'It is impossible!' he exclaimed to his assistant, Potz.

'What shall we do, sir? Should we get rid of them? We have men ready to go directly to St Petersburg and Moscow and dispose of them.'

'That would be too easy. Perhaps that is what Vienna is expecting us to do. If we destroy them, we will never know if they were working for us or our enemies. This could be a plot to destroy our best men.' He paused, 'Recall them from their duties. We will interrogate them. If it is true, then our best sources have been feeding us lies. But I think this is too tidy. Many of these men have been hand-picked by me and their information has always been accurate. No. It cannot be correct. Recall them from their posts. If they return directly, then it will be an indication that they are on our side.'

The fifteen spies were sent orders to return to Berlin. They were to return at different times and on different days. The baron decided that until he could ascertain the truth, he would not rest.

'And direct Sophie Schmerling to return at the end of the month,' he added. 'The Austrians know that she is one of our agents.' He looked again in disbelief at the list of spies. It contained some of his finest men.

Prince Karl possessed more money than he had in a long time. He could now satisfy his burning desires.

He went immediately to the apartment of Lydia Savina. When she opened the door his heart began to beat and a nerve throbbed in his forehead. Despite the late nights she had spent at the gambling houses, she still retained her milk-white skin, her childlike exuberance for life.

She put out her hand and touched him lightly on the face with her fingers. The dainty gesture sent waves of pleasure through his body. He wished to take her in his arms at that moment, throw her on the bed and tear the clothes from her body.

'Shall we eat,' she said. 'I am ravenous. Let us go to Café Cubah. Then we can go to one of the islands. Perhaps later we can sail in the Gulf of Finland. There are so many islands we could visit.'

'Very well,' he said, never taking his eye off her lithe figure. She moved with grace and ease. Her training as a ballerina had given her assured elegance.

She placed a light wrap on her shoulders and they left the apartment.

They walked down the boulevard that ran between the Admiralty and the Winter Palace gleaming in the bright light. They crossed the bridge to the stock exchange and the great Rostal Columns almost as high as lighthouses. Karl was proud of the beautiful young woman sitting beside him. The smell of her young flesh filled his nostrils.

He tried to put his arm around her shoulder but she playfully set it aside. 'Later, perhaps on our way to the casino.'

He knew that he was a fool. The woman was dangerous. She had destroyed his life and yet he could not live without her. He had enough money in his pockets to indulge every taste he could imagine with the finest prostitutes in the world. Yet he chose a young slip of a girl who could be his daughter and who dismissed his advances.

He knew that by dawn he would have lost a small fortune.

The casino was crowded. Several officers from the south had returned to St Petersburg after manoeuvres in the Caucasus, dressed in their regimental colours. The tables were busy.

'Which table will bring me luck?' Lydia Savina asked.

Karl picked out a table close to the open window, where a summer breeze lifted the gauze curtains in easy billows. It would give him a chance to escape from the crush of officers and their women.

'I know I will be lucky tonight,' she told him.

Soon she was the centre of attention. The officers were attracted to her fragile beauty, her coquettish manner. Prince Karl watched the money he had been given by Sophie Schmerling pass through the young woman's fingers like golddust.

He was standing on the veranda very late in the night looking at the light in the eastern sky when she came to him.

'I need more money,' she told him. 'I know my luck will change.'

He argued with her. 'But you have lost a small fortune.'

'And what of it. I will find a young officer. He will give me money to gamble. Several of the officers have expressed the desire to be my escort.' Her voice was shrewish.

She left him and walked down the veranda towards the French windows. He ran after her and gave her the rest of the money.

It was early morning when she emerged from the casino. She had lost all of his money.

'Let us go home,' she said. 'I am tired.'

'No, let us take a yacht out into the Gulf of Finland. The sea air will do you good.'

She hesitated for a moment then she decided to go with him.

The automobile took them to the docks at Vasilevsky Island. Soon they were sailing out into the Gulf of Finland under a moderate wind. The yacht moved gracefully through the waters.

An hour later they were moving across the open sea. Here and there they could see a wooded island, set on the wide waters.

Soon Lydia Savina began to complain of the cold. 'I wish to return. I am wearing light clothes. It is too chilly.'

As Karl looked at the lithe figure of the woman he had pursued for so long, his love turned to bitter hate.

He secured the tiller and moved towards her, his expression dark and sinister. Surges of hate and frustration passed through his mind.

She looked at him. Suddenly she sensed danger. She could not flee from him. 'No,' she said as he took her by the shoulders and began to shake her.

'You have destroyed me, you bitch. You have rejected me and gone to the bed of the old man Fedorov.'

'At least he has balls,' she screamed. 'He does not play

about with young men. He is not a Hapsburg pauper.'

He ripped the clothes from her shoulders, exposing small, well-shaped breasts. He pulled her to him and kissed her on the mouth.

She drew away and spat at him.

Then he began to beat her in blind rage. Again and again he hit her with his closed fist until she no longer cried out. Her neck was broken. In his anger he had killed her.

She lay like a broken doll on the deck.

He stared at her. Her body was as fragile as that of a child. Her cheeks were puffed where he had beaten her and blood ran down the edge of her mouth.

He looked about him. The great sea was empty. Carefully, he began to make his plans. For a moment he contemplated lashing her body to the anchor and throwing it into the sea. They would never find it at the bottom of the Gulf of Finland. He decided that it would be safer instead to throw her overboard and report that there had been an accident. It was the best course of action.

He took the body in his arms and threw it on to the blue waves. For a moment Lydia Savina floated, her light dress spread about her, then she disappeared from sight.

All that day Karl sailed amongst the islands. He felt free. He had destroyed the object of his passion. When the incident came to light, people might express their doubts but they could never prove his guilt.

The fact that he was a Hapsburg would throw a ring of safety about him.

Eight hours later he sailed back into harbour. He immediately reported that Lydia Savina had been swept off the deck of the yacht and drowned.

Chapter Thirty-six

Vienna lay in a summer dream.

At the Schönbrunn Palace Franz Joseph had risen early from his military bed and was working at his desk.

He opened a letter from St Petersburg. It carried a report on Prince Karl, and the old Emperor was startled by its implications. There was an extraordinary rumour in St Petersburg that he had murdered a young ballerina while sailing in the Gulf of Finland. Her body had not, as yet, been discovered.

Franz Joseph left his desk, went to the window and looked down on the gardens now in full bloom. Once he had been moved by such beauty. Now his mind was troubled.

Old age had not brought him any comfort. His son had taken his life along with that of Mary Vetsera at Meyerling. It had been a messy business. Rudolf had shot the young woman and six hours later, had shot himself at his hunting lodge. There had been the fear that his son might be denied the right to a Christian burial. Five doctors had to sign the death certificate, declaring that his son had been unstable when he had committed the act. And then the Pope had to be persuaded to give permission for the burial.

The shooting lodge at Meyerling had been turned into a cloister and the room where Rudolf and Mary Vetsera had died was now a chapel.

Now it seemed that the same madness seemed to possess the mind of Prince Karl. The Emperor was reluctant to recall him to Vienna.

At midday Prince Eugene visited him. He was now his adviser on the Balkans.

'I have accepted a poisoned cup,' the old Emperor told him when they studied the map of the Balkans. 'We should not have annexed Bosnia Herzegovina. It was a foolish mistake. These people now strain against our yoke.'

Prince Eugene, who spent six months each year travelling through the rugged country, knew better than most that it was a powder keg, divided by religions, race and political beliefs. He had flown across the region in one of these new planes he loved and had gazed down at the beauty of the landscape, disturbed by what lay in store for it.

'What should one do?' The Emperor broke into his thoughts.

'Perhaps a visit to Sarajevo might cement the factions within Bosnia Herzegovina. You are a popular figure and your presence could only do good,' Prince Eugene suggested.

'I am too old to travel,' the older man said gruffly. 'I rule the empire from the Schönbrunn. Let them come to me. Besides, if a war breaks out, it will be a small war. We will be able to contain it. If necessary, I will move troops south.'

'The Russians could move against us. Prince Dmitri has set up agitators in the region.'

'A most dangerous fellow. I always knew that he was dabbling in the area.'

They talked for an hour, but when Prince Eugene left the Schönbrunn, he felt frustrated. The old man had lost his grasp of what was happening. A war in the Balkans would draw Russia immediately into the area. Germany would come in on the side of the Austrians. At the moment there were too many voices calling for different solutions.

As he was driven from the Schönbrunn to the Belvedere Palace he considered some additional information he had received from St Petersburg.

He, too, had heard the rumour that Prince Karl had murdered some obscure ballerina. He wondered if Alma knew the truth of what was going on. He still loved this woman. Her face still haunted him and he could not put the memory of the happy days they spent together in Vienna out of his mind. But he knew he had to consider the prospect of a more suitable marriage. He did not want their liaison to shame Alma any further. He must marry, for her reputation and his political future.

So, the next day he visited his aunt. She was politically astute and knew what was going on in the larger world.

'Marry one of your own,' she counselled. 'Cement the relationships between families. Someday we may break free from Austria and the old kingdom could be restored. The union of two families at this time would secure your popularity. You can no longer follow the dictates of your heart. You must think of the old kingdom.'

'You are right, Aunt Edith,' Eugene replied, then anxious to change the subject he indicated the new plane he had purchased, now lying on the rough runway in front of the palace. 'I will carry you over the mountains,' he told her.

Like a child his aunt entered the plane. It vibrated with power as it accelerated. Then it moved into the sky like a great bird.

As she passed over the kingdom she loved, looking down into the heart of the valleys and over the impenetrable crags, she called to him, 'It is wonderful. I feel like a Greek god looking down upon my world.'

When they returned to the airstrip, Edith's husband was waiting for them. Dressed in his military uniform and waving a sword, he galloped beside them as they landed.

'He belongs to a barbaric world,' she laughed. 'This is the future. We are no longer isolated.'

* * *

Baron Von Hertling had travelled all the way from Berlin to Vienna, with the curator of the National Gallery, which lay on Museum Island between the Spree and the Kupfergraben.

The curator was a small man with glasses and a bird-like face. His life had been spent in art galleries and for him art was more real than life. His mind was an encyclopaedia of knowledge. He knew the title of every painting in the Louvre and the Hermitage as well as those in the London art galleries. He knew the great houses where pictures hung which had not been seen by the public for a hundred years.

He was most eager to build up the Italian collection at the National Gallery. It would enhance Berlin and underpin its importance as a cultural centre.

'This is wonderful, wonderful,' he said when he studied the catalogue of Joseph Steiner's collection. 'This man has discerning tastes. And he has concentrated on certain Italian schools which are becoming very valuable. He moved into the market when they could be bought in Italy for a pittance. Imagine having the masters of the Siena school hanging in Berlin. We will be the envy of every gallery in the world.'

'How much are they worth?' Baron Von Hertling asked.

'The Kaiser could not afford to purchase them,' the curator said firmly.

'Are they worth the title of Baron? That is what we are going to trade for them.'

'Then you get them for nothing,' the curator replied.

It was on his recommendation that the Kaiser agreed to confer the title of Baron on Joseph Steiner.

Von Hertling had not alerted anyone in the embassy to his arrival in Vienna. A whisper about his movements would start a diplomatic wrangle. The paintings must be out of Vienna and hanging on the walls of the National Gallery in Berlin, before anyone would be aware of it.

When he had arrived at Hauptbahnhof Station some days previously, Baron Von Hertling had carried with him a large leather case embossed with the Kaiser's insignia which was now concealed. It had been tooled by the best leather craftsmen in Berlin.

The Baron and the curator had walked briskly along the platform, eager to get away from the multitude of people milling around the platform. Two German agents located in Vienna and carrying revolvers in their pocket, followed them at a distance.

They had called a cab and drove along the Ring Strasse with its public gardens and impressive buildings and across the grey Danube. Great barges were moving along the river, heading towards southern Germany. But the Baron looked only towards the west. The paintings would be carried along the great river out of Austria in a wheat barge.

The warehouse was a building without any architectural merit, covered with a faded, pink wash. The windows were secured by iron grids.

Joseph Steiner was waiting for them. 'You are very punctual,' he said, looking at his watch.

The baron introduced the curator and immediately the two men began talking enthusiastically. There was much they had to say to each other.

'I can't wait to see the Sienese school,' the curator said. 'It is incredible to think that so many exist under one roof. How did you manage to assemble them?'

'It was a painstaking task. I sent a young man to Italy to make a catalogue of the various Sienese paintings there. They had never been catalogued properly and were dispersed all over the place. Then, as they came on the market, I purchased one by one. The collection is far from complete. There are some in the Vatican which I could not get my hands on and there are others in England. They may perhaps come up for sale. I believe that there is a collection, too, in Russia.'

'I know,' the curator smiled.
'Where?'
'On the estates of Alexander Federov.'
'Have you seen them?'
'Yes. I made the journey once to the estate. The paintings there glow with colour and with feeling. I thought perhaps he might bequeath them to our gallery, but he scoffed at me. The great house is loaded with treasure. He possesses an original Bellini and a slender David, not unlike the one in Florence.'
'I have never heard of it.'
'I can assure you that it exists. Delicate beyond words. A boy on the verge of becoming a man. I almost wept. But what could I do. I am the curator of a museum.'
By now they had climbed to the upper storey of the warehouse. Joseph took a key from his pocket and opened an iron door. It swung heavily on dry hinges.
The curator entered the room. He gasped. Hanging on the walls, sometimes two or three rows deep, stood one of the finest private collections in Europe. He recognised each individual piece, except for a section devoted to a modern artist.
Even in the semi-light of the room the pictures glowed. And they were all arranged in their proper order. 'It is perfect,' the curator sighed. 'I know the rooms in which they will hang. Only indirect light will fall upon them. They will glow.'
He touched the surface of the paintings. The texture and the brushstrokes assured him that they were original.
After a cursory glance at the paintings Von Hertling went for a walk along the quays. When he returned they were still talking. 'I have arranged to have them crated and transported to Berlin. Tonight several workmen will bring specially made crates to the warehouse. Tomorrow they will be on their way to Berlin,' the baron told them
And then he remembered the leather case he had carried with him from Berlin.

He removed the covering and handed it to him.

'A present for you, Baron Von Steiner,' he said, handing Joseph the leather case bearing the Kaiser's crest.

He opened the leather case and inside lay the illuminated parchment granting him the title Baron. At the bottom was the Kaiser's signature and his official stamp.

Joseph Steiner looked at the parchment. His eyes glowed. He was now a titled gentleman, a member of the aristocracy.

'Congratulations, Baron,' Von Hertling said, bowing from the waist.

'I feel honoured,' Joseph stammered.

'And we feel honoured to have such a fine collection bequeathed to our nation.'

If only I could acquire the Russian paintings. If only I could acquire the Russian paintings then the collection would be complete, Joseph thought to himself.

As they left the room Von Hertling turned once more and looked at the priceless collection of work. Then he looked at the strikingly modern paintings in one corner. 'It strikes me as odd that you should hang such modern works beside the old masters,' he said. 'Who is the artist?'

'His name is Fieldmann. You would not have heard of him. He lives in exile in Siberia. Someday, his paintings might be considered as great as the Italian masters.'

Fieldmann. The name rang a bell in the baron's mind.

Then he remembered. He had lived for several years with Sophie's sister. He was a dangerous revolutionary who had tried to assassinate the Tsar.

They left the warehouse. From the quay front it looked no different from all the other buildings which stood along the banks of the river. The curator would remain nervous until the paintings were hanging in the National Gallery in Berlin.

Chapter Thirty-seven

A fortnight after her disappearance, the body of Lydia Savina was found floating in a rolling sea off the coast, close to St Petersburg. The sailors who found her secured a boathook in the white cloth fabric and drew the chalky corpse to the side of the boat. They placed a net beneath it and lifted it on board. The woman's face was puffed and bruised almost concealing her eyes, but even to the sailors, it was obvious that her slender neck had been broken.

Fearing that ill-luck would follow them, they immediately returned to their anchorage at Vasilevsky island.

The body was taken and set on a table in one of the fishing warehouses and ice set about it. Then a tarpaulin was placed over it. It lay in a corner until the doctor arrived.

The fishermen returned to their boat and set off for the fishing grounds in the Baltic Sea, far away from their discovery.

The police and the coroner were informed that a body had been picked up at sea. Two hours' later the police arrived in a lorry and the body was carried to a hospital where Dr Kiliya performed the autopsy.

'This is the body of the young woman taken from the sea this morning,' the sergeant said as they trundled the corpse into the morgue.

They were on familiar terms and often talked while the coroner was carrying out his work in the cold building.

'I will attend to it later,' the doctor said, not taking his eyes from the marble slab on which lay the body of a young soldier who had been accidentally killed during rifle fire at a local barracks. He continued to examine the gaping wound in the head of the soldier. A young assistant wrote down his observations in a ledger.

The sergeant told him that it was necessary to examine the body of the young woman.

'Can it not wait? I have several other bodies to examine. Some are beginning to stink. What makes this one so important?'

'I believe that this is the young woman who was associated with Prince Karl. You remember the accident. It was widely reported in the papers. However, there is a rumour in the city that she was murdered. The suspicion remains.'

The doctor suppressed his excitement. The implications of what the sergeant said to him were abundantly clear. Perhaps the sergeant did not know how far-reaching the autopsy report might be. It could shake the Hapsburg Empire.

He was surprised that the autopsy had been left in his hands. Other coroners could be relied upon to falsify the report and the whole matter would end, but not he.

Now, as he took scissors and cut away the fine shreds of clothing from the body he believed that he had been handed a unique opportunity.

The shreds of clothing were placed in a basket and the body of the young woman lay naked on the slab.

He examined her toes. Then he described their condition. It was obvious to him that the young woman had been a ballerina.

He then gave a superficial account of the body: the general condition, the estimated age, the contusions and lacerations caused by the sea.

When he felt her neck and her jaw he knew that the woman had been murdered. Her neck was broken and her jaw had been fractured in several places. Some of her teeth were loose.

All this was written down carefully by Dr Kiliya.

The final evidence came when he cut into the ribs and sternum and exposed the lungs. They did not contain salt water. She had obviously been dead before she fell into the sea.

The sergeant had been following the autopsy with care. He would have to carry the report to his superiors.

The doctor said, 'I believe the young woman was murdered. Her neck is broken and her jaw is fractured in several places. This could only have been done by a heavy object like a fist.'

'Are you certain? Is there any doubt in your mind?'

'Any independent coroner would bring in the same verdict.'

'Then we have a murder on our hands.'

'Beyond any reasonable doubt.'

The implications of the autopsy suddenly dawned on the young sergeant. 'The Prince is a Hapsburg,' he said.

'Yes. The House of Hapsburg has blood on its hands,' the doctor said grimly.

'I must have the report and bring it immediately to my superiors,' the sergeant said anxiously.

'Very well. But I must go to my office and make it out in its official form.' Dr Kiliya took the notes from the young assistant and went to his office. He immediately began to make out the report in triplicate, working as quickly as possible.

An hour later he returned to the morgue and handed the sergeant the report.

'I would also like to have the notebook in which your original comments were made just to assure my superiors that they tally,' the young man said nervously.

The doctor handed him the notebook and the official report, and continued his work in the cold grey room.

When the sergeant had left he considered what had happened. The young man who often stood in the morgue while Dr Kiliya performed autopsies had never been so anxious to leave the place. He wondered what the next step would be and when it would be taken.

That evening Prince Dmitri was already taking steps which would ensure that the public would know nothing of what had happened, not because such a disclosure would harm the House of Hapsburg, but the Tsar. It would be used by the revolutionaries at home and abroad to stir up disaffection.

Dmitri wished to deal with Prince Karl in a more subtle fashion. He was clearly an undesirable, both in Vienna and St Petersburg. He was a danger to both empires.

A vague plan began to form in Dmitri's mind. It was both devious and delicate, but might solve a difficult problem.

As dusk fell a lorry drove into the hospital grounds and parked beside the morgue. The door was opened and the sergeant entered with two men. They lit a lantern. Around them lay trolleys, each covered with a white sheet. There was the strong smell of putrefying corpses in the air. One of the men rushed outside and vomited in the bushes.

The sergeant went from trolley to trolley lifting the sheets and looking at the chalky faces.

'It is not here,' he said, a tremor in his voice.

'Are you certain it was here or did you imagine it?' one of the other men asked sarcastically.

'I have handed the reports to your superiors. I was here when the autopsy was performed.'

'Then let us check again. It cannot have disappeared.'

By now the two secret police felt ill. The cold seemed to be entering their bones. They felt uneasy amongst the corpses.

They passed from trolley to trolley, shining their lanterns on the grey faces.

'The corpse is not here,' the sergeant said, barely containing his panic. 'She had long, dark hair and puffed cheeks, which almost concealed her eyes. She must have been removed to some other section of the hospital.'

'Have you any suggestions where she might be,' one of the secret policemen demanded. 'The corpse must be found and buried. These are our orders. Very soon we will be observed. Let us leave the place and make some further plans.'

They drove away from the hospital grounds and continued driving about the streets while they decided on a plan.

'Is it a common practice to remove corpses from a morgue?' the driver asked.

'No. Normally they are buried in the morning.' The sergeant replied.

'Did the doctor suspect that there was anything exceptional about this case?'

'We discussed it. He mentioned that blood was on the hands of the Hapsburgs. Now that I think of it, he was aware of the implications of the autopsy. He is a very clever man. I was told to keep a careful eye on his activities.'

It became increasingly clear to them that they must move quickly.

They returned to the hospital and found Dr Kiliya's address. Then they drove hastily through the twilight to the outskirts of the city.

'There is a simple answer to everything,' one of the secret police told them as they pulled up in front of the doctor's home.

The sergeant knew that the doctor lived alone. His wife had died some years previously of tuberculosis. He had not married again.

'You remain here,' they told the sergeant as they left the lorry. 'It is better that you are not a witness to what we may have to do.'

They knocked on the door. There was no answer. Anxiously they knocked again. Then they heard some bolts being opened and a key turning.

The door opened slightly and an eye peeped out. 'Who is there?' a voice asked.

They smashed open the door, knocking the doctor against the banisters of the stairs. Blood spurted from his nose. Before he could recover from the shock the barrel of a revolver was put in his mouth. The agent cocked the hammer. The doctor looked in fear at the hand holding the gun. One tremor and it would go off. He had seen the effects of such gun blasts in the morgue.

'I have one question to ask you and one question alone. Where is the corpse of the young woman who was brought to the morgue today? I will give you time to think. Then I will take the barrel of the gun from your mouth and give you exactly three seconds to begin talking. If you do not talk, I will blow your skull off.'

There was silence in the hallway. Nobody moved. Slowly the agent took the gun from the doctor's mouth.

Dr Kiliya began to talk immediately. He told them that he had removed the body to the theatre where the young interns could examine it. It was a common practice at the hospital.

'Strange that you should pick a young woman who might be the source of a royal scandal.'

'If the case is interesting, I send it to the theatre.'

'And what made this case so interesting?'

'You will find that in the autopsy report,' the doctor said.

'Now, old man,' the agent began, 'I am going to say something to you. Listen clearly. This corpse never existed. You never saw the body of the young woman and you never wrote a report on her. Nothing ever happened. Do you understand?'

'I understand,' he said, his whole body shaking.

'And the reports?' the agent asked.

'What reports?'

'The reports on the autopsy. We believe that more than one exists.'

It was a guess on Prince Dmitri's part that the old doctor might make out several. It was obvious that he knew how important the case was.

Dr Kiliya began to tremble. He searched about and produced the second report.

'Good,' the agent said. 'You have taken out a pension on your life. If part of this report is leaked to the papers then your pension will cease. Do you understand?'

'Yes,' he said.

They left the house immediately.

The doctor gathered himself together. He closed the door but did not bolt it. He went to his study and poured himself a glass of vodka. With shaking hands he drank it. Then he sat down and began to weep. He wept at his own weakness. He wept at the injustice of things. A prince of the House of Hapsburg, whom he knew was a murderer, would walk free.

Two nights later Prince Dmitri Shestov took the autopsy report, placed it in an envelope and addressed it to Alexander Federov. He was pleased at the subtlety of his plan.

'Dig,' the secret policeman told the sergeant. 'We don't want to wait here all night. We have had enough of morgues and corpses and graveyards.'

The sergeant dug into the muddy earth and threw the heavy soil onto the side of the grave. He began to sweat. He had not worked so hard in a long time. His asthma was catching in his chest and he had to draw in large mouthfuls of air.

'I have a bad chest,' he wheezed. 'I have not done heavy work in a long time.'

'Think of the poor bastards in the camps,' one of the agents replied.

Finally, the grave was finished. The secret policemen pulled the sergeant out of the muddy grave. His shirt and trousers were soiled. He had always taken pride in his uniform. It was firm and smart and gave him an air of importance.

The driver of the truck pushed the body of Lydia Savina into the grave with his boot. It rolled over on the earth, gathering mud about it, then it fell face-down into the grave.

'Now fill it in,' the driver told him.

It took the sergeant half an hour to fill in the grave. His body ached.

They drove him to his house in the industrial section of the city, where great stacks poured out smoke night and day, and where the furnaces never went out. The sulphurous smell of coal smoke filled the alleys.

'You have heard nothing, you have seen nothing and you have done nothing,' the driver said before he drove away.

The sergeant felt humiliated and empty as he stood in the narrow street and watched the lorry disappear.

Alexander Federov spent the summer on his estate, surrounded by his children and grandchildren. His sons had married young women from the province. They belonged to old families and they cared little for the delights of St Petersburg. They preferred their estates and their families.

He took pleasure in the activity of his property: the early morning when the workers gathered in the yard and prepared for work in the fields; the sound of slow trundling carts making their way down ribbons of road which led to the hazy horizon.

His mansion lay on a hill, close to a wide river. It was large and firmly built in the English manner.

During these summer months he lived in close harmony with the landscape. Despite his years he had the energy of a young man. He could ride all day across the endless steppes, stopping at a village for food, then continuing until he reached some friend's mansion.

One morning, as he was walking down towards the river, the postmaster appeared. He came once a week and felt very important delivering a large bundle of letters to Alexander Federov, who often engaged him in conversation. He would give him all the gossip of the area and fill him in on all that was happening on the neighbouring estates. They would walk towards Alexander Federov's favourite seat on the bank of the river, discussing many things of concern to them. Sometimes the postmaster made requests on behalf of the townspeople which Alexander Federov noted in a diary.

That morning, when the postmaster left, Alexander sat for a while and looked at the broad river flowing past, slowly and evenly. Some fishermen had launched their shallow boats on the far side and had begun the day's fishing. He looked at them and listened to their voices as they called to each other. They had not changed their methods since he was a boy.

He read through his correspondence. Finally, he came across the letter bearing the St Petersburg postmark. It was in a poor quality envelope and he did not recognise the handwriting.

He opened it and read the contents.

During his months at his estate he kept only tentative links with St Petersburg. He had been saddened by the drowning of Lydia Savina. She had been his mistress and her youth had brought a satisfying freshness to his life. He was aware of her failings which had cost him a small estate in the Ukraine.

Now, as he read the letter from the capital and the autopsy report, anger began to burn in his heart. He had never liked Prince Karl and he detested the Hapsburgs. The whole affair had been brushed under the carpet. He decided to act.

Each morning for the next week he set out with his servant for the forest. He carried a brace of pistols. He practised for several hours on the bowls of trees, stepping back from them the recognised distance, then firing.

His fingers became supple and after a week he was satisfied with his performance.

He took leave of his family and told them that he would return in a few days. Urgent business had recalled him to St Petersburg.

Before he left he drew up his will which was signed in the presence of his solicitor and witnessed by two old friends.

'I will return in a week. Then we shall go hunting in the forests. If I do not return, then carry out the directives of the will.'

The incident occurred on the broad sweep of staircase leading down from the private boxes at the Mariinsky Theatre. Prince Karl was making his way up the shallow, carpeted steps for the second act of *Giselle* when Alexander Federov, dressed in his military uniform, blocked his way.

Prince Karl looked into the flashing eyes of the old man set in his firm head. He was still handsome with his great mane of grey hair. He was dressed in full uniform, his medals pinned on his shoulder.

When Prince Karl made an attempt to pass the old man, Federov slapped him on the face with his white leather gloves. There was silence on the great staircase as the upper classes of St Petersburg witnessed that Alexander Federov had insulted one of the Hapsburg Princes. It was obvious what would follow.

Prince Karl attempted to strike the old man back, but found his hand grasped in a grip of iron.

'I believe that we can settle this in a proper fashion. Let us meet tomorrow morning at a place of your choice. I believe that pistols are acceptable to you. I will have my second with me.'

'I accept,' Prince Karl replied loudly and in anger.

With that Federov swept down the steps, walked across the crimson carpet, and out through the great doors.

There was a whisper of excitement among the onlookers. Then they began to move up the steps towards their boxes. Little attention was paid to the second act of the ballet. On several occasions the conductor looked about him into the semi-darkness. The place was alive with the sound of rustling silk as the women passed word of the incident to each other.

Finally the curtain fell on the second act and the lights came on. The box in which Prince Karl and his friend had been sitting was now empty.

'He is an old man. It will be over after the first shot. There are many in St Petersburg who would like to see the end of him,' Prince Dmitri told him as they made their way to his palace. 'The whole affair will enhance your reputation.'

Prince Karl was far from assured of the outcome. He feared the old man.

'He is still virile. The women flock to him. I am sure he can handle a pistol. No, I must find some other way out of the dilemma. Perhaps Nicholas should be told. Duelling is illegal.'

'It is carried on in the provinces despite the law. You are expected to behave like a Hapsburg. You were always an accurate shot. Old Federov's hands tremble.'

'I was foolish to accept. I had to accept in front of all those people. He did insult me.'

'And the insult must be avenged,' his friend told him firmly. 'If you do not accept, you will be the laughing stock of the city.'

They opened a bottle of champagne and Prince Dmitri toasted Prince Karl. 'Tomorrow night I will throw a lavish banquet for you. You will be celebrated throughout the city and afterwards we will go to one of the islands.'

Prince Karl drank the champagne quickly. Another bottle was opened. Soon he was light-headed. His mind began to play tricks. 'Of course I can outshoot him. Bring me some pistols and let me practise in the long gallery.'

Prince Dmitri ordered a brace of pistols to be brought to the long gallery. A plaster bust was placed on a plinth. The pistols were loaded. Prince Karl took one and weighed it in his hand. It was beautifully balanced. He took aim and fired. The ball shattered the plaster ear.

'Excellent. Try again.'

Prince Karl fired again. The bust exploded into dust fragments and fell to the floor.

He was satisfied that he could kill Federov.

'We will use this set of pistols,' he said. 'I feel they will bring me luck.'

They drank two more bottles of champagne. Then a servant brought Prince Karl to bed.

As Prince Dmitri sat in his armchair, he considered many things. He knew that Prince Karl had murdered Lydia Savina. A copy of the autopsy lay on his desk. He also felt that it was time for Prince Karl to die. He knew too many secrets and he had already sold information to the Germans. He was a traitor not only to his own country but he had betrayed Russia too. Now, the instrument of his death would be Federov. The incident would be a convenient way to close the scandal. He did not deserve to live.

It was a pleasant morning as Alexander Federov set out for the clearing in the birch wood outside the city. He could detect the scent of wild mushrooms in the air. They reminded him of the pleasant life he had left on his estate.

There was a light mist on the ground, swirling about the trees. It was a magical time.

When they reached the spot Prince Karl was waiting with Prince Dmitri. Close by stood a surgeon, dressed in a long black coat. He looked a mysterious figure, almost like somebody from the legend, waiting to carry off the souls of the dead, or the ferryman on the banks of the River Styx.

The two seconds measured off the paces. The firing lane was clear.

Federov inquired if Prince Karl was satisfied with the deadly path between them.

'I couldn't care less. Let the duel be finished with.'

The seconds began to load the pistols, beautiful instruments tooled in Italy. They placed the balls in position.

The two adversaries looked at each other. The mist was dissolving and the sun began to shine through. It played on the green leaves of the birch wood, casting dappled shadows on the ground. A horse whinnied with impatience, tossed its head and set the harness jangling. Then there was silence.

The pistols were loaded. The adversaries took them. They faced each other and waited for the signal, then they walked forward to their positions.

Before Prince Karl reached his position he raised his pistol and fired. It caught Federov on the left shoulder. Federov held his ground. He fired. Prince Karl dropped his pistol and held his stomach. Blood poured through his fingers. He fell onto his knees then forward on to the ground.

Prince Dmitri called to the drivers and ordered them to carry him to his automobile. They immediately set off for the Austrian Embassy. They moved slowly across the open land in order not to cause Prince Karl undue pain. His face was ashen.

'I am dead. I am dead,' he cried out, his face drenched in sweat.

They drove into the city, moving slowly through the traffic. Prince Karl's clothes were now soaked with blood.

Finally they reached the Austrian Embassy.

There was a brief explanation given to the door keeper and then the dying prince was carried indoors and up to his spacious room overlooking the Neva.

He was laid out on the bed. The blood soaked his trousers and his underclothes. The doctor cut away the soggy clothes to reveal the neat wound where the ball had entered the prince's abdomen.

The doctor felt Karl's fluttering pulse. He knew that the prince was dying. His life was haemorrhaging away.

Alma, who had been called from her private rooms, looked at her husband. Soon it would be over.

He returned her look with hate, envious that she would live, that she would carry his title. He screamed at her to leave the room.

When Alma returned to her room, she stood for some time looking across the river at the fortress of St Peter and Paul. Soon the gun would boom out to mark the hour.

There was work to be done. She was at peace.

Prince Karl died at six o'clock.

It was a warm evening and the windows had been thrown open to catch a cooling breeze. The body was washed and dressed for the Russian vigil customary in St Petersburg. The prince's coffin was lined with lead and his head wreathed in purple velvet. On his chest lay the insignia of the House of Hapsburg.

All evening important visitors arrived at the embassy. They moved silently through the halls and spoke in whispers.

The next morning the coffin was removed to the Cathedral of St Isaac.

Margit Schmerling had hastened from Vienna, distraught at the news. She arrived at the embassy before the removal of the coffin. 'What a tragedy!' she cried. 'He had such a promising future.'

'Don't be a fool, Mother,' Alma told her brusquely. 'He had no future. His death is most convenient.'

'You are a hard-hearted woman,' Margit said to her daughter. 'What will happen to your child?'

'He will be reared as a Hapsburg should and he will inherit his father's title.'

'And so I am the grandmother of a prince.' Margit's eyes suddenly lit up.

'That is correct, Mother. You will be titled because of your husband and your grandson.'

'Will Sophie attend the funeral?'

'I do not think so. She has been recalled to Berlin. She has brought her young man with her.'

'She was always a rough girl. There was something coarse in her nature. And will Joseph Steiner be present?'

'I could not tell you. He comes and goes.'

'I must talk with him. He is tight-fisted. He owes me money.'

Alma knew that her mother would now enjoy her visit to St Petersburg. She would meet the best of the nobility and thanks to her son-in-law and her husband, be able to choose her title.

The Archbishop of St Petersburg officiated at the funeral. The great cathedral was filled with dignitaries including the Tsar, who came to offer his sympathies to Alma and her mother. The vast dome of St Isaac's, almost as great as the dome of St Peter's in Rome, resounded to the voices of a Russian choir.

After the service the coffin was brought directly to the railway station to begin its journey to Vienna.

Three days after the funeral, Federov returned to his estate.

The wound to his left shoulder had been superficial. As the funeral train was making its way out of Finland Station, he was hunting boar in his forests.

Chapter Thirty-eight

Fieldmann would never forget the journey into exile in Siberia. His destination lay beyond the Urals, beyond the River Ob. The journey took place that autumn, before the first of the winter snows.

He had been taken from his cell and brought to a siding at the station along with other prisoners. There they had been loaded onto freight cars by their guards, armed with guns, who prodded them forward like cattle into pens. The small windows were gridded with iron bars.

Some of the men were hardened criminals, vicious men who looked sullenly at the political prisoners, seeing if they carried valuables or an article of clothing which would protect them against the harsh Siberian winter.

Rough bunks made from planks were arranged along the walls in tiers. The toughened prisoners took the bunks closest to the windows in order to breathe the last of the summer air. The others took whatever bunks were convenient. Before the carriages were closed bread and herrings and barrels of water were brought on board.

Then the train set out on its long journey through Russia. Soon, the carriages became stifling with the body heat of the prisoners. The train rolled east. Only the monotonous sound of the wheels marked the passage of time.

Men began to talk: apart from the criminals, some were political exiles, others intellectuals who had been rounded up by the Tsar's secret police, quickly tried and banished into exile. One was a professor of linguistics, a small frail man who Jakov though might not survive the northern winter. He belonged in a library and not in a freight car moving through Russia.

The professor had managed to carry a bundle of books with him, strapped to his body with a leather belt. 'They will keep my mind occupied,' he said. 'As long as I have books, I can survive.'

He introduced himself to Jakov. 'My name is Leonid Urusov.'

Jakov found him an interesting companion and discovered that both were exiled to the same village.

'I know the area. I have been there in summer, studying local dialects. It is surrounded by swamp lands. In winter the whole area is frozen over.'

'And escape?'

'Almost impossible. Prepare for a long exile.'

Soon they were engaged in deep conversation. Fieldmann told him of his travels through the Balkans. The professor was interested in all that he heard. He knew the various Balkan dialects. He believed that there was a language beyond the Indo-European source. 'It goes back further still. It came out of Africa. I have argued this and written papers on the subject but they scoff at my ideas.'

Jakov was struck by the strangeness of the conversation in such a wretched place.

After a time, they fell silent, until Professor Urusov cried out, 'I need water, the air is so stifling. I believe I will faint.'

Jakov pushed his way forward towards the barrel. As he was about to draw off a mug of water, a hand grabbed his wrist.

'Wait your turn. You will get your mug of water later when we have supped,' a voice said. Jakov found himself looking into the heavy face of a thief. He and some others had formed a circle about the food and the water.

'An old man requires a drink. He will faint if he does not receive it.'

'Then let him die of thirst,' the thief said roughly

'No. I will not let him die,' Jakov retorted.

With that the thief produced a knife and pointed it at his neck.

There was silence in the freight car. Men looked at the two opponents. Perhaps the journey might be enlivened by a fight.

'Pour the water back into the barrel,' the thief ordered.

Fieldmann spilt some of the water into the barrel, then with a quick turn of his hand, he dashed the water into the criminal's face. He grabbed the man's throat and threw him on the floor and began to vice his neck in his powerful hands. He put his knee on the man's arm to protect his back against the knife.

The thief's eyes began to bulge with fear. Jakov gave a final squeeze and the man's head rolled to one side.

It was the second time in his life that Fieldmann had killed a man.

He took the knife and placed it in his belt. Then casually he took the mug, filled it with water and carried it to the old man.

No word was uttered. Men understood the unwritten law of captivity.

That night the body was dragged from the train by the soldiers who were checking on the prisoners. They did not ask any questions. It would make their work more difficult.

The murder made life easier for Fieldmann and his friend. He insisted that Urusov sleep close to the window and that he be unmolested.

In a sense he did not feel the time pass by on the long journey into exile. He discovered a fellow revolutionary in Urusov.

The professor had a clear mind. He set out in precise lines the directions a revolution should take. 'The Tsar may be on the throne today but tomorrow he could be swept away like Charles the First and Louis the Sixteenth. There is a precedent for such things. Then, and only then, will the whole rotten edifice tumble.

'But you must make good use of your exile. Read all the revolutionary material you can get your hands on – there are ways of ensuring you receive it. And remember, there is going to be a war. Germany is only waiting to move on Russia. The pieces are set in order. A small spark will blow the whole of Europe apart. When it happens, we will be waiting in the wings,' Urusov advised him.

They passed through the Urals and then through the remote lands beyond, flat and monotonous. Everywhere the steppes stretched out, bleak and bare. There was rarely a sign of life and very rarely a patch of forest. Eventually, they passed across the Ob River and they knew that their exile had truly begun. During the journey they had been sustained by fish and bread and they had had water to drink, but the carriage now smelt of urine and semen.

When they arrived at the disembarkation area, the doors were thrown open and the dishevelled prisoners were lined up on a platform with their few belongings. The political prisoners were marched through the town to the banks of a large river. There, they boarded a barge and sailed north. They passed through the endless landscape of steppes and skies. In the distance they sometimes saw the onion dome of a church indicating a village set in a wood. Otherwise the landscape was empty and without interest.

After two days' voyage they eventually arrived at the village of Tarko, which would be the home of Jakov and the old professor during their time of exile.

A policeman was waiting to meet them at a small jetty. He had heavy jowls and sad eyes and he looked quizzically at the two political prisoners placed in his custody.

'Take your things and follow me,' he said.

He set off up the small incline from the bank and they followed him, clutching their small bundles.

Tarko was a primitive place, bare-looking and miserable. Alder trees grew about here and there and in the centre of the village was a small church, decorated with primitive pictures on the outer walls. Jakov studied them and found that they were badly drawn icons of St George and the dragon, along with other saints from the Russian faith.

The village was situated on a small hillock which overlooked the endless steppes with their woods and swamps.

'This is the highest place to be found within thirty kilometres,' their guard told them. 'That is why the village is built here. You cannot escape. In wintertime, you are bound by snow and in summertime, by swamp. So you must resign yourself to your plight. Some have tried to escape. They have never been seen again. The steppes have a large appetite. They swallow fugitives.' He made the speech in the centre of the village, probably as he had to all the prisoners who had been sent here.

The dour peasants looked at the small group making their way to the policeman's office, a small room attached to his house. In the corner stood a stove. In the centre, a desk with some yellowing files on it. Dull posters sent from some head office or other had been glued to the wall, the boards visible through them.

The policeman opened the register and asked them to sign their names. 'Each day you must report to me and sign your names in a register. For the moment you will live here. If you have money, you can rent a house. I will show you your room.'

It was a spartan place with two camp beds, an enamel basin on an iron stand and a shard of mirror, leaning against the small window.

The two prisoners looked at one another.

'Well, what do you think?' Jakov asked.

'Spartan. It will be cold in the winter,' Urusov shivered.

'We will not be here in the winter,' Jakov replied. 'I

intend to move out as soon as I have organised things. I have been in places like this before. We may be at the ends of the earth but it is not the end of the world.'

They sat on the edge of one of the beds and talked for a while. The professor was exhausted after his trip. He needed rest and he needed food.

'I will visit the village and see what are the prospects for us,' Jakov told the professor. When the old man was in bed and snoring lightly, he left the room.

On the front veranda, he took out his pipe and filled it with his last tobacco. Then he looked at the village. It was a miserable place and of little interest except for the church which possessed a simple beauty.

He walked down the street. People looked at him with an introspective glance. They were suspicious of prisoners. They were either thieves or political figures, some of whom had threatened to assassinate the Tsar who was father of all Russia.

Jakov knew that eyes were following him as he moved through the village. He stopped in front of the church. Soon he heard the door opening. A young priest emerged, curious about the stranger in the village.

'Are you one of the prisoners?' he asked.

'Yes. I am here at the Tsar's wish,' Jakov told him.

'You have seen the Tsar?'

'Many times. He is the father of our people,' Jakov said, wryly.

'Is it true he works miracles?'

'I have seen him work miracles in the great Church of St Isaac at St Petersburg. An old man shaking with palsy fell before him and begged him to cure his affliction. The Tsar laid his hand on his body and the man was cured.'

The young priest was greatly impressed. 'And the monk Rasputin, have you seen him?'

'Indeed I have seen him. Another worker of miracles.' Jakov was amused at the young man's innocence.

'I wish I had such power.'

'Very few are granted such power.'

'And what power have you?' the young priest asked.

'I paint churches. I have painted churches all over Russia.'

'And what do you think of my church?' he asked anxiously.

'I have seen the outside and it is terrible. Such a weak St George and such a poor dragon. '

'Could you paint a better picture?'

'Given the paints and given the money. I would like to see the interior.'

'Follow me then.'

They entered the church. It looked like a large empty barn. The walls were white and plain and rough beams supported the roof.

'I am not very proud of my church. The people here are ignorant and they do not come to my services. Some of them are heathen. I was sent here to bring them back to the faith. It is a difficult task,' the young man sighed.

Fieldmann was fascinated by the great empty walls. He had travelled in Russia and he had studied the murals in many of the great churches. In his mind's eye he could see the walls covered in icons.

'I could bring them into this church,' he said, after studying the walls and the roof.

'That is not possible! I have visited them and pleaded with them but only the women come to church. My heart grows black with despair. I doubt my vocation.'

'Of course I could not work such a miracle unless I were paid. Not very much. All I need is a small comfortable house in which to live. Logs for a stove in winter. Food and drink. An artist needs drink. For all that, I will paint your church outside and inside with pictures of saints and demons and all the choirs of angels and finally, with a great scene from hell.'

'And how will that bring them into the church?'

'Those who will not come to church and pray beneath this roof will be painted in the fires of hell. They deserve to be placed there.'

The priest looked at Jakov nervously. 'I must think about it. And what will it cost, all this work?'

'I have told you. A house, food and drink, logs for the winter and some small monies to buy paint and tobacco. I have just arrived and I am without money.'

'Then I will fetch you some. I have only a little but my metropolitan will send me some. Soon he will visit me and he will see that I have failed. I must do something about it.'

'No, you will see, you will not fail.'

They talked for an hour, then the young priest invited him to his house and offered him a meal. Jakov liked the innocence of the young man and his trusting nature. Perhaps he would work a miracle for him.

He left that evening with a pocket full of roubles. On his way to the guard's house he visited the local shop where he purchased some vodka and bread.

That night he sat with Urusov on the side of his bed. They drank vodka and ate the rough bread of the peasants. He told the professor of his plans. Urusov began to laugh uncontrollably. When at last he had finished, he said, 'I have not laughed since I was brought to prison. You have made my life sweet. But you are an agnostic.'

'The heart has good aspirations. These I will place on the walls. It will shorten my exile.'

A week later Jakov began work on the village church. The painting of St George and the dragon was obliterated and a thick skin of lime applied to the walls. As the gaudy figures disappeared under the great sweeps of lime, interest was stirred in the village. Some complained that the icon had brought good luck to Tarko, but nobody could demonstrate the good luck. Then it was said that St George protected them from evil spirits which roamed the tundra; large hairy beasts who devoured the aged and the young. But nobody had ever seen these fabulous beasts.

When the great, white limeface was ready, the priest, whose name was Father Sergius, and Fieldmann erected a scaffold and squared off the wall into segments with charcoal. Assisted by the professor, Fieldmann set out one morning and mounted to the top level of the wooden structure. He began to draw a cartoon on the wall. He worked quickly with rapid sweeps, not stopping until the whole area was blocked out. St George in dark silhouette and mounted on a horse looked large and noble and the dragon ferocious. Great plumes of fire and smoke issued from his nostrils.

After the great cartoon was completed and Father Sergius had studied it, he knew that the miracle he had prayed for was beginning to happen.

As he had promised, he placed a house at their disposal. It was set in a small wood and had a private and quiet air about it. Urusov set about placing it in order for the winter. With Father Sergius as his custodian he was permitted to make three trips downriver to the local town. There, he sold several drawings by Fieldmann. With the money he purchased a store of tobacco and vodka and several reams of paper, enough to last them through the winter. It was late autumn and the tundra spread brown and purple to the end of the horizon, but when the winter set in the river froze over, then the village would be an island in a waste of snow. It would remain an island until the thaw in spring when the ice would break into shards and flow towards the Kara Sea.

Urusov also purchased a gun and several boxes of cartridges which he gave to Father Sergius.

'Fieldmann intends to have meat during the winter. He is a good shot.'

The professor also obtained two boxes of books from

the library. The librarian knew of his reputation and was only too anxious to assist him. These were trundled through the streets in a barrow and placed on board the steamer. He also carried several back copies of the newspapers for Fieldmann, who wished to know what was happening in the outside world.

During the mellow autumn days, Fieldmann continued to work on the mural. It became the centre of interest in the village. The villagers had quickly forgotten the old icon and now they believed that only such a beautiful painting would draw good luck down on the village.

'You work too hard on the mural. You give too much of your talents to such a work. And who will look at it? In time the ice will crack the plaster and the wind blow it away in fragments,' the professor warned him.

'I do it because I have to do it. There is no other answer. Have you not noted that St George is Pushkin, dressed in medieval armour? And the dragon is the Tsar, and beneath the dragon are the bodies of those who have been crushed by oppression. Even here on the wall of a church I can make a statement.'

As the birds began to wheel down from the Arctic in migratory formations, filling the maroon evenings with moving silhouettes, Jakov finished the great icon. The scaffolding and the canvas which had obscured it were taken away and suddenly it came to life. It glowed on the church wall. The figures were filled with movement and strength and in the corner two angels, who were the image of two of the village children, looked down on the scene.

With great solemnity Father Sergius blessed the icon. The villagers were extremely impressed by what they saw. Clearly Fieldmann was a genius. They gathered about him and offered him their congratulations.

He had as yet only fulfilled half his promise to Father Sergius. Now he set about the second half with good humour. His life in exile was bearing some fruit.

He visited the local tavern every evening while the professor pored over his books, and made notes. It was run by a thick-set young woman with a heavy breasts and a round face, called Olga. Jakov had already enjoyed her favours, her rough tongue and massive strength.

'And what will you paint on the inside of the church?' she asked one night.

'I will paint a scene from hell on one wall and a scene from heaven on the opposite one,' Jakov replied, smiling.

'Neither hell nor heaven exists,' one of the young men said. 'It is a fairy tale told by Father Sergius to frighten people.'

'Oh, *this* hell and *this* heaven will exist. They will be filled with the population of this village.'

'And who will you put in hell?'

'I will place those who scoff at Father Sergius and those who do not attend service.'

'And what of yourself? You do not attend the service.'

'In this case, I am God and I can do what I like.'

There was a nervous guffaw of laughter from the young man. 'And what position will Olga occupy?'

'She will be close to the side of God,' he said. The humour was not lost on the tavern's clients.

Before the river froze and before the final steamer made its visit to the village, Fieldmann began to work on the two murals inside the church.

While he set about this work, Marie received permission to travel into exile to join him.

Jakov's exile had made her more ruthless and determined than ever. During her stay in St Petersburg she joined the Communist Party. She sustained herself by teaching English and German to children of the upper class and continued to read the works of Lenin, now an exile in Switzerland. He was biding his time there. Marie had been in communication with him regularly.

In the working-class areas of St Petersburg, Marie founded several revolutionary clubs. She visited the slums and noted the poverty there. She helped to collect money in order to feed those who were destitute. The eyes of hungry children haunted her and the memory of exhausted women trying to breastfeed their babies troubled her mind.

Beneath the surface of the city there was great dissatisfaction. Marie knew that there were others who would take the place of Jakov's group and make an attempt on the life of the Tsar. Three years before, the premier, Peter Stolypin, had been assassinated at Kiev, before the eyes of Nicholas II. It was only a matter of time before the Tsar would meet the same fate. And Rasputin was destroying the royal family. The papers were full of rumours. It was said that the Empress shared the peasant's bed; that he had raped all the grand duchesses and that he had ordered Nicholas to pull off his boots before he entered the Tsarina's bed.

Confidence in the Tsar was waning and tension was growing between Britain and Germany. The British fleet had been ordered into the North Sea from its base in the Mediterranean. All over Europe, factories were turning out arms and munitions at an accelerated rate.

Marie had noticed in the papers that her sister Alma had assumed the responsibilities of the Austrian embassy. There were rumours around the capital that her child was the bastard child of a Prince Eugene from the Balkans. In Berlin, her sister Sophie was quietly amassing a fortune.

She had received several letters from Fieldmann. He explained to her that he found exile burdensome, and to relieve the tedium, he was painting a church in the village of Tarko. His companion was a professor of linguistics who had been with him in the freight car which carried him into exile.

She missed this man with whom she had shared the vagaries of her life for more than ten years. Despite her work in the city, she wanted to join him before the winter set in.

Finally, the papers came through. She said goodbye to her friends in St Petersburg and set off across the wide steppes of Russia to an insignificant village situated in an endless tundra.

News that Fieldmann had begun his great mural of hell passed quickly through the village. Many of the men came to the church door and peered in. They could make out the great mass of red flames which writhed up the wall of the church and wrapped their arms about the bodies of the damned, but they were refused entrance by Fieldmann.

'If you wish to see the inhabitants of hell, then come to the service given by Father Sergius,' he told them.

Fieldmann's words were passed through the village.

Gradually the men began to stir. Old peasants with great beards and sad eyes, whose lives had been spent in arduous labour and misery, entered the church for the first time in many years.

They looked anxiously at the wall. The great mural was almost complete, but for the heads. They remained blank. The villagers felt unsatisfied.

Week after week they returned for the service. Still the faces of the damned had not been painted except for old Nikolai Kurpin. He occupied the lowest pit of hell, dressed only in a loincloth.

Jakov admired the old man's courage, but Kurpin replied, 'I fear neither the Tsar nor the priest. I am my own man. Christ will have more mercy on me than Fieldmann.'

The metropolitan arrived in late autumn. He had sent Father Sergius a letter announcing his arrival. The villagers had gathered at the jetty to welcome him. He was dressed in magnificent vestments and a gold cross encrusted in jewels hung from his neck.

He walked up the village, through the rutted streets, dispensing his blessings as he moved along.

From the tavern, Nikolai Kurpin and Fieldmann watched his progress.

'Here we are, good and evil,' the old peasant remarked, drinking his vodka.

Even Olga had left the tavern, dressed in her finest costume for the occasion. 'Why do you not pay honour to the metropolitan? He represents God and the Tsar,' she upbraided him.

'If he wishes to speak to me, then I will go to him. I have no truck with the church,' Fieldmann replied

'You are as bad as old Nikolai,' she said stomping out of the tavern.

'She has a fine backside, Fieldmann,' Nikolai said as she left.

They spent many hours drinking in the tavern and later in the evening Fieldmann staggered back to his house.

At ten o'clock Father Sergius knocked on the door. He was very excited. 'The metropolitan wishes to speak to you. He would feel greatly honoured to meet you.'

'Are you sure?'

'They are his very words.'

When he arrived at Father Sergius's house he found the metropolitan dressed in the simple clothes of the priest. He was eating a spartan meal of bread and a glass of water stood beside his plate.

He arose when Fieldmann entered. 'I am privileged to meet you,' he said simply. Fieldmann was surprised at his words. The metropolitan invited him to sit beside him. They talked for an hour about the murals and Jakov was surprised at the priest's insight.

'It is very good work. Perhaps you could come to the city. I could arrange it. Your exile would be made sweeter there and there is much work you could do in the churches.'

It was a tempting offer. Jakov considered it for some time. 'I cannot accept your offer,' he said finally. 'I have been condemned to live in this place. I will stay here. It will give me time to think.'

'You believe that there will be a revolution?' the metropolitan asked.

'Yes,' Jakov replied firmly.

'You are correct. The church has lost its intellectuals.' It was a blinding statement and Jakov knew that the metropolitan spoke out of conviction.

The priest continued, 'But some day, when they have tested and tasted the revolution, they will return. It may take a long time.' Then he brought the interview to a close. 'I will not bless you, for that would be arrogant on my part but I will pray for you.'

They shook hands and then by some instinct, they embraced each other.

When Jakov left, ice was forming close to the banks of the river. The steppes were freezing over. Soon the ice would form across the whole river and then it would deepen into a hard road.

Some days later, the final steamer of the year forced its way through the thickening ice to the village with supplies.

Marie had watched the flat tundras on her way up river. They were bleak and empty and she felt an oppressive weight on her mind.

At Tarko, she climbed off the barge and walked up through the village.

'Fieldmann's woman has arrived,' the villagers whispered.

She made her way directly to the church, where the door was slightly ajar.

She looked in. A great brazier burned in the centre. Fieldmann was working on a scaffold.

She pushed the door ajar and entered the church. Fieldmann thought it was some village woman come to pray and continued to work on the mural. The woman continued to stand beside the brazier.

'I have come as I promised, Fieldmann,' Marie Schmerling called.

Chapter Thirty-nine

Berlin was a thriving, vulgar city. Along the Leipzigerstrasse and the Friedrichstrasse, department stores and head offices of banks and mercantile houses were evidence of the opulence of the place.

Life moved to a Prussian drum beat. Wilhelm II wore operatic uniforms which he had designed for each and every possible occasion. Seven tailors were kept busy at the palace.

Society was stiff, dull and tiered. The various circles kept to themselves: the wife of a doctor did not speak to the wife of a tradesman and the wife of a tradesman did not speak to the wife of an artisan.

Everything was certain and in its proper place.

Baron Von Hertling loved the sinew and muscle of the city. Life had been good to him. His heavy, dutiful wife had presented him with five sons. They would follow in his footsteps and join the army.

By now his organisation had grown into a huge network extending across Europe. The young men he had gathered around him at the beginning were now in charge of their own departments, each accountable only to him. It gave him incredible power and he had a direct telephone link to the Kaiser. Wilhelm liked to meddle in his affairs, so he constantly fed him inconsequential titbits on the scandals of Europe. It kept him satisfied.

Baron Von Hertling knew that there would be a war. All that was needed was a small spark, then it would ignite. The great guns would be called into play along all fronts. The great ships would engage in naval battles.

Even the skies above Europe would echo to the sound of battles.

Already they had tested aerial bombardment from great balloons, but the new planes had greater war potential.

Now, dressed in his military uniform he set off in his chauffeur-driven car to meet General Moltke and his officers in the red brick General Staff building on the Konigplatz.

He admired Moltke. He was dour and introspective. In his spare time he painted or played the cello. But he possessed the courage of his convictions.

The general was standing with his officers in the military room when Von Hertling arrived. He saluted stiffly then he joined the others in front of the great model of Europe with mountain ranges, lakes, rivers, railroads and towns. They often stood before this model as they made out the plans of war.

'When the German army begins to move, it cannot be recalled,' Moltke told them. 'It will move forward like an avalanche.'

They were all aware of the plans. They would move swiftly against France. Seven-eighths of their military might would move west. It had been calculated that it would take the Russians six weeks to mobilise their army. By then France would be defeated and the army could be recalled and thrown against the Russians.

During the years Baron Von Hertling had meticulously gathered every train timetable in Europe. He had studied them carefully. He knew precisely the number of trains and carriages necessary to move both the army and its munitions to the various fronts. Every train would have its kitchen. Food would be cooked in transit. Not a moment must be lost. There must be no back up of trains or confusion at railways, he had decided.

To facilitate easy transport of troops they had rehearsed their mobilisation and movement, using models.

Now, as they studied the Russian front, Moltke asked, 'And what is the morale of the Russian troops?'

'They can put two million into the field against us. But they are badly armed and ill-prepared. There is always the danger of a revolt in Russia. It is seething with discontent, particularly in the cities. The Tsar is unaware of how dangerous the position is. And General Sukhomlinov lives in the past. He boasts that he has not read a military manual in twenty-five years. He believes that machine guns and rapid firing artillery are unworthy of brave men. His military ideas belong to another age.'

'Then the fool is on our side,' Moltke remarked.

He considered the model once again. 'What is the present strength of their artillery?'

The Baron drew a dossier from his leather case and gave Moltke details of the strength of the Russian army.

'It will be a pigeon shoot,' the general told his officers. 'Now, let us consider the Belgian position again,' he said, directing his attention towards the west.

Molkte had no intention of meeting the French on their borders. The German army would move rapidly through Belgium and sweep down into France at its weakest point.

'This is the Achilles heel,' he told them.

Baron Von Hertling knew that if war was declared they were ready.

That afternoon Von Hertling had a visitor at his office, a Russian émigré, a cultivated man who spoke several languages, just arrived from Switzerland. He had a round, soft face which belied his intelligence.

Kropov was Von Hertling's contact in Bern.

The baron welcomed him and invited him to sit down. They never engaged in pleasantries.

Von Hertling sent for a file. A secretary placed it on his desk. Inside the cover was a photograph of Lenin. Von Hertling was always impressed by the intensity of his gaze, the wide brow above the brooding eyes. He had followed the course of his vagrant life for many years. He even had an itinerary of the revolutionary's day.

'Does he continue to work at the same pace?' he asked.

'He never rests,' Kropov replied. 'Intellectual work is a drug. And he attracts people to him. They are drawn by his logic.'

'He seems to be familiar with all the revolutionaries in Europe. Rosa Luxemburg is one of his associates, I believe.'

'He may well be the enemy that you need within Russia. I can assure you that more than anyone else, he is capable of throwing Russia into chaos if the occasion arises. His articles are smuggled in on every train, on every boat. He is no armchair revolutionary. I have sat and listened to him and I admire him greatly.'

Von Hertling listened to his agent speak. He was a shrewd judge of men and he valued Kropov's judgement.

'There is always money available if necessary to oil his palm and sweeten him,' he told him.

'Perhaps at another time. At present, I would advise you to let him continue his revolutionary work.'

'Germany will be attacked on both borders when war begins. Our only ally will be Austria. So, victory must be quick. We cannot afford to get bogged down in some morass in Russia,' the baron told him.

'You have laid out your plans. I weep that so many Russians will die in a futile war. That is why I wish to rid the world of tyrants.'

'Do you believe that the Kaiser is a tyrant?'

'It is up to Germany to decide that matter for itself,' Kropov answered shrewdly

They argued for more than an hour on the subject then they parted amicably. As he left the building Von Hertling looked at the heavy-shouldered figure walking down the avenue of trees, until he passed out of sight. He thought it interesting that, although motivated by patriotism, Kropov should turn to the Germans.

He returned to his desk. He had much to consider. He opened another file, thicker than that of Lenin. Inside the cover was the picture of Rosa Luxemburg with Karl Liebknecht, taken at Leipzig in 1909. He considered the large figure of the Jewess, the shawl thrown across her shoulders, the leather bag she held in her stubby hands. He took a magnifying glass and studied her face. It was fleshy and her lips were small and full. He left it aside and considered her file.

Like the agent who had just left she believed in her cause.

Now he considered if she should be assassinated. He had only to give the order and trained killers would murder her in some dark corner. However, as he considered the plan, he found that it had its disadvantages. He would give the Communists a martyr. The incident would draw accusations from all over the world. The times did not justify such an act.

He closed the file and turned to another, a list of five spies who were gathering military information for the French government. One was working in Berlin.

Again he considered the idea of eliminating them. However, he believed that it was better to pass them false information. In that way the French would be confused. He set out his plans in a brief letter and passed it to one of the young men he had trained in counter-espionage. Having tidied up his desk he rang for his secretary and dictated some letters to her.

Then he left for his home. That night he was giving a party for some generals. He looked forward to the occasion.

Joseph Steiner was respected in Vienna. The title of Baron had conferred on him the aura of nobility. Sophie had been correct. He felt more certain of his position. And he could wield influence if he so wished.

He established a small bank in Vienna. Because of his discretion, many investors placed their money with him.

As he had wished, his new position and influence allowed him also to begin quietly to work against the anti-Semitic poison of the city. He financed a small Jewish newspaper and a musical scholarship at the Vienna Academy.

His wife, too, was pleased with her title and the coat of arms embossed on her stationery. She lived in her own house, surrounded by a coterie of friends. The life of the court engaged all her energies.

The fact that Prince Karl had died in a duel and her daughter had given birth to his son, brought her into the magic circle of the court. Even Franz Joseph had granted her an audience and was most anxious about her grandson.

Now, it was her ambition that Joseph purchase some of the estates which her son-in-law had squandered.

But her husband preferred to live in his own mansion in a wine valley close to the city and refused either to answer her calls or her letters.

After Karl's funeral, they had argued fiercely. 'The matter is settled. I will not purchase the estates,' he had told her firmly.

'It is not settled,' she had screamed at him. 'I will pursue you until you ensure our grandson's inheritance. He could be Emperor some day.'

'If fifty members of the Hapsburg family are wiped out at once,' he had answered sarcastically, reflecting on their happy separation. He had grown tired of her petty demands.

Now, he sat in his library surrounded by precious books. In the small wood there was birdsong and the city seemed far away.

His journey to the small village in Russia had given him firm roots in old earth. He wrote each year to old Father Alexei and enclosed some money for the upkeep of the cemetery. He had received a photograph of the plot as an assurance that his money was being well used. He was certain that half of it was expended on vodka but that was of little consequence.

His collection of rare Hebrew manuscripts and books was impressive. From the great cities of Europe booksellers sent him rare editions which he placed in a large library. These he treasured more than all his other books. They came from London, Cordoba, Constantinople. Each one bore testament to the genius of his race.

And in the basement, locked away, lay a library of anti-Semitic literature. It consisted of small newspapers and magazines as well as books. Amongst the most vicious attack on his race was *The Protocols of the Learned Elders of Zion*. Its authorship was uncertain but he believed that it could have been commissioned by Nicholas II of Russia. In the book a mythical council of Jews were plotting to take over the world.

It disturbed him when he read it.

On a great map drawn by a rabbi Joseph had employed were marked out the cities and towns, century by century, where pogroms against his race had taken place.

The scholar, Steinmann, was an old man, with a grey beard and a skullcap, who lived in the ghetto. Each day he made the journey to Joseph's house, his back bent with the burden of history, a mystical look in his eyes.

'You are the wandering Jew,' Joseph often said to him when the old man recounted the history of the Jews. 'You seem to have lived in all the centuries.'

'Perhaps I have,' Steinmann would answer in a serious tone.

They had often argued on the future of the race, but the old man was firm in his thinking. 'They must return to

Israel. They must possess their own borders again. The Diaspora must be reversed. It is the only answer. Until that is done, we will all be wandering Jews.'

'Is this possible?' Joseph Steiner asked.

'Of course it is possible. At least that is the dream of some and they are not old rabbis like me, filled with dreams. No, these are practical men. I will prepare a map for you. I will show you what is happening and what can be achieved.'

It was the beginning of Joseph Steiner's interest in a new Israel.

The old rabbi spent weeks bent over large parchment, drawing maps of Palestine, on which he set out Jewish settlements. They extended from Yesod in the north to Hebron in the south. The greatest clusters of settlements were centred about Jaffa, Zikhron Yaakov and the Sea of Galilee.

'It is not a dream,' the old man said. 'It is already beginning to happen. The Russian pogroms began this new course of history. The Jews are moving towards Jerusalem. We will not be equal with the others until we have our own state.'

Steinmann brought Joseph a small, badly printed newspaper, which he read with enthusiasm. There was an optimistic note in the articles. They had a ring to them which pleased the old man. They were not the words of a beaten people.

'What can I do for these settlers?'

'What all rich Jews can do for poor Jews. Send money to one of the settlements. It will be well used.'

One morning, Joseph went for a walk in his garden behind the house, a large lawn, surrounded by mature shrubs and flowers. He considered his life. Only he knew his wealth, where it lay and how dispersed it was. His title had given him pleasure and protection. Yet he felt alone.

He thought of the Jewish settlers working in swamps

and barren land in Palestine. Perhaps he would visit the country and see for himself. It was a thought which gave him some satisfaction and a sense of purpose.

He returned to the house. As he walked up the marble staircase, he stopped and examined the Gobelin tapestries hanging on the wall. They were objects of great beauty, depicting an enchanted forest, with hunters and deer and a hermit bearing a cross. On the landing stood a brooding Rembrandt, one of his final portraits. Joseph stood and examined it. The bulbous nose, the doughy folds of flesh of the sitter, the round head, testified to old age. From beneath busy eyebrows bright and critical eyes looked at him, questioned him as he stood on the gallery of his mansion.

He entered his office. There was much to be done. He sat at his desk and studied the newspapers. Then he took the phone and began calling his brokers all over Europe. It was a ritual which lasted an hour. At four his chauffeur knocked at the door of his office.

His bag had been packed and a first-class compartment booked for him on the Berlin train. He reached the city the next morning. He had slept fitfully during the night but it was sufficient for him.

Sophie was waiting for him at the station. He noticed the changes in her. She had grown heavy, almost Germanic in her appearance. Her flesh was opulent like that of a Rubens nude.

Berlin was bustling. The great avenues seemed to go on forever. The suburbs had extended and trees gave the flat, sandy land their own beauty. And everywhere there was frenetic movement. The motorcar had taken the place of the horse and cart. The Berliners had a cocky, confident appearance. They did not possess the elegance and charm of the Viennese. Joseph noted, too, the presence of the military uniforms. It was more marked than in any other city in Europe. Wagner and Bismarck had welded the German states into an empire.

'You like this city?' he asked.

'I have always liked it. I have grown with it. It is now part of my blood. It is the greatest city in the world,' she stated proudly.

'And what of Vienna and Paris?'

'They are beautiful but not great,' his stepdaughter replied smartly.

They exchanged gossip on the family as they passed down Unter den Linden to the art gallery.

The building had been designed by Sinkler and it was impressive with its Greek façade. Its location by the Spree gave it added prestige.

The curator was waiting in the great hall to receive them. 'You are most welcome, Baron,' he said, bowing from the hips. Joseph felt a sense of importance in the great art gallery. The curator had set his collection in its proper place in the art gallery, part of the Renaissance collection.

A special catalogue had been prepared, which Joseph Steiner examined closely. The curator waited for his approval.

'I commend you for your excellent scholarship,' he told the man, not taking his eyes from the de-luxe edition. 'I note that you have traced the location of the missing paintings,' he continued, smiling.

'Yes. When we acquire them, then the collection will be rearranged,' the curator told him.

'And when will that be?'

'One never knows. These paintings originated in Italy, now they are in Russia. We may acquire the others in time.'

'I hope we acquire them sooner rather than later. The collection will never be complete until they are brought together under one roof.'

Together with Sophie Joseph spent two hours in the gallery, going from painting to painting. He knew the figures better than he knew his three step-daughters. He was more familiar with the Renaissance landscape than he was with any other in the world. It glowed with southern light.

When they left the gallery he turned to Sophie and said, 'I must go to Russia. I must make another attempt to purchase the paintings. My life will be incomplete until they have been brought together.'

The completion of the collection had become an obsession. Russia beckoned.

Chapter Forty

When Joseph set off for St Petersburg, the winter of 1913, which had held Central Asia in its iron grip, had passed. The thick sheets of ice on the great rivers began to crack and loosen. Soon small slabs of ice moved towards the seas.

'Is it wise to go to Russia at this time?' Sophie asked before her stepfather left.

'It is never wise to go Russia,' he replied. 'But it is at these times that art collectors go in search of art and move it across national boundaries.'

'I have phoned Von Hertling. He tells me that there could be a general strike in St Petersburg. There is unrest in the working-class districts in the north of the city.'

'And that is all the more reason that I should go.'

Sophie now watched the lonely figure of her stepfather, dressed, as always, as a businessman, enter the train. He waved from the door and then disappeared.

Joseph had planned his journey into Russia. He knew that war would soon break out. He had a nose for such things. Great hatreds were stirring in the soul of Europe. Beneath the thin patina of civilisation lay the demons of war.

In the event of this war, he wondered, would the great paintings survive in Berlin. In the event of a revolution in Russia, would the treasures of the Hermitage be reduced to ashes. 'Will Europe destroy its own memory?' he asked himself as the city passed out of view and the agricultural lands came into sight.

The journey to St Petersburg would be a long, tedious

trip, but Joseph's mind was excited. He had located a bookseller in St Petersburg who had come into possession of valuable Jewish manuscripts. He wished to see them.

And then there was Joseph, Alma's son. He must visit him and give him a present. He had not told his wife that he had already purchased an estate in his name close to Vienna. It would come into his possession when he was twenty-one. In the meantime, it was managed by an honest Englishman and the profits would be left to accrue in an American bank.

Two days later he arrived in St Petersburg. As always, he stayed in a second-class hotel close to the Nevsky Prospekt.

He did not immediately let his stepdaughter know that he was in the city. His first visit was to the antiquarian bookshop in a small side street off one of the canals. The interior was dark and smelled of the leather-bound books which were stacked in columns on the floor. The walls were crammed with books on every conceivable subject. Customers stood in front of the columns, reading silently.

'Ah, Mister Steiner,' the owner said when he introduced himself, 'I am so glad to see you. I received your letter some days ago. Come with me.'

He led him into a small office, more confused than the shop itself, lit by a single gas lamp. He took some correspondence from the high desk at which he worked and lifted the lid. He took out several old manuscripts and books in Hebrew.

'They came from central Asia, Simbirsk to be exact,' he explained.

'How did they come into your hands?' he asked, looking at the precious books.

'A soldier brought them to me. I did not ask any further questions.'

'They are stained, I notice,' Joseph told the bookseller.

'Yes. I tried to wash off the stains but they remained, despite my best efforts. Of course, I will allow for such stains. I know they are not in pristine condition. But I believe that we can come to an agreement.'

Joseph purchased the books, ordered them to be parcelled up and paid for their postage to Vienna. He did not tell the bookseller that the marks on the books were bloodstains. There had been a pogrom in Simbirsk in 1906. It was marked in red on one of the maps drawn by the old rabbi.

He left the shop and walked along the banks of the canal. St Petersburg was a beautiful city but it was a city built on bones. Joseph knew its history only too well.

Now, he was curious about the social unrest which lay beneath the even tenor of the city. As he walked down the Nevsky Prospekt, everything seemed normal. It was thronged with people; the shopfronts were as elegant as those in Paris or London; automobiles were as prevalent on the wide boulevards as in Berlin. But he knew that this was only a veneer.

He met Professor Ivovich of the St Petersburg Lycée, at eight o'clock in the morning. Joseph had invited him to have breakfast and he had accepted the invitation.

'I want to know what is going on in the city,' Joseph told him. 'I read what is going on in the papers but they are censored by the secret police.'

'Where are you from?'

'Vienna, but I was born in Russia a long time ago. I have only a vague memory of what happened there. My parents had to flee to Vienna, where they died.'

'You are a Jew then?' Ivovich asked.

'Yes.'

'Your rights will be protected when the revolution happens. We have little time for race or creed or colour or religion. These ideas will all be swept away.'

'I hope so,' Joseph Steiner replied. But he was cynical about great social changes. The Jews would always be scapegoats for every ill, as they had been scapegoats during the Black Death.

'I talk better when I walk,' the professor interrupted his thoughts.

'And I need the exercise,' Joseph Steiner laughed.

They left the hotel and began to walk through the city.

They passed the Winter Palace, its delicate lines reflected in the Neva. The professor looked at it scornfully. 'Some day it will go up in flames.'

'And what of all the works of art inside?'

'We will create new art; people's art. When the proletariat are free, a new art will flourish,' Ivovich declared.

They strolled across the wide bridge leading to the islands. Joseph looked up the river to the thin, golden spire of Saint Peter and Paul's Cathedral, gleaming in the air. They passed it and continued along the Schlusselberg road which led to Ladoga lake. The road took them through the manufacturing district. Mills were built on both sides of the river, iron works, cotton mills and candleworks.

'This is not the city of the Tsar. This is the city of the workers,' Ivovich said. 'Here they eat soup made from bad meat and their bread is black. On Sunday they spend the day drinking vodka to forget their misery.'

They passed through a warren of streets, where the houses were wooden huts, with whole families living in one room. Their furniture consisted of a table, stools, beds and a chest for clothes.

'Are these people organised?' Joseph asked.

'More than you know.'

Joseph Steiner was tired when he returned to the hotel. The intensity of the professor and the poverty of the narrow streets had wearied his mind. He rested for an hour in his room, trying to pull all the strands of the conversation together.

There would be a revolution, but he did not know when the spark would be put to the tinder. Only a spark could cause the revolution. It could sweep the nobles and princes with it, as had done the French revolution.

He hoped that he could rescue the Sienese masters from the Federov estate before the revolution brought chaos to an old world.

Next day he sent a letter to Alma telling her that he was in the city.

She immediately sent the official embassy limousine to collect him.

She was waiting for him in the main hall when he arrived. She had changed little in the past few years. She had the bearing of a countess and her clothes were fashionable and expensive, but she still retained the youthful appearance which had brought her to the attention of Franz Joseph so many years ago.

'Prince Joseph is having his lessons,' she said, kissing her stepfather on the cheek. 'His day is quite full. Never a dull moment for him.'

'But he is so young,' Joseph said. 'What can one teach him?'

'Russian, French. A child can pick up a language very rapidly. But come, tell me of your new home in Vienna. I believe that it is set in the woods close to the wine villages. Mother was quite furious when you moved out,' she laughed.

'She left me no choice. Day and night the conversation centred around the court and the gossip of the court. I sat at so many dinners listening to court gossip that I felt my mind was growing soft.'

'Come to my rooms,' Alma directed, 'there we can discuss matters of great and little moment.'

Joseph looked at her suite of rooms with appreciation. On his advice, she had purchased some Impressionist paintings which suited the light quality of the decor. He examined them for some time.

'You can no longer purchase a Renoir or a Manet,' he told her.

'I know. The French ambassador never fails to admire them when he visits me. He brings all the gossip of the court. He is the most informed man in St Petersburg.'

'And what is the gossip from the Court?'

'Rasputin's hold on the royal family grows stronger daily. It is almost impossible to approach the Tsarina or the Tsar but through him. Of course, his influence on the Tsarina is profound. He healed Prince Alexis when the doctors gave him up for dead.'

'A peasant ruling Russia,' Joseph Steiner commented.

'A peasant ruling the country. They say that many of the great ladies of St Petersburg have been in his bed; that he has made a brothel out of the royal palace and that the young daughters fight with each other to gain his attention. He is an unwashed, filthy boor, half mystic and totally debauched. Alexandra uses him to evaluate ministers, I am told. His word in many cases is final. All this is false of course. However, many believe the rumours.'

They spent a long time gossiping and reminiscing about the past, then that night they had a private dinner at the embassy. It was at this dinner that Joseph presented Alma with Prince Joseph's birthday present.

'Do not let your mother know,' he told her.

She opened the envelope and looked at the deeds to an estate close to Vienna.

'Until he comes of age it will be run by a manager. I believe that he will be a wealthy young man, but this will ensure that he will be independently wealthy.'

'You are a good man Joseph Steiner,' she said, tears in her eyes. 'How can I thank you?'

'Perhaps you might have Fieldmann's sentence lightened. He is a great artist. He will waste his talents in the steppes of Russia.'

Her eyes hardened. 'Many years ago my sister refused my help. I detest all that she stands for. I cannot help him. He is lucky that he was not hanged with the others.'

The subject was closed and the enthusiasm went out of their later conversation. When she walked with him to the embassy door he knew that he should not have asked her for such a favour.

All his stepdaughters had gone their different ways.

Next day Joseph left St Petersburg.

His journey took him across endless steppes. It was late spring and the young wheat was growing on the vast tracts of land. Sometimes he saw a lone horseman in the distance or a gilded spire which marked the presence of a peasant village. Now and then the plains were broken by woods or small copses. The air was filled with the scents of spring, which had been locked in ground during the harsh winter when the snows wheeled down from the north and covered the steppes with a great white blanket.

It was an empty landscape, part of a landmass which stretched as far as the borders of China. Joseph wondered how a collection of Sienese masters had found their way this far east.

The driver of his automobile told him that if he watched the horizon he would soon notice the first appearance of the great estate. Some time later he saw it, standing alone on a hill.

Joseph Steiner knew that Alexander Federov was one of the richest men in Russia. He was descended from a Tartar who had been a friend of Peter the Great. He knew also, that his mansions teemed with precious works of art. Many of them had not been catalogued. As he crossed the river and approached the great palace he felt that he should not have made the journey. But then he wished to see the paintings and admire them.

They entered a great courtyard at the back of the estate,

a vast place with the walls of the house stretching in a semicircle about it.

He was met by one of the servants dressed in livery. He led him through shimmering corridors hanging with a hundred portraits. The servant explained that they were the mistresses of Prince Federov's great-grandfather. In another hall he noted several Dutch masters. He wished he had time to study them.

Finally they entered the Italian wing. Every treasure, from the tapestries to the furniture, had been purchased in Italy. Joseph finally discovered the paintings he desired hanging on a wall with many others. They had not been correctly attributed or positioned. Their ethereal beauty was destroyed by the presence of later schools.

'Could I remain here for a time and study them?' he asked.

'Very well. If you wish to speak to Count Federov's secretary he may be available in two hours' time,' the servant said and left him alone with the paintings.

His instinct was to rearrange them and set them in the correct historical order, but he restrained himself and instead looked at the paintings he had read about in art books.

He knew the history of each work. He was familiar with the figures, the landscapes, and the style. They did not belong in this palace, stuffed with treasures, but in Berlin with the others. Their impact was lessened by the company they kept.

Joseph stayed in the room for three hours, going from painting to painting, studying the familiar techniques, the use of brushstrokes, the composition of the groups.

Time passed rapidly. His mind was filled with immense pleasure and he felt that the journey had been worth undertaking.

At four o'clock he entered the secretary's office, a walnut-panelled room along which bookcases, crammed with books, ran.

'Ah, Baron Steiner,' he began 'I hope you have enjoyed your visit. Not many Germans come to this district.'

Joseph did not explain that he was a Jew.

'Yes. I have marvelled at Count Federov's Italian paintings.'

'Oh yes. I do remember that you wished to see some. We have quite a collection. One of the Count's ancestors purchased a whole palace in Italy and had the contents brought to the estate. It is said that a freight train with forty carriages brought them across Europe to Moscow. There they were brought by road to the palace.'

'How very interesting.'

'Not as interesting as the animals which were brought from Africa for the zoo here, by the Count's grandfather. The animals died during a severe winter, as the old Count had lost interest in them. However, some of them were stuffed. They are at one of the hunting lodges.' He chuckled. 'But why come such a long way to see some paintings? Surely the art galleries of Europe are crammed with such wealth?'

Joseph did not feel like explaining to him that the galleries were not 'crammed' but the paintings were arranged in schools and that attention was given to the finest details when hanging them.

'I thought I might perhaps purchase some of these paintings. They belong to the school of Sienna. They should be hung together with others in my possession.'

The secretary looked at him in disdain. 'Sell our paintings? What would Count Federov say when he saw the empty walls? He has a quick temper. You do not offer to purchase paintings from Count Federov. They are part of the palace. You were permitted to visit the Italian wing because he is at Baden Baden in Germany. Only your rank guaranteed you entry to the wing.'

Joseph Steiner realised that his journey had been futile.

He would never possess the paintings. The collection would remain forever divided.

He thanked the secretary for the time he had granted him and was shown through the palace to the great courtyard. He had not been invited to have a light meal before setting out, and he felt humiliated as he entered the carriage. Before him lay a long journey across the endless steppes.

As he went down the avenue he turned about and looked at the great mansion equal in splendour to anything he had seen in St Petersburg. Later, it became a small dot on the long horizon.

Joseph had found an hotel in a lonely small town in the middle of the steppes. In his room, he checked his map of Russia. The village of Tarko was five days' journey away, by train and boat. He felt that he must visit Fieldmann and Marie.

On his way to Tarko, Joseph visited the humble churches and studied icons which were blackened with smoke and time. Many of them were of low quality, but some were as great and as moving as the early Sienese masters.

As he moved north, oak gave way to birch. The land became waterlogged and soggy. The villages became less numerous. There was a brooding emptiness in the landscape. He wondered how Fieldmann and Marie could survive in such an isolated place.

Several days later he reached the village, set on an elevation above the dreary marshes. He felt odd, dressed in his city clothes and coat, standing on the small, wooden pier. He inquired after Fieldmann from one of the villagers.

'Fieldmann. Of course I know Fieldmann. Everyone knows Fieldmann. He is a mad artist who lives in one of the church houses with his wife and a professor. You will find him in the church.'

'Not praying, I hope,' Joseph said.

'He has a black heart. He could not raise his voice in prayer. He is painting the walls and the ceiling.'

'And the woman?'

'She is trying to teach the children to read and write. But why do they need to know how to write. Ignorance is a good and pleasant thing. We are born here and we die here and you only need education in the big towns.'

Joseph made his way through the village, conscious of the eyes on him, until finally he reached the small school. The children were playing in the yard and Marie was standing amongst them.

She had changed. Her tall figure was slightly stooped. She was dressed in heavy, drab clothes. She wore the peasant blouse buttoned on the shoulder and a scarf on her head. Even at a distance he noticed that her red hair was turning grey.

Marie looked up at the approaching figure. She could not believe her eyes. She left the group of children and rushed over to him.

'Joseph Steiner! What brings you here?' she asked.

'Hardly the stock exchange. I wanted to see you.'

She kissed him on the cheek and linking his arm in hers, walked with him to the schoolyard.

'I will dismiss the children. It is a special day. We do not have many visitors here.'

Later they sat down to a meal in her small house, at a table which she had covered with a fine linen cloth. She had made him some simple food.

'Do you find exile harsh?' he asked.

'No. I like the simple life. We receive books and I read a lot,' she told him.

'And what do you read. Karl Marx?'

'Yes Karl Marx and Engels and many others. I keep my mind occupied.'

'And Fieldmann?'

Marie sighed. 'He is growing irritable. During the wintertime he was very morose, and kept recalling our days in Odessa. But, he has continued to paint. He is completing the interior of the church. People travel from everywhere to see his work. But I fear the future years of exile. They will be a burden upon him.' She paused. ' And you? You seem to grow richer by the day.'

'And more disillusioned. I am now a Baron, but I still feel a stranger in Germany.'

'The Jew is always a stranger, Joseph. He never rests. He is accepted nowhere. He moves from place to place like a nomad. I know the meaning of loneliness. I live in this vast waste and I, too, have no roots. That is why I believe in the people. I am one of them.'

Joseph looked at his stepdaughter sadly. 'My mind turns more and more to Palestine. I think a lot of Jerusalem. It has become a mythical city in my mind.'

'So, Europe has changed you?'

'Yes. I have discovered much about myself and about my ancestors.'

As if to ward off such introspection, Marie turned the conversation to the subject of Margit. 'So, Mother is now a titled lady. Well, she has achieved her foolish wish. I am sure that she is insufferable.'

'She is now engrossed in the life of her grandson, Prince Joseph. She believes that he may one day be Emperor,' Joseph chuckled, 'She still entertains illusions of grandeur.'

'And Alma and Sophie?'

'Eminent women. Each has achieved their ambitions, but they no longer see eye to eye. Something happened in St Petersburg to which I was not party and they became bitter enemies. In fact, you are all bitter enemies. It is very strange.'

Marie noticed again the change in her stepfather. He had become unhappy and thoughtful. The conversation returned to the fact that he was Jewish and that Jews were wanderers.

'We must have a homeland; a place to call our own; our own earth and our own government and our own schools, and a language of our own. We are the scapegoats who carry the sins of Europe and Russia on our backs.'

'You think too much, Joseph. You cannot carry the burden of the world upon your shoulders.'

'Yes. I have become too introspective.'

'Even at wakes there can be celebrations. In this isolated place we celebrate life and we celebrate death.'

'There is no great logic in life.'

'No. There is not.'

There was much they had to talk about, but Joseph would remain with them for a week. 'You must see Fieldmann's work,' Marie said the following day, as she prepared the midday meal. 'Go to the church and you can make your own judgement.'

Joseph left the house and walked the small distance to the church. He stood before the outer walls and studied the great murals. He could recognise Fieldmann's brushwork amongst that of a hundred artists.

He entered the church, which was cast half in shadow and half in light and gazed about him. On the walls and ceilings the whole of Orthodox belief was celebrated: saints and devils, sinners and demons in colourful profusion. On a rickety platform close to the roof Fieldmann, dressed in a rough smock, was at work, unaware of Joseph Steiner's presence.

Joseph gazed in awe at the wealth of creation around him. The primary colours of the mural were used with massive force and the surfaces pulsated with life.

He stood there for a long time before he heard a booming voice from the platform above him. 'Who are you and what do you want?'

'It is I, Joseph Steiner.' His voice echoed off the ceiling in a hollow fashion.

'Do not tell me. You have been sent into exile for embezzling the Tsar,' Fieldmann laughed.

'I was doing some business in central Russia. I realised that I was a week's journey from the village. I decided to pay you a visit,' Joseph replied seriously. He was surprised at how well Fieldmann looked. He had a healthy and athletic appearance.

Jakov descended from the platform and wiped his hands on a cloth. He looked at Steiner for a time. 'You have not changed,' he said.

'This then is your Sistine chapel,' Steiner commented.

'Yes, this is my Sistine chapel. What do you think of it?' he asked, never taking his sharp eye from Joseph's face.

'It exceeds belief. It exceeds belief,' he repeated, gazing in awe at the work. 'It seems perfect in every way: the colours, the iconography, the composition. It is your best work, but it will never be seen. When you leave, some fool will whitewash over it.'

'What does it matter? What does it matter? I would have been troubled had I not done it. I exorcised some demons out of my soul,' he explained.

Joseph was not listening to him. Unconsciously, he began to walk along the aisle of the church, taking in the whole pattern of the composition. 'I would like to visit this place tomorrow and study it more closely, so that I do not interrupt you.'

'There is a moment when the mind becomes exhausted. I have reached that point,' Jakov smiled.

They left the church and made their way back to the house. Marie had prepared the meal and Urusov, the professor, had come to join them. He picked at his food, but his mind seemed far away. He had received a book on phonetics from St Petersburg and he had spent the morning studying it.

They talked of many things during the meal and over the

next few days. Their discussions were long and heated, particularly about the prospects of a war.

'Germany is armed to the teeth,' Joseph argued. 'They have laid out their war plans and they are spoiling for a fight. The least incident will spark off a war and let me assure you, everyone will be drawn in, including Russia.'

'This is what we have been waiting for,' Marie said eagerly. 'The workers and the soldiers will mutiny. Why should they fight with their compatriots. Let the generals fight amongst themselves.'

'So it appears in theory. But war is a strange thing. It sucks whole nations into its vortex. And remember, this war will not be fought with sabres. Great armaments have been built up. I have seen them. I know the massive power of the guns and the bombs,' her stepfather told her.

Knowing she was beaten, Marie changed the subject. 'Are you returning to Vienna soon?'

Joseph laughed, aware of her tactics. 'No. First, I must make a pilgrimage to a small village in Russia from which my ancestors came. I have traced them to a cemetery there. Then I will leave for Palestine by way of Odessa. I have taken an interest in the Jewish settlements there. Some day the Jews will have their own state, you know.'

The Jewish state became the subject of argument for some time. 'You must call on my old friend, Ibram, who lives at Loslov,' Fieldmann told him. 'I left some paintings in his possession, but they would be of little interest to him. They belong in this new state you dream about. Take them. They are a gift. You saved my life. I am grateful.'

Next morning, carrying a small bag and out of place amongst the rough peasants, Joseph climbed up the gangway to the river steamer. As the boat moved up the river he waved to Fieldmann and Marie, a small, tidy figure with a sad expression in his eyes.

Father Alexei had grown older and more careless. He

drank continually and had become almost incoherent. When Joseph visited, he told him that he had seen several visions and had held long conversations with all the saints of Russia. But he had attended to the cemetery.

Before he left the town, Joseph visited the cemetery for a last time. He looked at the shallow mounds of earth where some of his ancestors lay and he reflected on the long migrations which had brought them to this lonely spot. Then he set off for Odessa.

'And how is my friend, Fieldmann, and his good lady, Marie?' Ibram asked when Joseph arrived at the town of Loslov.

'He is exiled in Siberia,' Joseph said.

'In prison?' Ibram was shocked.

'No in a village surrounded by marshes. It is in all respects a prison.'

'Fieldmann will escape. I know his mind. He will stir up trouble. He should have remained a painter – he is mad. But I liked him and I liked Marie. She educated my young son. Now he is an engineer. I am very proud of him.'

Later he brought Joseph Steiner the paintings, unrolling them and placing weights upon them to hold them down.

When Joseph saw them he knew that they belonged in the new State of Palestine.

He left Odessa and took a ship to Istanbul. Then, after a few days in the city, he managed to find passage through the Greek islands to the port of Jaffa.

Jaffa was built on the slope of a hill. Five thousand years of history lay beneath its foundations: it was to this port that the Lebanese cedars had been shipped for Solomon's temple; Richard the Lionheart had conquered this strategic place during the Crusades; it was at Jaffa that the first Jewish immigrant settled and it was through this port that the Jews had arrived from Europe. Here they had a toe-hold in an ancient land.

Joseph spent some days in the company of a Jewish

scholar travelling along the coast to the north of the city, where a new Jewish town called Tel Aviv had sprung up on the sand dunes. Here he saw the dream of a new homeland taking shape.

But he was more interested in pushing into the hinterland, where the Jews from Russia, Galacia and Romania had settled. He travelled to one of the new settlements, a primitive place of small buildings set on a hillside, overlooking a narrow, fertile plain. It had been a dry, dusty bowl when the group had purchased it. Now, through careful irrigation, they had build a series of walls on the hillside. Here olives had established themselves in the earth, their roots drawing upon its moisture.

The little town had been the sight of an ancient synagogue. Now, in early summer, small flowers grew amongst the ruins; bees were busy gathering nectar for their hives; the vegetable patch was tended each day by members of the community and the hay, which would sustain the cattle during the winter, had been saved and carried to the barns. In the evening the townspeople sat around a table and discussed the work of the day and made their plans for the future. Joseph Steiner listened to them intently. They were practical idealists.

The leaders of the community were a lawyer from the Crimea and his wife, who had been a concert pianist.

He laughed when he examined his callused hands. 'I took a law degree. Now I till the land. My wife, who has been trained to play Mozart and Brahms, hoes a vegetable patch and milks cows. Have we made a correct decision, Joseph Steiner?'

The older man reflected for a moment. 'Yes,' he said. 'You made the correct decision. You own the land. You have made this deserted place bloom.'

Joseph stayed in the settlement for a week. During that time he made a visit to Jerusalem. When he stood beside the Wailing Wall tears sprung to his eyes. He could not say why he wept in front of the great blocks of stone. It was a strange experience for a man whose heart had been dry for as long as he could remember.

On the 14th of July 1914, Joseph set out for Europe.

That day, in London, the worst thunderstorm in living memory struck the city. Torrents of rain fell on the city for three hours.

In Vienna, the Hapsburg heir, Archduke Franz Ferdinand and his wife, the Duchess of Hohenburg, were making arrangements for their visit to Sarajevo.

Chapter Forty-one

'Not Sarajevo!' Prince Eugene exclaimed.

'Yes,' the Archduke insisted.

'I know the city. This is a dangerous time, your Highness. There are those in Belgrade who have already planned to assassinate you or any other member of the royal family, given the chance.'

'But something must be done about Slav nationalism. It will tear the Empire asunder. You have said so yourself. Besides, I wish to travel. Vienna has become oppressive. My wife will accompany me. At least in the Balkans she will be treated with the respect that is her due.'

Prince Eugene could see the Archduke's point of view. His Czech wife, Countess Sophie Chotek, had been considered an upstart by the Hapsburgs: she was excluded from the intimate functions of the court; she could not appear with her husband in the royal box at the Opera and their children would not inherit the throne.

'And you understand that the Slav nation must be given a certain independence within the Empire. You even advised a federal solution to the problem of the Balkans. Let us be seen to have some sympathy with their cause,' Prince Ferdinand continued.

Prince Eugene silently agreed – under a new agreement he would become ruler of his own people. It was something which his father had dreamed of. But he continued to pace the long room at the Belvedere Palace. Periodically, he stopped to look out on the gardens, now in full bloom. Eventually, he sighed, 'You are right. I agree with everything you say, but I wonder if this is the correct time?'

'There will never be a more correct time. It will be a ceremonial visit, nothing more. We can dispense with the troops. There should be sufficient police in Sarajevo to guard the streets.'

'Very well. I will work out the itinerary,' Eugene said, saluting the Archduke and returning to his offices which he used whenever he visited Vienna.

The Archduke slumped down into his armchair. His heavy Hapsburg jowls poured over his stiff, military collar. He began to brood darkly over his decision.

From the very outset he had been doubtful about the arrangement. He had a premonition that something dreadful would happen. He had expressed his reservations to the Emperor but the old man insisted that the visit to Sarajevo must take place. He was expected to review the summer manoeuvres of the Austrian Army Corps in the mountains of Bosnia. As future Emperor, he was expected to attend such events.

He took up the telephone and considered cancelling the visit. Then he thought of his wife. For her, he would continue with the plan. He would go to the Balkans.

He replaced the telephone and went to the window to look out over Vienna. Some day he would be crowned Emperor at St Stephen's cathedral. The great empire would be his to command. The protocol would be changed to facilitate his wife.

Belgrade swarmed with student refugees from Bosnia. In the cafés they planned vengeance on the Austrians who had annexed Bosnia-Herzegovina in 1908. Their minds were filled with the vision of a pan-Slavic nation, free from the power of Vienna.

The plot to murder the Archduke was hatched in a Belgrade café, The Golden Sturgeon, by two students, Gavrilo Princip and Nedelkjo Cabrinovic.

The secret police in Belgrade had found amongst its fiery

students the volunteers they needed to carry out such an assassination: young men, eager to revenge themselves on some member of the Hapsburg dynasty, their minds fed on hate.

Now, after training, they were ready for the task.

Princip and Cabrinovic began their secret journey into Bosnia. In order to avoid border guards and Austrian agents, they passed down rivers and along paths known only to the secret society The Black Hand.

It was a journey fraught with danger: on the last part Cabrinovic met an Austrian agent who had been acquainted with his father; then there was always the danger that the bombs and revolvers, stuffed in a black sugar box and covered with newspapers, would be discovered before the attempt on the life of Franz Ferdinand.

It was by luck more than anything else that the assassins and the fatal box arrived in Sarajevo on the 3rd of June. They immediately went into hiding and waited for the single chance to satisfy their desire for revenge. It was never certain that the Archduke would visit Sarajevo, but they must be prepared.

That same day the fatal journey began for Franz Ferdinand. He and his entourage came on board the Traits-bound train at Vienna. There was a certain amount of gloom amongst the entourage.

The Archduke sat with Prince Eugene and discussed his itinerary until, suddenly the electric lights in the saloon car fused. The train passed south lit by funereal candles.

The summer manoeuvres would be carried out to the south-west of Sarajevo, in the barren Karst region – high ground exposed to the hard heat of summer. Franz Ferdinand and his wife arrived at the mountain spa of nearby Illidze which had been placed at their disposal during their visit. In the mountain air and amidst the military excitement, the fears and premonitions which had plagued Franz Ferdinand's mind were set aside.

The summer manoeuvres, spread over the 26th and 27th of June, were satisfactory. There had been no evidence of any danger. Telegrams were dispatched to Vienna full of praise for the performance of the military.

Then it was time to visit Sarajevo. It would be a visit of little consequence, after the glory of the manoeuvres.

A hot Balkan sun shone down on Sarajevo. It was the 525th anniversary of the great Serbian battle of Kossovo. The morning light was pleasant and the earth was warming to the early summer sun.

There was great excitement in the city. The people had begun to line the road leading to the centre of the city early in the morning. They wished to see the middle-aged Hapsburg prince who would one day be their emperor.

That morning, Franz Ferdinand dressed in the green uniform of an Austrian field-marshal. Green cock's feathers fell from his military cap. Sophie, his wife, dressed in a high-necked white dress and a picture hat.

General Oscar Potiorek, the military governor of Bosnia, was waiting for the Archduke and his wife when they arrived at the station. They would drive to the city in a six-car motorcade.

The Archduke sat in the second car with his wife. Everywhere there were smiling faces along the route, hands raised to greet the royal couple; brightly coloured rugs hung from the windows of shops and houses.

They passed down the Appel Quay beside the Miljacka river towards the city hall. The crowds were dense along this part of the route and the Archduke's chauffeur feared that somebody might be pushed in front of the automobile. Suddenly, he caught sight of a shape, arching towards the open car. Sensing danger, he accelerated. The bomb, which would have landed in Sophie's lap, bounced off the rear of the car and exploded under the wheels of the following car. Prince Eugene was shaken by the explosion. Two of the officers beside him were wounded. He jumped from the car and hurried forward into the crowd.

Meanwhile, Cabrinovic, who had hurled the bomb from the pavement, swallowed a cyanide capsule and jumped into the river. He had fulfilled his patriotic mission. But some of the angry crowd leapt in after him and he was quickly dragged away.

The Archduke's car stopped and Ferdinand saw to the safety of the wounded who lay about the street. Then he turned to his chauffeur and said, 'Come on. The fellow is a lunatic; let us get on with the programme.'

The assassination attempt had been thwarted.

The Archduke was pale when he arrived at the city hall for the official welcoming ceremony. He was furious at the incident. 'Mr Mayor, one comes on a visit,' he shouted, 'and one is received with bombs. It is outrageous!'

When he had recovered his temper, he told the mayor to begin his speech.

When it was finished the Archduke replied, ending his address in Serbo-Croat. The gesture towards their identity impressed the gathering. Perhaps this Hapsburg might accommodate their political aspirations.

Prince Eugene, who had reached the hall just after the Archduke, held an urgent meeting with the provincial governor. There was an angry exchange between them. Prince Eugene asked if a military guard could be arranged for their return journey. The governor was furious.

'Do you think that Sarajevo is filled with assassins?' he asked. 'I can assure you that the young man who threw the bomb is in custody. There will be no further attempt on the Archduke's life.'

'We will return by a different route, then,' Prince Eugene

replied firmly. 'The assassins must already know of our plans.'

They quickly changed the return route and new orders were issued immediately.

The Archduke was eager that his wife should return to Illidze but she insisted on accompanying him to the city hospital, to speak to those wounded in the incident. The motorcade set off from city hall to the hospital, the streets still lined with crowds.

The chauffeur of the first car forgot his new instructions and took a wrong turning into Franz Joseph Street. Then confusion set in: the chauffeur of the Archduke's car started to turn and follow him. An official called to him excitedly from the street, 'Wrong way. Straight down Appel Quay.'

The car stopped. The Archduke's chauffeur began to shift the gears. Franz Ferdinand and the Countess looked apprehensive. The cheering crowd was almost on top of them. Princip, the young student, could not believe his good luck. He would never have such an opportunity again to avenge himself on the Hapsburgs. He moved forward in the crowd, drew the pistol he was carrying in his pocket, aimed it at the car and fired twice.

Princip tried to turn the gun on himself but he was quickly seized and beaten up, then taken away.

The Archduke and Sophie sat upright in the car as it reversed. It appeared that the assassination attempt had failed.

Franz Ferdinand continued to sit stiffly in the car. Then, as the people gazed at the royal figure, blood spurted from his mouth.

His wife cried out and fell on to her husband's chest. The Archduke knew that she, too, was wounded. 'Sophie! Sophie! stay alive just for our children,' he pleaded. Then his body slipped forward. Blood covered his green uniform.

Sophie was the first to die. She had been shot through the lower abdomen.

The royal couple were quickly driven from the scene. A quarter of an hour later the Archduke died at the Governor's residence, close to the ballroom where the waiters had prepared chilled champagne for his reception.

Two iron bedsteads were brought into one of the bedrooms and the bodies were laid out on them, covered with flowers from the banquet tables.

Prince Eugene had been at the Archduke's side when he died. At that moment he felt the whole Balkan world would explode.

His worst fears had been realised.

Tsar Nicholas and Alexandra learned of the assassination on board their yacht, the *Standard*, anchored in a Finnish fjörd. The Tsar did not feel it necessary to return to St Petersburg, as his ministers did not believe the event would lead to war. The couple continued with their vacation.

The day after the assassination, a more interesting piece of news reached the newspapers. Khina Gusseva, a pretty young prostitute, had been Rasputin's lover, later cast aside. She wished to have her revenge. She followed him to his village and, finding him alone in the street, she had plunged a dagger into his stomach, crying out, 'I have killed the Antichrist!'

When he was found, Rasputin's entrails hung out of the long gash. He was at that moment in a hospital in Tyumen, fighting for his life. The Russian people hoped that the licentious monk would die and that his hold on the royal family would be broken.

The Kaiser received the news from Sarajevo on board the *Meteor* in Kiel Harbour, where he was presiding over the German national regatta. Immediately, he ordered all flags to be flown at half mast, beside the battle flags of Austria-Hungary.

The regatta was cancelled and the Kaiser returned to Berlin. He was eager to attend the funeral of the Archduke in person, together with one or more of his sons, as in his mind he saw the theatrical possibilities of such a grand occasion.

The expectation was that all the crowned heads of Europe would gather in Vienna.

It might be the harbinger of peace.

Sarajevo was stunned by the death of Franz Ferdinand and his wife. They mourned as the coffins were carried through the city and placed aboard a train to be taken to the coast. From there they were brought to Trieste on board a battleship.

In Vienna the pomp and circumstance which had attended previous royal funerals was abandoned, as, even in death, old scores had to be settled. Count Montenuovo, the Emperor's chamberlain, who had hated the royal pair, now set about having his revenge, as he made the funeral arrangements.

Sophie, who had been despised by the royal circles, would none the less be buried in the imperial vault in the Capuchin church, against the wishes of her husband, who had stated many years previously that he wished to be buried with his wife, and had a vault prepared for both of them at the town of Artstetten some distance from the city.

The coffins were taken to the vault.

Ferdinand's coffin was surmounted by the regalia of empire. Sophie's coffin lay at a lower level in the vault, and upon it lay a pair of white gloves and a fan – the marks of a lady in waiting.

The lying-in-state was brief, almost an embarrassment to the royal family. No royal mourner from abroad attended. The whole ceremony lasted for two hours, then the doors were closed and the waiting crowds turned away.

Prince Eugene was angry at the treatment of the heir to the throne. But his mood lightened as he left the chapel and noticed Alma outside. She had hastened from St Petersburg when she received the news. Beside her walked her young son Prince Joseph.

Eugene walked towards her. 'Will you share my automobile?' he asked.

'Yes,' she said smiling. She introduced him to Prince Joseph. 'Meet a close friend of mine,' she said to the young Prince.

As they travelled through the city, Alma saw that it had changed. Some of the enchantment it once possessed had vanished from it.

'How long are you remaining?' he asked.

'Until the funeral is over, then I will return to St Petersburg. This assassination has created international tension. I hope Russia is not drawn into a foolish war with Austria.'

'It depends on the next move by the Emperor. I have always feared such a moment. It could be used as an excuse to settle greater scores.'

They had both changed during the last few years. They now occupied important positions. Part of the destiny of eastern Europe lay on their shoulders.

'Will you dine with me tonight?' Alma asked. 'I am alone at home. I need company.'

'Very well,' he replied, delighted at the invitation.

From the balcony above the garden, it was a pleasant evening. The light still held in the sky and the Danube ran quietly between the leafy banks below. A pleasure barge passed and the music of a Strauss waltz drifted across the water with the silver gaiety of young women's voices.

'Their world is coming to an end and they do not know it. In two months' time their young lovers may be dressed as soldiers, marching towards some front or other,' Prince Eugene said sadly.

'So you think there will be war?' Alma asked.

'I am certain.'

They drank the light wine and reminisced about the grand days of Vienna.

'I must tuck in Prince Joseph,' she said at eight o'clock.

'I shall go with you.'

They went indoors and walked to the nursery.

The young Prince lay asleep. Alma looked down at him and arranged the clothes about him.

'He is a Hapsburg,' Prince Eugene said.

'No,' replied Alma. 'Someday his father may be king of Transylvania.'

They looked at each other and said no more for a time.

'It all could have been so different,' he said.

'Perhaps. But we cannot recall the past.'

'You should not return to St Petersburg. It is too dangerous. You are free to come with me.'

'Would we return to our island and the hunting lodge?' Alma smiled.

'That seems such a long time ago. They were golden moments. No, now you could come east with me. Someday Transylvania might be a kingdom again.'

'It was a dream, Eugene. Remember it as a dream.'

'So you will return to St Petersburg,' Eugene sighed.

'I must. I am needed there. Perhaps when all this is over we will meet again.'

'Yes. We will meet again. But we may meet in a Europe that is changed beyond recognition.'

They returned to the balcony, where they talked seriously for many hours.

As he left he said, 'I will not see you tomorrow. But if at any time you need me in Saint Petersburg, contact me and I will immediately come and help you.'

'I will remember.'

Alma watched him walk down the steps to his gleaming

automobile. He cut a dashing figure. Before he climbed in to car he turned and waved to her.

She knew she would not see him again.

Already the people of Vienna were becoming aware of the insult heaped upon Franz Ferdinand and his wife. There was gossip in the court circles and in the cafés that the old Emperor and the upstart, Prince Alfred Montenuovo, were having their revenge on Sophie. Sympathy for the dead couple stirred in the city. The people felt insulted at the measures taken by Montenuovo. It should have been a royal occasion. Heads of state, kings and emperors should have flocked to the Imperial city. It was nothing less than Vienna deserved.

Next day there was a Requiem Mass.

That evening, when the coffins set out on their journey to Artstetten, there was a spontaneous demonstration in the city: unit commanders turned out their men in uniform; the aristocracy turned out in full regalia. The dim little funeral cortège was turned into a State occasion.

It left the West Station for Artstetten at ten o'clock. At twelve o'clock it passed on barges across the Danube. A thunderstorm broke out as the coffins sailed across the river. The rain sheeted down on the royal barge and the river became turbulent. The horses champed at the bit, fear charging their eyes. It was thought that at any moment they might bolt into the raging waters and the coffins might be lost.

Finally the cortège reached the far bank and made its way to Artstetten where they were quietly buried.

With the death of the Archduke and his wife reason died in Europe.

It waited for reprisals against Serbia.

An ultimatum was delivered by Austria to Serbia on 23 July.

The reply was immediate.

War was declared on 28 July.

At five o' clock the next morning Austro-Hungarian artillery began shelling Belgrade. The bombardment continued all day.

The Tsar ordered the mobilisation of his troops on 30 July, deciding that he must stand by his allies in the Balkans.

Immediately the Kaiser warned Russia that Germany would mobilise her armies within twenty-four hours.

The deadly moves were played out, as Europe slid into war during the following week. All the great nations found a reason to mobilise: patriotism, fuelled by propaganda, reached a fever pitch. Old scores had to be settled. It would be a final war; the war to end all wars.

This is what Europe had been preparing for during the years of peace.

As soon as Von Hertling realised how dangerous was the situation, he left his family in the safety of the south of the country, where he had been spending a week at his estates. His automobile had carried him directly to his office in Berlin.

His mind was filled with the excitement of the hour. Events had moved so rapidly in the last few weeks that he was taken by surprise.

Now, sitting at his desk, he set in motion certain plans which he had drawn up to take effect in the event of war. While he was doing this, a network of his spies in France began sending in dispatches, giving a clear indication of the buildup of military forces.

Von Hertling had calculated with Von Molkte the capability of each country to mobilise. Most of the German army would be thrown into the western front and, when Paris was conquered, they would be switched to the east to fight against the Russians. The invasion of France had to move to an exact pattern. For years he had built up the schedule of invasion through Belgium, as precise as a timetable. He telephoned Von Moltke. The armies were ready to move.

The German armies moved in a great, six-pronged sweep through Belgium, moving forward at a rapid pace. The great mechanised army met with little resistance.

In St Petersburg Alma followed the course of events intently.

She quickly ordered the burning of all secret documents in her house. At any moment she expected the secret police to descend upon her.

Everything was chaotic. Patriotic fever gripped the city.

It was difficult to follow the war on all the fronts. Like everybody else, Alma was surprised at the manner in which the Russians mobilised: they invaded East Prussia and defeated the German 8th Army at Gumbinnen, who then were forced to withdraw to the Masurian Lakes. There was panic in Berlin. Von Hindenburg was recalled from retirement and moved to the Eastern Front. In the battle of Tanneburg which followed, the Russians suffered a complete defeat. But the Germans never reached Paris. They were halted at the Marne.

On land, Europe settled down to a tedious trench warfare.

At sea, the German submarines went hunting for enemy ships.

Joseph Steiner made his way to his villa outside Vienna. His mind was in turmoil. As he walked up the avenue of trees, now in full bloom, he no longer felt secure. At the station troops were embarking for various fronts. He noted their faces. They were young men filled with a passion for war.

Only the middle-aged and the elderly would remain in the city.

Joseph read the various newspapers avidly. His shares were falling. Each day of the war would destroy his wealth, most of which was invested in Germany.

'The Kaiser is a fool,' he said to himself. 'Germany is not ready. Perhaps in ten years it could dominate Europe, but not at present.'

The German strategy was based on the Von Schlieffen plan – destroy one enemy, then turn on another. It had been prepared by a German military officer and called after him. Von Hertling had often discussed it with him: 'It is a plan on paper. Von Schlieffen has a cold, arid mind. He plays war games on paper. You cannot play war games on paper,' he had argued. 'Do you think the French and the Russians will stand idly by while you put some idealistic plan into operation. War is not a game. It is a set of uncertainties.'

When Joseph reached the villa he was greeted by his servants, many of whom were in tears. Sons and nephews had been mobilised. One had already been killed on the Serbian front.

'What shall we do, Herr Steiner?' they asked.

He looked at the small group of uncertain people. 'Perhaps it will soon all be over. Perhaps by the New Year. In the meantime, continue with your work. Order must be preserved even during times of great doubt.'

The old rabbi, Steinmann, was waiting for him in the library. His tasselled shawl was thrown across his back and he was bent over his work. When he worked over parchment and books, his whole face glowed with some inner light.

'I have received the books from St Petersburg. How wonderful they are; so rare and rescued from such a barbaric country.'

'Soon we will all be barbarians, Jeremiah,' Joseph Steiner told him.

'It is dreadful news. Two of my grandsons have been called up. Intelligent boys. One is a musician. Why should they fight? They were reared to add something to society. I search the Bible. I question God why these things happen. He does not answer me very clearly.'

To distract the old man's mind Joseph Steiner handed him a book which he had purchased in Trieste. The old man fondled it carefully. 'I have a place for it in the library. It will be safe there. It has found a good home.'

When Steinmann returned Joseph told him that he had visited Palestine.

The old man immediately began to ask him questions. 'Did you visit the wall of the temple? You know it will be rebuilt some day and the keys of the city, thrown to heaven two thousand years ago, will be handed back to a Jewish keeper.'

They talked together for a long time, and when Joseph returned to his own rooms he realised that they had only briefly spoken of the war. The subject of their conversation had been the New Jerusalem.

In Berlin Sophie walked along Unter den Linden. The trees were in leaf and the city looked pleasant. She had come to love Berlin more than any other place in the world.

Now, it seemed euphoric: crowds marched up an down the boulevards singing German war songs, 'Die Wacht am Rhein,' resounded from a thousand throats; sometimes a squadron of soldiers passed down the road westward, dressed in the new grey uniforms. The crowds cheered them forward, handing them flowers and food parcels; others cried out against the enemies which now surrounded them. Already several Russians had been killed and the windows of foreign embassies smashed by yelling crowds.

Sophie's mind was on more serious matters. She had visited the stock exchange in which she had invested so much of her money. It had once been an ebullient place filled with confidence, but as she studied the shares she realised that something was happening. Before her eyes they began to shed their value.

The financial markets were becoming unstable. Her mind was charged with fear. What if the war did not move to the rhythm of Von Hertling's plans? What if victory was not achieved in a few weeks?

The future looked hostile.

Sophie decided to invite Von Hertling to supper. He arrived at nine o'clock, dressed in his military uniform.

'You have not had supper with me for a long time,' she said as they went to her luxurious dining room. They sat together at the end of the great oak table. Candles burned in silver candlesticks. The French windows were open and they could heard birdsong from the garden.

'Is this a last supper?' he asked.

'You can tell me. Surely you have your finger on the pulse of everything which is happening on all the fronts.'

Von Hertling looked at her intently and Sophie thought he looked the perfect military figure, cold and distant with others but at ease with her. They had shared a life together. They had lived in Berlin during its great years. They had watched it grow in stature and importance.

'The news is gloomy. We have become bogged down in France. They have organised themselves against us and Britain has now entered the war. By now, we should have been in Paris. I believe that we have gone into a second phase and we are facing a long and tedious war. Already the dead are being brought home. Soon, they will be buried on the battlefield. Perhaps we might make a breakthrough in France, but I doubt it.'

Sophie could not believe it. She had been sure the war would not outlast the summer. 'And Russia? Will the eastern front hold?'

'Russia is a vast swamp. The whole German army could be swallowed up in its marshes. But the Russians are poorly armed. We are already hearing that the Tsar believes that he made a mistake with his people. He is out of touch. A revolution in Russia could save us.'

'Will there be a revolution?'

'We have friends in Russia who are working against the Tsar,' Von Hertling said grimly. 'I can tell you no more.'

'And the stock exchange?'

'That too could fail.'

'Then it is a last supper,' she said in a serious voice.

When they had finished, they sat on the veranda and looked at the pleasant garden, barely visible through the leafy trees. They could hear water splashing in the fountain and the air was filled with the scent of flowers.

'What a beautiful place,' Von Hertling sighed.

It was late when he left the house. He returned immediately to his office.

Sophie mounted the stairs to her bedroom.

Like people all over Europe she was doubtful of her future.

Chapter Forty-two

News of the war reached the village of Tarko and the inhabitants became apprehensive. A detachment of soldiers, dressed in their finest uniforms, reached the village in September of 1914. The young men of the village were quickly mobilised and ordered to assemble at the wharf under the threat of death. The soldiers, with bayonets on their rifles went from house to house in search of any young men who might be hiding from them. Even the village idiot, whom they discovered in a loft, was taken out and pushed forward with the others.

His mother protested to the soldiers. 'He has the mind of a child. He knows little of this world. He cannot take care of himself. Please let him come home with us.'

'He is twenty years old,' the sergeant replied gruffly. 'We will find work for him. There are horses to be fed and stabled. He is needed by the Tsar. He is needed by Mother Russia.'

'Then why not take Jakov in his place,' she protested.

'He is a revolutionary! He would be dangerous. We must keep him isolated from the soldiers or he will sow the seeds of revolution amongst them.'

'It is unfair,' she cried.

'Your son serves this glorious cause,' the sergeant replied blandly.

She tried to argue with them but they pushed her aside. The idiot did not understand what was happening. He continued to smile and wave to people as he passed down the dusty street feeling that he had suddenly become important to some cause or other.

The new recruits gathered their few belongings and marched down to the jetty. Father Sergius blessed them before they departed, handing them pictures of the Tsar and the Tsarina. They waved to the whole village who had gathered to say goodbye. As the villagers watched the tramp steamer disappear into the infinite horizon many of them began to weep.

'Their father the Tsar will take care of them,' one of the women cried. 'They will return with great honour from battle.'

That evening Jakov and the professor were visited by Vlasov, father of one of the village boys, who had been taken away that morning, himself too old to be conscripted. They opened a bottle of vodka and began to drink. He was morose and began to ask Fieldmann many questions.

'You have travelled to distant countries. You have been to the great capital, St Petersburg. What will happen to my son?'

'I do not know,' Fieldmann sighed. 'Perhaps the war will be over before they reach the front line. Russia is a large place. One never knows.'

'I had a bad dream last night. I saw the horseman of the apocalypse, not unlike the horseman in your painting, pass through the village. After he passed the place was red with blood. It was a bad dream and I woke screaming.'

'Do you believe in such manifestations?' Fieldmann asked.

'I do. I have been troubled before. I have seen such visions before. They have always been the heralds of disaster.' Then Vlasov's mind turned sour. 'Why were you not taken, Fieldmann? You would make a good soldier. You are strong and intelligent. You know the ways of the world. The peasants do not.'

'Soon they will take me,' Jakov told him. 'Soon they will need me.'

'I will watch you, Fieldmann,' Vlasov said. 'I have a file from St Petersburg. I know more about you than you think.'

Fieldmann listened to this wild assertion. Clearly, Vlasov was drunk and emotional. He plied him with more drink.

'I drink too much, Fieldmann. But I should drink. My son has been taken from me. And what does your friend the professor think of all this? I have also a file on him. He is a dangerous fellow. But I should not tell you all these things.'

He paused and waved his glass in the air. 'You cannot escape. You think that the villagers are your friends. You drink with them. But there is a price on your head. If you should attempt to escape and one of them brings you back he will receive many kopeks.'

'Am I worth kopeks to you?'

'Yes. You attempted to assassinate the Tsar. But the Tsar will take care of my son. He is the father of all Russia.'

The morning sun was well into the sky when they led Vlasov through the streets to his home. He was very drunk. They placed him on his bed and drew the blankets over him. Soon he was asleep.

When Jakov and the professor returned to their house they sat around the table and discussed the events of the night.

'He is more intelligent than I thought,' Jakov muttered.

'He is treacherous. The whole village is treacherous. They would sell you for a few kopecks,' the professor said. 'Now they have good reason to hate us.'

'The priest and the whore would not,' Fieldmann said.

'Perhaps they would not but the others would,' Marie said.

'What shall we do?' Jakov asked. 'We have spent the winter here and now there is nothing left for me to do unless I paint every house in the village. The long winter nights and the cold are a burden upon me. I can no longer endure this barren solitude. Let the professor give us his counsel.'

The little man, who had been poring over some books he had been sent, looked at them for a moment. He considered their position. 'I, too, find exile laborious. I believe that the government will soon recall all political prisoners. What better way to get rid of them than throw them onto the front lines? It is justifiable murder. I have no doubt in my mind that the military will soon look towards the vast Siberian wastelands and calculate how many prisoners are in the camps. We are cannon fodder. We must plan our escape.'

Jakov had listened to the professor during their years of exile. Of all the men he had ever met he was the finest. His mind and his ideals were clear.

The morning light poured in the window. Fieldmann opened another bottle of vodka and filled their mugs. 'Continue,' he said. 'We can sleep all day and night if necessary. Nothing very much happens in Tarko.'

'The summer will soon pass. When the marshes freeze over and when the village is snowbound, then is our only time to escape. In two days and with the proper rations we could be sixty miles west of Tarko. They would never find us. We could reach the railway within a week. From there we could board the train to St Petersburg.'

'Do you think you could survive the freezing cold?' Jakov asked.

'Better die in the centre of Russia than on some battlefield where I would be fighting against the working classes. The Tsar and the generals have no regard for us. Remember, we are cannon fodder. We must escape. Sooner or later the boat will take us as it took the young men of their village.'

'And what of Marie?' Jakov asked.

'She is not a prisoner. She can leave at any time. She must leave before the river freezes over. Let her travel to St Petersburg and establish herself there. We will follow in the winter.'

'What do you think?' Jakov asked Marie.

'I will leave for St Petersburg. The longer the war continues, the better for the Communist Party. This war will expose the weakness of the whole system. Perhaps now they are filled with fervour. It is always so at the beginning of a war. When the snow comes and the cold winds blow and they run out of food they will change their minds.'

It was an argument which would continue for many weeks. Each week the boat brought newspapers which they studied intently. It was obvious that the war had bogged down on all fronts. Men were digging the long trench which stretched down through half of Europe.

One day a captain arrived at the village. He was dressed in his ceremonial uniform, a red jacket and buff trousers, with a bright sabre by his side.

He had come from the Tsar, he said, to present medals to the parents of those who had died for Mother Russia. Only the village idiot's mother did not receive a medal.

'Did my son not die for the Tsar?'

'Your son is not mentioned in dispatches. He is at the barracks. He is performing heroic work preparing the horses to be sent to the front.'

'Blessed be God that he was born an idiot,' she called out.

It was at that point that the other parents realised their sons would not return to the village. They began to cry out in prayer.

That night Vlasov visited the house. He was drunk. 'You live well in this village, Fieldmann. I know your tricks. They sell your paintings in the city for a good price. You are rich. You can afford your vodka. My son is dead. He would have gone to the university and become a civil servant. He would have married a city wife and done well for himself. They give me a medal. Look at it. It is made of iron. A son's life for an iron medal. It is you who should have died, you and the professor.'

Jakov noticed that he was carrying a pistol. It was the first time that he had carried a weapon.

'Leave your pistol aside and have a drink,' Jakov said firmly.

'The pistol stays with me. You make one false move and I will shoot you. You should have died and not my son.'

Next morning they carried him back home.

'He is dangerous. His mind is that of a peasant. He may be able to read and write but that makes him more dangerous. He will shoot us given the chance,' the professor said.

They had noticed over the weeks that the villagers had become hostile. They did not talk to Jakov when he visited the tavern. Some tried to pick fights with him.

'It is time for you to leave, Marie,' he said as autumn approached. 'Take the boat and the train to St Petersburg. I have sufficient money to sustain you for a month. By then you will be able to take care of yourself.'

A week later she left with a bag, clutching a manuscript by the professor. He had finally finished his book on the dialects of the region.

'Secure it in a safe place,' he told her before they left. 'And have someone type out three copies. It is a valuable manuscript. It is the best work I have done.'

Jakov watched as Marie boarded the boat, remaining on the jetty until it disappeared. Then he returned to the house.

For the next two months both he and the professor remained aloof from the villagers. When the river froze and the snows swung down from the north they would attempt their escape.

The war continued. News of the great battles reached even the far corners of Siberia. Jakov and the professor studied the newspapers carefully trying to determine exactly what was happening along all the fronts.

'This is a new kind of warfare,' the professor told Jakov. 'The most powerful weapons are at the generals' disposal and the war is being fought on land and sea and in the air. The casualties are mounting. The British have lost a hundred thousand men at Ypres. If that is happening on all fronts then a half million men are already dead. Men will revolt against such slaughter.'

'Soldiers do as they are told. They obey orders.'

'There is a point when the strain will be too much. At that moment you can expect your revolution.'

Night after night they considered the reports on the war. Winter was setting in. Already the river had frozen and the last ship had departed.

'Soon the snows will come and then Vlasov will remain indoors. When the blizzard descends, we will make our move,' the professor said.

'You should remain. You will not stand the harsh weather and I cannot tell you how long it will take to cross the tundra.'

'It is a chance I am willing to take.'

They prepared quietly for the departure. They had discreetly purchased heavy fur coats, strong boots and caps. Fieldmann had made two satchels to carry food and he had cleaned his gun. Without the knowledge of Vlasov he had exchanged one of his paintings for a case of cartridges in the next town.

From the window of the timber house they watched the snow fall on the village. The inhabitants remained indoors. The winds wailed in the trees around the church and among the houses.

'Tonight we leave,' Jakov said. 'Nobody will venture out, and the snow will cover our footsteps.' He turned to the professor and looked at him intently. 'I still beg you to consider your position. You are very frail to venture out into such a hostile countryside.'

'It is either that or rot here,' Urusov said. 'I wish to be in

St Petersburg when the soldiers turn on their captains and generals.'

Darkness fell early and soon lights began to burn in the village. The snow fell in large, soft flakes.

At five o'clock they slipped out of the village, moved north for a mile and crossed the river. Then, taking a torch from his pocket, Jakov looked at the compass he carried with him.' Follow me,' he said, and they began to trudge through the heavy snow.

It was a slow, tedious journey. Several times the old man fell and Jakov had to pull him up out of the snow. He wondered if he could continue. All that night they moved forward. Periodically Jakov would check his compass. In the blizzard he feared that he might take a wrong turning and end up back in the village.

Then the wind dropped and the snow stopped falling. A cold moon stood above them and the stars were cast in bright diamonds across the arc of heaven. From the moon Jakov could take his bearings.

Several times they stopped during the night to eat some food and drink the vodka they carried with them. They did not speak. Instead they bent their will to the dreary journey.

And finally a faint grey light appeared in the east. They now could see the landscape through which they were passing, an endless tundra with only small islands of feather trees breaking the monotony. A white mist lay about the countryside. There were no houses or villages to be seen anywhere.

Finally they reached a small hill covered by silver birch.

'Let us rest here,' Jakov told the professor. 'We are well out of range now and Vlasov will not follow us.'

They built a fire and Jakov roasted some meat which he had secreted in his leather bag. They ate it, although it was half cooked. Then they crawled into a low shelter made from branches and leaves and tried to sleep. But the Arctic cold seemed to penetrate their bones. Jakov wondered how long they could continue across the wide expanse. If they were lucky it would take them two weeks to pass across the frozen marches. Their journey would now take them south-west.

A week later the old man died of exhaustion, in one of the birch woods where they often found rest and shelter, during the night.

'You should have remained behind. You could have returned to St Petersburg later,' Jakov cried in anguish.

He buried the old man beneath some snow. Then he set out on the lonely journey across the tundra.

On several occasions during the following days he almost lost heart. He had run out of food and managed only to shoot an Arctic hare whose warm blood he drank. He ate the raw meat to sustain him.

Then the landscape began to change imperceptibly. Small forests of fir trees made their appearance and he knew that he was reaching the beginning of habitation.

Finally, he reached a wide beech wood, much larger than the copses to the north. He felt totally exhausted. He fell on the ground and could barely rise.

'I must make a fire. I must find shelter,' he repeated to himself.

Drawing on his last ounce of strength he made a fire. Soon the branches were crackling and the warmth seemed to give energy to his body. He lay against the trunk of a tree. Sleep began to invade his mind. He tried to keep awake.

Then he felt a gun barrel at his temple.

He opened his eyes.

A hunter stood beside him. His features were Mongolian and there was a suspicious look in his eye.

'Who are you?' he asked.

'An escaped prisoner,' Jakov told him honestly.

'Are you hungry?' the hunter asked.

'Hungry and exhausted,' he admitted.

'Then you are lucky I came this way. Here, eat this,' he said and he took some venison meat from his bag.

Jakov nibbled at the solid meat. It was dark and strongly flavoured. His appetite began to return. Soon he munched resolutely at the meat until only the bone remained.

'You are lucky,' the hunter said stolidly. 'Not many make it this far. They lose their way in the blizzards.'

'I used a compass,' Jakov said, indicating the instrument which hung from his belt.

'Are you a political prisoner?'

'Yes. From St Petersburg.'

'Where is St Petersburg?'

'Many miles to the south-west.'

'What is your name?'

'Jakov.'

'It is a strange name.'

'I am from Europe. It is a long way away.'

'And what are your plans?'

'To return to St Petersburg. I will go there by train.'

'I can show you where the train passes through the forest. It carries great timbers to the saw mills. It never stops, but it does slow down as it climbs a hill. A man could board a train there. I have often waved to the drivers but I have never spoken to them.'

Jakov began to entertain new hope.

The hunter led him to a hut in the forest. It was a simple log building, secure from the sharp wind and the snow. Along the wall hung animal traps with savage teeth. The southern wall was built from stone and here the hunter set a fire. Soon the place glowed with heat.

The hunter shared his bread and his vodka with Jakov and told him of his life on the edge of the tundra. Further south he had a family. With the animals he trapped he could secure a living for them, selling the pelts to traders.

'I prefer the woods to the village. All my ancestors were hunters. It is the only way of life I know. But tell me of your life and your travels.'

Jakov, sitting in the inglenook, told the hunter of his travels. He was quite amazed to hear that there were places in Southern Russia where snow never fell and where flowers bloomed, even in winter. Jakov offered to draw his portrait with a pencil but the hunter refused. 'No, I would lose part of my soul. But draw a Siberian tiger. That would give me control over him.'

Jakov drew a Siberian tiger from memory. The hunter was greatly impressed. He studied it carefully. 'Now I own the spirit of the beast,' he said. 'I will have a successful season.'

Jakov stayed with him for a few days until his strength had returned.

One evening, as it was growing dark, they set off for the train. The hunter was correct. After dark, drawing great pine logs, the train advanced across the plain and made its way up the incline. They could see men feeding the furnace with timber blocks. As it slowed down Jakov raced beside it and drew himself up on one of the couplings. He found a space amongst the great tree trunks and sat in this protected place. He drew his great coat around him and drank from the bottle of vodka the hunter had given him. He could hear the wind crying in the forest through which they passed.

He slept in the comfortable space. In the morning the train passed through the white, empty plain. Only the black outline of forests gave some relief to the vast landscape. Then the train made its way slowly through the Urals.

It took a whole day to pass through the majestic passes until finally, it chugged onto a plain again, gathered speed and continued through the empty Russian darkness.

When Jakov awoke in the morning the train was drawing into a large timber yard.

Everywhere he looked he could see lines of carriages drawn up, waiting to discharge their loads. He slipped out from his position and made his way along the tracks.

Suddenly a man appeared. 'What are you doing here?' he asked.

'Gathering fuel,' Jakov lied.

'No, you are not. You are an escaped prisoner. I know from your appearance. Many of them end up here. The police check all the trains. Come with me. I am a friend of prisoners.'

He led him across several tracks until they came to a long, brick wall with a door in it. He took a key from his pocket and let him out.

'If you are looking for help you will find it at Number eight St Nicholas' Street. Be careful how you go.'

Jakov discovered that he had covered three hundred miles during the night. It took him an hour to find the address, a tailor's shop in the artisan quarter of the town.

'You are welcome, friend,' the small tailor told him when he entered the shop and identified himself. 'I hope that you have not been followed.'

'No. I can recognise one of the secret police at a hundred yards,' Jakov smiled.

'Good.'

The tailor directed him into the back of the house, where four children sat in the kitchen. They had curious eyes, but remained silent. They were used to strangers passing through the house.

'You look hungry and cold,' the tailor's wife said. 'I will make you some warm soup.'

In the small kitchen, sitting beside the oven, Jakov felt the heat enter his body for the first time since he had left Tarko.

* * *

He stayed in the house for three days until he had time to make arrangements to depart. In the meantime, he caught up with the war news. A new Russian army of almost a million was advancing to the eastern front. They, too, would be slaughtered, like the other armies sent to fight against the Germans.

'I must leave for St Petersburg,' he told the family. 'You have been most kind to me. I know that I have been a burden upon you and I have taken the food from the mouths of your children.'

'We share what we have. It is our Christian belief. God will provide. He always does,' the tailor's wife said with a simplicity that moved Jakov greatly.

Two days later, with his beard shaved and wearing respectable clothes which he had purchased with the money he had carried with him in his pouch, Jakov boarded a train for St Petersburg.

He sensed the excitement as he passed westward. He felt in his mind that the great revolution would soon take place.

Chapter Forty-three

The war wore on. Soon people became confused at the great battles which were taking place on all fronts: there was no certain victory; it consumed men and munitions; every village in Europe mourned its dead. Each month added new names to the lists which appeared on the papers.

In November of 1916, Franz Joseph began to die. The Emperor's personal physician, Dr Kerzl, watched helplessly as the old man's chest was wracked with coughing. He preferred to sit in his chair at nighttime rather than sleep on his iron bed.

Vienna, now hungry and dull, waited for the old man to die. Almost all the able-bodied men had been called up; the coffee houses served only a brew made from chicory; pastries were a rarity; the wine taverns in the Vienna woods remained silent. Only old men, or soldiers on leave, would drink the young wine.

For sixty years Franz Joseph had ruled his vast and vexed empire. Now it was disintegrating about him.

His death was unheroic. He suffered a severe attack of bronchitis and was forced at last to take to his bed.

He told his valet that he was behind in his work and wished to be called early in the morning.

That night he died at nine o clock.

He was laid out in the Schönbrunn on the plain iron bed in which he had died. Carriages immediately began to arrive at the great place. Ministers and generals stood in small groups whispering together. Many grieved for the passing of a golden age, marred in the end by war. Others prayed for the old Emperor's soul. Lights burned all night in the palace he loved so much, which had been embellished by Maria Theresa.

In the morning the high officers of state arrived at the palace. With fine etiquette they prepared him for the last of the great Hapsburg funerals.

The Emperor's body was coffined and then drawn through the streets of Vienna in an ornate hearse to the Hofburg chapel. There it lay in state for a week.

Joseph Steiner ordered his chauffeur to bring him to the Hofburg chapel. As they made their way through the dreary streets of Vienna, they passed several companies of soldiers making their way to some front or other.

Joseph had asked to be dropped off at some distance from the Hofburg chapel. Then, on foot and in dark clothes, he made his way along the road to the church, where he joined the long queue of mourners: young soldiers not yet tested in the war, the war wounded, old men and women who had lived through his long reign.

'It is the death of the monarchy,' one old man said.

'I was a child when he was crowned emperor,' his friend remarked.

'And this war. Will it ever end?'

'When they all grow tired of the slaughter. Last week my neighbour's child was killed. He had been a student at the university,' one man declared.

'I have lost a grandson,' another replied. 'I wanted him to be buried in the family plot but he was torn to pieces with shrapnel.'

'Everyone has lost some relative or other. It should not have happened.'

Thus they shuffled forward on flat feet, their coats drawn about them against the bitter cold. Finally, they reached the door of the church and passed through.

It was dim inside and the coffin was laid out on a great

catafalque bearing the Austrian eagles. Thick candles burned firmly on candlesticks beside it. Young soldiers drawn from many regiments guarded the coffin which was closed because the corpse had been disfigured during the embalming.

Joseph gazed at the great stained-glass windows. He was impressed by their luminous beauty. He bowed like the others before the coffin, then he shuffled towards the door. He felt lonely. He could not say why he felt lonely but he did.

When he had finished paying his respects, he walked through one of the parks and visited a banking friend .

'You were wise, Joseph Steiner,' his friend said. 'You saw what was going to happen and switched some of your money to America. Somebody will have to pay for this war. Each day it costs many millions to service. It is always the ordinary man in the street who has to pay for it, but America is booming.

'On the other hand, I have lost a fortune and food is almost impossible to purchase. It is even worse in Germany where there is a terrible food shortage. I remember days when I sat down to meals of quality. Now I eat to live. What will happen?'

'I do not honestly know. I do not honestly know,' Joseph replied sadly.

Much later he left his friend's apartment. As he wandered through the twisted streets of the old part of the city, he considered many things. He wondered how his stepdaughters would survive the war. Would Sophie's fortune be wiped out in Berlin? Was Alma foolhardy remaining in St Petersburg. And where was Marie, the most strong-willed of them all?

His chauffeur picked him up at seven o'clock and brought him home through the silent streets. Joseph could not take his mind off the sad thoughts of death. He was fascinated by the Hapsburg ritual.

* * *

The Emperor's coffin was taken from the Hofburg chapel and carried with great pomp through Vienna on 31 November 1916.

For the occasion, the street lamps had been covered in black crêpe; units of foot soldiers and cavalry marched behind the coffin to the beat of muffled drums.

At the doors of the imperial vault they set the coffin down. The master of ceremonies knocked three times on the doors of the vault with his mace.

'Who seeks entrance?' a voice called out from within.

'His Apostolic Majesty, the Emperor,' replied the master of ceremonies.

'I know him not,' a monk called.

Again the master knocked three times.

'Who demands entrance?' the monk asked.

'The all-high sovereign, the Emperor Franz Joseph,' came the reply.

'I know him not,' the monk called.

The master knocked again three times.

'In the name of God, who wishes to enter?' the monk called.

'Your brother Franz, a poor sinner.'

The doors were opened and the great coffin was carried in.

Franz Joseph was laid to rest between the tombs of his assassinated wife and his son, who had committed suicide.

The haunting words echoed in Joseph Steiner's mind. As he returned home after the funeral he reflected on what he had heard.

He wished that he was in the new land of Palestine, with its dry earth and clear skies.

He decided not to go home immediately. Instead, he made his way to the old Jewish ghetto. He felt a strange comfort here. It was pervaded by a sense of serenity.

He made his way to the old Jewish graveyard where his mother and father lay in a mass grave.

All about him Europe was falling apart. Soon Jews would be on their way again, down all the pathways of the continent, seeking refuge in another ghetto.

For them there was no end to wandering.

Joseph recited a prayer in Hebrew over his parents' grave. Then he left the cemetery.

In Berlin hope of a final victory had died. At the beginning there had been delirium in the city. Now, as the winter of 1916 set in, hunger gripped the city. Step by step, meat, sugar, potatoes, eggs, fat and milk were rationed. The Kaiser, it was said, munched rusks, thickly spread with butter and maintained that he lived on soldiers' rations.

Luxury goods had long since disappeared. Coffee was made from acorns and everything was synthetic: honey, marmalade, soap was largely made of sand which left the skin raw; wool and cotton were requisitioned for army uniforms; turnips became part of the staple diet.

When Von Hertling visited Sophie at her villa, he looked strained. His gestures had become nervous and he was taking drugs to keep him awake and to help him sleep.

During the meal he could not relax. That day he had received information from America.

'It is preparing for war,' he told Sophie bleakly. 'It will find an excuse for joining our enemies. When it does, it will throw fresh troops into the field. Then we are destroyed.'

'Why does the Kaiser not return to the city from the front? Every day some new party is formed. Revolution is preached in the squares. It is like a bomb waiting to be lit,' Sophie remarked anxiously.

'The Kaiser is a meddling fool. There should be a *coup d'état* and the army should take over. Perhaps we could sue for peace. It is the only real solution. Otherwise we will be defeated and I dare not consider the consequences of that.'

'And what will you do, flee the country?'

'No, I will remain. My organisation will go underground. Already, I have plans set out to hide our documents in underground bunkers built in the north of the city. Very few know of their existence.'

'I have watched my shares slide until they are worthless,' Sophie told him angrily. 'The only objects which will be of any value after the war are my paintings. But I wish to remain in Germany. It will rebuild on firmer foundations and more political sense will prevail.'

'You are a brave lady,' the baron said as they drank the last of Sophie's wine stocks before the fire.

'Do you know the city is starving?' she said. 'Women are prostituting themselves for food.'

'If you need food, telephone me. I will send one of the trucks to deliver some of our war rations.'

This was the gesture Sophie had been waiting for. Already, her food supply was low, and now there was barely a week's supply left. Every morning she sent one of the servants to the station to buy some of the food carried from the countryside by the farmers, but it was becoming more expensive and almost impossible to obtain. And she no longer had any money. It had been tied up in the stock exchange.

Despite her calm appearance, desperation was beginning to disturb her mind. She did not sleep at nighttime. Instead she lay awake, considering her future. It was possible that, as well as her wealth, she would now lose her beloved house. Like Von Hertling, she was taking drugs to help her sleep.

She did not tell him that when she walked through the city, she dressed like a servant in order not to draw attention to herself. On several occasions she had been taken for a common prostitute.

Von Hertling said goodbye to her in the darkness. His car drew away and passed down the quiet street. There was nobody about.

He did not return immediately to his office. He had his driver take him to the brothel area of the city.

During the last two years, he had become impotent. Now he paid to watch young men and women copulate in his presence.

Two days later Sophie decided to take a walk in the Tiergarten. In the great park, surrounded by trees, she could clear her mind. The sharp winter air stimulated her. It gave her a chance to put her thoughts in order.

She was beginning to grow desperate. The city had become a rough, unmannerly place. Any elegance it had once possessed had been destroyed by shortage and hunger. And there were more women than men in the city. They had lost their husbands and their fiancés. Now, they slept with any stranger they met. Many of them were infected with venereal disease.

She should have followed the advice of Joseph Steiner. Even before the war had begun, he had quietly changed his stocks to America. Now they were booming.

She could not live a life of poverty. She must search about and find some elderly lover who could protect her.

As she returned from her walk she passed through a market street, off one of the main roads. Suddenly she noticed a group moving towards her. From their clothes she knew that they were ordinary people but there was something menacing about them. They stopped in front of a baker's shop and somebody broke the window. It was a signal for them to advance. They poured into the bakery and emerged with loaves of bread and bags of flour.

As they walked down the street one woman lost her balance. The loaves she were carrying fell at Sophie's feet.

The sight of the food released some savage instinct in her. She got down on her knees and began to collect the small loves of bread and put some in her pockets.

'They are mine, you bitch,' the woman screamed at her.

She grabbed her hair and began to pull her away from the precious loaves. Sophie hit her in the face. Then she joined the crowd and rushed along the street.

It was only later, as she regained her composure, that she realised what she had done. She knew at that moment that her world was slipping into chaos.

A week later she phoned Von Hertling. She told him that she would accept his gift of food.

In 1914 the Russian soldiers had marched gaily through the streets of St Petersburg on their way to the front. They had been blessed by the Tsar and they had called out, '*Batiushka, Batiushka*, lead us to victory.'

Alma knew that they were unprepared for modern warfare. Even her vague knowledge of statistics had proved to her that the great Russian army was badly armed and that the German artillery would destroy them.

But wild excitement had gripped Russia from St Petersburg to Odessa.

She would wait fearfully for the results.

When the war turned quickly sour, she realised she should have returned to Vienna. One day, shortly after she had moved from the embassy to take up residence in a discreet mansion close by, she watched a crowd attack the embassy. Precious paintings were burned and Renaissance statues broken on the steps. Embassy records were carried away by the secret police. Less important documents blew down the broad road and were trampled on by the crowds.

The war became a disaster: five months in, one million Russians had been killed, wounded or taken prisoner; the front consumed men and ammunition; soldiers rioted and turned on their officers; the Tsar moved from his palace at Tsarskoe Selo to the front.

Nicholas II liked the simple, bustling life of military headquarters. He felt that he had some control over the fortunes of the war. Early in the struggle his presence could still inspire a mystical confidence. But the Germans soon moved through the red summer dust and the winter mire in Poland, with little opposition.

St Petersburg became a grey city: the palaces were silent; there were no flags and no cheering crowds; when they gathered before the shop windows on the Nevsky Prospekt it was to read the casualty lists; shops and homes belonging to Germans were sacked and burned; the Tsarina was called a German spy.

Having recovered from the assassination attempt it was widely thought that Rasputin wielded control over Russia through her, while her husband was away. The whole affair was the talk of St Petersburg. The people believed that Alexandra Feodorovna was the monk's lover. Even the Tsar's friends at the parliament were now turning against the royal family. There were many in the officers' ranks who would have assassinated him, given the chance.

Alma listened to all this gossip carefully, when she visited old friends who still held quiet dinner parties. Despite the war, she retained their friendship and they were protective of her and her young son.

On 30 December 1916, Rasputin was murdered.

On the first night of the New Year, 1917, Alma sat around an oval table in her apartment and talked quietly with her friends. They were in a sombre mood. Being serious-minded people, cultivated and informed, they were well aware that the whole fabric of Russian society was now in danger. The death of Rasputin confirmed this.

'It was planned by Prince Yussoupov, while the Tsarina was in the south. There are two others involved,' one of the company said, 'including one of the Duma, Purishkevich.'

'The Empress has ordered a complete investigation,' added another. 'One of the murderers told a policeman that he had murdered the enemy of Russia and the Tsar. At present they are looking for the body.'

'What will happen Yussoupov and the others?' Alma asked.

'Only the Tsar can order the arrest of a grand duke. But the Empress has ordered him to be confined to his house.'

'He has done a patriotic deed. At least the Tsar will now be free to govern.'

'It has gone too far,' a journalist on St Petersburg's most important newspaper added. 'The war has taken its toll. There is dissatisfaction everywhere. People are crying out for food. I believe that a revolution is already on the way.'

'I see no evidence of it,' an embassy aide replied, startled.

'I have been to the front. I have travelled with the soldiers. I know their feelings. The Tsar is no longer the father of all his people. And the intellectuals are at work. They no longer believe in the government or the war-lords.' The journalist's words were ominous.

Alma asked him several questions and discovered that he believed that soon there would be a mass surrender of Russian troops. She decided that she must still try to get the information to Vienna. She had still some tentative connections with the spy network. If there was a revolution in Russia then there was every chance that Germany and Austria could transfer troops to the hard-pressed fronts in the west.

As she walked home that night she considered all that she had heard. To pass information to Vienna, she would need help. Perhaps it was time to contact Sophie. Alma had been betrayed by her sister, but she had since come to believe that Sophie had helped her. On Karl's death, Alma had been set free.

Next day, Rasputin's body was discovered by divers in the Neva. He had died, not from a bullet wound, but from drowning.

Two days later, in secrecy, Rasputin was buried in a corner of the Imperial park. The sky was clear, the snow crisp underfoot. The Tsar and the Tsarina were at his graveside. Inside the coffin the Empress had placed two objects. One was an icon, the other a personal letter.

From her window Alma looked across the Neva at the fortress of St Peter and Paul. She had grown to love the splendid city and the river itself, now bound with ice. Every day, despite the war, skaters passed across the frozen surface, blithe as birds, the ringing of their laughter reaching up to her window.

Her thoughts were interrupted by a knock on the door. Her maid, Masha entered with her young Prince Joseph. Now a young boy, he strongly resembled Prince Eugene. He was tall for his age, his limbs long and aristocratic. She looked forward to the day when he would take his place at the Viennese court.

Masha always brought news of the city. 'And what have you seen and heard today?' Alma asked.

'What I see everyday, madame. The people have come to hate the Tsarina. They would have her sent to a convent in Siberia. Worse still, some would have her hanged.'

'And do you hate her?'

'Yes. I hate her and I hated Rasputin. He slept with her. Now people like me are growing angry. The factories are closed for the want of coal and the workers have nothing to do but mill about the streets. Even in the barracks the soldiers grumble. The revolutionary agitators go amongst them. The streets will run red with blood, madame, you will see.'

Alma shivered. 'How do you know all these things?'

'My brothers and my sisters tell me. And I can see with my own eyes.'

Alma decided she must see for herself.

That afternoon, she dressed as an ordinary housewife and set off to walk through the city.

Snow was falling gently on St Petersburg, reducing the sense of distance and space. People wrapped against the cold passed her by in troikas, with the jingle of harnesses mixed with the noises of trams on the main boulevards.

Alma quickly noticed a new phenomenon: lying on the side of the street were the new beggars; the maimed from the battlefront. They called out, 'In the name of Christ and his mother give me a kopeck.'

Alma passed on, deaf to their pleadings. She had no money left to give them.

Next, she saw the long, patient queues in front of the bakeries and the meat shops. The patient women did not speak. They waited in silence, hoping that the doors of the bakeries might open.

Alma was crossing the great square in front of the Winter Palace when she heard the brass band. As it grew louder, great columns of protesting workers from the Vyborg section of the city entered the square. Behind the men marched a long parade of women.

They called out 'Give us bread.'

The cry for food soon filled the square. Others joined them as they marched down Nevsky Prospekt. Alma followed them along the sidewalk, noticing that they were men and women who were hungry and in need of food.

Suddenly, and without warning, they stormed the bakeries. They broke open the doors and emerged minutes later, their arms filled with bread.

Alma saw the Cossacks, trotting alongside the crowds. Once the formidable force of repression all through the turbulent history of Russia, they had been ruthless, but now she noted that they did not carry their whips in their hands. The people were quick to appreciate the absence of the weapons, and called to the horsemen to join them.

She discreetly joined the crowd and eavesdropped on the conversation of two young students.

'They are coming over to our side. The very instruments of the Tsar's repression are with us,' one said.

'Have you noticed their faces? They are afraid. They are young men fresh from the villages. The best of the Cossacks have perished in Galacia and Poland.'

'And the infantry at the barracks are old men who are not wanted by the generals at the front. Power is passing to the people.'

Alma had not seen such open defiance of law and order before on the streets of St Petersburg. The Tsar, at the front, was not obviously aware of what was happening in the capital.

She looked about her at the milling crowd. Then, her gaze fell on a tall woman, carrying a red flag. She looked intently at her, thinking she had seen her somewhere before. She suddenly recognised her sister, Marie. Her skin had grown coarse during the years and strands of grey hair now mixed with the flamboyant red.

Alma watched as she called out to the crowd and they began to assemble about her and behind her. The band reformed and they began to march along the Nevsky Prospekt towards the Winter Palace.

And then their eyes met. They stared at each other for a moment. Perhaps Marie recognised Alma. Perhaps she did not. If she did, she gave no sign, but lifted the red flag and marched forward to the music of the band. The snow began to fall heavily and soon they were hidden by the falling flakes.

Alma returned home, knowing she must make plans to escape from the capital. What she had seen had convinced her that the revolution would now take place.

She called on her old friend Von Schoon and explained her plans.

'It will be difficult but not impossible,' he said.

He took out a large map of Russia and spread it on the table. He pointed to the Ukraine. 'It will be difficult and dangerous, but there are unguarded passes in the mountains and from there you could find your way into Austria. There is no other route. You must make your way into Transylvania, taking as little as possible with you. Stick some gold coins into your clothing and some diamonds, if you can lay your hands upon them.'

That evening as light faded over St Petersburg, Alma began to make arrangements for her escape.

On the runway, in an airfield north of St Petersburg, the planes began to prepare for battle. Prince Eugene had formed his own squadron. At first they had merely flown observation missions over the enemy lines. Now, mounted with guns, they were a formidable force.

He taxied down the runway, then turned into the wind. Quickly he was airborne and the earth fell away beneath him. He circled the airfield. Soon his squadron had joined him.

They headed west, not expecting to meet enemy aircraft, but suddenly the French squadron appeared from nowhere.

Immediately, they engaged in a dogfight. They circled about the sky like birds of prey. Eugene watched as a French plane caught fire. Trailing a tail of smoke it plunged towards the earth.

He knew then that he had made a fatal mistake. He had taken his eye off the enemy.

As they approached from behind and from above, he opened fire. The bullets strafed his back. Blood spurted from his mouth. Desperately, he gripped the controls, but they would not respond. His plane began to swing down in lazy circles towards the mountains.

Then it exploded.

Chapter Forty-four

For eighteen months, Jakov, under an assumed name, had been reunited with Marie, and had worked in the steel yards to the north of St Petersburg. He had shaved his beard and dyed his hair. Each morning he made his way to the great complex of buildings and furnaces fuelled by coal from the Ukraine. Since the war, it had to be transported a great distance from the Donets basin.

St Petersburg was an ideal city for revolution. First reports of the war arrived there and the first food shortages would occur in this city, so remote from the wheatfields of Russia.

Already food supplies were running out, particularly bread. The railway lines were overloaded with trains carrying munitions and men to the front.

If the Tsar had sense he would propose that the great warehouses of the city were filled with food, Jakov thought, as he watched the chaos deepen during the winter of 1916 and into 1917. The extreme cold froze the locomotive boilers and they burst under the pressure, now lying like useless hulks in the railway yards. The lines were blocked by snow drifts. With their supply lines cut, children began to starve and women began to complain.

'This is the hour we have been waiting for,' Jakov told Marie as they lay, during a freezing night, under a layer of blankets which could not keep out the intense cold.

'Lenin does not think so,' she told him.

'Then Lenin is out of touch. Write to him again. His last letter suggested that he is depressed. Describe the conditions in the city. Even Kerensky calls for the removal of the

Tsar. The parliament is crying for his blood. Describe what happened yesterday. The Cossacks are ready to come over to our side.'

'But what if Nicholas gives them direct orders? They will fire on the people.'

'I have visited the barracks. I believe that they are as dispirited as the workers. If the crack regiments come over to the people, then victory will be ours. The soviets of St Petersburg are well organised.'

For two years Marie had worked as secretary to many of the unions. They had been brought together under one banner, led by men of grim determination, who had grown tired of the war and the waste. They believed that it was time for the workers to make their voice heard. The city continued to fall apart: the great factories fell silent – there was no coal to fuel the furnaces. In their small, brick houses and in their wooden cabins the workers shivered.

'We have come a long way, Jakov, since you spoke to me the first time in Vienna so many years ago,' Marie mused.

'Nobody could have told me then that I would be a communist agitator living with the working classes in St Petersburg.'

'At least it has been useful. And perhaps we are only at the beginning of things. Yesterday, I saw my sister on the pavement in front of the Winter Palace. Our eyes met, but I pretended I did not recognise her.'

'How was she dressed?'

'Like a Russian housewife.'

'Then she did not wish to be noticed. What brought her into the city? She should know that Austrians and Germans are hated. They would have hung her from one of the trees if they had known.'

'She would have deserved it,' Marie said bitterly. 'She has worked against Russia. She has lived the good life for several years, while the poor starved. She was the mistress of Franz Joseph, did you know? Otherwise, how would she have been appointed to her position in the city. Her son is titled, too.'

Jakov made no further comment, and they fell into a fitful sleep. The cold seemed to penetrate their very bones.

Although they did not know it, members of the Russian cabinet were meeting in the city that same night. They were seeking desperate measure to solve the food crisis.

Saturday 10 March was a fateful day in the life of the city: most of the workers went on strike; the city closed down; the trolley cars stopped running; the newspapers did not appear; huge crowds poured into the streets calling for the death of the Tsarina and the generals and an end to the war.

Jakov and Marie hurried into the centre of the city and joined the crowds. They had never been so angry or so numerous.

St Petersburg was in chaos.

That night the cabinet met again. They sent an urgent message to Nicholas to return to the city. Instead, he ordered General Khabalov, Military Governor of the city, to put down the riots. It was a fatal error of judgement.

General Khabalov made immediate preparations to deal with the crowds. On Saturday night posters were printed and pasted all over the city. All public meetings were banned. Force would be used to disperse crowds and those not returning to their jobs would be drafted for the war.

General Khabalov, too, sent orders to all the barracks. The troops began to move into their positions.

The crowds read the notices and ignored them.

'What will happen now?' Marie asked Jakov. She held his arm, fearful of what might occur, now that all their plans would really bear fruit.

'We must wait and see.'

At half-past four that Saturday evening, the soldiers, obeying orders, opened fire on a crowd of protesters on the Nevsky Prospekt. Marie and Jakov were amongst them.

Around them the wounded and dying cried out as their blood soaked into the slush.

'Are you wounded, Jakov?' Marie asked as they lay on the ground.

'My arm is bleeding a little. We must attend to the wounded when the soldiers move away.'

A doctor walked among the wounded and the dead. 'The fools,' he cried. 'There was no reason to open fire on innocent people.'

All over the city the dead were being counted. Two hundred had been killed.

However, some soldiers had mutinied and refused to fire on the crowds. They were disarmed and returned to barracks.

Night descended and the Tsar ordered more troops into the city. He also ordered that the parliament be suspended.

There was quiet in the streets and an uneasy night passed in the barracks.

The soldiers of the Volinsky Regiment who had refused to shoot at the people argued all night.

On Sunday morning, a sergeant killed a captain who had struck him the previous day. It was the spark the revolution needed.

Fear spread among the officers and soon they abandoned their barracks; the soldiers mutinied; news spread quickly through all the barracks in the capital. When the Preobrajensky Guard, created by Peter the Great joined the mutiny, it was obvious that the tide of rebellion would be halted with difficulty.

On Monday morning, the troops joined the crowds pouring into the city. The law courts were set on fire and became a raging furnace. The revolution spread. Soon other buildings were torched.

Prince Dmitri looked in anger at the destruction of the city.

'They are fools,' he cried. 'What do they expect to achieve?'

Nikka, his faithful servant, stood beside him. 'They wish to be free, master. They are tired of the war. They are tired of the Tsar. I have heard them say these things.'

'Then we must make preparations, Nikka,' Dmitri said sadly.

That night he took several boxes of documents from his office and, with the help of Nikka, placed them in an automobile and drove around, hiding them in various secret locations in the city.

Then he returned to his villa and, taking several precious paintings from their frames, rolled them up and placed them in a cylinder which he hid behind a panel.

He took his most important files, of which Nikka was unaware, and splitting them up, hid them in several places in his mother's home.

It was obvious to the cabinet, as evidence of the mutiny and disorder reached them, that Nicholas should return from the front and attempt to restore order in person.

They knew that they no longer served any purpose. They felt that their lives were in danger from the mutinous soldiers now moving through the streets. By nightfall, many of them had made their way to the Tauride Palace and placed themselves under the official protection of the parliament. Now they feared for their lives.

Jakov and Marie were quick to grasp that the whole political system was crumbling. With workers and soldiers they made their way to the Tauride Palace, where the Soviet of Soldiers and Workers' deputies had already taken over one wing. They stormed the building, determined to take the lives of the most detested ministers and officials of the government. Senior minister Karensky managed to bargain for their lives, but, shorn of power they became whimpering cowards, wandering the corridors of the palace aimlessly.

Marie, with some other secretaries, manned the switchboards. They were now in communication with groups all over the city. Each hour brought new evidence of the revolution's growing power. Only the Winter Palace held out for the Tsar.

Wild mobs ran through the streets destroying mansions, flinging precious objects onto the streets, and setting fire to the buildings. When firemen arrived to put out in fires they were prevented by the mob.

It was late in the evening when the noise began to reach the quiet street where Alma lived with her son, Joseph. She heard it growing louder. She recognised the sound of angry voices and looked out of the window. A mob was running up the street. She gasped in horror as she watched a neighbour's house being attacked by the marauding crowd. They set upon it like wild wolves on a carcass: they broke the windows, threw the contents of a library into the front garden, set the books on fire and then proceeded to throw the furniture on top of it.

Immediately Masha rushed up to Alma's room. 'Hurry. There is no time to lose. You are next. I heard them talking. They know that you are the Austrian woman. Take what small valuables you can and run.'

Quickly Alma put on some warm clothes. She opened the safe and filled her purse with gold coins and some jewellery. Then she placed some letters and documents in a small travelling bag.

Masha gathered the child in her arms and they fled from the house, passing down a small alleyway used by servants.

'What shall we do?' Alma asked.

'Come with me. I will put you up for the night.'

'What will they do to the house?'

'They will loot it. Then they will burn it, but it is of no matter now,' Masha said bleakly.

They made their way through the streets, hurrying

across the Neva to Masha's house, in the industrial area of the city, a small wooden shack, housing two families.

They hurried inside. 'You will be safe here for the moment,' Masha said, indicating that they should enter a very small bedroom where an old woman lay in bed.

'Remain here until I return.'

Alma looked at the old woman. She was toothless and her mouth had collapsed. She grinned at her with a foolish expression.

She wondered at that moment what the future held for her. She was too confused to think. She held her young son in her arms and tried to reassure him.

An hour later the door burst open and Masha appeared, with four soldiers behind her, her face filled with a hatred that Alma had never witnessed before.

'That is the Austrian woman. She is an enemy of the people. She has fled from her house, carrying a suitcase of papers. No doubt they are documents for the enemy.'

The soldiers took the suitcase and opened it. They studied the documents. They could not read them but it was obvious that they were of some importance.

'In the name of the Soldiers' soviet, we arrest you,' they said and one of them reached out to grab her by the arm. Alma, taking her child by the hand, followed them without saying a word.

As she passed, Masha clutched at her purse containing the gold coins and the diamonds. 'This is mine. This is my reward,' she called, hugging the purse to her chest.

The soldiers did not bother to investigate, but marched Alma out the door, leading her through the streets to the fortress of St Peter and Paul, to join the other diplomats and aristocrats who had been rounded up and placed in the dungeons.

The cell was cold and only a little light filtered in from a small window set high on the wall.

Alma held her young son, who was crying, in her arms. 'Everything will be alright ,' she assured him.

Jakov and Marie were at the centre of events in the capital. They barely had time to sleep during the days which followed.

On 16 March 1917, in the royal train a hundred miles from St Petersburg, Nicholas, Tsar of all Russia, abdicated.

The news was received with disbelief and delight.

Many old men and women wept openly. They had always lived under the shadow of the Tsars. Now Nicholas, the appointed one of God, had abandoned them.

'This is only the beginning,' Jakov told Marie. 'He has brought down not only his own family but all the nobles with him, their great estates and houses. Their time is over. The coming months will see the end of all they stood for.'

His words were prophetic.

Chapter Forty-five

St Petersburg was in chaos: officers had been turned upon by soldiers and murdered; dishevelled soldiers loitered in front of their barracks or in mess rooms expecting some new era to dawn. Some officers tried to escape across the Neva but were pursued and shot as they fled. The police fared no better: most of them were caught and executed. Young agitators, armed with guns, moved through the city. They became the newly appointed police force. For many it was a time to settle old scores.

There was confusion in the steel mills. The workers, spurred on by agitators, demanded vast sums of money from the owners to continue working. Many of the mills ground to a halt.

The first days of the revolution were days of anarchy.

Jakov Fieldmann moved cautiously through events. Their vision, forged during the bitter years, was that Russia had to pass through a crucible of destruction before a new society would emerge.

'Society will rid itself of the dross. Soon we can begin all over again. This is what we planned for,' Marie argued when he had preached caution. 'We must throw care to the winds. The landlords are fleeing and the peasants are taking over their estates. At last the serfs are landowners.'

Marie had become obsessed with the revolution and the war. Soon, she believed, people would turn against the generals at the front. Soldiers would return home and society would have a new beginning.

At the fortress of St Peter and Paul new prisoners arrived

each day from all over the city. Some belonged to the diplomatic corps; others had been government civil servants; all were enemies of the revolution.

Each morning a jailer opened the door of the prison and Alma made her way up the stairs to the wide exercise yard. She brought her son Joseph with her. Silently, she walked about the compound which was covered with snow. Her feet dragged and she felt hungry. She was not permitted to talk to the other prisoners who took exercise at the same time. She recognised some; they had once been friends of hers, who had sat around her table during happier times.

They were dressed in a variety of old clothes. Some had been robbed of their furs by the soldiers and given in their place long military coats which trailed along the ground. The food was meagre and arrived at irregular intervals. After a week the dark rye bread became sweet to the palate and wholesome to eat. When one of them cried out in hunger they were beaten into silence.

Fear hung over the compound.

Sometimes during the night, a screaming prisoner was taken from his cell and brought up the stairs to a kangaroo court. The trial was brief and the outcome inevitable.

They always knew when someone or other had been executed. There was fresh blood on the snow.

Now Alma feared for her life. There was no-one she could turn to for help.

One night, just as she was falling into a chill sleep, the cell door was opened. Two soldiers with lanterns stood outside.

'What is wrong?' she asked.

'You must appear immediately before a court,' she was told.

'And my child?'

'We will take care of your child,' they told her.

'No,' she cried, gathering him up in her arms, 'He comes with me.'

One tried to wrench the young boy from her arms but his companion said, 'Let it be. Soon it will all be over.'

She did not weep. Stoically she walked up the steps from her underground dungeon and walked across the quadrangle to the Commandant's house, which now served as a headquarters for the new guard.

Alma believed that her execution was imminent. There was only one slight hope left to her now.

When she entered the well-heated room she felt faint. The officer sitting behind a large table noticed her pale face. He indicated that she should be given a chair.

She looked at him. He was about thirty and obviously well-educated from his accent. He looked sharply at her. His cold blue eyes frightened her. She noted that beside him stood the pile of documents that she had brought with her from the embassy.

Now she regretted that she had not burned them.

The young commander took a file and opened it.

'I wish to be brief. I will read out the accusations against you. If you have anything to say at the end, then you are free to do so.'

He began with a brief account of her life. Then the list of accusations, based on the evidence contained in the files.

'This evidence is damning. It is obvious that you have sent information to Vienna of troop movements and other military matters. We have already captured several spies and they have admitted that valuable information passed through your hands.'

'I would like to see my accusers,' Alma said.

'You cannot. They are dead,' the commandant retorted curtly. He closed the file and looked at her. 'Many of our troops have died because of you. It is not an easy thing to condemn a woman to death but I have no choice. You will be taken from here and executed.'

At the sentence the soldiers, who had been leaning

against the wall, began to move towards her, taking their rifles and falling into line.

Alma turned pale. 'I believe that you should contact my sister, Marie Fieldmann. She may have something to say in my favour,' she stammered.

The commandant recognised the name. 'This is not in the file,' he said, opening it again and running his finger down the central events of her life.

'I can assure you that it is true.'

'Perhaps you are playing for time. Perhaps you think you will receive a stay of execution,' he smiled coldly.

'Telephone her and see,' she said.

The commandant ordered the soldiers to leave the room. Then he took the phone and made several calls. Alma listened to the snatches of conversation.

Finally he got through to her sister. There was some conversation and then he paused. 'Very well. I will wait,' he said and replaced the telephone on its cradle.

'What did she say?' Alma asked.

'She told me that you are sisters but that you took separate paths many years ago. She believes that you should be executed. However, she is coming to see you. I believe that she has a proposition to make. She is a lady of some importance in the city and is secretary to one of our soviets.'

He opened a silver cigarette case and took out a cigarette. He began to smoke thoughtfully.

As Alma sat down again on the hard chair she heard confusion and shouting in the corridor. The door was thrown open and Prince Dmitri and Nikka were pushed through into the room. The Prince looked haggard. The epaulettes had been ripped from his military uniform and his shirt was torn. Alma and he recognised each other. But they looked away.

'He is one of them. So is his servant. Shall we shoot them?' one of the soldiers asked. He was a nervous young man who had been placed in charge of a group of rebels.

'Yes. I recognise this man and his servant. He has sent men to their deaths,' the commandant replied.

Prince Dmitri's eyes bulged with fear. Nikka remained stolid.

'No,' cried Prince Dmitri. 'I have documents of immense value. They will help your revolution.'

'Where are they?'

'All over the city in various locations.'

The commandant looked at him. 'If you do not divulge the information, I will shoot your servant.'

It was then that Prince Dmitri made a fatal mistake. 'Shoot him. It makes no difference to me.'

Nikka roared in hate. His voice was like that of a great bear wounded by hunters. 'I will join the revolution. I know where the papers are hidden,' he cried.

'Another comrade has seen the light,' the commandant laughed. 'Take this enemy of the people out of my sight.' He indicated Dmitri. 'I will talk with him later.'

The prince was led away.

Nikka was released. They gave him a gun and told the great giant to guard the door. He was pleased with his new position.

It seemed an age before Marie arrived with Fieldmann at the fortress. She entered the room with a new confidence that the revolution had given her.

She did not greet her sister. 'Take the prisoner, Schmerling, outside,' she directed.

Two soldiers caught Alma roughly by the arms and pushed her through the door.

'Well,' asked the commandant, 'What shall we do with your sister?'

'She is worthless dead. But her stepfather, Joseph Steiner, is a wealthy man. Perhaps he could be persuaded to pay a high ransom for her. The revolution needs money at this moment, as we are making arrangements for the return of Lenin through Berlin. We are dealing with a

Baron Von Hertling, a German spy. This could be a very useful way of raising the money. We will use him as a broker for Alma's life. If Steiner does not come up with the money, then we will execute her.' She spoke without emotion.

'Is it so easy to deal across frontiers during these desperate times?' the commandant asked.

'Yes. If we operate through Berlin.'

'And the child? Should we execute him?'

'No. He will become a ward of the state.'

They considered the plans for a long time then Alma was ordered to return.

The commandant directed her to sit down. She sat on the chair and her small son stood beside her.

'Under normal circumstances, you should be executed. However, these are not normal times. You are of little use to us dead, so we have come to the following decision. Some of our agents will contact Joseph Steiner in Vienna. If he is willing to advance two million roubles' worth of gold, which will be transported to St Petersburg, then your life will be spared.'

Alma gasped when she heard their decision, but she held her silence.

Her sister looked at her with derision. The times had changed Marie. She now carried a pistol and Alma believed that she would have used it to execute her. Fieldmann watched in silence, looking like the rough Russian peasant he had become.

'If the gold is not forthcoming from Steiner, then you will be summarily executed,' Marie told her. 'You are an enemy of Russia and an enemy of the Revolution.'

'Return her to her cell,' the commandant ordered. 'Bring the next prisoner.'

Alma walked with Joseph across the cold snow. Her execution had been stayed. Now her life and the life of her child depended upon Joseph Steiner. For some strange reason she now recalled her first New Year's night in Vienna all those years ago, at the turn of the century. Then the whole world and all the empires seemed stable. Now she was an insignificant being, dying in a freezing fortress in Russia.

Marie left the fort with Jakov.

'Would you really shoot her?' he asked.

'Yes, and without compunction. But I owe Joseph Steiner a life. He will have to pay for it.'

Prince Dmitri looked at the bleak cell around him. He felt trapped. Events had moved too rapidly for him. They had moved too rapidly for all the aristocrats. Now many of them languished in jails all over the city.
There was no escape.

Some time later the lock turned and the door opened. A lantern was placed on the floor and the commandant entered.

He stood in the centre of the floor and offered Prince Dmitri a cigarette.

'I once was captain of the Cossack regiment which guarded the Tsar. I know court intrigue. In fact, I still possess a small estate in the country. It was the slaughter of my best friends in a useless war which turned me against the monarchy,' he told the prince bluntly.

Prince Dmitri looked carefully at him. He wondered what suggestion he was going to make.

'We know where the secret files are. Or at least where most of them are hidden. I'm afraid Nikka is not too bright.' He paused. 'I have had the chance to examine them. They are of value, but they point towards a central secret which is not there.'

'There are other files. I would not confide such secrets to my servant, or should I say "comrade" in the new parlance. The others are hidden in the city.'

The commandant looked at Dmitri for a long time. 'It would be a barbarous and useless thing to torture you. There are more diplomatic ways of doing things. So, let me make you an offer. Come over to our side. Bring the secret police with you. Serve our cause.'

'Have you the power to guarantee my safety?'

'Yes. Perhaps it may change but at present I have it and it can buy you time.'

'Very well. There is no other decision I can make.'

They sat in the cell for another hour, while Prince Dmitri traded many secrets to stay alive.

It was early morning when he breathed the fresh Petersburg air again.

A truck carried him to an office in the city, dressed in decent but nondescript clothes.

That day he set about reorganising the country's new secret police. He was playing his part in the dawn of a new Russia.

Joseph Steiner had watched the progress of the war from his mansion set in the Viennese woods. His thoughts had become dark. He rarely visited the city which was now grey, without music or youth. Its young men were buried in nameless graves; its young women's voices no longer rang with laughter. Like all the other citizens of the imperial city they had grown hungry and morose.

Now, Joseph often sat with the rabbi and pored over the old Jewish books which he had purchased all over Europe. They were a source of consolation for him.

His wife, Margit, had tried to approach him on several occasions but he refused to see her. The imperial world of Vienna to which she had aspired was falling asunder. With the abdication of the Tsar it seemed that all the crowns of Europe were in danger, but they no longer seemed significant to Joseph. Margit pleaded with him to return to America, but he refused to listen.

'But you must find out what has happened to Alma. Prince Joseph must be brought back to Vienna. Why did Alma insist on staying in St Petersburg. Some day Prince Joseph might be Emperor,' she cried over the phone.

'They suffer now because of your ambition,' Joseph retorted angrily. 'You filled your daughter's head with foolish notions when she was a child.'

'If they die now, then their blood is on your hands,' she screamed.

Her husband put down the phone. In her way, Margit was right. He had already received confirmation from St Petersburg that Alma and her child had been taken prisoner. He felt helpless. He could not save her. There seemed no one to whom he could turn.

Joseph rarely entertained visitors. In fact many of his friends thought he had left Vienna for America. But one morning two men approached the house in a motorcar. The gardener ordered them off the property but they brandished pistols and he had been forced to let them pass.

They knocked at the door and demanded to see Joseph. When his servant told them that his master was having his breakfast and had no wish to be disturbed they produced their pistols for the second time.

'We have not come to take him away. We wish to talk to him about a serious matter.'

The servant led them into a bright room with a pleasant view of the garden. The small, Jewish figure who was nibbling small morsels of food was surprised to see them. He was about to ask how they had entered the house but he was interrupted.

'Could we see you in your office, sir? We have important information which concerns the life of your stepdaughter, Alma, and her child,' one of them said.

He started when he heard her name.

'Well,' he said, when they were sitting in his office. 'What news have you of my stepdaughter?'

'She is to be executed for treason,' one of them began. 'At present she is being held in St Peter and Paul Fortress.'

Joseph Steiner grew pale. 'But she is a woman. Do you execute women in Russia?'

'She is a spy. We execute spies. However, in this case, we will make you an offer. Listen very carefully.'

The instructions were precise.

'How can I be certain that this is not a confidence trick? You are asking for a great sum of money.'

'You are acquainted with Baron Von Hertling, no doubt?'

'Yes, he is familiar to me.'

'We are using him as an intermediary. He will contact you about the arrangements. In the meantime you can assemble two million roubles in gold, ready to send to Russia.'

As they left, the older of the two men turned around. 'And one final message. Marie Schmerling wishes you to know that this is the life she owes you.'

Joseph watched the two sinister figures enter the car and drive down the avenue. Then he returned to his office, sat at his desk and stared at the wall. He reflected on the situation. He must do everything in his power to save his stepdaughter and her son.

He made a series of phone calls to various addresses in Vienna. He could bring two millions roubles' worth of gold together in a matter of days. It could be moved to his villa during the night and be prepared for transport.

He did not consider the loss significant. During the war his fortune had doubled in America and each year he gave considerable sums of money to the Jewish Land Bank in order to purchase land in Palestine.

Now, he was anxious only for the safety of Alma and her son.

While he waited for his instructions from Berlin, he began to consider certain aspects of the deal.

How was the baron involved? Germany was at war with

Russia so the deal must favour Germany too. And who in Russia would receive the money? It would not end up in the coffers of the Tsar. He was a virtual prisoner in his palace. There must be collusion between Germany and one of the Russian parties, perhaps the Bolsheviks? If Russia withdrew from the war then Germany could pour her forces into the western front. That could be the only reason. He knew how devious the mind of the Baron was.

And then another thought entered his mind. He recalled his visit to the Federov estate. If the owner had fled, then the precious paintings from the school of Siena were in danger. Some peasant might easily destroy them. Perhaps he could make a deal with the Russians to assemble the whole collection in Berlin.

He would split the delivery of the money and make a further offer. Fieldmann would understand his motivation. One-and-a-half-million roubles' worth of gold would be sent to Berlin and another two million when the paintings were in his hand.

He believed that it was a clever deal – it would save Alma's and little Joseph's lives, while allowing him to possess the paintings he had always wanted.

Von Hertling needed little proof that the war was going against Germany: on every front the German forces were hard pressed; the Russian front alone was engaging a third of its army; America was contributing food and munitions to the allies. Now, time was against Germany. She was bound by her enemies in a hoop of steel.

He reflected on these matters as he made his way to his office. He passed through the bleak city of Berlin. The weather was freezing and a harsh wind blew down from the north. He could see hunger written on the faces of those making their way along the streets.

Von Hertling knew the statistics. The potato crop had yielded only a half as much as the preceding year and there was no-one left to work on the farms. The horses had been requisitioned by the army.

There was only one bright spot on the horizon. The Russian Empire was collapsing. A revolt among the soldiers would give Germany the time it needed. The baron had already been in contact with his agents in St Petersburg and discovered that the city was in chaos. A new government might sue for peace. Germany might yet be saved. And he would play an important role in her salvation.

When he reached his office an agent was waiting for him.

'Have you made the final arrangements with Lenin?' the baron asked.

'Yes. He is ready to receive our offer and our aid. He is only too willing to return to Russia. We have made it easy for him. We will transport him through Germany, Sweden and Finland.'

'And the gold?'

'It is ready. We will place it on board the train in Germany.'

Four days later, he had a strange call from one of his agents in St Petersburg. The members of the Communist Party wished to do a further deal. They would exchange a political prisoner called Alma Schmerling for gold bullion to the value of two million roubles. Joseph Steiner, a Jew from Vienna, was willing to pay. The baron was to broker the deal with a woman named Marie Fieldmann.

Von Hertling held his breath.

He considered informing Sophie for a moment, but then he refrained. He realised that she would try and block the exchange. She had not forgotten her humiliating experience at her sister's hands in St Petersburg.

Then he considered the irony of the situation. 'And so, Joseph Steiner, you have been scalded. The peasants have robbed you,' he laughed.

Through a series of dispatches to St Petersburg the whole

situation became clearer to him. Alma had been convicted as an Austrian spy. Her execution had been stayed while the deal was worked out.

The whole family was at war with each other.

Von Hertling set up the whole intricate deal. Several coded messages passed between the three imperial cities. As soon as Joseph Steiner delivered the gold to Berlin, into the keeping of Von Hertling, Alma and her son would be released.

The days dragged on in St Peter and Paul fortress. Each day, Alma expected to be taken out and executed. There was no news from her sister Marie.

The cold was intense. No matter how she wrapped herself and her child against it, it seemed to enter their bones. And now she was beginning to starve. She believed that the guards were eating all the food which belonged to the prisoners.

Each night she heard people being taken from their cells. They screamed as they were dragged up the steps to the interrogation rooms. There was silence for a half an hour, then she would hear the volley of rifle fire and the dense silence which would follow. Next morning there would be fresh bloodstains in the prison yard.

Her small son began to cry out for food. She called to the jailers but they banged on the door with the butts of their rifles and called to her to remain silent.

The days and the nights passed. The stench from her clothes no longer offended her. Her body was filthy and her hair fell about her in a dishevelled mess.

Sometimes to pass the time she talked to herself. 'I was too ambitious. I should have settled for less. I should have remained with Prince Eugene. I could have been happy with him.'

She recalled her lover many times. Like all the other members of the golden circle at Vienna, he was probably dead on some battlefront. The last she had heard of him was that he was commander of his own flying squadron. He had always been fascinated by the freedom of the air. 'I am an eagle when I am in the sky. I can look down upon the mountains and the lakes from the very seat of the gods,' he had laughed.

Perhaps he was still alive. Perhaps they could make a life for themselves in Transylvania. There, she would live amidst rural delights.

'I am a fool, a fool,' she told herself. 'I am no longer attractive. I have grown grey and thin and old.'

But soon her anxieties were centred upon her young son as he began to cough violently. Alma patted his back and tried to break the phlegm which was choking him. His forehead burned and he called out for water.

'Let him die. It will be a mouth less to feed,' the guard roared at him.

'Have you a family?' she asked.

'I have. Many of my children have died from hunger and the illness that hunger brings on,' he said bleakly.

She lay the child on her bed and wrapped her coat around him, hoping that it would warm his body and break the fever. Night after night for the next week, she attended carefully to him, praying that he would live.

Steiner had by now delivered a million-and-a-half roubles' worth of gold bullion to Berlin. He would deliver a further million when the Seinese paintings arrived in Vienna and a final million when they were in his possession in his villa.

'The deal should have been closed a week ago,' Marie cried. 'My stepfather is cutting it fine. Why should we bother with these paintings? Sell them to someone else, if they are worth anything. We need gold now. If not, destroy them.'

Jakov was astonished at the changes the revolution had wrought in Marie. Her mind had grown coarse. He would not have great paintings destroyed. He knew that in the hands of Joseph Steiner they would be safe. He, too, was determined to save them.

'I will travel to the Federov estate and requisition the paintings. Steiner has often spoken about them. Let him have them. We need gold, not art. Why destroy what we can sell to the bourgeoisie?' he said.

'Very well. Go and fetch them. We will agree to his offer,' Marie said.

She was anxious that the deal should be sealed. Lenin was coming from Switzerland. The gold could be loaded on board the train in Germany. Otherwise, they would have to find another way to bring it into the country.

Joseph received the news through Von Hertling. He was delighted. At last the paintings would be his.

The Sienese group arrived in Vienna on the day they buried the small corpse of Joseph in the mass grave in the Fortress of St Peter and Paul.

Two nights later Alma was awoken from sleep. Dully she accompanied her guards up the frozen steps and across the snowbound quadrangle to the commandant's house.

Inside sat the officer with her sister. Fieldmann was not present.

Marie was surprised at Alma's haggard appearance. During the short period of her imprisonment, her hair had turned partially grey, her face had aged and she looked dishevelled as she looked in a glazed fashion at her sister.

'An agreement has been reached. You will be brought to Germany by submarine. You are lucky. Prepare your belongings. Tomorrow night you will be brought to the island of Kronstad. There arrangements have been made to transport you over the border.'

Alma looked at her sister. Her gun was on the table. For a moment she wondered if she could reach it and shoot her.

'I refuse to go. Execute me. You killed my son. I have nothing to live for. Execute me.'

Marie was taken aback. 'When did this happen?' she asked the officer.

'A few nights ago.'

She felt pity for Alma. She had her revenge upon her, but now it tasted sour in her mouth. She had not foreseen Joseph's death.

Nevertheless, she could not let her sister see her emotions. 'His death is on your head,' she responded grimly. 'All revolutions consume their young. Someday you too will die and it will be sooner than you expect.'

'You and your foolish dreams. You have pulled my world apart. Now, put it back together in your own fashion. You have destroyed civilisation.' Her sister was standing before her, leaning over towards her, the foul smell of her clothes filling Marie's nostrils. Suddenly she lunged forward and grabbed the pistol. The two sisters struggled for the weapon and it discharged. Marie felt the bullet pass through her arm.

By now the officer had separated them and wrenched the pistol from their hands.

'Get the bitch out of my sight. I have no wish to see her again,' Marie roared.

Alma was taken back to her cell.

Next day a woman officer came to the cell and brought her to a bathroom, where she was ordered to undress. She looked at her naked body in a long mirror. It was thin, almost starved.

She had the luxury of a long bath and later, when she was dressed in incongruous clothes stolen from some fashion boutique on the Nevsky Prospekt, she was given a warm meal.

'I would like to visit my son's grave,' she said when she had finished.

'I will see if it can be arranged,' the guard said.

Half an hour later she was brought to a long mound beyond the northern turret of the fortress.

'He is buried here with the others,' she was told.

Alma looked at the frozen mound. Her son lay with so many of those who had been executed. She bowed her head and reflected on all that had happened. She had no desire to belong to the future. She wished that she was lying dead beside the body of her son.

That night a motor launch brought her to the island of Kronstad. There she was transferred to a ship which set out immediately in a westerly direction across the Gulf of Finland.

Two hours later, she was transferred to a submarine.

Lenin set out from Zurich for Russia on 9 April 1917.

When the train stopped in Germany nobody knew what passed between Lenin and the German officers who met him at one of the railway sidings. But during the brief stop, gold bullion, which had been secured in strong wooden boxes by Joseph Steiner at his mansion in Vienna, were brought on board.

When Lenin returned to his carriage the train set out for the Finland Station.

A week later Alma stood on the platform of Vienna's central station. Joseph Steiner was waiting to greet her. His heart was filled with joy.

'Where is your child?' he asked, when he had embraced her.

'He died ten days ago,' she said bleakly.

Joseph Steiner put his hand on her shoulder and led her away. 'I am sorry,' he said.

His plans had worked against him. He had sacrificed life for art and he would carry the burden of this knowledge with him for the rest of his life.

The blood of the young prince was on his hands.

Chapter Forty-six

On the eleventh hour of the eleventh day of the eleventh month 1918, the guns fell silent all over Europe.

The old, bloody, year was ending. In graves all over Europe and Russia lay the remembered and the unremembered dead of the war. The trenches were waterlogged, the landscapes scarred and winter silence brooded over the abandoned battlefields.

Prisoners of war were making their way home to villages and farms and towns. Revolution simmered in the cities of Vienna, Berlin and Saint Petersburg.

The Tsar and his family had been assassinated in Siberia. Their bodies had been set on fire and the charred remains thrown into a mine shaft.

The Kaiser had abdicated. He had removed himself to Holland with his servants and some of his possessions. There he would live on in comfortable exile, his imperial fantasies in ashes about him.

When he arrived at Amerongen Castle in Holland, his first words had not been memorable. He remarked to his host, 'What I should like, my dear Count, is a cup of tea – good, hot, English tea.'

While his capital city was in the grip of fear and terror, his life in Holland would be that of an English country gentleman. He would chop trees and busy himself writing historical and scientific articles. His old age would be both tranquil and happy.

When Von Hertling read the conditions of surrender that had been accepted by his countrymen in the guarded railway carriage in the forest of Compiègne, he felt betrayed.

The old ideals had perished. The Teutonic Knights had been dishonoured. Chaos reigned in Berlin.

Sitting at his desk on a dark November night he felt that he did not belong to the new world. He took his revolver and shot himself.

Next morning an officer found him, lying face down on a file. A pool of blood lay on the desk and on the floor around him.

At the Schönbrunn Palace the new Emperor, Karl, and his Empress, Zita, presided over the dying days of Franz Joseph's empire. Four million Austrians had perished in the war. Now the royal family feared for their lives. Their royal guard had disappeared and nothing stood between them and the revolutionary crowds which surged through Vienna.

On 9 November, Karl signed the document of abdication in the blue Chinese room.

Two days later some cars drew up at the palace. The new socialist leader Karl Renner announced, 'Herr Hapsburg, your taxi is waiting.'

This was the beginning of their journey into exile.

Vienna, capital city of the Austro-Hungarian empire, which had been a thousand years in the forming, was a husk. It was now the capital of Austria.

When Baroness Steiner heard the news of the abdication she collapsed. She had built her dreams about the imperial family. Now they were commoners.

It was approaching midnight in Vienna.

Joseph Steiner told his stepdaughter that it was dangerous to visit the city. 'Let us go to a wine village in the woods,' he suggested.

‘I have little desire to celebrate the New Year,’ Alma said. Ever since her return she had watched the empire collapse. She had nothing more to live for.

‘We must celebrate. The war is over. It is time to look forward. Soon spring will be in the air and grass will grow over the battlefields. Nature recovers and we, too, must survive.’

‘You are a brave man, Joseph Steiner,’ she told him.

He ignored her compliment. ‘Now get dressed and let us go.’

Alma went upstairs to her room to prepare for New Year’s Eve, 1918.

Sophie sat alone in her room. A meagre fire burned in the grate, as she had managed to purchase some coal on the black market.

She had much to consider. Most of her fortune had been dissipated by the war. Now there was a run on the German mark. Each day it seemed to devalue. Great families had become impoverished. The imperial city was in confusion. It was believed that the communists would take over.

She had ventured out during the day. Everywhere she saw defeated soldiers confused at the defeat which they had returned from.

A heavy war debt now burdened Germany and she, too, was worthless.

Soon some bell would ring out the New Year. It was most unwelcome.

In St Petersburg, Marie walked with Jakov along the boulevards which led to the Winter Palace, which stood ghostly and beautiful on the left bank of the Neva.

The revolution had succeeded beyond all their wildest dreams. The Tsar lay dead, and two Emperors were in exile. It would be the century of the common man.

They looked forward in expectation to the coming year.

They had found their place in a new world.

It was pleasant and warm in the wine-village restaurant. An old man played some sentimental music on his violin and it filled the room with nostalgic sound. The food was simple, the local wine tasted sweet on the palate.

Joseph checked his watch. It was approaching midnight.

And then the bell in the local church rang out.

The New Year had arrived.

Outside, snow was drifting downwards in gentle flakes.

He turned to Alma. 'Happy New Year,' he said to her. 'We are the lucky ones. We have survived. Let us toast Life.

'*Lechayim*.'